THE DEAD SONGBIRD

By Harriet Smart

THE DEAD SONGBIRD

by

Harriet Smart

Published by Anthemion

Fourth Edition

ISBN 978-1-907873-55-3

Made with Jutoh

Chapter One

Northminster, March 1840

Felix Carswell sat in his consulting room, scowling over the latest edition of The Lancet. He had skimmed through two papers written by contemporaries of his at Edinburgh. They were excellent papers, and their authors were men he had not thought capable of anything much. It was galling, for he, the winner of several university prizes, had published nothing. He had not even submitted anything. It was true that he had a couple of half-worked-up ideas but they were languishing in a drawer and, in the light of what he had just read, he was tempted to throw them into the fire.

He lit another cheroot, despite all his resolutions to quit. Major Vernon, the Chief Constable, had told him that the Duke of Wellington abominated smoking in a gentleman. This meant that the Major himself disliked it and Felix did not wish to displease him unnecessarily. But it was a struggle to forgo the pleasure of it, and having enjoyed a long, sweet breath of smoke, he hooked his arm over the back of his chair and turned to watch the woman who was sweeping the floor of the adjoining room.

Usually this was not a matter to excite his attention, but Mrs Craven, the usual charwoman, had sent her widowed daughter Mrs Parkes to clean his rooms in her stead.

Mrs Parkes was tall and clearly accustomed to hard labour, but she was graceful in her movements, and Felix found her well worth looking at. She had handsome, determined features that put him in mind of antique statuary.

He liked the way a few dark curls were escaping from the restraint of the plain but fetching linen cap she wore. Her cheeks were reddened, as were her lips, and as she swept she hummed an old and wistful tune.

She made him think of the maids in his parents' house: those bare-armed Highland girls, who had first awakened his senses to the bewitching possibilities of the other sex. He had spent hours in his boyhood idly dreaming of those girls, and how he might possess one for himself. Now he wondered how it would be to possess Mrs Parkes, with her long neck and her rounded hips. He mentally removed her calico print dress and gingham apron, and laid her on a freshly made bed, with her knees raised and an expectant smile on her face...

Just then her baby, lying in a basket that was set down on the threshold between the two rooms, stirred from sleep and began to scream. Mrs Parkes rested her broom against the wall and loosened the front of her bodice, apparently unaware that he was looking at her. She scooped up the child and put it to her breast, without much modesty. He knew he ought not to be remotely stirred by the sight of a woman feeding a child but he could not help himself. The tantalising curve of the milk-swollen breast entirely caught his attention.

She at last realised he was looking at her. Their eyes met, and from her level gaze, he could have sworn she was daring him to look directly at her, to discover if he would be so insolent as to continue to look back.

He did continue, and then, feeling himself flush with shame, forced himself to look away and back at the irritating words of the periodical in front of him.

He wondered if she was available, if she was perhaps that sort of woman. He knew she was a widow of a year, with a posthumous child, and several others to feed. Would she be amenable to such a proposition and how much did it cost to make such an arrangement? Was there a going rate? How did one even go about making such arrangements? How did one broach the subject? Other men seemed to manage these things, with ease.

At that moment he could only think about the monumental beauty of her swollen breast, which he longed not only to touch, but which, just like that greedy bairn, he wished to thrust into his mouth. He stared down fixedly at his desk, wretched with shame and desire.

"I'll be done in a minute, sir," she said.

"You should sit down," he managed to say.

"If I sit down I'll never get up again," she said. "And I'll never get through the half of it. Now, sir, about your laundry – my mother told me to tell you that if you want things mending, she will have to charge you extra."

"Of course," he said.

"Just to make it clear," she said.

"Is money tight?" he said.

"We manage, sir," she said.

"If you find yourself in any difficulty, you know you must only ask," he said. He stubbed out his cheroot, and got up, but was careful to avoid looking at her, but instead at the bookcase on the far side of the room. "There are perhaps other things you can do for me. We might come to some arrangement."

Even as the words fell from his lips he was appalled at himself. It was at once too vague and at the same time outrageously graphic. He might as well have specified some indecent act.

There was a long silence and then she said, "I know what you are trying to say, and the answer is no."

Her tone was so sharp he could not help but look at her again. To his regret he saw she had covered herself with a shawl.

"What did you think I was trying to say?" he said, flushing in spite of himself.

"I've seen the way you've been looking me over, and it isn't decent. I think you should spend more time reading your

Bible and thinking about your immortal soul, sir, that's what I think."

"That is not what I meant," he said.

"Whatever you say, sir," she said, reaching down and picking up the baby's basket. "My mother will come and clean in here tomorrow, as usual."

As she pulled open the door, she was met by the sight of Major Vernon. She dropped a brief curtsey.

"I hope your mother improves," Major Vernon said.

"Thank you, sir – I hope so too," she said, and gave a fierce glance back at Felix, before she deftly slipped past Major Vernon into the corridor, her child still at her breast.

"May I come in?" Vernon asked. "No patients this morning, Mr Carswell?"

"All dealt with," said Felix.

"And no calls to make?"

"No, unfortunately."

"Your practice will pick up in time," said Major Vernon, his glance taking in the dish of cheroot stubs on Felix's desk. "I am sure of it. In the meantime, I have a diversion for you. What do you make of this?" he said, holding out a small, pale grey envelope made of good quality paper. The hand on it was feminine, elegant and pleasantly legible. Felix turned it and saw it was sealed with dark blue wax, with the pattern of a lyre pressed into it which made a rather charming effect. "Hardly typical of my usual correspondence. Delivered by hand."

The seal had been broken so Felix drew out the letter and glanced over it.

> Mrs Morgan presents her compliments to the Chief Constable and begs the favour of an interview with him. Mrs Morgan understands that the Chief Constable must have great demands upon his time, but the circumstances in which she finds herself are such that she can only think to put the matter in the hands of the appropriate authorities. She hopes therefore he will not consider it a great imposition to wait upon her at the

above address as soon as is practical.

"What do you think of that?" said Major Vernon.

"Mrs Morgan?" said Felix, handing the letter back to Major Vernon. "Am I supposed to know her?"

"You haven't heard of Mrs Morgan?" said Major Vernon. "Haven't you noticed the bills all about town for the Handel Festival, announcing 'Mrs Morgan, the famous soprano'? I wonder what that all means."

"Probably some hysterical triviality," said Carswell. "These prima donnas are well known for it."

"You had better come with me and see for yourself, then," said Major Vernon. "I am going to wait on her."

"I take it you do not have a great deal to do this morning either, sir," said Felix.

"I cannot overlook it."

"You could send a constable."

"I could. But I admit I am interested to see her for myself. And she may be in some real difficulty. My brother-in-law thinks she has a remarkable voice – and it is, he tells me, a considerable coup for the Handel Festival to get Mrs Morgan to come all this way. So, Mr Carswell, get your hat – we have a call to pay."

"With all due respect to Canon Fforde," Felix said, as they went downstairs, "I do not know how anyone can get so excited about a soprano. Have you ever heard her sing?"

"No, but I should like to."

"I do not like over-trained voices," said Felix. "They sound artificial to me. I hate all that trilling around and warbling on the high notes."

"Mrs Morgan is supposed to have the voice of an angel."

"Whatever an angel might sound like," said Felix. "How can one know?"

Chapter Two

If he had time at his disposal, Giles Vernon never liked to walk straight to an appointment, but to use the walk as an opportunity to see that all was well in Northminster. That morning, although they were headed for the Minster Precincts, he chose to take a detour through All Souls, an area that had once been one of the most respectable parishes in the city, with its own ancient and vast church, topped with a gilded cockerel. But now it had lost its foothold on the ladder of prosperity. The merchants who had built the large houses and paid pew rent to sit in All Souls Church had long since moved away, and the lesser, middling sort had come to occupy it. It was the kind of place you would go to get a fiddle mended or have a dress made over. But it was obvious that this was changing too. All the houses had now been subdivided and the shops looked shabby and uncared for. The stench of the river was noticeable, and the smoke from the factories added to the unpleasant note of sulphur.

As they turned into All Souls Green, he saw that the churchyard railings had become the gathering place for a rag-bag assembly of hawkers and handcart men of the sort who usually kept their trade to the most distressed parts of the city. There, their cheap but dubious goods found a ready market. Yet they seemed to be doing good business in All Souls.

One, a print and ballad seller, had set up a veritable exhibition along the railings. He was announcing his presence with a handbell and a lively line of patter.

"All the famous faces! All the famous faces! Best quality – three for sixpence. Her Majesty and the German Prince – lovely wedding portrait – Her Majesty's own favourite likeness of her new lord. The Noble Duke himself, our Wellington, England's saviour, on or off his horse, whichever you fancy. And here, just in — Madame Morgan, the divine diva, soon to be here in Northminster. After a painting by the famous Italian Signor Pastcarlini. Best quality and only to be had here! Come on! Murders for a penny, if that's your taste!"

"I don't suppose for one minute he has his token," said Giles.

"Token?" said Carswell.

"A trading licence. The Guild of the City attempts to regulate the street trades with it, but they have set the price so high that no one ever bothers to buy one, and my men are forced to waste a great deal of time chasing such people up. I did suggest that they reduce the price a little to encourage them, but I was given a stiff lecture for my presumption. The system is wretched beyond belief but they will not think of reforming it."

By now a sizeable crowd had gathered to be entertained by the patter, and Giles was about to make his way through to the front of it to challenge the print seller, when suddenly from the ranks of the crowd a stout woman burst forth and began to harangue the man.

"Off my patch, you filthy tinker!" she screeched, her vast mushroom of skirts shaking with fury. "Haven't I told you? Haven't I told you before? I'll have the law on you, you dirty beggar. Transported you should be, and hanged, you dirty, stinking Paddy!"

And as she screamed at him she upturned the baskets and boxes of prints onto the muddy ground. The man rushed to retrieve his stock and she took the advantage to raise the knotty stick which she was carrying and began to lay it upon him with some force. Giles now pushed through the crowd, which had spontaneously compacted itself to get a better view of such a good 'going-on', and ripped the stick from her hand. She stared up at him with utter astonishment and rage.

"If you please, ma'am," he said. "Or I shall be forced to charge you."

"Charge me?" she exclaimed. "Charge me?"

"Calm down, mother, please." A small man came scurrying up behind her. He was carrying a sulphur-yellow shawl which he tried to drape about her shoulders, but she was having none of it, and brushed him away with a mighty sweep of her arm as if he were an insect. "Mother, your heart, remember," he said.

"Charge me?" she said again to Giles. "With what?"

"Malicious damage and assault," said Giles. The print seller was scrabbling about, trying to retrieve his stock from the puddles.

"He's not allowed! He's not allowed to sell that rubbish here. I know the law, mister high and mighty, I know the law. He can't sell that here."

"That is for me to decide," said Giles.

"Then ask him for his token. He won't have one. They never do, these tinkers. Filthy tinkers, ruining the trade for the likes of us."

"That may well be, ma'am, but this is not the way to deal with it." He turned to the son, who was still standing with the shawl stretched open, ready to wrap her in it should she ever signal she wanted it. "Take your mother home, Mr...?"

"Fildyke, sir," he said. "Now, mother, you heard the gentleman." Mrs Fildyke gave a snort of disgust at the word 'gentleman'. "Let's get inside before you make yourself ill. Now take my arm, please," he added with excruciating humility, but she pushed away the arm he offered and stomped away. Giles handed Fildyke her stick and he went after her.

Mrs Fildyke wrenched it off him and turned back to Giles for a moment.

"This is not the end of the matter. I shan't let it rest! Mark me, mister, mark me!" She concluded with a filthy look and a flourish of the stick as if she fully intended to lay it across his face. It was clear he had spoiled all her pleasure.

Giles turned back to the print seller.

"Your token?"

The man began to pat the many pockets of his old-fashioned plum-coloured overcoat.

"I seem to have mislaid it, sir," he said with the charming but practised smile of a person who has always lived on the margins of legality.

Giles pulled out his notebook.

"Name and address?"

"Hopkins, sir. Tannery Lane."

"You know the penalty for trading without a token?"

"I have a token, sir, of course, I do. I've just lost it. I'm all legal. Swear to God!"

"It may come to that," Giles said. "I want you to report to the police headquarters in Castle Street in the next twenty-four hours with your token."

"Yes, yes, of course I will, sir."

He would not, Giles knew well enough. He would clear out of Northminster, at least for a while. Technically he ought to have arrested him, but Giles was inclined to be lenient.

"If you cannot find your token you cannot trade here," he said.

"No, sir, of course not. I would not dream of it. I wouldn't have set up here today if I hadn't a token, would I?" he added with such an insolent grin that Giles was tempted to change his mind and arrest him. But he reflected it would only be a matter of time before the man was caught at it again, and then he would not have the excuse of not having been warned. He would send a constable up to Tanner Lane to look him out. It was a little shoddy to leave it as it stood, but the problem was endemic, like an outbreak of cockroaches – insoluble unless the root cause was tackled: the iniquitous token system. It was the *de facto* criminalisation of the many for the benefit of the few, and for all his dishonesty and obvious guilt, Giles could not help having some sympathy for the print seller.

"So pack up and be on your way," he said.

"Yes, sir, at once, sir."

"Major Vernon!" Carswell calling was out.

He turned and saw Carswell running across the green. Mrs Fildyke appeared to be collapsing.

Chapter Three

"I want Dr Joyce!" said Mrs Fildyke, her arms flailing, as Felix tried to take her pulse. "Get off me!"

"I'm a surgeon, Mrs Fildyke."

"No, no, you're nothing but a boy. Where's Dr Joyce? Edwin, go and get Dr Joyce. I don't want no 'prentice surgeon. And get me my pills... Oh God, my poor heart... I'm going to die, I swear it."

They had got her back to her house with some difficulty. She was not unconscious but her bulk was considerable and she was complaining of severe pain, and every move had seemed only to increase her distress. The three of them – her son, the Major and Felix – managed to manoeuvre her through the tiny shop and into a back room which contained a large sofa and a great quantity of bird cages, all filled with frenzied little creatures, who set up a din at their interruption.

It was soon clear that this noxious apartment was where she spent most of her time. Her excursion onto the Green had been an exceptional one, and she was so unused to exercise that it had brought on a violent attack of dyspepsia.

"You insolent beggar!" she said, as Felix again tried to examined her, albeit cursorily. "Edwin, get him out of here. I must see Dr Joyce."

"He's trying to help you, Mother. You might have died out there."

"I don't think it's as grave as that. What did you have for breakfast, Mrs Fildyke?" Felix said, noticing the dish of sugar plums and the port bottle on the table.

"Just a little gruel. That's all I can bear first thing. I don't eat a great deal."

"You ought to loose your stays," he said.

"How dare you!" she screamed. "Edwin, get him out of here!"

"Very well, ma'am," said Felix, stepping back from the couch. "If you will not take my help –"

"No I will not!" she said. "Get out!"

"I must apologise for my mother," said Mr Fildyke as they went back into the shop. Major Vernon was waiting there, apparently absorbed in studying the cluttered shelves. "She takes on so and that rascal has been here every day this week."

"Dyspepsia, I should say. She should observe a stricter diet," said Felix. "And take more exercise. Tell her that, won't you?"

"Yes, yes, I shall try. I shall try. Thank you, sir – thank you both," he added, turning to Major Vernon who had picked up a print and was examining it closely by what scanty light came through the glazed panes of the door. "Do you like that, sir? Lots of gentlemen have been in enquiring for Mrs Morgan's picture since we heard she was coming to sing. That's the last one I have in stock."

"That's just as well, for I'm not sure this is legitimate, Mr Fildyke," said Major Vernon.

"What do you mean, sir?" said Fildyke, all apparent innocence.

"That this is a pirate copy of a Hill & Co engraving. You should be a little more wary about who you buy your stock from if you do not want to get yourself into trouble."

"I don't know about that, sir," said Fildyke, a little flustered now. "No one else has remarked on it. All our customers have been satisfied."

"They would be for that price if it were genuine," said the Major. "Who is your supplier?"

"I don't know, sir, off-hand. I should have to ask my mother, and I don't like to disturb her now."

"Perhaps in the near future you will remember," said the

Major rolling up the print. "I would advise you to do so."

"Yes, sir, I will, of course."

"I will take this with me, if you don't mind, Mr Fildyke? You don't want to sell it by accident, I'm sure."

Fildyke looked as though he were about to protest and then thought better of it.

"A very dubious establishment," said Major Vernon, as they walked away. "Half the stock was counterfeit or adulterated, and all sold at vastly inflated prices." He handed Felix the rolled-up print. "Pirate copy or not, I wonder if that is a good likeness."

Felix unrolled the paper to reveal the figure of woman, leaning on a pillar with a bland, sweet and abstracted gaze. She had large spaniel eyes and glossy ringlets.

"I doubt it. No woman ever looked like that. Why do people waste their money on such things?"

"We like to have our idols, our great men and our beautiful women. It is in our nature. Well, at least we weak mortals do. Obviously not you, Carswell."

"I could see the point of a portrait which did a person justice, which had some honesty in it. It is the utter falsity of it that offends me. That is not a woman. That is a doll." He handed it back to the Major.

"We shall make a scientific comparison," said the Major, tucking the print inside his great-coat, "when we see the lady for ourselves. A great many would envy us the opportunity. After you," he said, indicating a narrow flight of steps hidden behind a crumbling old wall.

"Where does this go?"

"Up to the far side of the Minster Precincts. This is Jacob's ladder," said the Major.

Some thirty steps later they were following a narrow lane that led to a wooden handgate.

"Avonside Row?" said Felix, glancing up at the cast iron sign fixed to a high brick wall.

They had emerged into a short but handsome street in a secluded corner of the Precincts. He had not taken in the address at the top of Mrs Morgan's letter, but was now surprised he had not. The name Avonside was always one to make him uneasy. "Is this part –?"

"Of the Rothborough estates? I believe so."

"What is Mrs Morgan to do with that?"

"It is a good address," said Major Vernon, his hand on the elaborate wrought iron gate that led to a generous front garden. "I should live here if I could afford it. She clearly can – at least for the time of her engagement here. Very pleasant indeed. A fine house – especially that large garden at the side. No common lodgings for the great diva."

Felix followed the Major up the flagged path, with its trimming of clipped box, to the immaculately-proportioned front door, topped with a fanlight. It was, he supposed, a desirable house, but he could not dissociate the property from its owner. It had too much of the stamp of Lord Rothborough about it – glossy and aristocratic. Above the door was the Rothborough coat of arms, the three diamonds set in an oval, topped by a raven's head. Felix knew the pattern well from the watch-chain seal that Lord Rothborough had given to him when he turned one-and-twenty.

A maid of striking looks opened the door to them and enquired haughtily, in a strong foreign accent, "Yes, what is it?"

"Your mistress is expecting me," the Major said. "Tell her the Chief Constable presents his compliments." He held out his card to her, which she took and examined dubiously.

"You are sure, Monsieur?"

"Yes," said Major Vernon crisply. "Take that up to your mistress and you will see that I am expected."

"Wait here," she said, gesturing to the row of hall chairs that skulked against the wall. "I will see for you."

"She's clearly used to weeding out the riff-raff," said

14

Major Vernon, when she had gone.

"That doesn't excuse her insolence."

"Swiss," the Major went on, "if I am not mistaken. Extremely smart indeed."

"What is?"

"To have a Swiss maid. So I am informed. And for a married woman to keep a maid that beautiful – well, the mistress must be sure of her own charms, don't you think? A girl that handsome would be a serious provocation to a husband."

"About as provocative as a quart of vinegar," Felix said, turning quickly away from the painting he had found himself facing: a perspective view of the park at Holbroke, with a large coat of arms in the corner, supported by flying angels.

Upstairs someone began to play the piano – the introduction to a song which Felix vaguely recognised. Then someone began to sing; not, as might have been expected, a woman, but a man. He sounded ordinary enough, neither good nor bad – a respectable drawing room tenor – and Felix recognised it at once.

"What the devil?" he muttered, and pushed his hands through his hair. "That's –"

The Major, who had been looking at the other paintings, turned to him. "Yes?"

"My Lord Rothborough."

"The solicitous landlord, of course," said the Major, with an amused but sympathetic smile.

"Collecting his rent, I suppose," said Felix, taking up his hat. "We won't be allowed to intrude on this."

"We owe the lady a little more than that," said Major Vernon, going to the stairs. "It would be better for her if we were to intrude, I think. After all, she did ask to see me."

"To save her from Lord Rothborough?" Felix said. "I think not."

"Do not judge her until you know the facts," said

Vernon, climbing up. "Come along."

"She wrote to you," Felix said, going towards the door, "not me."

"Mr Carswell," insisted the Major, with an emphatic gesture to follow him.

Felix did so, but with great reluctance. The Major was now striding upstairs with jaunty confidence, like a sportsman with his gun crossing a field in search of a bird. Felix felt his own steps were leaden, especially when on the half landing he noticed a man's great-coat lined with cherry-coloured silk tossed carelessly across a cane settee. He began to dread what it was that Major Vernon was so determined to burst in upon.

The icily beautiful maid was standing on the landing, her ear turned to the half-open door. She spun round with a guilty start when Major Vernon tapped her on the shoulder.

"Announce me, won't you?" he said, and propelled her gently through the door.

The piano continued for a moment, the singer for a note or two more.

"Yes, Berthe, what is it?" said a woman's voice.

"This gentleman, he insists..." responded the maid.

"What gentleman?" said Lord Rothborough.

"Forgive me, my lord," said Major Vernon, taking his cue and going in. "Mrs Morgan – I am Major Vernon, the Chief Constable. I have come about your letter."

"Oh yes, I see," she said. "How prompt you are, sir."

Felix remained on the landing, hoping he might not be seen, but the Major pulled the door open.

"How could we not respond promptly to such a request, ma'am?" said the Major. "We could not ignore it, could we, Mr Carswell?"

Felix could not now avoid going in, and not wanting to look at Lord Rothborough, instead found himself staring straight into the lustrous blue eyes of Mrs Morgan.

Chapter Four

She smiled at him across an expanse of shining rosewood – for she stood on the far side of a large piano. He sensed a constriction to the vessels of his heart, which was of course nonsensical. At the same time he felt his mouth go dry and he could do nothing but stare back, aware that he must look like a slack-jawed fool, but he was unable for a moment to do anything about it. Her appearance struck him as something beyond remarkable. He felt he might faint if he continued to look directly at her, but neither was there any question of his looking away.

She was too ravishing for that. She was tall, slender and crowned with pale golden hair, braided and wound about her head. There was a becoming pink flush on her high, finely-sculpted cheeks, and long, dark lashes framed extraordinary eyes that seemed to know him in a glance. He felt scorched and yet comforted in the same moment. It was like being in the presence of a goddess.

"Mr Carswell?" she repeated. "Lord Rothborough has mentioned you."

Damn him, thought Felix, reddening.

"How delightful!" said Lord Rothborough, rubbing his hands. "Felix, my boy, and Major Vernon! How excellent to see you both. But, my dear, what letter is this?"

Felix's heart sank at that careless endearment. How close were they, he wondered, and at what point in this story had they blundered in? The thought of the two together made him faintly nauseous. For Lord Rothborough's reputation in these matters was by no means unblemished, and their situation could not be anything but suspicious.

"Just a trifling business," said Mrs Morgan.

"With the police?"

"It is nothing, I assure you. Nothing of any concern. I wanted a professional opinion, that is all."

"You could not have summoned a better man," said Rothborough. "Though I wish you had asked me first. Major Vernon and I are well acquainted."

"I did not like to bother you. You have so many calls on your time already, such important business to attend to. Indeed, I think I must be keeping you from –"

"Not at all, not at all. What could be more important than seeing that you are comfortably settled, Mrs Morgan?"

"More than comfortably," said Mrs Morgan. "I am honoured to have such a house put at my disposal."

"We could not have a national treasure putting up in ordinary lodgings. Such places are full of draughts and are most insanitary. If you had caught cold and lost your voice in Northminster, it would be a disaster. And this time of the year is dangerous. I have known so many people drop dead in March. One can never be too careful."

"Please be assured, Lord Rothborough," she said, with a laugh that made Felix want to sit down and luxuriate in it, "I have no intention of dying in Northminster, especially not in your beautiful house. Your generosity has sustained my will to live. And now that you have seen for yourself that I am completely comfortable, I really cannot take up any more of your valuable time."

It was a dismissal; clear enough, though sweetly done. But Rothborough seemed disinclined to leave.

"My time is at your disposal, Mrs Morgan."

"No, no, I will not believe that, my lord," she went on.

"It must be. How can it not be?" he said. "And this police business. You cannot think I will not help you?"

"I know you would move continents for me. But I do not think that continents will need to be moved. It is a trifle, as I said. I do not want you to trouble yourself, truly. And remember, I shall expect you at the rehearsal this afternoon. If you are not there I shall be disappointed. I need your opinion on which arias I should sing."

"You know I shall be."

"And if Mrs Morgan's business turns out to be anything but trifling," Major Vernon said, "we will at once enlist your assistance, my lord."

"Very well, very well. I shall hold you to that, Vernon," said Lord Rothborough. He turned to Mrs Morgan and took her hand. *"A bientôt, ma chère Madame."*

He bent to kiss her hand, and seemed to take such a devil of a long time at it that Felix wanted to manhandle him away for his presumption.

When Rothborough had at last gone, there was a moment of awkward silence and then she turned to Major Vernon and said, in a quiet, grave tone, "I hope you didn't mind my writing. I couldn't think what else to do."

"Then it is not entirely a trifle?" said Major Vernon.

She shook her head and walked away down the room.

"No," she said, with her back to them. "I was not sure to whom I should speak. It's such a strange matter, and I thought of going to Bow Street, but..."

"Perhaps we should sit down," said Major Vernon, reaching for his notebook.

She turned back to them.

"Yes, of course, gentlemen, do sit. I'm sorry, I have forgotten myself. Shall I ring for tea?"

"No, we have everything we need. But you, ma'am, you are not at your ease. Please won't you sit down? Carswell, get a chair for Mrs Morgan."

Felix moved a chair and set it opposite the Major.

"Now, please, ma'am, sit, and you can begin from the beginning."

Felix positioned himself on a sofa next to the wall, where

he could observe her completely. He saw her folding her pale hands neatly in her lap, but then after a moment she began to play with one of her rings. She did not need such decorations, he thought; her hands were perfection already.

"I have never spoken of this to anyone before," she said, after a brief silence. "I thought if I did not, then it would go away, but it did not." She glanced from Major Vernon to Felix with a half-smile. "Oh dear."

"Think of me as a Roman cleric in a box, hidden behind a grille," said Vernon. "Anything you say is quite safe."

"So long as I do not get a penance for my sins," she said, with nervous levity.

"So?" prompted the Major.

"Yes, yes, of course," she said, and reached in a pocket in the folds of her skirt and took out a folded piece of paper. She fingered it for a moment, and then held it out to him. "This is why I called you. It is probably nonsense."

Vernon took the paper, unfolded it and looked it over.

"That is not nonsense," he said after a moment. "May I show this to Mr Carswell?"

"Yes."

Felix crossed the room and took the paper. It read:

> Death is too good for a whore like you.
> But He may show you mercy yet.
> BE PREPARED.

It was not written out, but made from printed letters, chopped up and pasted, a violent jumble of typefaces and capitals, so that the words seemed like blows. He stared down at it, appalled that anyone should think of doing such a thing to her.

"Good God," he said, under his breath.

"This was delivered to you here?" Major Vernon asked.

"Yes."

"Amongst your usual letters?"

"Yes."

"But delivered by hand, apparently," said Vernon. "There's no stamp, I think?" Felix turned the paper over, glad not to look at the message. The name and direction had been carefully printed but the Major was right. There was no stamp. "You don't recognise this hand at all?" the Major continued.

"No. I have puzzled over it before."

"You have had such letters before?"

"Yes."

"How many?"

"I don't know."

"Two or three?"

"More than that. Usually I throw them straight into the fire. That seems the best place for them. After all, they are just little bits of gummed paper; it's just some horrible, childish game. I decided I would not let myself be hurt by them. To take them seriously, well, that seems to play into their hands. I should have burnt that one."

"But you decided not to on this occasion. Is the language stronger?"

"Yes, somewhat."

"And why did you decide to speak of this now?"

"Because I have not given out my address here. I had thought it was just some nonsense that happens in London. People do write to me a great deal there. It is a hazard of being well known, and I tried to make light of it. But finding one here, when I am supposed to be away from all that – it disturbed me."

"When did it arrive?" Felix asked.

"Yesterday afternoon, with my other letters. It was waiting for me when I arrived. That disturbed me, and last night I did not sleep. A strange bed in a strange house I suppose accounts for that, but to find it here already, waiting for me..."

"How long have you been receiving these letters?" Major Vernon asked.

"I cannot say when it began. I have pushed it from my mind, I suppose. It was too unpleasant. When it came I threw it straight on the fire. It was last summer, I think."

"And you have spoken to no one of this?" he said.

"No one."

"Not even your husband?" the Major said.

She shook her head.

"My letters are a slightly sensitive matter between us," she said, after a moment. "I get a great many letters. I do not invite them. It is simply that people of my profession seem to attract admirers."

"Especially female singers?"

"Yes. Of course, that is hard for my husband. It is an affront to his pride. So I do not speak to him of my letters, good or bad. I do not want to wound him unnecessarily, and these letters would make him angry. Perhaps that may seem strange to you, gentlemen, but I have been trying to make light of this. I should have carried on like that," she said, getting up. "Really, I have been wasting your time. After all, what can be done about this? I cannot send the police after a shadow who is trying to scare me out of my wits – but who has not succeeded." She held out her hand to Felix, who stood still holding the letter in his hand. Before he knew what she had done, she had taken the letter from him. "This should go in the fire like the rest of them. And I will lose no more sleep."

She walked over to the fire with it, but the Major leapt up and stayed her hand.

"Sir?" she said, in surprise.

"If you burn it, I cannot catch him. And I will catch him. This cannot be allowed to pass."

"I would be happier if I could burn it," she said, "and think it all nonsense. I want to laugh at this wretch, not fear him." And she moved her hand again towards the fire, but the

Major again stopped her. There was a slight struggle between them, the great fire blazing behind them, and the light of it cast strange shadows on her face, making her beauty seem more other-worldly than before.

Suddenly she stepped back and yielded the letter to Major Vernon. She walked swiftly up the room away from them, then spun round, throwing up her hands.

"Yes, yes, you are right. Of course. I concede, but please give me credit for my defiance. Tell me I have courage for being so careless!" and then dropped a low curtsey, as if she was on stage. As she began to rise from the curtsey, Felix met her eyes again and he could not help himself: he rushed forward and took her hand.

"It is more than courage, ma'am. It is..."

She did not allow him to hold her hand for more than a moment. She stepped back from him and turned again to Major Vernon.

"It is less than courage," she said. "It is foolish. I should have spoken to someone long ago. I have let it carry on too long. Thank you for making me see sense."

"I think we should begin by questioning your household," the Major said. "These things often lie close at home. A disgruntled servant –"

"I cannot think of anyone I might have offended. But perhaps I am a bad mistress. I am so busy with my work that sometimes these things may escape me. You should speak to my sister-in-law, Mrs Ridolfi. She engages the servants for me, and counts my sheets and is the repository of all our domestic virtue. She's out in the garden now with my little boy," she said, going to the window. As she looked out Felix saw her face light up and wondered what it might be like to be the recipient of her unfettered affection.

"A handsome boy," Major Vernon said. He was looking out of the other window. "How old is he?"

"Harry is just three," she said.

"That's a charming age."

"I have not yet found an age at which he did not charm me," she said.

The maid came into the room again.

"Madame," she said, "there is a policier at the door. He is asking for Major Vernon."

"If you'll excuse me a moment," said Major Vernon and left with the maid.

Alone with her, Felix felt dry-mouthed again and struggled to think what he might say. He could not make small talk about her child. He was longing to ask her how things stood with Lord Rothborough, but that was not a question that could be asked.

She came away from the window and went to the piano, picking out a few notes as she stood there.

"I need to send for a tuner," she said.

"Lord Rothborough would probably insist upon you using his man," Felix said.

"Yes, probably," she said, glancing up at him for a moment. She played another chord and winced. "Oh dear."

"Do you know him well?" he managed to ask.

"Scarcely at all," she said.

"Then he presumes," he said.

"He is not the only one," she said. "And in my profession, you learn to expect it."

"But still, he ought not to," said Felix.

"It does not offend me. His attention is good-natured and generous. You know, Mr Carswell, he spoke warmly of you. You should not be too unkind to him – I hope you do not mind me saying such a thing. You, on your part, should not assume anything."

It was gently said, but he felt stung by it.

"Ma'am, I did not mean to imply..." He broke off, and found himself looking about the room, at anything but her. How had he managed to offend her so quickly when all he wanted was her good opinion? "I meant only to..."

He would have continued, but at that moment Major Vernon came back into the room.

"I'm afraid we will have to take our leave, Mrs Morgan. Something rather urgent has come up. But I will be attending to this matter of yours as soon as I can, I assure you."

"Thank you."

"In the meantime, if anything else unusual or disturbing happens, please let me know at once. I will put one of my men to watch the house. You can send messages by him."

"What could be more urgent than those threats?" said Felix as they hurried downstairs. He had no desire to leave at all.

"How about a dead body?" said Major Vernon.

Chapter Five

Giles looked about him, taking in the circumstances.

The room was large, cool and light, with a five-lancet window filling the entirety of one wall — that was the window that could be seen from St Anne's Street, Giles thought. The opposite wall was filled entirely with the organ pipes. Beneath the large window was a raised dais with a plain communion table with an equally plain cross upon it. There were two floor-standing candlesticks heavy with melted wax, and numerous other candlesticks, also containing half-burnt candles.

On the floor directly below the dais, lying on his back with his hands folded as if in prayer, was the body of a young man. His head was resting on a kneeler and his wavy, pale corn-gold hair had been carefully swept back from his forehead. His eyes were closed, his expression blank. He was the image of dignity and peace in death, yet there was something profoundly shocking about him.

He was scarcely a man, more a boy, and the clear midday light in the room showed his considerable beauty.

"And this is exactly how you found him, Mr Watkins?" Giles said, turning to the younger of the two men who had accompanied him and Carswell.

"Yes, exactly."

"You did not touch anything?"

"No, nothing. I may have touched him when I went to see if he was breathing — well, to see if he was dead. Then I locked the door and went straight to Canon Fforde."

"I'm surprised you didn't go to the Dean, Mr Watkins," said Lambert Fforde.

"I thought since — well, I knew your connection with

Major Vernon, sir, and I thought it better. Besides, the Dean..."

"The Dean will need this broken gently to him, yes indeed. I see your point," said Lambert.

"And you recognize him?" said Giles, turning to his brother-in-law.

"Yes, he's one of the Vicars Choral," said Lambert. "His name is Charles Barnes."

Carswell had knelt down and was examining the body. He felt the dead man's hand. "He's not been here long. He's still warm."

"Of course he is!" exclaimed Watkins. "He was alive last night!"

"When you're done, can you make a drawing of this?" Giles said. "Just as he is now – and all the objects around it."

"Yes, of course," said Carswell.

"It's so deliberate," Giles said. "But no obvious signs of violence."

"Well," said Carswell, "I'm not so sure about that. That looks suspiciously like a ligature mark to me." He loosened the stock and pulled back the collar, exposing the bare flesh of the neck. "Or at least bruising of some description." Then with a flick of his finger he had pulled back an eyelid. "Dilated pupils. That's interesting, certainly."

"A ligature!" exclaimed Watkins. "Are you saying –?"

"I'm not saying anything yet," said Carswell.

"A ligature – that means strangulation," said Watkins. "Dear Lord above! Strangulation! But who in the world would want to strangle poor Charlie Barnes? Why, he was practically a child!"

"Mr Carswell is only speculating at this point, Mr Watkins," said Giles. "What caused this remains to be seen."

"Something – somebody caused it," Watkins said. "You don't just lie down and die like that. Charlie was as fit as a fiddle. This – this is murder! There is no other word for it!"

Whatever it is, it is strange, thought Giles staring down at the carefully arranged body while Carswell continued his cursory examination.

"But who on earth would wish to murder young Barnes?" said Lambert. "I shall have to go and tell the Dean," he added with a sigh.

"Yes, you had better. And you, Mr Watkins, you can tell me everything you know about Mr Barnes."

Carswell stood calmly making his sketch while Giles led Watkins to one of the benches by the side.

"Everything?" Watkins said after a minute.

"Every little thing that you can," said Giles, taking out his notebook.

"Well, he's... he was," Watkins corrected himself with a gulp, "one of my best tenors, with an exceptional range. Very sweet, pure voice that blends well. Perfect top notes. Could sing alto at a pinch. And getting better every day. Just the sort of man one needs. Last Sunday, for example, I gave him the solo in the Nunc – Bryce in F – and he sight-sang it at short notice and did a good job. Perhaps you heard it?"

"I was away on Sunday," said Giles.

"Usually Harrison would have done it but he was ill. Or at least said he was – I'm not sure he wasn't exaggerating. Jos Harrison has a touch of the prima donna about him, on occasion, but I let him get away with it, because he is so exceptional." The words faded and Watkins glanced away, overcome for a moment. "What will I tell him, for God's sake? He will be heartbroken."

"Mr Harrison is another of the Vicars Choral?"

"My other first-class tenor, yes."

"And they were close, Mr Barnes and Mr Harrison?"

Watkins nodded.

"Like brothers," he said. "This will be dreadful news for Harrison. I should go and find him."

"All in good time, Mr Watkins," said Giles. "What can

you tell me about Mr Barnes' family? Was he a Northminster man?"

"I don't think so. Not by birth. But he lived with his uncle – can't recall the name – but he's that bookbinder down the little lane past the White Hart. Charlie was still apprenticed to him – that was the trade he was supposed to be learning but his heart was not in it, and I think with good reason. He was not just a fine singer but also a promising organist."

"Sledmere, perhaps?" said Giles.

"That's the fellow. Heavens, what a specimen he is! I took a few scores in there for repair and he treated me as if I was asking him to bind some obscene portfolio. Practically a Dissenter. He did not like Charlie singing at the Minster, I am sure of that. I think he believes that music is wicked." Watkins shook his head.

"And did Mr Barnes have a sweetheart?" Giles asked.

"I don't think so," said Watkins. "But you should talk to Jos Harrison. He knew him better than I did."

"I will," said Giles.

"I should like to have known him better. I had hoped to. I have not been here so very long, you see, Major Vernon, and perhaps I am a little preoccupied in my spare time with various matters." Watkins got up, walked over to the body, and stood gazing down at it. "And now I shall never know him, shall I? Or hear that wonderful voice again. I was writing a setting of the canticles with his voice in mind, and I don't know how I shall find the heart to finish it."

Chapter Six

Giles stood at the front door of a modest house in one of the narrow lanes of Northminster. It was marked by a sign: "Sledmere. Bibles and Bookbinders."

The blinds had all been drawn down; a "Closed" sign was propped up in the front window, while black crepe adorned the knocker. The house was already in mourning, for Giles had sent Sergeant Collins to inform the Sledmeres that their nephew was dead.

Giles knocked and waited for some time to be admitted. At last the door was opened by a woman. She was dressed in black which did not look much like mourning, but rather her habitual attire. She frowned at him.

"Mrs Sledmere?"

"Yes?"

"Major Vernon, of the City Constabulary. I have come to speak to you about your nephew. I think Sergeant Collins will have mentioned that I would call?"

"Yes, yes, I suppose he did," she said. "I'll get my husband."

"I should like to speak to all the household, if I may."

"Yes, well, if you like..." she seemed nonplussed. "I'll just get Mr Sledmere."

"Thank you," he said. "May I come in?"

"Yes, yes, you had better," she said, closing the door behind him. "Wait here, sir, will you?"

So Giles waited as she disappeared into the back of the house. As he stood there, he sensed he was being watched, and stepped forward a fraction so that he could see up the stairs. He peered up into the darkness and thought he saw a pale white face and some white skirts, but only for a moment. Whoever she was vanished into the shadows.

Sledmere came out of the back of the house, pulling on his coat. He looked displeased at the interruption.

"I am sorry to have to intrude at such a difficult time," Giles said. "But any help you can give me now will more quickly bring to justice the person responsible for this."

"Then it is murder?" said Mrs Sledmere.

"I am afraid there is little doubt of it," said Giles.

"As they sow, so shall they reap," said Mr Sledmere, with a fierce shake of his head. "The vengeance of the Lord is a terrible thing, sir, a terrible and wonderful thing. A stubborn, wicked soul has been cast down into the fiery pit, and no mistake about it. The Lord God hath acted against his iniquity and sent him down. This is a great lesson to us all. For the Lord your God is a jealous God, and shall not suffer a sinner to live!"

"I am sure you are right," Giles said, formulating his words with care, somewhat astonished by this outburst. "Perhaps you might explain a little more to me? How had your nephew offended you?"

"It was not I who was offended!" exclaimed Sledmere. "It was against the Lord he sinned, and now he must pay for eternity. I warned him, many the times I warned him. I have been up many a night attempting to save his soul and bring him into the light of faith but he would not go. He was resolute in his sin, and this is the result."

"And the person who did this to Charles, what do you think of him?" Giles asked, turning to Mrs Sledmere. "He has denied your nephew the chance to come to repentance. Surely he must be punished for that?"

"You will not find him, not in mortal form," Sledmere broke in, for Mrs Sledmere seemed about to answer. "It was the hand of the Lord. He has sent an avenging angel. That is the long and short of it."

"You must forgive me, sir, if I offend you, but that I cannot believe. Your nephew Charles was wilfully murdered by a fellow human, who must be found and punished for their wickedness. As a good Christian you must assist me in this. You know it is your duty."

There was a long silence, and then Sledmere jerked his hand towards the stairs.

"We will go up to the parlour," he said.

They went into a grim little room, more like a waiting room than a place a family might use for their recreation. But Giles supposed that the comforts of this world were of little interest to Mr and Mrs Sledmere. Above the fireplace there was a large framed text, which had been draped with black gauze. Catching sight of this as he came in, Mr Sledmere snatched it down and threw it into the empty grate. "Woman, I thought I told you that we would have no signs!" he said to his wife.

"It was not me," said Mrs Sledmere. "Rose must have —"

"Did you not make it clear to her?" he said.

"I cannot. She will not listen to reason. She is too —"

"You must be firmer with her," Mr Sledmere said. "It is for her own good. Her soul is in as much peril as his if you do not!"

"Rose?" enquired Giles as mildly as he could.

"Our daughter," said Mrs Sledmere. "Our only child."

"Is she close in age to Charles?" Giles asked.

"She is seventeen," said Mr Sledmere. "And not yet saved."

"May I speak to her?"

"She is not well," said Mrs Sledmere. "This news, it has…"

"She is very upset?" Giles said. Mrs Sledmere nodded.

"Perhaps you might tell me when you last saw your nephew?"

"At breakfast this morning," said Mrs Sledmere.

"Mr Sledmere?" said Giles.

"He was at his work – well, he was supposed to be at his work with me in the shop, but he took offence when I rebuked him, and went – well, I don't know where. He left the house."

"He said nothing to indicate where he might have gone?"

"No," said Sledmere with a shake of the head. "No, he went and that was it. And the Lord's judgement is on him now!"

"He took offence – you mean you quarrelled?"

"I rebuked him and he took offence," Sledmere said, as if Giles were simple-minded.

Giles turned to Mrs Sledmere again.

"Has Charles been living with you long?"

"He came to us at three years old," Sledmere answered for his wife. "His mother left him here."

"Your sister, Mr Sledmere?"

"Aye."

"Who was his father?"

"A dirty rogue of a soldier. My father had to pay him to marry her. An Irishman."

"Is he still living, do you know?"

"No. If he was, I should have gone after him for the boy's keep."

"And his mother?"

Sledmere shrugged. "I think she is in London. If she is still alive, she is beyond hope. She took to a life that..."

"She was very pretty," put in Mrs Sledmere. "In a showy sort of way."

"And you brought him up as your own? A great act of charity."

"The idea was that he should take over the business," said Mrs Sledmere.

"He was your apprentice?" Sledmere nodded.

"And before that? He was a singer, I understand. Was he at the Minster school?"

"He was. A grave mistake. He got his schooling free and I thought it was in God's service, but I see now it was a snare. He was corrupted by it. I thought myself a Christian then, sir, but I was not. I did not know the Truth. I had not opened my heart to the word of God. Mercifully God showed me the Way, but that boy..." Sledmere shook his head, and turned away a little, showing something that might almost be interpreted as grief. "He would not be guided. He would not. He was seduced by all that vain pomp and show."

"Mr Watkins tells me he was an extremely talented musician."

"Music is the work of the Devil, sir!" said Sledmere with something of his former fire. What wretched sect do these people belong to, Giles wondered, to preach so hotly against something as innocent as music?

"It is music that is at the heart of that boy's destruction!" Sledmere went on. "And Watkins and those Vicars Choral are the tools of Satan himself. We can only pray that they will see this business for what it is – a dreadful warning from their true and loving Redeemer!"

"Amen," muttered Mrs Sledmere, her head bowed.

Giles had a great fear that the pair of them were about to sink to their knees and start to pray, so he said quickly, "Perhaps I might see Charles' bedroom? Mrs Sledmere, would you show me? I am keeping you from your work, I think, sir." He was anxious to speak to her alone. He had hoped she might give a more straightforward recitation of the facts, without the constant embellishment of hell-fire. And he was also anxious to speak to the mysterious Rose.

"If you think it necessary," said Sledmere, "but I do not know how you will profit from it."

"God sets us all to our labours," Giles said. "And we must endeavour not to disappoint Him. I must do as my duty directs and find the man who killed your nephew, Mr Sledmere."

Sledmere went off downstairs – rather reluctantly, Giles felt. He knew he would not be allowed to leave the house without a few tracts, or at least being asked if he knew his Saviour. He would need to have a response ready for that.

Mrs Sledmere showed him up another two flights of stairs – the house was like a tower, the rooms stacked one above the other – and stopped in front of a closed door, indicating with a brief wave of the hand that he might go in. Even in the gloom of that top landing, Giles could see the reason for her reluctance to do anything more. Her emotions had overcome her.

"You should go and sit down," he said. "You have had dreadful news today. Sometimes it takes a little time to feel the smart."

She nodded and turned away, her hand over her mouth. She let out a muffled cry and then she hurtled downstairs and Giles feared she would tumble head over heels and break her neck. Then a door slammed and he was alone. Or so he thought.

A moment or so later he became aware that he was being observed again, this time through a chink in another door on the landing. He could hear the person breathing.

"Rose Sledmere?" he inquired. "Is that you?" The door opened a fraction more. "You should go to your mother if you are able. She needs you."

The door opened slowly, but still not entirely, but enough for Giles to see the spy: a fair-haired, grey-faced girl in a white dress. She was extremely thin and not very tall. She did not look seventeen, he thought.

"I have come to look at your cousin's room," he said.

At that she dashed in front of him and stood with her back to the door to Charles' room. She shook her head, and all her wild, unbrushed hair with it, and mouthed, "No, no, no..."

"I'm afraid I must, Miss Sledmere. I want to help you. I am going to catch the man who killed your cousin."

"No!" she shouted, and stamped her foot. "You cannot go in there. You cannot!"

He would have answered, but he found suddenly that he could not. A memory had risen up unbidden, awakened by the girl's demeanour: Laura barring the door to him.

It had been one of the first manifestations of her illness – those violent but childish tantrums. On that occasion she would not allow him into the now empty room that they had used as a nursery. She had stood in there, in her nightgown and bare feet, her hands clasping the knob behind her, a manic expression on her face, while he had reasoned with her, then wheedled and begged, and then, his temper breaking, he had raged at her, which had of course made her own hysteria all the worse.

He tried to tell himself this was just a girl suffering from shock, wild with her grief. But he could only think of Laura and the wretched degeneration of her mind, the decay and waste of it all, and for a moment he stood there unable to do anything but try and master himself, let alone deal with this creature in front of him. Every painful scene that he had ever witnessed with her, every step away from him and into the possession of her demons, seemed to rise up in his mind like a noxious vapour and threaten to choke him.

It was with some difficulty that he managed to speak, reminding himself as he did so that if there was any profit in such trials, then this was a moment to realise it. He knew what he must not do. He had done it all wrong with Laura. A hundred times he had done it, and more, and he had paid dearly for every lesson. But he had, he realised, a faint glimmering of what he must do now, and it would be easier. As his clouded mind cleared he remembered that this girl was nothing to him. She had not shared his bed or his breakfast table. She had not slapped or bitten him, or broken his heart a hundred times over.

He went and sat down on the top step, so that his back

was to her. He took out his notebook and began to make some notes. He was not sure for how long he waited but at length he heard a door latch being lifted and the door being opened. He waited another long moment, slowly putting away his notebook, before he got to his feet and turned.

Rose Sledmere had vanished but the door to Charles Barnes' room was open.

"You mustn't touch anything," he heard her say as he came quietly, cautiously into the room, as into the lair of an animal.

A plain white quilt covered the bed, with a cross lying on the pillow. Rose stood making minute adjustments to its position.

Giles glanced about him: white walls, a scrubbed floor, a shelf of folded linen and a row of hooks upon which Barnes' clothes were hanging. There were rather more clothes than might be expected for a young man in such circumstances. There were several coats, a silk hat, some fancy waistcoats, and a striking dressing gown in crimson satin, which Rose now took down from its hook. She wrapped her arms about it, as if she were cradling a child, stroking it. She walked away with it towards the window.

Giles used her distraction to take a closer look at the coats – they were of expensive cloth, with vivid silk linings. There were only a few tailors in Northminster who would make such coats, and they did not look as if they were second-hand. Charles Barnes had been particular about his clothes, even extravagant. He would have run up large debts for clothes like this.

He turned his attention back to Rose. She was still standing in the window, cradling the dressing gown. Could it be possible that she had something to do with his death?

"Is there anything you would like to tell me, Rose?" he said softly.

He saw her bend her head and sniff at the satin.

"Are you sure?" She shook her head, but he could see she was shaking. "Do not be afraid," he went on, but in asking her to trust him he felt the lie sting his lips. If this poor, unhappy girl was the author of her cousin's death, then she had a great deal of which to be afraid. He wished he did not have to ask. He wished he might leave her there alone with her grief. Her pain was tangible to him, and the possibility of her guilt too easy to contemplate.

The light was fading now, and his zeal for the task in hand seemed to be fading with it. He left without another word.

Chapter Seven

"Cause of death: asphyxiation, by strangulation, using a ligature," said Felix. "Time of death: sometime this morning. Can't be more precise than that. There was a partially digested meal in the stomach. His breakfast, most likely."

Major Vernon was pinning his notes to his office wall. "Do you have your sketch?"

Felix handed it to him.

"Excellent," he said. "A good likeness. You are perfectly justified in being an art critic."

He went to the wall and pinned it up at the centre.

"So what do we have?" He stepped back, his arms folded, regarding the collection of papers. "A handsome young bookbinder's apprentice, strangled and then laid out with care. Not just left in a heap, but laid out."

"Out of remorse?" said Felix.

"That occurred to me. A fit of destructive rage leading to a horrible outcome – and then an attempt to make it better. So this person, our murderer – will he be in mourning? Has he perhaps destroyed something he loved?"

"Watkins seemed quite distressed," Felix said. "And very quick to talk about murder, don't you think?"

"Given that he is apparently the keeper of the only key to that room, we cannot rule Mr Watkins out," said Major Vernon. "However, is it possible for a female to strangle a young man?"

"Barnes was not well-developed for his age," Felix said. "Undernourished, certainly."

"So a woman – it's possible. Would one put up a struggle with a sweetheart? It would help if there had been some witnesses about the place, but we have so little to go on. Nobody in the Precincts seems to have seen anything – or if they have they are not admitting to it yet. We shall have to be patient."

Vernon turned from his display of papers on the wall and looked at Felix for a moment.

"You are clearly dressed to go somewhere," he said.

"I have been asked to dinner at the Deanery. I don't know why they asked me, though. I'd rather not have to go. If you need me this evening –"

"No, you had better go. It is a great honour. They are sparing with their invitations."

"Then why on earth have they asked me?" said Felix.

"You will find out when you are there, I am sure. And you can be useful to me, pouring bland assurances in Dean Pritchard's ear. Tell him that our investigation is perfectly in hand and will be solved in the blink of an eye, without any attendant scandal."

"That's not very likely, surely?"

"One can at least hope for such a miracle. That this puzzle is not a puzzle at all."

"I'm not sure I can manage bland assurances," said Felix.

"You'll find they come easily enough," said the Major. "There is always very little to excite anyone in that house."

Felix had not dressed with such care simply for his dinner at the Deanery. He intended first to look in at Mrs Morgan's open rehearsal – the one to which she had invited Lord Rothborough.

He had sat in his bath, debating whether or not to go. The more he thought of it, the more he was convinced he must go. It would be in the nature of an experiment. He wanted to know if the dazzling, confusing impression she had created in him was anything more than a momentary madness – something like the temporary damage to the eyes made by looking directly at the sun.

He profoundly wanted to see her again. He felt thirsty for her presence. Yet at the same time he wished to be free of her allure. His rational mind wanted to be swiftly disillusioned by her. He hated the feelings she had produced in him. He felt wretched for being enslaved by her smile, yet at the same time extraordinarily alive. As he had gone about his business that afternoon, performing the post-mortem on Charlie Barnes, he had felt a heightened awareness of every action he took, as if the brightest of lights was shining upon him. It was disturbing and yet incredibly invigorating.

He had put on for the first time the new suit of clothes that he had had made by Major Vernon's tailor. After his old rusty black coat had been ruined by bloodstains, the Major had gently suggested he think about replacing it, and had invited Loake to call upon him. Loake had made the case for two new suits, one in professional black and one for dress in a deep inky blue, and at such a price that Felix could not object. After being sneered at by the servants at Holbroke he felt the need of a little armour, and the dress coat, with its dove-grey satin lining, gave him the air of a gentleman without veering towards dandyism. He was slightly shocked at himself for entertaining such worldly considerations. The Rev. James Carswell would have had some sharp words to say about it, but his father was not there, and he felt that Major Vernon's advice in such matters ought to be heeded. However, he had not replaced his old overcoat nor his broad-brimmed hat, and these made him feel less like a stranger to himself as he set out for Mrs Morgan's rehearsal.

If he had hoped for objectivity, he knew the moment he pushed open the hand-door in the great west door of the Minster that he would not find it. A woman was singing, and with a voice of such unbearable beauty that he knew it must be her.

It was like a heady, potent scent escaping from a flask. It surrounded him, embraced him and then seeped its way into every pore of his skin. It was as if he had never heard a woman sing before. Those high, pure notes slicing through the chilly air of the Minster were like a well-honed blade through his heart. He was astonished at the corporeal nature of it. It caused him pain and pleasure in the same instant. He wanted it to cease and at the same time he wished she never would be silent.

He stood, hardly daring to look for the source of the sound, but then forced himself to look directly at it, and saw she was standing, alone, in the great transept crossing under the canopy of stone arches. She was dressed in black, a close bonnet covering her glorious hair, looking more austere than she had done in her pale morning gown, more majestic and even less approachable. She held no music. She knew the aria perfectly, and she was entirely given up to the performance. As he looked at her, she seemed to be singing to him, and this increased both his discomfort and his joy. A tender, rippling succession of sweet notes reached out to him as she entered the ending of the piece. "Of endless light" were the final words, and he was left astonished by the raw emotion she had produced in him, while the organ accompaniment continued to the end. He scarcely heard it.

The organ finished but there was no silence, rather a lingering vibration in the great space, as if the stones were as unwilling as he to let go of the music.

He walked up the great centre nave of the Minster, determined to speak to her, but utterly unable to think what he would say. She turned away towards the east end and he saw she was no longer alone. Lord Rothborough, who must have been sitting in the quire, was coming towards her, clapping his hands together quietly.

"Magnificent, quite magnificent," Felix heard him say. "What can one say, what can one say?"

He wanted to turn on his heel and run, but it was too late. Lord Rothborough had seen him, and was waving him towards them. He was forced to go and join them.

"I have heard a great many interpretations of that aria in my life, Mrs Morgan," Rothborough said, "and none to equal that. Felix, you have been fortunate to hear it."

"Yes, I believe so," he managed to say, as Mrs Morgan bestowed a smile upon him. He stared at the distant south door of the Minster as if it mattered. "It was..."

"I can take little credit for it," she said. "This is a powerful space. It is made to carry the human voice. A wonderful piece of ingenuity. Our ancestors were clever men."

"I cannot agree, ma'am," Rothborough said. "It was the interpretation that was particularly moving."

"Thank you," she said, with a slight incline of her head. "But how could I not sing with feeling in such circumstances? Mr Watkins told me about the case just when I arrived here to rehearse. He was so upset – I wonder he managed to play." She glanced about her. "I should go and speak to him."

"About Mr Barnes?" said Felix. She nodded.

"What case is this?" asked Rothborough.

"A death," said Felix. "Rather unusual circumstances. It is under investigation."

"I suppose that was why you and Major Vernon were called away," she said.

"Yes, it was."

"Another murder in Northminster," said Lord Rothborough. "Good heavens!"

"That has not yet been established," Felix said quickly.

"You have brought a curse on the place, Felix," said Rothborough. He turned to Mrs Morgan. "So, ma'am, will you sing again? I rather think you should not after such a performance. Allow me to escort you home."

"That would be an honour, Lord Rothborough," she said. "But I have more work to do yet, and Mr Watkins will make sure I am taken safely to my door. His mother is a great friend of mine, and I must question him about a dozen trivial things in order to quiet her mind about his life here. Although perhaps I will not tell her of this sad business."

At that moment, as if on cue, Watkins appeared at the far end of the quire and came down towards them. He stopped at the sight of the three of them and was about to walk away, but Mrs Morgan went straight up to him and put her hands on his shoulders, pressing her forehead to his, whispering something to him. Felix saw him nod and then kiss her on the cheek. She took his arm and they walked away, their heads bent together in confidential conversation.

"She is a most generous creature," said Lord Rothborough, gazing at her in such a way that Felix wished to step in front of him and block his view. At last, Lord Rothborough turned his insolent eye on Felix. "So," he said, "what is the occasion?"

"I am going to dinner."

"Where?"

"At the Deanery."

"Ha," said Rothborough. "He is dangling for a mitre, you know. I dare say he would ask me if he could. Perhaps he wants you for one of his girls and thinks it would serve him to have such a connection with me. Take care, Felix."

"I assure you, sir, I am in no danger there," said Felix.

"You have been a fool before," said Rothborough. "A great one."

"Thank you for reminding me," said Felix.

"Woman are a great risk," said Lord Rothborough, unperturbed by Felix's sarcasm. "A necessity, but a risk never the less. Particularly at your age and in these provincial circles. All these dangerous young ladies with absolutely nothing to recommend them except their manners and their complexions. They are all about love, and that is a luxury none of us can afford."

"I would have thought you could, my lord," said Felix. "Of all people."

"Do not be vulgar, Felix," said Rothborough. "You know as well as I do that sentimentality in the matter of marriage is the last thing that people like us can afford. Marriage is too important a business to be clouded by it."

"People like us?" Felix said, with some incredulity. "My lord, whatever you may be, you know I never can be!"

"You play the same tune again and again, and you play it badly, sir!" exclaimed Rothborough.

"As do you," retorted Felix. "Now, I must go or I shall be late. Naturally I do not want the young ladies to think I am anything less than a paragon! A perfect potential husband, in fact."

Lord Rothborough looked for a moment as if he was extremely provoked, but then, with the control that he was famed for in public life, he paused, and said, in a quiet, surprisingly conciliatory voice, "Felix, I know I offend you when I speak like this. I know how it must seem to you. You are young and full of passion. I was like you once, though I dare say you cannot believe it, and I learnt bitter lessons from my mistakes, of which there were many, the good Lord only knows – so many. I only wish to spare you that pain. Love is a game for fools. Do not play it, I beg you."

"But –"

Lord Rothborough held up his hand to silence him and took a step closer. Speaking in almost a whisper, he said, "Admire women, yes, kiss them, take them, get the best of them, but do not give them your heart. You must remain the captain of your own soul, Felix – that is the best advice I can give you. Now go – you certainly must not be late."

Chapter Eight

"So this is the only key?" Giles said to his brother-in-law, holding up the key to St Anne's Chapel by the scrap of black-and-white ribbon that Watkins had presumably put on it to identify it. "The one that Watkins used?"

"I very much doubt it," said Lambert Fforde. "Sherry?"

"Just a small one," said Giles.

Canon Fforde's study in the Treasurer's House was a room of some state. It had been fitted up a century ago in the most fashionable style of its day, with an elaborate plaster ceiling of shells and scrolls, all touched with gold, while the walls were covered in scarlet damask trimmed with gilt fillets. The damask was faded to rose now and the gilt was tarnished, but the impression remained of sumptuous but discreet grandeur, of easy dignity. In this Giles considered it suited Lambert's character well.

"See what you think of this," said Lambert handing him a glass. "It's a nice little Oloroso. I wouldn't waste this on my commonplace visitors." He held his own glass up to the light, examining the colour. "This is only for those who appreciate such things." He took a sip and relished it, and then, as if ashamed of his pleasure, put the glass down on the baize-covered wine table, next to the key for St Anne's Chapel. "But it's a terrible business that brings you here, Giles, however glad I am to see you."

"So there may be other keys?"

"I am sure there will be, but where they are and to whom they were issued, is something of a mystery. I have been racking my brains all afternoon on this, for I knew you would want to ask me about it. Of course, this is an imperfect institution at the best of times, and the keys are always going astray. It is a source of some annoyance, I can tell you."

Giles sipped his own wine, which was rich, mellow and warming. Lambert was looking enquiringly at him, waiting for his verdict.

"Very good indeed," Giles said, wishing that the business of the keys was as straightforward.

"Isn't it?" said Lambert, pleased. "Quite a discovery, if I say so myself. But we shall not tell Sally what it cost me."

"No, of course not," said Giles, smiling. "So, to return to these keys – I think we had better get together every Minster employee and inspect their key sets. From the Dean to the assistant verger – Old Walt? Is that his name?"

"Old Walt indeed," said Lambert. "He has a little cubby hole where goodness knows what may be found."

"Watkins tells me he was expecting him to come and blow for him this morning. Did you see him about when you came back with Mr Watkins?"

"No," said Lambert.

"And how did Mr Watkins seem when he came and spoke to you?"

"Agitated – and out of breath. He had run all the way. And he just ran in here, without waiting to be announced. It was a good thing I was alone."

"And would you say he looked genuinely shocked?"

"Yes. Goodness, you don't think –?"

"I am just considering every angle. That is all I can do, disagreeable though it may seem."

"Not to you, I think, Giles," said Lambert. "I think you have a decided taste for all this." Giles shrugged and drank some more sherry. "It is just as well you do and that you have the aptitude for it as well. Given the circumstances – that business with Rhodes, and now this."

"Tell me some more about Mr Watkins," said Giles. "I get the impression he is not fond of the Dean, and that the

Dean –"

"Is not fond of him. It's all rather unfortunate," said Lambert. "Especially as I pressed for his appointment. He is an excellent musician and we are lucky to have him, but the Dean is perhaps not so interested in music as I am. He doesn't understand the importance of the post, I think. He believes we are paying Watkins too much, for a start – and I am sure of course that Watkins does not think we are paying him enough."

"Of course," said Giles, with a smile. "What man ever thinks he is getting paid enough?"

"I did manage to get him a better house but it was a close run thing. The Dean thought that only a man in orders should have that house. That it was a gentleman's house, and by implication, Watkins is not a gentleman."

"Who are his people?"

"His father was organist at one of the City churches, and his mother – well, of course, we shall have a great treat when we hear Mrs Morgan, but she will never match Miss Collier, as Mrs Watkins was then. Quite the most exquisite voice I have ever heard. Not showy – but with such feeling and truth to it. And wonderful diction. I am rather hoping she will come and visit her son, so I might have the pleasure of hearing her again. She might be persuaded to sing in private."

"And there is nothing about Watkins that you have found fault with?"

"No, not really. Well, he was a trifle high-handed at first – in the matter of removing some of the dead wood in the choir, for example. There was a fellow called Fildyke; well, there's no doubt he did that badly. And Dean Pritchard was not pleased with him. Neither was I, for that matter, but for different reasons. It had to be done, but there are ways of doing these things that cause less pain. And he did cause pain. But he is a young man and inexperienced, and who of us have not made such mistakes in our careers? When I told him he had done it poorly he admitted as much to me. He was suitably penitent and I do not think he will do such a thing again."

"But he is still at loggerheads with the Dean."

"Yes," said Lambert, examining the colour of his wine again, "but to be frank, I think we are all at loggerheads with the Dean to some extent. One can only hope he gets his mitre before too long, and we will be rid of him."

Giles could not conceal his surprise. He was aware that Lambert found the Dean irksome at times, but had not understood the extent of his irritation.

"Strong words, for you," he said.

"I know," said Lambert. "I ought to endeavour to be more patient, but these last few months I have found it increasingly difficult to bear all his little peccadilloes. I would say he is like some old woman in his fussiness, but that would insult the old women I know, who are far more sensible and forgiving than he is. You know he will not come to dinner with us because Mrs Morgan is coming? Can you imagine it? It is one thing to refuse to receive a person but to turn up his nose at another man's hospitality and take issue with his choice of guests!" Lambert broke off. "I am as bad as Mr Watkins. But I am sore on this one, I can't deny it. I feel the insult. God knows, how foolish of me that is. For we shall have a much more amusing evening if they are not there, but it is a pity for Miss Kate that she will not get the chance to meet Mrs Morgan. She is such a sensitive musician and it would be of great interest to her, I am sure."

"And is Mr Watkins coming?"

"Yes, of course. He is the whole reason she is here. She is one of his mother's pupils. And," he added, rather sheepishly, "we will need a competent pianist, if Mrs Morgan decides to favour us with a song after dinner. Not of course that I expect it, but..."

"No, of course not," said Giles smiling.

"And you will join us, I hope?" said Lambert. "And Mr

Carswell?"

"Of course – if it does not go to his head to be asked out to dine twice in one week. He is bound for the Deanery tonight."

"Poor fellow."

At this moment, Giles' sister Sally came in. "Who is a poor fellow?" she said.

"Mr Carswell, for being asked to the Deanery for dinner. I don't think he is sensible of the honour of it," said Giles.

"If honour equates with three hours of bad food and worse conversation," Lambert said, "and liquid that cannot be described as wine except by the loosest definition."

"Lambert," said Sally with a frown. "Must you be so sardonic?"

"I am amongst friends," he said waving his glass. "Will you have a glass, Sal? We will drink to poor Charlie Barnes."

"It is so sad," said Sally with a sigh. "Poor man."

"I cannot imagine he will be anywhere but Heaven," Lambert said, handing her a glass. "But that anyone would want to murder a sweet soul like that!"

"You are sure it is murder?" said Sally.

"Unfortunately, yes," said Giles, sinking back in his chair. "I shall be kept busy by it."

"Then perhaps this is not the right time to have taken that house for Laura," said Sally. "To bring her to Northminster, now, with all this..."

"No, Sal, you shall not make me reconsider that. My mind is made up," Giles said.

"You are sure?"

"Truly. I am only more convinced of it. It is the right thing to do."

"Well, if you think so. But I cannot help but think –"

"Sal," Lambert said, "let it be, for goodness' sake."

"I cannot help thinking you are being swayed by sentiment," she said.

"That may be the case – but since when was sentiment such a bad thing?" Lambert said.

"I am not saying that," she said. "But it may cloud the judgement on occasion, and this is a business that demands the clearest thinking."

"Yes, I know," said Giles. "But I have to live with my conscience. I cannot consign her to oblivion any longer. It is does not feel right."

"You have hardly done that, Giles," said Lambert.

"I know, I know – she is well cared for there and doing as well as can be expected, but I do not feel comfortable with it any more. I want her within reach."

"But you say she does not know you," said Sally.

"She might know me again if she sees me more often. And even if she does not, then at least... well, it has to be better than that place. A real home for her. That is all I am trying to do."

Sally sighed and said, "I do not mean to quarrel with you, Giles, you know that. I just want to make certain that this is the right thing to do. What if – well, what if she becomes agitated again, as she was before?"

"Then we will deal with it. And that house is well suited. She will not be able to wander off. She will be watched day and night."

"It will be expensive," said Sally.

"Perhaps, but what else am I to spend my money on? I don't have any children to educate, do I?"

"God may still grant you that, in time. Things change," said Sally, "in the most surprising ways. You should not be profligate."

"This is hardly being profligate," Lambert said. "What is it that worries you so, Sally?"

There was a long silence and then Sally said, rather quietly, "It is just that... that I find her so difficult. I do not have your faith or your courage, Giles, I have to admit it. I find her a challenge. It is so distressing." She got up from her chair. "And I know how weak, how un-Christian that must sound, but –"

"You do not have to do anything," Giles said. "I do not expect that."

"And how could I not? My own sister?" she said, throwing up her hands. "I must!"

"Sister-in-law," Giles said. "You owe her nothing. You need have nothing to do with this. I know what you mean. She *is* disturbing and distressing. I do not expect either of you to feel in any way obligated towards her or that you have to become involved in this. It is my responsibility alone."

"If only we had known," Sally said. "If only we had known that when you married her there was –"

"It would not have stopped me," Giles said. "I would have dismissed it as a slander."

"Yes, yes, of course," she said.

Giles caught her hand and pulled her towards him.

"It may work. It may not, but I must try. Please do not trouble yourself about her. I can manage everything."

She passed her hand across his hair.

"I will do all I can," she said. "I just must find some of your courage. That is all. And we can spare Ned and his boy one day a week to keep that little garden in trim. He does not have enough to do here as it is."

As he walked back to the Constabulary Headquarters, Giles turned over her words in his mind, thinking of that clean, sea-swept place, the white house in the meadow with its pretty gardens, surrounded by high walls, where Laura was presently lodged. It was a sweet, secluded spot, the very definition of asylum. He thought of the quiet room where Laura sat with her dolls or fiddling with bits of twine, as if she were doing some great work, but only ravelling and unravelling them. Those were the good passages.

Then there were the times when she was sullen with her

private miseries and did nothing but sit, rocking back and forth, never meeting the eye of another soul, least of all his. Perhaps Sally was right and he ought not to move her. But at the same time he knew it would prey on his conscience more not at least to attempt something new.

It had been an exceptional marriage, in the sense that it was rare for English officers in Canada to be married there. Any wives remained at home, and most of his fellow officers were unmarried. Laura was an Englishwoman stranded in Ontario by an accident of family circumstance. She was the niece of the colonel of another regiment who was pleased to get her settled and off his hands. He had no inclination to live respectably and the girl was something of an inconvenience. He committed himself only to finding her a good marriage in as short a time as possible. Giles was an unblemished prospect – letters went back and forth across the Atlantic, all parties were mutually approved and Miss Romney and Captain Vernon were allowed the uncustomary indulgence of making a match of it.

The local girls were annoyed to see that one of the red-coated gentlemen who formed a necessary part of their assemblies had been allowed to marry after all. They wondered in vain if any other exceptions might be made, but then learnt the hard truth – Englishmen only married in their own circles. They flirted a great deal but it was never to be taken seriously.

As a result, the new Mrs Vernon was not popular with the local girls and ladies, especially as the other officers made such a pet of her. They had no colonel's lady, but they had Mrs Vernon, and gave her her due and much more, as the senior woman connected with the regiment, and the doyenne of an already constricted society.

For a high-spirited girl of twenty, not entirely sensible, with only a patchy education, this was not the best of situations. But she was sharp as a needle – that was what had drawn Giles in from the start, and he thought that her intelligence would grow with her years and that marriage and his protection would settle her. Colonel Romney was more explicit. He told Giles that he would not have trusted her to a lesser man – he would correct that slight giddiness she exhibited from time to time. There was nothing to fear. They were well matched in temperament, fortune and position. It augured well.

For the first six months they were happy. The novelty of their situation was enough to keep them cheerful. Giles liked the comforts that a domestic establishment brought him – her cat, his well-cared for linen, the posies of flowers about the house. He liked the intimacy – having conversations in bed, sleeping with her locked in his arms, his face buried in her hair. He liked the unrestrained pleasures of marital love and discovered, once beyond her innocence, that she was saucy and as eager as he was.

He knew that these pleasures would soon be interrupted, imagining in the normal way that there would be children. He had anticipated this to the extent that he gave up one of his horses, and made a few what he hoped were prudent investments back in Northumberland. He acquired a couple of small farms near his brother's estate, to which he hoped to add in future years, much as he hoped to add to the stock of Vernons on the earth. Indeed all his family wished them well in this endeavour. His siblings professed to love Laura without ever having seen her, in their typically generous way. Johnny, his elder brother and the squire, was a settled old bachelor and had put a substantial amount of money down on the table on the occasion of Giles' match, rather expecting him to take the trouble and the risk of getting an heir for his property.

The trouble and the risk proved great enough. As he ploughed through the fraught months of Laura's pregnancy and then all the disasters that followed, Giles began to see why Johnny had never married. Edward's death and Laura's subsequent descent into that miserable, impossible state of living death which now afflicted her, made him think that an obsession with perpetuating a family name was folly. The world existed balanced on a knife edge. One could fall either way – into happiness and prosperity or into unimaginable tragedy. Giles, who had never had much of a stock of self-love or any taste for amateur dramatics, had never fancied he might become a tragic hero. He had tried to live a practical, cheerful, energetic life and had married in hope, not of a great love affair, but for a contented family life, such as that he had known from his own boyhood. His own parents had married in obedience to their parents' wishes and had made a good bargain of it. He had hoped for nothing more, and had been prepared to work to achieve it.

But with Laura, he soon found that her illness was not one that could be dealt with easily. He found he was in possession of a broken-down house, through the empty rooms of which starlings flapped their inky wings and fouled the floors. Good landlords kept their properties in repair but the more he tried, the less viable the structure became. It had crumbled in his hands, leaving nothing to repair.

But that, he told himself as he walked briskly along, was no reason not to try again.

Chapter Nine

After dinner, Felix found himself standing next to Miss Kate Pritchard at the piano, as she searched through her music at his request, looking for the aria he had heard Mrs Morgan singing.

"I think it is an air from Theodora," she said. "With Rosy Steps," and she picked out the melody.

"That's it," he said.

"I can't sing it for you, I am afraid. For one, it is too hard for me," she said, "and I have no wish to spoil your memory of hearing Mrs Morgan sing it. You were lucky."

"It was remarkable," he said, looking over the music.

"And I don't think my father wishes us to have any music tonight," she said, glancing across the room to where the Dean sat talking to another of the dinner guests, "in the circumstances."

"Yes, yes of course," said Felix.

"A ridiculous idea," she said. "Not at all what Mr Barnes would have liked."

"Did you know him?"

"I knew his voice well," she said. "And his playing. And we shared a teacher."

"Oh, who?"

"Mr Watkins," she said.

"Is he a good teacher?"

"Yes. I was getting on very well with him until my father —" She broke off with a sigh. "He has notions, you see."

"Your father?" Felix said.

"I am sure your father has notions too. He is a clergyman, is he not?"

"Yes. Plenty of notions."

"It seems to be a feature of the profession," Miss Pritchard said.

"Not just the clergy," said Felix, thinking of Lord Rothborough and his little lecture in the Minster. He would not like to see him standing there in the corner of the drawing room with Miss Pritchard, having what a casual, conventional observer might label a flirtatious conversation.

"Papa's idea was that I was taking it all too seriously. That composition was not an appropriate study for a young woman. And since that terrible business with my sister and Mr Rhodes, well, he is apt to be..."

"I understand. Then perhaps I ought not monopolise you. I wouldn't like to cause any difficulty, pleasant though this is," he added.

"I can't keep you against your will," she said. "And we ought to see to the proprieties, but..."

"But?"

"I would rather you stayed. I know everyone else so well. They have nothing new to say. You heard the conversation at dinner, and how thrilling it was not?" He nodded. "And although my father might be disquieted, my mother will not be."

"Oh," said Felix, thinking that he really ought to move away. "I see."

"Please, Mr Carswell, do not be afraid. I am not my mother. I am not looking for a husband. Just for a little interesting talk – talk that does not involve the Christianisation of the savages or the impudence of Dissenters."

Felix burst out laughing and found that everyone else in the room was looking at them.

"Now we have given them something to talk about," he said.

"Good," said Miss Pritchard, meeting his eyes with a warm, disarming smile. She really was a charming girl, he thought, and in other circumstances he felt he would have been in all the danger that Lord Rothborough had predicted. But pleasant though it might be to stand and talk like this, it was nothing to the feelings that Mrs Morgan had produced in him. He had never felt anything like that for a woman before, not even for Isabella. That was something new to him.

"You are a mischief-maker," he said.

"No, no, I am not," she said. "It is a distraction for them. To see us talking like this and drawing all their conclusions – well, we do good by our actions. We are entertaining them."

"No, I think it was pure mischief on your part," he said, grinning. "And you know I find that far more amusing." It occurred to him that if he were seen to flirt with Miss Pritchard, a report of it would inevitably find its way to Lord Rothborough. It would be an excellent way to ruffle his feathers.

"Oh, do you?" she said, in such a manner that he realised that she perhaps also wished to be seen flirting with him.

It was clear they had begun to play a game, and one which he found diverting. So he took a half step closer to her and said, "I like to think you are not a paragon."

"I should, of course, be insulted."

"You should – but you are not. Which proves my point."

She smiled and said, "Come and admire these watercolours, Mr Carswell. There is nothing much to admire in them, but we will be able to stand with our backs to everyone."

So they moved away from the piano.

"This is positively scandalous," he said, as they went and stood in front of a pair of landscapes.

"Our alliance will be the talk of Northminster. They will be choosing wedding bonnets."

"They will have to be disappointed," said Felix. "I thought we would elope to Gretna. That would upset the apple-cart, wouldn't it?"

"Oh yes, it would," she said. "Now, will we be rehabilitated in time, or shall we die in penniless squalor, never having been received in polite society again, exiled from all those we love?"

"It depends what sort of a novel you are reading," Felix said, and glanced at her. She suddenly looked rather grave.

"This is not really anything to joke about," she said.

"I think we might be forgiven," Felix said as lightly as he could. "Almost certainly we would be."

"*We* might be, yes," she said, with something in her voice that sounded like bitterness. "I think, Mr Carswell, that we had better circulate after all." And she walked away and went to talk to an old lady about her embroidery.

Chapter Ten

The party broke up shortly after that, and on leaving the Deanery, Felix turned his steps towards Avonside Row. He had decided that he would walk the long way home down Jacob's Ladder, retracing the route they had taken that morning. That this walk took him under Mrs Morgan's windows was a fact he chose not to dwell on.

As he came up on Avonside Row he saw Constable Eakins walking towards him.

"Anything to report?" he asked when they met.

"Next door has had a few callers, but no one here, sir."

"And Mrs Morgan came home safely with Mr Watkins?" said Felix.

"Mr Watkins? The gent that conducts the Minster choir?"

"The Master of Music, yes."

"Well, he brought her home, but he left her at the front gate. She went in alone. Why do you ask, sir?"

"No particular reason," said Felix. "And that back lane – no one has been along there?"

"I've walked around the property every five minutes, just like Major Vernon told me. So I couldn't have missed anything."

At the sound of a sash being raised, Felix glanced over his shoulder, hoping that he might catch a glimpse of her at the window. There was nothing to be seen but the glow of a lamp within, and he turned back to Constable Eakins.

Then a second later a shriek ripped through the air.

It came from the open window – a sustained, hysterical, high-pitched scream, terrifying in itself, as well as for what it implied. What nameless horror had provoked such an extraordinary reaction?

Eakins and Felix rushed round to the front door. As he knocked, Felix turned the handle and was surprised to find that the door was unlocked. He was horrified that the door had been left open in such circumstances. What were her servants thinking?

He ran in and started to sprint up the stairs, his heart pounding at the thought of what might have happened to Mrs Morgan, only to be forced to stop in his tracks. On the landing above him stood the lady herself.

She was holding a candle and was dressed in only her nightgown, her hair cascading down over her shoulders. She looked pale, but it was evident that she was not the source of the scream.

"Mr Carswell!" she said. "What are –?"

"Where? Who?" he said.

She indicated the room from which the sound had come and Felix ran into it, only to find another woman, also dressed in her nightgown. But he scarcely noticed her, for the lamp was on the floor and flames were starting to lick the rug. Felix was obliged to attend to that first, stamping it out, while the woman fell sobbing into Mrs Morgan's arms. A jug of water from the washstand put out the rest of the flames, and then Felix turned and saw what it was that had caused such a reaction.

Lying on the bed, in the centre of the quilted white counterpane, was a small dead bird, with a piece of scarlet ribbon about its neck, like a ligature. Felix glanced at Mrs Morgan who was holding the now howling woman against her, comforting her.

"Get it out of here! Get it out!" the woman shouted.

"This is your bedroom, Mrs Morgan?" Felix said, taking the bird up and putting it into his pocket.

"We share it," said Mrs Morgan, who was already leading the woman out of the room and across the landing. Darkness fell in the room, for she still held the candle, so Felix followed them.

Mrs Morgan crossed the landing and went into a small bedroom. She sat her companion down on a low chair, wrapping a shawl about her and kneeling in front of her, holding her hands.

"Now breathe, Paulina, breathe steady and true. Remember how we were taught? In and then out. In and then out, nice and slow... There, that's better, isn't it?" After this admirable treatment, the woman's hysterical fit seemed to subside. Felix felt he could not have done better himself, and found another score of reasons to admire Mrs Morgan. "There is nothing to be afraid of."

"I know, I know," wailed Paulina. "It's just that... d...d...dead birds... I cannot bear the sight of them, and to turn round and see one!" She buried her face in her hands. "I could have burnt the house down. I could have killed us all!"

"No, no, it would not have come to that," said Mrs Morgan. "And our landlord will forgive us a singed rug," she said. "Do you not think, Mr Carswell?" she added, shooting a gentle smile at Felix as he stood at the door way.

"Certainly," he managed to say, stunned for the moment by the beautiful movement of her pale gold hair as she had turned to look at him.

"Nothing to worry about, then," said Mrs Morgan, stroking Paulina's hair. "Nothing at all."

Felix was even more impressed by her courage than he had been that morning. For it was evident that the bird had been left there deliberately, presumably by the same person responsible for those vile letters.

"Mama?"

Felix looked round and saw that there was a small child in his nightshirt standing by him. He looked sleepy and disorientated.

"Oh, Harry, darling," said Paulina and put out her arms to

him. Mrs Morgan also stretched out her hand and the boy went into the room, and hesitated, as if he did not know which of them to choose. But Mrs Morgan caught his hand and said, "Give your dear aunt a hug, Harry," and propelled him gently into Paulina's arms. Paulina proceeded to give him the most suffocating embrace imaginable, but it clearly soothed her.

"Why don't you go and put Harry back to bed?" said Mrs Morgan. "You could sleep there, if you like." Choking back her tears, Paulina nodded, and stood up, lifting up the boy in her arms now, the shawl falling from her. She carried him out of the room. Mrs Morgan followed with her candle and stood at the foot of the stairs as they climbed up. She waved at the boy, then turned back to Felix.

"Mr Carswell, I can't thank you enough," she said.

"Your servants did not lock your door," he said. "Which one of them should have done it?"

"Berthe, I suppose," said Mrs Morgan. "She must have forgotten."

"It seems gross negligence to me, given that... given that..." He was suddenly disturbed by her lack of clothing. Her nightgown seemed the flimsiest lawn item, slipping from her shoulders. He went and fetched the shawl that had fallen to the floor and handed it to her. "You must keep warm. The shock..."

She smiled, and took it from him, and then proceeded to wrap it about herself with an elegant gesture which seemed to emphasise her lack of dress. He felt his mind cloud with inappropriate desire. He had wild thoughts of falling to his knees and kissing her hem, her bare feet. He wanted to say so much and also to do too much. With difficulty he said, "You must bolt it when I have gone. And I will join Constable Eakins on his watch."

"No, no, that I cannot permit," she said. "You must go to bed. You have been working all day. You must rest. You have a murder to attend to."

"And you are being tormented. I cannot –"

"It is just a dead bird. It does not scare me, let alone torment me. It is just unfortunate Paulina saw it first. I should not have been so rattled, I promise you. Now, you must go home." She wrapped her shawl about her a little more tightly. "Is there no young Mrs Carswell to draw you back to your own fireside?"

"No," he said.

"You should look to it," she said, gently. "It would be good for you."

He managed a smile, though the remark stung him more than he cared to admit.

Chapter Eleven

The next morning, Giles went in search of Watkins and found him marshalling his gaggle of choristers after their morning rehearsal in the song school, before sending them off to their lessons. He had his arms full of music and a flustered air as Giles approached.

"One moment, sir," he said, "if you don't mind."

"No, not at all," said Giles, watching the boys fidgeting and chattering in their places.

"Silence!" Watkins shouted, and they fell silent. "Now, Decani, I want you boys back fifteen minutes early this afternoon for extra rehearsal. You were all very sloppy. Cantores, that was adequate, but only just. And Herbert, your organ lesson today is in the Minster, not St Anne's Chapel."

One of the older boys stuck up his hand.

"Please, sir, does that mean the body is still there?"

"Mr Barnes to you," said Watkins. "No, he has been taken away. And this is not a subject for idle conversation! No matter how odd the circumstances of Mr Barnes' death, it is a great loss to us all and I hope you have all remembered him in your prayers."

"A good point," said Giles, stepping forward, "and there is another way you can help Mr Barnes. If any of you saw or heard anything that seemed out of the ordinary around the Minster Precincts over the last few days, I want you to talk to a member of the constabulary about it."

~

"You have a fine house here, Mr Watkins," said Giles, following him into the spacious hallway of a pretty double-fronted house in the Minster Precincts, tucked into a little yard behind the Minster school.

"It needs furniture and a wife," said Mr Watkins, going into a large room containing only a grand piano made with glowing yellow satinwood, and a dilapidated bureau bookcase. There were no curtains at the window, no rugs on the bare boards, and no pictures on the wall, only patches of darker paintwork where the previous occupant's pictures had once hung.

"And I am unlikely to get the one without the other," Watkins went on, dumping his pile of music on the piano. "Now, the names of all the Vicars Choral – I have them in a ledger. Canon Fforde gave it to me and he was insistent about proper record-keeping – he is right; such efficiency does not come naturally to me, but I am trying. I don't like to disappoint him. He has been good to me. I think it is only because of him that I have this position. The Dean does not much like me." He spoke as he searched through the various pigeon-holes on his desk. "He wanted a man in orders for the job. That was the important thing with him. Not musical ability. Here we are." He brought a battered ledger to the piano and flipped through it. "Most current list – well, it isn't now, if you take my meaning." His finger was resting on the entry labelled "Barnes, Charles." He shook his head, and walked away down the room, wrapping his arms around himself, leaving Giles to study the ledger.

Giles looked down the list of names.

"May I borrow this?"

"Yes, of course, take it away."

"Which of these men would you say Mr Barnes was particularly friendly with? His drinking companions?"

"As I said yesterday, Jos Harrison. And Fred Taylor, I suppose. He was at the Minster school with Charlie, I think. I know they sometimes go drinking together at the Vine in Saddler Street."

"And do you know of any animosities among them? Any quarrels?"

"Not that I know about. But I don't always notice that sort of thing. I don't know them that well. I don't go drinking with them – well, not often. I have to try to maintain a little distance – it makes things clearer, and there is of course the question of my professional standing. The Dean, you see, thinks little enough of me as it is, and wouldn't care to hear of my going out drinking with the Vicars Choral. What I am supposed to do for amusement I do not know, for I am not invited there. Your sister and brother-in-law have been kindness itself, sir, but Dean Pritchard –"

"They entertain very little," Giles pointed out.

"They entertained last night," said Watkins. "And your surgeon Carswell was not too low for them."

"I am never asked," Giles said. "And Mr Carswell was somewhat surprised to be asked. You should not make anything of it, Mr Watkins."

"Of course I should not," said Watkins, sitting down at the piano. "But I cannot help being offended. Not for myself, but for my people. The Dean seems to think that my people are no one. He is offended by the notion of my mother having performed in public, that is at the root of it, and that I will not –" He broke off and played a rapid succession of loud, dissonant chords, then stopped and went on, "She never appeared on the stage, sir, perhaps you might tell him that. He would listen to you, I am sure. Only ever in oratorio. She has never acted. My grandparents would not have dreamt of allowing such a thing."

"Yes," said Giles, returning to his study of the names in Watkins' ledger. "Whose name is this crossed out? I cannot make it out." He brought the book over to Watkins who was still sitting at the piano.

"Oh, Fildyke," said Watkins, starting to pick out a figure which soon turned into an elaborate fugue.

"That is what I thought," said Giles.

"It is crossed out because I dismissed him," said Watkins, continuing to play. "One of the first things I did when I got here. What he was doing in the choir I can't imagine. He can't sing. And of course I had no idea that he was a pet of the Dean's. Not an auspicious start."

"Does this Fildyke have a shop in All Souls?" Giles was forced to speak rather loudly, for Watkins was now going at his fugue fortissimo.

"Yes, I think so," said Watkins ending with a flourish. "I didn't deprive him of his livelihood."

"Was that Bach?" said Giles.

"Yes," said Watkins, with some surprise. "Do you like Bach?"

"Yes, I suppose I do," said Giles, thinking of Laura playing to him on the old piano he had rented for her. How imperfect and yet how delightful it had sounded.

"I want to do one of his Passions," said Watkins. "Nan Morgan agrees with me – they should be performed more widely here – and it would be a great thing for Northminster and the Festival. Herr Mendelssohn has brought out some new editions. If there is a taste for Handel, I think we may develop a taste for Bach."

"Do you know Mrs Morgan well?" Giles said, a little astonished at such a casual reference to the lady.

"She's known me since I was a drooling babe," said Mr Watkins. "She was one of my mother's pupils – one of the best, my mother says. Not that she listened to all her good advice. She would be in a better situation now if she had not been seduced by the idea of doing opera. My mother told her it would not do."

"You think she is in a difficult situation?"

"A woman artist must guard herself more carefully than a

man. It is a fact. And the opera house stage is no place for a respectable woman. But when she fell for that wretch Morgan there was no stopping her. He convinced her to do it."

"Did her family consider it a bad match?"

"Her parents were dead by then, and her brother did little to stop it. He was thinking only of the money – and she made vast sums in those early years. My parents certainly advised her against it and the match with Morgan, but Nan was so in love with him, and in love with the opera. I went to see her début as Cherubino – a friend of mine was depping in the pit and I could not resist going. It was shocking – brilliant, but shocking, none the less."

"Then you are pleased that she only sings at sacred concerts now?"

"Yes, but the damage is done. It is a great shame. For such an extraordinary talent to be tainted in that way."

"I had the honour of meeting Mrs Morgan yesterday," Giles said, "and I see no damage. She was every inch a lady."

"Of course, of course she is, but that is not what the world thinks. And until the world changes, then..."

"But perhaps a woman such as Mrs Morgan is what is required to change that reputation. If women on the opera stage, indeed women on the stage in general, are seen to be as uncorrupted and incorruptible as any ordinary decent woman, then the reputation of the professional will change. She can be an exemplar."

"Perhaps. That was her argument, of course, Major Vernon. She will be pleased to find you espousing it. But I have no great faith in it happening. People will always think ill of women on the stage, no matter how they conduct themselves."

The sort of people who write malicious, anonymous letters, Giles thought, closing the ledger of names. As he picked it up, he revealed a name, hand-written on the unbound folio of music he had put it down on: *K. E. Pritchard.*

Furthermore, Watkins appeared to see him see it, for he at once picked it up and dropped it on another pile, in a manner that was too casual to be anything but deliberate.

"Is there anything else you remember from yesterday, from when you found Mr Barnes? Anything that struck you as unusual? I suppose you got up there regularly. You give the boys lessons there sometimes?"

"Yes."

"And that was why you were going there that day?"

"No, I went to practise. It is a good organ."

"Without anyone to blow for you?"

"No, old Walt would have been along presently. I was expecting him. He has very little to do and I can usually get him to come and blow for me as and when I need him."

"And you asked him yesterday?"

"Yes, I suppose I did."

"But he did not arrive."

"He did. I turned him away when I got downstairs again. After I had locked up. Why?"

"I just want to know exactly when and how it all happened, Mr Watkins."

"Surely that hardly matters – what matters is who put poor Barnes there in the first place, and in that terrible condition."

"You may not know it, Mr Watkins, but it happens often enough that the person raising the alarm on a murder, is the person responsible for the crime."

"What are you alleging, sir?"

"Nothing, I am only explaining my method. I must know all your movements so I may eliminate you."

"Yes, yes, of course," he said, quickly. Giles wondered if he detected nervousness in his voice.

Chapter Twelve

Josiah Harrison was employed as a clerk by Archibald Carr and Sons, one of the largest cloth merchants in the city, so Giles headed to their premises in Greyfriars Street. It was one of several opulent new buildings that had recently been put up in the street. The rest of the street was a building site, as the other merchant enterprises of Northminster were in the process of rebuilding their premises, anxious to keep up with their neighbours. What it would look like when it was all done, Giles could not imagine. At present the new buildings seemed too tall for the street, which was not a wide one, while the variety of fanciful architectural styles and the great expanses of glistening plate glass windows seemed at odds with each other. It was a battle between the quaint and old, and the braggardly new.

Carr and Sons had gone for a tapestry of red and purple brick, with bright white stone dressings, and the impressive entrance took Giles into a showroom, furnished with shining counters and all lit brilliantly by gas. A clerk ran up to meet him.

"I am looking for Mr Josiah Harrison," he said.

"He's not here this morning, sir," said the clerk. "Least I don't think so." He glanced round towards a more senior clerk who stood at counter nearby, and seemed to be in charge of the room.

"No, he is not," said the senior man, with some annoyance.

"And he did not send word he would be absent?" Giles said.

"No," said the senior man, taking in Giles' uniform. "He

may of course deign to show himself in due course, but I don't expect you'll want to wait that long, sir."

"He is often late?"

"More often than not," said the senior clerk. "It is a wonder he has a place. It is only to please Mrs Carr that he is kept on."

"Your employer's wife?" said Giles.

The clerk nodded and then straightened at the sound of footsteps behind them. Giles turned and found himself facing Mr Carr, with whom he had a slight acquaintance.

"Major Vernon?" said Carr. "What brings you here?"

"I came to speak to Josiah Harrison. In connection with a case."

"Who is not here, sir," chimed in the senior clerk. "Again."

Carr frowned. "Perhaps you'd like a glass of wine, sir," he said to Giles, and indicated his office door.

"I have been too tolerant with that young man," Carr said, once they were inside. He poured out the sherry. "I have known for some time that I have made a misjudgement, and now you are here. What was it you wanted with him, Major Vernon? What has he done? Nothing, I trust, that will bring this firm into disrepute."

"I wish to talk to him about a friend of his who has died in odd circumstances."

"That singer boy from the Minster?" said Carr, handing a glass to Giles.

"It's all about town then, Mr Carr?"

"It is," said Carr. "And I am not surprised by it. Pack of rascals."

"You mean the Vicars Choral?" Carr nodded. Giles went on, "Tell me about Mr Harrison. How long has he been in your employment?"

"Couple of years. He came here from Winchester. He'd no background in the cloth trade. He was clerking in an attorney's office. His references were excellent, one from a clergyman at the Cathedral – he was one of the singers there. I was short-handed at the time, and glad to have a presentable man, but he has not proved his worth. Very lax in his timekeeping and the other men do not like him. They do not like his airs."

"Airs?"

"He has a great opinion of his talent. He does sing well, if you like that sort of thing, which I don't much, but my wife, who knows about these things, tells me he does. But it is one thing to sing well, and another to regard yourself as better than your fellows because of it."

There was a knock at the door and a clerk came in.

"Harrison has just arrived, sir," said the clerk. "Shall I send him in to you?"

"Yes," said Carr.

"Might I speak to him alone?" said Giles.

"My office is at your disposal."

Harrison came into the office, looking neither defiant nor penitent. He had the air that Giles had seen many times in court as defendants shuffled into the dock. He knew that he was about to be judged. He was tall and good-looking, but any distinction he might have had was extinguished by the humiliation of the moment. He looked as if he had passed the night in a police cell having been discovered in the throes of debauchery – he had that sallow, dirty look, not helped by the brilliant red of the long scarf he had wound about his neck. With exhausted, nervous eyes he glanced from his employer to Giles, clearly trying to work out what was going on. His glance took in the sherry glasses too – Giles' was still untouched. A sniff had been enough to establish it was not worth drinking after Lambert's fine Oloroso.

"This gentleman is Major Vernon, the Chief Constable, and he would like to speak to you," said Mr Carr. "And then you and I shall have words, lad."

"Save your breath," said Harrison. "I quit. There – that's what you wanted, I'm sure." Carr looked a little startled. "I've no damned stomach for this place any more. This whole stinking town."

It was evident from the slurring of his speech that Harrison was still somewhat under the influence.

"Don't expect a character, Harrison," said Carr, on the way to the door.

"I don't!" said Harrison. "I don't want one. I shall make my living by my voice. This is slavery and I want no part of it. I was a fool to waste my time here."

Carr stopped and turned back.

"You ought to be grateful I did not put you out on your ear months ago," he said. "I should sue you for the return of your wages. You did so little work I reckon I would have a fine case."

"Oh, go boil your head!" said Harrison, with a flamboyant wave of his hand. Carr left the room without further words but he banged the door behind him.

"Sit, won't you, Mr Harrison?" said Giles.

He did so, wearily, like an old man. He rubbed his face with both hands and then looked at Giles.

"Chief Constable," he said. "So, this is about Ch–"

"Charles Barnes," said Giles. "Yes."

Harrison closed his eyes for a moment. Then he gestured towards the full sherry glass.

"Is that going begging?" he said. "I'm rather dry. It's thirsty work quitting."

"You'd be better putting your head under a pump," Giles said.

"I am not ready to be sober," said Harrison, each word punctuated with a pause. He reached out and pulled the sherry glass towards him. "And how sad for this poor glass to go to waste."

"Talk to me a little first," said Giles, removing the glass

and putting it on the mantelshelf. "And then you may have it. Tell me about Mr Barnes. You were friends?"

"Yes."

"Close friends? Like brothers?"

Harrison looked up at him, blinking.

"Yes, close." He exhaled nosily.

"And when did you last see him alive?"

"Night before last. Tuesday night. About eleven."

"And where was this?"

"Top of Saffron Lane. Near The Fox and Grapes."

"And what were the circumstances?"

"We parted there. We were walking back from an evening party." He winced as he said it. "Oh, God."

"Where was this party?" asked Giles.

"At Mr Geoffrey's in Martinsmount."

"A fine address," Giles said. "Were you working there or were you guests?"

"We did sing for our supper," said Harrison. "But it was a generous supper. Mr Geoffrey is hospitable."

"So a pleasant evening?"

"Not really."

"Oh, why was that?"

"He was..." Harrison broke off. "He was... Well, I was vexed with him and we had words. The party was..."

"You quarrelled?"

"How that must look to you," said Harrison, pushing his hands through his hair.

"I merely want the facts," said Giles, sitting down opposite him. "I have formed no judgements. A man can quarrel with another man without it being cause for murder." Harrison looked slightly more at ease. "So," Giles went on, "you say you were vexed with him? Why?"

"He would not see my point of view."

"About what?"

"I... I am thinking of going to London. I thought we

should both go, try our luck together. But Charlie, he has... had never been out of Northminster. He was scared of the notion, so I told him he was a coward and that if he wanted to rot in provincial obscurity he was welcome to, but I was going and that was an end to it." He paused. "I was in my cups. Mr Geoffrey is liberal, as I said."

"And what was his response?"

"He said he could not leave. That there were people he could not leave."

"His family?"

"His family. Though God only knows why. Those ghouls."

"His cousin, though?" Giles suggested. "Rose?"

"Rose," said Harrison bitterly. "Briar Rose, with her little thorns."

"There was not some understanding between them?" Giles said.

"Her fancy," said Harrison. "He was not inclined."

"But she was enough to keep him in Northminster?"

"Out of guilt. They had him on a long chain, like a dog in a yard," said Harrison. "I told him as much and we quarrelled."

Giles put the sherry back on the desk. Harrison drank it in one gulp.

"Did you often quarrel?" Giles asked.

"Yes," said Harrison after a moment. "But we always put it right again. But not... not this time."

"So," said Giles, "you left the party together, but in an ill humour. You walked down from Martinsmount, along Greyfriars?"

"Yes," said Harrison.

"You did not stop anywhere, for a nightcap or a smoke?"

"No. We hardly spoke, and then, at the corner of Saffron Lane, which is where he always turns... turned off, I let him have it. I told him that he was a coward. That if he did not consent to go to London with me, then I would no longer consider him my friend. That I would not write to him when I was gone. I told him I'd had enough."

"Just words? Nothing more? The argument did not come to blows?"

"No."

"And there was no one with you? No one witnessed this argument?" Harrison shook his head. "And how did the matter end, then?"

"When I said my piece, I walked off."

"He didn't respond? And you did not expect an answer from him?"

"I thought he might come after me, I suppose. But he did not. I wish to God he had."

"And you never saw him alive again? Not yesterday morning?"

"No, I did not manage to get to Matins. I was ill."

"Did you miss your work that day, then?"

"Yes, I stayed in my bed until four. I got up and went to Evensong and that's when... when I heard what had happened."

"In your bed all day?"

"Yes."

"Your landlord can vouch for that?"

"I don't know. I didn't see anyone. I was asleep."

"You were ill from drinking?" said Giles.

"I suppose," said Harrison with a shrug.

"And you went straight home to your bed after you had your argument with Mr Barnes?"

"Yes."

"You did not stop anywhere to drown your sorrows, after your quarrel? You were still angry. You lodge, I think, in Malthouse Lane? There are places there that you might have stopped on the way."

"I did not. I went straight home."

"Anyone see you come in? One of your fellow lodgers? Your landlord?"

"No idea," said Harrison. "I didn't speak to anyone, certainly. She may have heard me come in. You ask her."

"I shall," said Giles. "One last question for the present, Mr Harrison. Have you ever had any of the Minster keys in your possession?"

"No," said Harrison. "Why should I?"

Chapter Thirteen

Harrison's lodgings were in Malthouse Lane, one of a network of narrow streets that lay in the shadow of the Minster Precincts, known locally as the Lanes. The houses were ancient and many-storied, and had it been a little closer to the river it might have descended into a rookery. Yet it preserved its respectability, for many of the older, better shops remained there, patronised by those within the Precincts and in the new square at Martinsmount.

Harrison's lodgings were in a slip of a house, half-timbered, neatly painted and well kept up. The landlady, Mrs Marling, opened the door to Giles. A young widow, she was in her apron and looked flustered when he explained his business.

"Why do you want to talk to me about Mr Harrison?" she asked, showing him quickly into the front parlour, and closing the street door. "What's he done?"

"Do you think he's done something?"

She did not answer.

"Mrs Marling?" he prompted her.

"I must just check on my little boy. He's not been well. He's asleep in the kitchen."

And she ran out of the room.

He seemed to wait a long time, so he followed her, and found her on her knees by a small truckle bed by a roaring fire, dabbing a cloth on the forehead of a sleepy but obviously miserable child.

"I'm sorry, sir, he just woke up and he's burning up again, and..." She looked up at him, helplessly.

"Why don't you move him into the front parlour? A

cooler room might help him."

"Oh, do you think, sir?"

"I'll move the bed for you if you like."

She nodded, so Giles carried the little bed through, put it down, and took off a couple of coverlets.

"Can you tell me when Mr Harrison came home on Monday night? Did you hear him come in?"

"Oh yes, I did. He was so noisy he woke Tom," she said with a frown. "And I would have gone out and had words with him, but I was in my nightgown by then and I thought I would leave it until the morning. And this little one was so sickly that night and I was tired, too tired to deal with anything else. I told myself it could wait. But then I clean forgot about it, because of the bother with Tommy – he had the most awful cough all night, and I didn't like to leave him, so I hardly got a wink, and then I fell asleep with him, and when we woke up it was halfway through the morning already."

"So, did you have words with him?"

"Well, no, because I didn't get a chance. He went out before I could. Yesterday morning, that is. I heard the door banging again – he does bang it so. I've told him enough times about it, but he never seems to remember. He bangs it hard enough to shake the house."

"And is that what happened yesterday morning?" Giles said. "Do you know what time he went out?"

"I can't be sure, because I went straight back to sleep. But the next thing I heard was the Minster bell striking ten. Not that I usually lie in my bed so late, sir, you understand, it was just because my little boy had been so ill. You understand, sir, I'm sure?"

"Of course. And I think he's looking better already."

"So he is," she said, going and pressing her hand to his forehead. "Maybe that's the end of it coming on... the Lord be thanked!"

"Tell me about Mr Harrison," said Giles. "How long has

he been staying with you?"

"Almost a year. It was just after Tommy's second birthday," she said, pulling up a stool to the child's bedside.

"And he has a key to come and go as he pleases?"

"Yes," she said.

"What time does he usually leave for work?"

"Just before eight, properly, I suppose. But he never is one for getting to work on time. That Mr Carr should have put him out on his ear long ago – that's what my mother says. She thinks I should put him out as well, of course."

"Does she not approve of him?"

"He is a bit wild," she said. "Coming back in his cups often enough. I didn't tell my mother that, because she'd have had a fit. But he pays when he should and I like to hear him singing about the place. He's got such a lovely voice. My mother was worried that I was getting ideas about him. She thinks I want to marry him. As if I would be so daft!" She gave a nervous laugh.

"But you always get your rent?"

"Always. Never been a problem with that. And he can be as charming as you like."

"Did you meet his friend Mr Barnes, by any chance?"

"Oh yes, a few times. They came and drank tea with me once, when my mother was visiting. A nice young man, and he seems to put Mr Harrison on his best behaviour. Very fond of each other they are, I'd say. Almost like sweethearts – if it isn't silly to say that about two lads, sir, but that was how it strikes me."

"Not silly at all, Mrs Marling," said Giles. "You've been very helpful."

Chapter Fourteen

"I'm glad to see you at last," said Carswell. "You need to call on Mrs Morgan. There's been a most unpleasant development. Someone left a dead bird on Mrs Morgan's bed last night. A linnet – with a scarlet ribbon tied about its neck."

"Just that?"

"Hardly 'just'!"

"There was no letter or anything else with it?"

"No. Just the bird."

"I suppose we had better call in after we have seen Mr Geoffrey."

"Not before?"

Giles repressed a smile at his eagerness.

"Before, then – it makes no difference, I suppose."

"I think we should question that maid," said Felix. "The door was left open. Anyone could have gone in."

"And you spoke to Eakins?"

"Yes, and he saw no one go in or out. Nothing suspicious."

"He's a reliable man," Giles said.

"Yes, yes, of course, but we are obviously dealing with..."

"We don't know what we are dealing with," said Giles. "So how did Mrs Morgan react?"

"Magnificently," said Carswell. "It was Mrs Ridolfi who was hysterical. She almost burnt the house down."

~

Giles sensed that Mr Carswell was disappointed that Mrs Morgan was absent. Instead, they found Mrs Ridolfi at home. She was sitting at her work, close to the fire, wrapped in several shawls.

"My sister-in-law is out walking with Harry," she said.

"You seem to be suffering in this cold snap," Giles observed, as she pulled her shawls about her more tightly.

"I should not complain, but this house has not a warm corner in it," said Mrs Ridolfi. "It seems to catch the wind in two directions. I knew it was a bad idea to accept Lord Rothborough's offer of this house. I did try and tell Mrs Morgan that it would be more trouble than it was worth, but she is..." she paused for a moment. "I do consider her friendship with him unwise," she said softly. "No matter how innocent it may be, people will draw the worst conclusions. They always do, and by staying here she does not help her case."

"Your husband no doubt thinks the same. I understand he is her manager?"

"Yes, he is, but sometimes, well, she is unmanageable. Sometimes there is no telling her. She does not see it. She just sees a charming gentleman who admires and understands her work. She does not see... well, I think you know what I mean, Major Vernon."

He nodded and asked, "So who is in the household here? Which of the servants came with you from town?"

"Berthe, our maid, and Hannah, who is Harry's nurse."

"And they have been in your service how long?"

"Hannah has been with Harry since he was born and Berthe has been with Mrs Morgan before she married, I think. She used to be her dresser at the theatre."

"And who came with the house?"

"There is a cook and a kitchen maid, two housemaids and an outdoor man who is a queer sort of fellow, but he does keep the garden well. But they are difficult to deal with, I must confess."

"In what way?"

"They look down on us. It is really obvious. And I think they are used to a lavish way of living, and will expect outrageous tips, no doubt. I would not put it past them to have put that horrible thing there." She gave a shudder. "I think you had better question them all, Major Vernon. I think you should soon get the truth out of them."

"I shall question them, certainly. But first, Mrs Ridolfi, you could explain everything that happened that night. You dined alone?"

"I ate with Harry and then put him to bed."

"You don't recall asking one of the servants to go in there and make up the fire? Or warm the bed?"

"No," she said. "I did not order a fire for the bedroom. We are not so extravagant."

"And Mrs Morgan's maid did not attend you at bedtime?"

"No, Mrs Morgan and I were the only ones still up. I had sent Berthe to bed earlier. She had a headache."

"When was that?"

"Some time after my sister-in-law left for the rehearsal. I found her frowning over some sewing. It is a sure sign of a migraine, so I sent her to bed with a compress. I think she slept. You must ask her."

"And where is Berthe's bedroom?"

"Upstairs. We gave her one of the better rooms as she is so dear and useful to us. Mrs Morgan and I decided we would share the large bedchamber down here. I have to confess I do not like to sleep alone and it seemed most convenient that way. And warmer too," she added. "It is so cold here."

"Mr Carswell found the front door unlocked. Can you account for that?"

"It should have been locked. My sister-in-law was supposed to lock it when she came in, but she did not. She came straight in and went up to the drawing room. She must have forgotten to bolt it."

"And you were in the drawing room?"

"No, I sat in here after I had put Harry to bed. The drawing room was too cold for me last night."

"And so she did not come up to you until it was bedtime?"

"No, she did her piano practice – as she does most evenings."

"For how long?"

"She usually does two hours. It was about ten when she came up and we began to get ready for bed."

"And you went first into the bedroom and found the bird there?"

"Yes."

"And the last time you went into the room it was not there? When was that?"

"Some time in the afternoon. I can't say when – but I went in to get an extra wrap."

"And you noticed nothing amiss then?"

She shook her head.

"Thank you for your help, Mrs Ridolfi."

~

"I did not like her implication about Mrs Morgan and Lord Rothborough," Carswell said, as they went downstairs again.

"It is perfectly understandable in the circumstances," Giles said.

"It is hardly loyal."

"Sisters-in-law do not have to be loyal," said Giles. He stopped in the hall and looked about him. "So someone could have slipped in, gone upstairs and put that bird there without anyone hearing them, especially if she was playing the piano

85

loudly."

"Yes."

"It is all very odd. You say she was not upset by it?" he asked.

"No, it was a great display of courage on her part. Mrs Ridolfi was the only one screaming," said Carswell.

"She seems a nervous individual," Giles said. "No doubt the author of this prank imagines Mrs Morgan will be scared easily. Someone who does not know her, perhaps? My impression of her is someone who has a steady nerve."

"Yes, indeed," said Carswell.

"The same with the letters. She has great mastery over herself. Other women would have been reduced to terror after such a campaign. Yet a dead bird – a dead bird is a commonplace enough thing. Not in itself terrifying, unless you are Mrs Ridolfi."

"It *was* a songbird," Carswell said. "A strangled songbird. Just like Charlie Barnes."

"There is no evidence that the two events are related," Giles said.

"But it is curious. Perhaps whoever dispatched Barnes is giving Mrs Morgan a warning? If you don't watch yourself you will find yourself in the same condition."

"Not necessarily the killer – but possibly they had knowledge of it. But then, how do we even know that bird was put there to scare Mrs Morgan, who is not afraid of dead birds? There is one person in that house frightened of dead birds – Mrs Ridolfi. You saw it for yourself. Perhaps the person who put it there knew that."

"But for what possible reason?"

"A servant with a grudge? You noticed she complained about the existing staff. Perhaps she has made one of them angry. That would seem to make a great deal of sense."

"But it is so specific – a bird with a ribbon ligature."

"There is probably gossip going around already about the

manner of Barnes' death – this person may be acting on that. Hoping to give one or both of the occupants of that room a good scare. We cannot say which one in particular."

"But surely those letters prejudice it in favour of being a warning to Mrs Morgan?"

"It is one thing to write spiteful letters and post them but another to enter a house and leave a dead bird on someone's pillow. That requires a bit of nerve, something writers of anonymous letters rarely display. I am not convinced these incidents are related. The person who left the bird knows all about the routine and the composition of the household – which points to an insider. But the letters may be from anyone. The dead bird will be a far easier nut to crack, so to speak, than those wretched letters."

"So how will you do it?"

"I shall send Superintendent Rollins to put the fear of God into the servants. He will get to the bottom of the situation."

"You will not interview them yourself? Surely..."

"We have a murder investigation, Mr Carswell, that must take priority. Mrs Morgan will understand," he added.

Chapter Fifteen

"So why are we calling here?" said Felix as they stood at the door of an elegant modern villa on the outskirts of Northminster.

"Mr Geoffrey hosted a supper party which Barnes attended the night before he died," Major Vernon explained.

A liveried manservant opened the door to them and said, "The master is indisposed this morning."

"Go up and tell him that Mr Carswell is here," said Major Vernon. "And that he puts himself at your master's disposal." When the servant had gone, he added, "He's bound to want to see you. He has a reputation as a professional invalid."

"What on earth shall I say to him?"

"Just find out what you can about that party and what happened." Felix frowned, not at all certain he had Major Vernon's skill as an interviewer. "Don't worry – you can send him a large bill at the end of it. You do need to build your practice, after all."

"And what will you do?"

"This time I am going to talk to the servants."

The servant returned a few moments later and informed them that Mr Geoffrey would see Mr Carswell.

Felix was shown into a bedchamber of staggering opulence. It had apparently been designed to evoke the splendours of far more aristocratic mansions. Felix, who had now seen the glittering enfilades and painted ceilings of Holbroke, was none the less astonished by it. It was covered with exotic, brightly coloured paper, an oriental confection involving long-tailed birds and blackamoors in turbans. It also felt as hot as India with a huge fire in the grate, and the air was over-sweetened by burning aromatic pastilles. The room felt more like a feverish nightmare than a pleasant retreat.

Mr Elias Geoffrey was sitting up in a bed that was hung with swags of puce-striped silk. He had a cashmere shawl about his shoulders and an embroidered, tasselled cap covering his bald head. Through the open door to the adjoining dressing room Felix could see a luxuriant, curly wig sitting on a stand. It would look absurd upon him, Felix could not helping thinking, looking back at the thin, whey-faced man in the bed. He scarcely matched his extraordinary surroundings.

"Mr Carswell?" he said. "This is Providence at work! I was on the verge of sending for you. I am in need of a fresh opinion – Woodcroft talks such nonsense to me. I fear he is trying to kill me."

"What is troubling you, sir?"

"What is not troubling me? What?" said Mr Geoffrey. "Where shall I begin?"

"Perhaps I should examine you?" said Felix.

"That would be a great kindness, sir," said Mr Geoffrey. "Perhaps you would look at my right leg in particular. I have an excruciating inflammation on my leg. Woodcroft has given me plaisters to draw out the pain but they do irritate the skin. And then there is something seriously amiss with my bowels. I have not passed a thing for twenty hours, at least! Just ask Nickson." He waved his hand towards the valet who was in attendance. "Is that not so, Nickson?"

Nickson nodded solemnly.

Felix began his examination. As he expected, Geoffrey was an obliging patient, even over-obliging. Neither was there very much wrong with him, and Felix soon concluded that he was of a type well known to those in the profession: the patient who took excessive pleasure from a doctor's attention and often faked symptoms to indulge further. It was usually reckoned to be a female trick, often practised by wealthy old widows who had nothing better to do than engage in medical flirtation.

"So, Mr Carswell? What is the verdict? You need not spare me the details."

"I think you are perhaps low in your mind because of Mr Barnes. A depression in spirits can often have a physical effect on the body. He was an acquaintance of yours, I understand?"

Geoffrey gave a heavy sigh.

"Poor Barnes. Yes, it is a great loss. But the inflammation – do you not think –"

"I agree that the plaisters were unwise. But the inflammation will soon go down of its own accord."

"But, but," said Mr Geoffrey, thrusting his bony leg out towards Felix again, hitching up the long tail of his nightshirt. "That is not temporary, surely? That is persistent, do you not think?"

Felix swallowed his impatience. There was no need to examine the offending limb again, but he pretended to. He was not here so much to diagnose but investigate.

"How did you meet Mr Barnes?" said Felix, putting his hands around Geoffrey's calf and pressing down on it with his thumbs, with some pressure. He hoped this would feel reassuringly vigorous.

"I like to gather talent about me," said Mr Geoffrey. "It is my pleasure to collect the brightest and the best that Northminster can offer." He paused a moment. "Are you musical, perhaps, sir?"

"No, not very," said Felix.

"Literary, then? A talent for verse? You look like a man who ought to have a talent for verse."

"Hardly," said Felix, who glanced up and saw he was being gazed at by Geoffrey. "I am not sure I have any talents."

"Nonsense, sir, you are talented. I sense you are a great healer. I am already feeling a great deal better. Your hands... ah, but... *omnium artium medicina nobilissima est*," he added with a suggestive sigh and Felix stopped at once.

"Massage and exercise might be something to consider. Your man there might –"

"Nickson does not have your delicate touch, Mr Carswell," said Geoffrey. "Really, I cannot believe that you think you have no talent. Every man has some aptitude or other, some claim to distinction. And a gentleman with your lineage, well..."

"I suppose Mr Barnes came here to sing," said Felix, hastily getting back to the point.

"Yes, poor fellow."

"I understand he was here the other night. That you had some sort of supper party."

"My reputation precedes me, I see," said Geoffrey. "Yes, he was here, at my *conversatzione* on Tuesday."

"A *conversatzione*?"

"You should come, Mr Carswell. You would be more than welcome. I hold them once a fortnight. It is the best society in Northminster – a confraternity of talent. Yes, you must come. I am convinced of it now."

"No ladies?" said Felix.

"Assuredly not!" he said. "I have nothing against ladies, *per se*, but for rational, philosophical conversation I find they are not useful."

"So who was there on Tuesday with Mr Barnes?"

"We were very select that night," said Geoffrey. "Harrison, Fowler, who plays the flute, and Mowbray, the antiquary. You know his establishment, perhaps?"

"I know of it."

"He sells the most fascinating baubles. You should make his acquaintance."

"Did you dine with them?" Felix asked.

"Oh, no, they are asked for half past eight. I only ever dine alone and I like to have a small rest after my dinner. It helps my digestion, I find."

"Very wise, sir," said Felix.

"I do think so," said Geoffrey. "And I am glad to hear you agree with me."

"So what is the usual programme for these *conversatziones?*"

"Usually we have a little music. I am fond of music. Are you sure you are not musical? Your voice is well modulated. I cannot believe that you do not sing."

"I'm afraid not."

"That is a pity, a great pity. But perhaps you would aid our other great amusement, hailing as you do from the Athens of the North. You certainly have the figure for it."

"For what?"

"*Les pose plastiques.*"

"Oh, theatricals, you mean?"

"Theatricals – hardly, Mr Carswell. It is not so frivolous. It is the representation of the great classical myths, inspired by the nobility and beauty of ancient Greek statuary. Need I elaborate? You have had a classical education, I am sure. You are an Edinburgh man, I have heard that."

"It sounds a novel entertainment," said Felix. "Do you take part?"

"I direct operations," said Geoffrey.

"And it involves dressing up?"

"You speak as if it were tawdry costumes," said Geoffrey, "not the pure and simple dress of the ancients."

Felix could not decide whether to be amused or disgusted at the thought of naked men draped in bed sheets pretending to be statues for the entertainment of Mr Geoffrey.

"Forgive me," he said, carefully, with a slight bow.

"You really should join us, Mr Carswell," said Geoffrey. "You would make an excellent Ganymede. Or perhaps Daphnis, being instructed in the pipes by Pan himself."

Felix strenuously ignored this and asked, "And all went off harmoniously on Tuesday? You were not aware of any tensions between any of your guests?"

"No. It was a delightful evening. Harrison and Barnes

were in magnificent voice, and then we did scenes from the Iliad. Achilles lamenting for Patroclus, as I recall. Very effective, and in the circumstances rather prophetic and tragic." He gave a heavy sigh.

"Did you know Mr Barnes well?" Felix said.

"A brief acquaintance, but a sweet one," said Geoffrey. "It is pitiful." He shook his head and fiddled with the edge of his bed sheet. "*Sic transit gloria mundi*, Mr Carswell," he said. "*Sic transit.*"

Chapter Sixteen

Having questioned the other servants in the kitchen, Giles found the butler, Holt, polishing the silver in the pantry. His sleeves rolled up, he was vigorously buffing up the gleaming belly of a hot water urn and he did not stop when Giles came in. Like all the servants, he was a handsome man. Geoffrey obviously chose his staff for their looks.

"I hear from the hall boy you were with the Rifles, Mr Holt," Giles said. "When did you leave?"

"Thirty-five, sir," said Holt.

"And you like service better?"

"Do you, sir?" said Holt, glancing up from his polishing for a moment.

"And Mr Geoffrey, is he a good master?" Giles said, ignoring this.

"He's the master, and that's all there is to be said about it," said Holt.

"But you've been in this place three years, so it can't be so disagreeable."

"It does me well enough. The food is good – that Frenchie cooks well, you can say that for him. I've a comfortable bed and the perks aren't bad."

"But you have no respect for your master?"

"I do what he wants, sir, and he pays me for it. There's nothing says I must respect him."

"He offends you, then?"

"I shall not say either way. You will only twist my words, sir."

"There is obviously something about this household that discomforts you, Holt. You must not be afraid to speak of it to me." Giles had already encountered a certain reticence from the other servants and was beginning to draw his conclusions from it.

"As I said before, he pays me and I do what he says. That is all you people want of folk like me, surely?"

"What do you do for him, Holt, other than polish the silver and wait at table? Do you turn a blind eye, is that it?"

Holt put down his cloth.

"It's a good place, sir. That is all I will say."

"Very well," said Giles. "Tell me about Mr Barnes and Mr Harrison. Tell me what you can remember of them on Tuesday night."

"They were at loggerheads. It wasn't news, though."

"You saw them quarrel?"

"Having words."

"About what?"

"That I couldn't say, sir."

"Are you being discreet, Holt or was it genuinely unclear?" said Giles. "Give me a sense of what they were saying, if you can. A man has been murdered."

Holt gave a long sigh and then said, "It was something about going to London."

"And they left together?"

"Yes, they always left together."

"But not with the other guests? Messrs Mowbray and Fowler?"

"They left earlier. That's the usual way it happens."

"And what state were Barnes and Harrison in? Drunk, sober, what?"

"Mr Harrison was as he usually is at these affairs – drunk as the lord he'd like to be, as full of himself as with wine."

"And Barnes?"

"He'd taken a few. They always do. Otherwise – well, how else could they...?"

"For Dutch courage?" Giles said.

"I'm not saying another word," Holt said, picking up his cloth again and starting on another piece of silver.

"You've implied enough. You've been most helpful, Holt."

Holt gave a grunt and said, "And what good will that do me when I'm turned out with no character? You've no notion of that, sir, I think."

~

"That is not a comfortable household," said Giles to Carswell as they walked away. "What did you get out of Mr Geoffrey?"

"I was invited to his *conversatziones*, which seem to involve dressing up like a Greek statue."

"Yes, the servants mentioned the dressing up," said Giles. "It's interesting. Harrison talked of singing for his supper. I suspect they were not so much guests as paid to come here, and do as they were told, be it singing sentimental ballads, or dressing up as Greek heroes, and perhaps something rather more questionable than that."

"Buggery, you mean, sir?" said Carswell.

"Perhaps. Certainly, something is going on there. Suppose Geoffrey has been taking liberties –"

"Undoubtedly," said Carswell.

"If he has been indulging himself there, then he is at great risk of being blackmailed. He is the perfect target for blackmail – a wealthy man with unfortunate habits. Barnes had money to spend on expensive tailoring. I shall have to search his room again. There may be money stashed away. Ditto Harrison. Perhaps they were both getting cash from him."

"And buggery – it's a hanging offence, is it not?" said Carswell. "He has to worry about that, surely? Could he have murdered Barnes to silence him? Or have had him murdered?

96

I can't imagine him soiling his hands and he didn't seem unduly upset that Barnes was dead. Regretful but not grief-stricken."

"It's an interesting theory. Certainly the man is playing a dangerous game. What did he say about Barnes' and Harrison's quarrel?"

"He said there was no quarrel. That the evening was harmonious. That Harrison and Barnes enacted Achilles lamenting the death of Patroclus. If that was all there was to it, of course."

"I am beginning to think it wasn't," said Giles. "I wonder, Mr Carswell, is there any way that such acts can be discovered forensically?"

"That rather depends," said Carswell. "I don't have any direct experience of these sort of cases myself, but the theory is that if the victim (if one chooses to put in that light) is habituated to the act, that there is very little evidence. If not, if it is a question of assault, for example, then it might be visible."

"You didn't notice anything unusual when you did your post-mortem?"

"No, but I will look again – and do a little more research. There is rather a variety of opinions on this, of course. Some men take a more liberal stance than others."

"It is a difficult question, certainly," said Giles. "Classical literature suggests that it was once perfectly acceptable for an older man to take a young man as a lover. But the Bible is clear on the matter, as is the law of the land, which is more to the point. Whatever the rights and wrongs of it," he said, "we must proceed with great caution and keep our judgements and feelings to ourselves. People are far less inclined to speak unguardedly if they think they are suspected of something. There is an undercurrent here that must be explored – it may be the key to the whole business."

He broke off, for he realised that Carswell was no longer

listening. He had stopped in his tracks to watch an open carriage drawn by a sumptuous pair of bays. The coachmen and postillion were wearing the gold and chocolate livery of the Marquess of Rothborough, and as it bowled towards them, the noble lord himself could be seen sitting with his back to the horses, while opposite him was a lady and a small child – Mrs Morgan and her son.

"What the devil does he..." Carswell muttered, and was about to stride over to the carriage, which was drawing up in front of Avonside Row. Giles caught his arm.

"We have work to do, Mr Carswell," he said.

"What is she doing driving with him? Mrs Ridolfi said they went for a walk."

Rothborough was now lifting the child out of the carriage.

His hand still on Carswell's arm, Giles said, "She does not have to answer to you for her actions."

"Don't you wish to ask her about the dead bird?"

"As I said before, I shall send Rollins in to talk to the servants. It is hardly our most pressing task."

"But, sir, you gave her assurances that it would be investigated."

"Yes, and it is in hand. However, I cannot simply drop a murder enquiry. She of all people will understand that. My impression of her is that she is not a piece of fragile china that must be protected from every shake and buffet."

"But she is being victimised by some unknown person. That can't be allowed to pass, surely?"

"It is not being allowed to pass. Really, Mr Carswell, you must attempt to keep your admiration in check. Of course, I know it is not easy in the presence of such a woman as Mrs Morgan." He said this with some sincerity, for the sight of her climbing out of the carriage was an appealing one.

"So you find her admirable?"

"What man wouldn't? But she is also a respectable

married woman."

"Something that Lord Rothborough seems to forget," Carswell said. "He seems to treat her like something else entirely! And that —"

"I am sure she knows perfectly how to deal with Lord Rothborough," said Giles, unable to repress a smile at Carswell's vehemence. "Besides, you will be able to see her tonight. She is dining with my sister and brother-in-law and we have been favoured with an invitation."

"But not Lord Rothborough, I trust?"

"I very much doubt it," said Giles.

Chapter Seventeen

"It was impossible not to ask him," said Lambert, catching Giles for a moment of private conversation on the half landing coming down from the drawing room at the Treasurer's House. The others were making their way into the dining room in a procession led by Sally and Lord Rothborough. "Sally has already burnt my ear over it, but my lord is... well, you know what he is like. When he heard that Mrs Morgan was coming..." He shrugged. "He does even up the table, we can say that for it!"

"I shan't burn your ear – but watch out for Carswell. He is feeling most protective of the lady," said Giles, watching as Carswell stepped back from the door to let Mrs Morgan and Mrs Ridolfi go in.

"Oh, the poor fellow," said Lambert. "Of course – he is just the age for a bad case. I had a *tendre* myself at the same age for Francesca Corti but of course, I never had to sit with her at dinner. This *will* be a great trial for him. Perhaps we should send him upstairs to supper with Celia. She'll be glad to see him and I'd rather his heart was broken than hers."

"She still intends to marry him?" said Giles. At the age of eleven, Celia had decided that Felix Carswell was her future husband.

"Yes, she's determined on it. I should send her to talk to Lord Rothborough. She would put him in his place, if anyone can." It was an entertaining thought. "Between you and me, Giles," Lambert went on in a quieter tone, "you don't think there is actually anything between Mrs Morgan and Lord Rothborough, do you?"

"I doubt it," said Giles.

"I hope you are right. But I sense there is a campaign under way," said Lambert.

"Success is not inevitable, even for Lord Rothborough."

"He managed to get me to invite him to dinner against my will. What havoc might he unleash upon a defenceless woman's heart?"

"You are poetic tonight, but I don't think Mrs Morgan is defenceless. She has us here to protect her. Not to mention Mr Carswell."

Lambert smiled at that. "I understand her brother is her manager. Where is he, then?"

"As curiously absent as her husband," said Giles. "It's rather unfortunate for her. She must wish them here in such circumstances."

"According to Watkins the husband is a scoundrel," said Lambert.

"Yes, he said that to me," said Giles. "What else did he say to you about the state of the marriage?"

"He didn't say it in so many words, but it is not reckoned to be happy."

"So she may be here alone by choice?" Giles said. "You don't happen to know if they have actually parted company, do you?"

"No. But then that's hardly the sort of thing I would be privy to, is it?"

They were eight at dinner: Lambert and Sally, Lord Rothborough, Mrs Morgan, Giles, Mrs Ridolfi, Carswell and Watkins. As was usual in the Fforde household, the table was elegant and liberal, and if he was on campaign, Lord Rothborough gave no sign of it. He was faultlessly attentive to his hostess and managed to choose all Sally's favourite conversational subjects. Giles wondered if his conscience was hurting him – having forced himself on them he was prepared to be the most agreeable and useful guest. He had opinions and information on everything – he was able to discuss the merits of German versus English organ-building with Mr Watkins and wild flowers with Mrs Ridolfi with perfect ease.

But for all that, it was still awkward. Mrs Ridolfi was pale and reticent, unable to hide the disapproval Giles knew she must feel. Mr Watkins also said very little out of turn, which suggested he was not at all at his ease, when Giles had previously observed him to be voluble, verging on the emotional. Carswell, he feared, was a muzzled, angry dog on too short a leash and Giles wondered if and when his patience would desert him.

As for Mrs Morgan – she was as smooth and polished as Lord Rothborough in her manner. She said nothing out of turn, only what was pleasing and apt. Giles saw the easy charm of it, but had no clear sense of the woman beneath. He knew she was a talented actress – did that mean that performance was part of her character?

He wondered again whether she had parted from her husband. It would make a great deal of sense if she had, and it perhaps gave some clue as to the source of those unpleasant letters. Perhaps they had been sent by an aggrieved and malicious husband. If Morgan was a scoundrel and had made her so wretched that she felt forced to leave him, well, that was hardly something that a woman, anxious to preserve her reputation, would readily admit to on first acquaintance, even in the context of asking the police for assistance. But if it was the case, he wished she had managed to tell the truth that first afternoon. It left a rather disagreeable impression.

Then there was this business with Lord Rothborough. If she was susceptible to Rothborough, then she was playing with fire, and accepting carriage drives and the use of his house was not going to help her reputation a great deal. But perhaps her world, which Giles felt he did not fully understand, demanded different actions. After enduring a scoundrel of a husband and a miserable marriage, she was perhaps vulnerable. Rothborough was no rich booby. He was a compelling man in the prime of life: sophisticated and worldly, yes, but not without charm and a certain sensitivity. He was making Sally laugh at that very moment. What woman in a dangerous frame of mind would not be tempted?

~

The gentlemen had not spent long over their wine. Usually Canon Fforde would not let them upstairs again until they had sampled at least two interesting vintages and given their opinions on them. It could be a lengthy business, but not tonight. There was just one decanter of port, but it had Lord Rothborough fairly raving and even Major Vernon, who was never intemperate, took a second glass.

Felix, for his part, could not see what was so remarkable about it, although it was easy to drink – perhaps too easy. He realised when they got up that he had taken a little more than he should have. He felt flushed and disorderly – the wine had amplified his already feverish state. Dining with Mrs Morgan would have been both a pleasure and torture in ordinary circumstances, but the circumstances were not ordinary. Lord Rothborough's intrusion had seen to that. Felix felt like a primed and loaded duelling pistol and he wondered how on earth he was going to get through the rest of the evening without losing his temper.

He had gone to relieve himself in the closet next to the dining room, and emerged to find that Lord Rothborough had not yet gone upstairs, but was waiting for him in the hall.

"A word, my boy," he said beckoning him over.

"We should go up," said Felix, gesturing towards the stairs.

"All in good time," said Lord Rothborough coming over. He gave Felix's cravat a tweak, then straightened his lapels, at which Felix flinched. "I wish you would hold yourself better," he said. "Even that young Watkins carries himself better."

"Do you not want to be upstairs, sir, with Mrs Morgan?" said Felix.

"Mrs Morgan can wait," Lord Rothborough said. "And I know what you are suggesting with that tone, and I request that you desist from it."

"That may be difficult," Felix said, "when you –"

"Desist, sir," said Rothborough calmly. "Now, listen, I have some important news for you. You know that our neighbour Sir Robert Arden has died?"

"No," said Felix, particularly disliking that 'our neighbour'. He had no wish to be encompassed into Rothborough's household.

"He has no heir and debts aplenty. The estate will go to auction. The house itself is practically a ruin but has a considerable piece of land, with a good income on it, and it borders Holbroke to the north-east. Naturally, I am going to acquire it."

"What of it?" Felix said, carelessly.

Rothborough tapped Felix on his lapel.

"Because, my lad, I intend to settle it on you. It is a nice income for you – and there may be considerable mineral rights there, which we would be fools not to investigate. It is a good piece of property, entirely suitable for our purposes. You need some land, Felix. Without land you can and will be no one." Then, before Felix had a chance to say a word, he added, "Now, let us go upstairs. With luck Mrs Morgan will be persuaded to sing for us."

There was some part of Felix that almost admired Lord Rothborough, or at least admired his guile, for choosing such a moment to impart this information, when there was no time to form an adequate rebuttal. Annoyed almost to the point of incoherence, he struggled to find some sort of retort. All he could manage to say was, "So, my lord, what precisely are your intentions towards her?"

"My intentions towards Mrs Morgan? Dear God, Felix, must you be so provincial?" He shook his head. "Of course you admire her, but –" He exhaled. "Indeed, I might ask you what your intentions are?" Felix could find no answer. It was a painful question. "Yes?" He sighed again as Felix remained silent. "What did I say to you about the dangers of love? Did you not listen to anything I said? You must guard your affections. Such a person can mean nothing to you. Of course, you could learn a great deal from her – a woman like that is a civilising influence on a man. It would do you good." Rothborough then began to climb the stairs and then stopped, and turned back to Felix. "And talking of the social niceties, you were not as appreciative of Canon Fforde's excellent port as you should have been, especially when you drank so much of it. You still have a most uncultivated palate. You should make more of a study of these things."

Then, before Felix had a chance to answer, he strode up the rest of the staircase and disappeared into the drawing room.

Felix stood for a moment in the hall, trying to master himself. He knew he must follow. It would have been most discourteous to do anything else, but he felt dry-throated with rage, and entirely unsuitable for company.

Finally, he made his way upstairs, his hands clasped behind his back, digging his nails into the palm of his hand. He went over to Major Vernon, who was standing by the fire watching everything with his usual acute gaze. He gave Felix a slightly encouraging smile, as if he understood his condition, and Felix felt a little better for it.

The ladies were sitting around the tea table with their work in their hands, while Canon Fforde was opening the piano and arranging candles.

"Will you sing for us, ma'am?" Lord Rothborough was asking Mrs Ridolfi.

"Oh, I do not sing," said Mrs Ridolfi.

"Mrs Ridolfi does sing," said Watkins, "and most beautifully. She is another of my mother's pupils."

"Really?" said Canon Fforde.

"It was a long time ago," she said, "and I do not sing any more."

"That is a great shame," said Watkins. "My mother always had the greatest regard for your talent."

"It's true – she did," said Mrs Morgan. "And Paulina, I think your technique was better than mine – and you certainly studied harder."

"That is such a pretty piece of work you are doing there, Mrs Fforde," said Mrs Ridolfi. "Did you design the pattern yourself?" She was examining Mrs Fforde's white work as if her life depended on it.

"Yes, that is a beautiful design," said Mrs Morgan, pausing at her tent stitch. "I wish I could master white work, but I always prick my finger and bleed on it."

"My interest is now thoroughly aroused, Mrs Ridolfi," said Lord Rothborough. "Mrs Watkins was such a wonder in her day, and to find not one, but two of her pupils in the same drawing room – well, I can only wish that at least one of them might favour us with an air."

He looked from one woman to the other.

"I will sing, if you will, my lord," said Mrs Morgan, returning to her sewing. She was working a vividly coloured parrot on canvas, and the intense colours of it glowed against the midnight blue of her gown.

"That is not an unreasonable demand," said Lord Rothborough. "But of course you are only hoping to make your performance more memorable by forcing them to sit through my indifferent one. Yes, ma'am, is that it?"

"I must do anything I can to add lustre, yes, of course," said Mrs Morgan, with a smile, snipping her thread.

"What shall it be, then, Mrs Morgan?" Lord Rothborough

said.

"Where Ere You Walk, by Handel," she said. "You have mastered that."

Watkins was now sitting at the piano and began, as if on cue, to play the introduction.

"You will not play for me?" Rothborough asked her. She shook her head.

He went away to the piano.

"You had better start again, Mr Watkins," he said. "And a trifle slower, if you please."

Felix endured the song as best he could. It seemed to last an eternity. He managed to salvage some pleasure from looking at Mrs Morgan with her head bent over her work, her quick needle pulling a bright blue thread to and fro, but it was only a small pleasure. He was tormented by the familiarity the last exchange implied. Then, as the song reached its conclusion, she put down her work, rose and walked across to the piano, without a trace of self-consciousness. She was clearly comfortable with being admired, and the eyes of every person in the room were upon her, even Watkins who was still playing the piano.

She was preparing for her cue, Felix supposed.

"Nicely done, my lord," she said, tapping her fingertips together, and making a slight but elegant inclination of her head when the song was finished. It was a gesture of submission, surely; an acknowledgement of his authority over her. Rothborough had had her, there was no doubt about it, and Felix's misery was complete.

She was talking to Watkins quietly, presumably about what to play, while Lord Rothborough, his side of the bargain concluded, took a chair and placed it in front of the piano, so as to get the best sight of her. It was for all the world as if no one else was there.

"I need some air," Felix muttered to Major Vernon. "I took too much port. It doesn't agree with me."

The Major nodded as if to give him permission to leave, and he crossed the room, just as Watkins had launched into a sequence of throbbing, lustrous chords, which in their beauty were a prelude to something yet more beautiful from Mrs Morgan.

He was right. As he went downstairs, her voice, like mercury, seemed to flow out from the drawing room, almost as if in pursuit of him. He was not allowed to escape.

He went to the front door, and out into the small courtyard that fronted the Treasurer's House. There was only a low wall separating the courtyard from the road, and he was surprised to see a woman standing on the other side of the wall. She moved at the sight of him, and attempted, not very successfully, to conceal herself to one side of the arch that formed the entrance to the court. Anxious for a distraction, he went to see who it was, and in a moment found himself face to face with Miss Kate Pritchard. She shrank into the darker shadows under the archway.

He would have greeted her but she raised her finger to her lips, with such a look of appeal on her face that he could not possibly have refused her request. They stood in silence while the music continued, clearly audible through the open windows of the first floor drawing room.

Despite the semi-darkness he saw that Miss Pritchard was in the thrall of it: her chest was rising and falling, and her eyes were half-closed. He found himself staring at his hands, ashamed to see her in such a condition. It felt like prying. There was so much passion and feeling in it, as she stood there, her back pressed against the wall.

The final note died, and she said softly, "Thank you." He was not sure whether she was thanking him or Mrs Morgan. "That was so..."

"Have you been waiting here to hear her sing?" Felix said.

"You will not say anything to anyone, will you?" she said. "About finding me here?"

"No, of course not. But your parents – won't you be missed at home?"

"I pretended to go to bed. You will think me wicked now, Mr Carswell, but I wanted to hear her so much." She glanced up at the window. "I wonder if she will sing again. But what are you doing out here? I would not have left my seat in that room for anything."

"I have a thick head," he said. "The port..."

"Oh, I see. How unfortunate. I hope you feel better soon."

"I feel better already," he said, and meant it.

"Then you ought to go in case she decides to sing again."

"I would rather keep you company, Miss Pritchard – as I did last night."

"But I am sure that is a much more entertaining party," she said. "Mrs Fforde's parties always are. Tell me, who was the gentleman who sang before? That was not Canon Fforde – he is a baritone and –"

"That was Lord Rothborough."

"Oh," she said. "I did not know he was asked."

"He asked himself. That is the sort of thing he excels at, and no one ever dares quarrel with it."

"It must be hard for you," she said after a moment. "Sometimes you must not know where your duty lies."

"That is exactly it," said Felix, feeling both surprised and pleased at having someone understand his peculiar situation.

"Very hard," she said again, with a nod. "Well, I suppose I ought to go home before I am discovered."

"Let me take you back."

"There is no need for that. And what if we were seen?"

"Let them see us!" Felix said with sudden defiance.

After all, what was he doing wasting his energy on an unattainable, impossible object like Mrs Morgan, when there was such a passionate, sympathetic creature so close at hand? A girl who was full of feeling and spirit. Mrs Morgan had told him to look for a wife and Miss Pritchard was exactly the sort of woman he might marry. Why should he not try and make love to her? Surely that was the best treatment?

"We might build on the beginning we made last night," he added.

"You have had too much wine," she said, with a smile.

"*In vino veritas*, Miss Pritchard," he said. "I thoroughly enjoyed the conceit – as I think you did. And I have great news for you: I am soon to be a man of property. So if you are discovered and they scold you, tell them that, and then you will be forgiven instantly."

"You are cynical, Mr Carswell."

"I suppose I am," he said. "Forgive me. That was unkind."

"But perhaps not so far from the truth," she said after a moment. She glanced back at the windows. "I really ought to go. I must not be caught out here, really I must not."

The front door opened and Major Vernon came out into the forecourt. Miss Pritchard seemed to take fright. She ran straight away, with a beautiful animal swiftness, like a hare, and Felix wondered again if he would be better engaged pursuing her than dreaming feverishly of Mrs Morgan.

"Who was that?" said Major Vernon, coming out of the courtyard.

"I can't say," said Felix.

"Can't or won't?"

"I promised I would not say." He pushed his hands through his hair, massaging his scalp as he did, for his headache had returned with a vengeance. "Are you leaving, or have you come to drag me back in there?"

"Come and take your leave properly. The party is practically over." Major Vernon was staring out in the direction Miss Pritchard had run. "Are you sure you can't say?"

"No," said Felix. "I really cannot. I gave my word."

"Very mysterious," said Vernon, looking about him. He crouched down and picked up a knot of ribbons that was lying on the ground, the sort that formed a trimming on a dress. Presumably it had fallen from Miss Pritchard's dress. "And extremely interesting."

Chapter Eighteen

Giles' instincts had been correct.

A moment's inspection in the grey light of morning revealed that the length of ribbon tied to the key for St Anne's Chapel was the same pattern as that forming the knot of ribbons he had found outside the Treasurer's House: a plaid ribbon in white, red and black, with a distinct figure woven into it. It was not a commonplace style of ribbon, he reflected; it was luxurious, probably expensive and doubtless fashionable. Of course, that did not prove that the two strips were related. The ribbon itself proved no ownership. Two different ladies could have been entranced by its elegance.

However, there was another crucial similarity between the ribbon on the key and the ribbon he had found last night. In both cases, the ends had been carefully cut into a deep 'V' shape, then rolled, and finished with identical tiny stitches to stop the silk from fraying. That detail seemed to remove the matter from being a simple coincidence and into the realms of potential significance.

How, he wondered, did such a ribbon come to be marking a key in the possession of George Watkins? That was the interesting thing. Watkins was not a man with women about him. There were no work baskets for him to raid for a piece of ribbon to mark an important key. And what man, in the ordinary course of affairs, would choose such a showy piece? A piece of herringbone tape would have done the job as well. It would be more than likely that the woman in question would have been annoyed at his taking such a prize for the purpose of marking a key, unless it had been freely given, for reasons that were not strictly utilitarian.

Perhaps he had acquired it as a keepsake from a woman –
and if that were the case, was it the same woman who had
been lurking in front of the Treasurer's House, the woman
whose identity Carswell, with irritating gallantry, had refused to
reveal? It suggested that she was someone in their social circle,
someone who ought not to have been there.

Giles put the key in his pocket, along with the knot of
ribbon. Later he would see if he could find any duplicates.
Lambert had summoned all the Minster employees for nine
o'clock for an inspection of the keys. In the meantime, he had
Rollins waiting to speak to him about Mrs Morgan's domestic
establishment.

"I am afraid it does not shed much light on the business,
sir," said Rollins. "Neither the foreign maid nor the nurse
showed a trace of any knowledge of it. I didn't reckon either
one of them was a liar. They could not account for it being
there."

"And what about Mr Morgan? Did the nurse and the
maid have anything to say about their absent master?"

"They didn't tell tales, no, sir."

"As if they had been told not to, perhaps?"

"I should say so, but not out of fear. Out of respect and
loyalty. Good women both of them, I should say. Respectable
and God-fearing."

"You might tell me something else – did they say
anything about Lord Rothborough's involvement in the
household? Did they imply, for example, that their mistress
knew him well?"

"It was hard to gauge, sir. Usually these things are clear
enough, and people are quick enough to speak, given a chance
to complain of their masters and mistresses, if they can."

This was true enough. Mrs Ridolfi had complained of it,
but Mrs Morgan's servants had not. It was certainly a puzzle
and Giles had no immediate idea how to solve it.

"I do not understand this preoccupation with keys, Major Vernon," said the Dean, meeting Giles a little later in the hall of the Chancellery where all the Minster employees had been bidden to gather. "Surely there are keys used by members of criminal fraternities that will unlock any door?"

"Yes, but not I think in this case. I do not think we are looking at the work of such people here. Now, I take it you have never had a key to St Anne's Chapel, sir?"

"No, never. The keys are the responsibility of the Chancellor, not the Dean."

"But I would imagine that your office means you do have a great many keys."

"I have some. I dare say the Bishop has some. I trust you will not be subjecting his Lordship to this humiliating procedure?"

"I am afraid I can spare no one, sir," said Giles.

"Oh, very well," said the Dean, and took his bunch of keys and put it down on the table. "If the owner of the key is so likely related to the crime, then you will be suspecting Mr Watkins – for he has the only key. Yes?"

"I am in no position to speculate on anything, sir. I have not enough facts." He examined the Dean's bunch of keys. There were only ten or so and he could see nothing that resembled the key to the chapel. He was surprised there were so few. He handed them back to the Dean. "Thank you, sir, your cooperation is greatly appreciated."

Dean Pritchard looked as if he were about to deliver a sermon, but seemed to think the better of it, to Giles' relief. Instead he stalked off to speak to someone else, perhaps to complain about the indignity that had been heaped upon him.

It was a frustrating hour that followed. Accompanied by Rollins, Giles looked over all the keys that were produced, but there seemed to be no match for the one given to him by Watkins.

"I didn't really expect to find one," Giles said to Lambert when they had dismissed the last key holder, "to tell you the truth. What I want them all to know is that there is a key missing – and that I know there is a key missing."

"That is clear enough to them now, certainly. Come, you will need a drink. I certainly do."

"I have not looked at your keys yet, Lamb," Giles pointed out, as they went into his private office upstairs.

Lambert turned out his great bunch onto the table.

"In comparison with you, the Dean has very few keys indeed," Giles remarked, when he had finished examining them.

"That is because I don't choose to let him have many. He would only lose them – or confuse them. He is not a practical man, and these details bore him. He has the keys he needs."

"I always suspected you were the real authority here, Lamb," said Giles with a smile. "But I have never dared articulate that truth."

"He who controls the purse strings controls everything," said Lambert, his hand on the decanter.

"So that's why you don't want preferment?"

"I like my post here," said Lambert. "I shouldn't want to be Dean of Northminster, or dean of anywhere else for that matter, let alone a bishop! Too many sermons to preach. Far better to balance the books."

"You preach very well."

"When did you last listen to me preach, Giles?" said Lambert.

"Only over the port," said Giles.

Lambert gave a slight shrug, as if he hardly expected otherwise.

Lambert's secretary came in and said, "Dean Pritchard would like to speak with you, sir."

"Perfect timing as ever," said Lambert, replacing the stopper in the decanter. "Very well, send him in, James."

Dean Pritchard came in with great briskness and looked annoyed to see Giles standing there.

"You are still here, Major Vernon?" he said.

"I'm afraid so, sir."

"However long it takes," said Lambert, with a wave of his hand. "Now, what can I do for you?"

"I wished to talk to you about Fildyke. You said you would find him a post."

"Oh yes, so I did," said Lambert.

"And have you?"

"Not yet."

"He is a loyal servant and he has been badly used. I would like this matter seen to with alacrity."

"Dean Pritchard, you will forgive me," Giles said, cutting in. "But there is good cause for Canon Fforde to hesitate to make another appointment. I have reason to believe that Fildyke's character is less than spotless."

"In what way?"

"I have visited his shop – his affairs are highly dubious, by my reckoning. He was selling counterfeit engravings."

"You are sure of this?" said Dean Pritchard.

"I have begun an investigation, yes," said Giles. "I would suggest that you hesitate before putting such a man back on the Minster roll."

"That I can scarcely believe," said Pritchard.

"I will soon have the evidence I need to put him in front of the Justices," Giles said.

"I think you must be mistaken, sir," said the Dean.

"He isn't usually," said Lambert, mildly.

"I find it hard, Major Vernon, very hard to believe that a man I have known these many years, an excellent pious man, who has served this house of God for so long and with such devotion, could be responsible for any wrongdoing."

"It is for the courts to judge him – not you, nor I. You may wish to offer him your support as a character witness, but the evidence is strong against him, and until the matter is resolved I suggest that you do not find him a post."

"I believe he is being victimised!" said Dean Pritchard. "A campaign is afoot against him and it pays neither of you gentlemen any compliments to be involved in it. You, Canon Fforde, you were eager to support Watkins in his intemperate dismissal of him from the choir."

"That is not fair, my dear Pritchard," Lambert Fforde, in his most conciliatory tone, though Giles heard the touch of steel in it. "We discussed the matter at great length, and I think you will recall that we decided that the Master of Music must be allowed to take such actions. The manner in which it was done was to be regretted, but the action itself was permissible."

"I think you recall the matter wrongly," said the Dean.

"I believe I minuted it," said Lambert. "I can have my clerk look out the record if you wish."

The Dean twitched his face in annoyance, apparently unable to find an answer to this.

Instead he turned to Giles. "And you, sir, seem determined to assert your authority where you have no authority. Within the walls of the Precincts, I would remind you, sir, I am sole authority, by ancient custom. You are only here with your investigations by my leave!"

"Well, sir," said Giles, "that is not strictly the case. Although ancient custom is something I always try to respect, I must also abide by statute. The Act of Parliament setting up the City Constabulary was clear to the letter. My force has equal jurisdiction within the Precincts as without. When we have such a grave matter on our hands as the wilful murder of a man, every step must be taken to find out who is responsible. I do regret the disruption to the Minster business, as I said to you earlier, but I must proceed as I think fit. After all, Charles Barnes was one of your own and deserves every effort we can make on his behalf."

"Quite so," said Lambert.

"Then I trust for your sake, sir, that your efforts will not be in vain!" said Dean Pritchard. "This matter of Mr Fildyke is not closed, Canon Fforde, you may be sure of that! Good day to you, gentlemen!" With which he left.

"Is it my imagination," said Lambert, "but is his temper getting worse? He is very quick to climb upon his high horse these days, don't you think?"

"Perhaps," said Giles.

"I think it is because he is never happy in his boots. His people – well, I believe his father was a grocer in Lincoln or some such and he thinks we don't believe him to be a gentleman."

"Perhaps we don't?"

"You may be right," said Lambert, with a sigh. "Sally would certainly accuse me of that. Whatever, he is always trying to be something he is not. It is rather tiring for the rest of us." He poured a glass of sherry. "And Fildyke is crooked! Ha! Well done, Giles, well done! You'll join me?"

Giles shook his head. He could not feel any satisfaction in it. The search for a duplicate key had proved completely futile. He had no sense of progress. He had only succeeded in closing down a somewhat tenuous avenue of enquiry. Perhaps there was only one key to the chapel, a key marked with a conspicuous ribbon which might or might not be significant.

"I have to go," he said.

Chapter Nineteen

Having finished his morning surgery, Felix was attempting to write up his notes, but found himself utterly distracted by thoughts of Mrs Morgan. It was more than distraction; it had all the qualities of a waking dream. He saw her smiling at him across the expanse of her satinwood piano, and then again recalled how she had been last night at dinner, in the austere majesty of her midnight blue silk. He could see every detail in his mind's eye – the bright parrot tapestry on her lap, her elegant hands plying her needle, the soft pale skin of her shoulders, even the pearls about the neck which he had longed to kiss. And then her voice which seemed to ring in his head – that clarity of tone, the sweetness, the passion that conspired to be so ravishing, like the touch of her hand on his own skin.

He had tried with some effort to think about Kate Pritchard instead. He wished she had not forced him into a falsehood. He did not like keeping such a matter from Major Vernon.

The discomfort she had produced in him by doing this offset any enthusiasm he attempted to whip up for her. Yes, she was a good-looking and amusing young woman, but that was all. She could not hold the stage of his mind with Mrs Morgan.

How perverse of him it was to discard that which was potentially available in favour of the unattainable!

He was just getting up from his writing table, having almost decided that he would go and see Mrs Morgan – as if that might do him any good – when there was a knock at his door.

It was Barker, Major Vernon's clerk.

"I have a Mr Fildyke here asking for you, Mr Carswell."

Felix went out into the passageway and found Fildyke standing there, hat in hand, revealing his greasy, over-pomaded hair.

"I'm sorry to bother you, sir – but it's my mother. She's so very bad today. I thought – well, if you would not mind stepping by, if you could spare a moment of your valuable time."

He had no wish at all to go back to that tawdry little shop, but he could hardly refuse. Perhaps there was a sort of providence in making him go there rather than to see Mrs Morgan.

"I'll come as soon as I can," Felix said, not wishing to walk through Northminster in the company of Fildyke.

"Thank you, sir, I'm much obliged."

Felix closed his door and managed ten minutes of writing before packing his bag and setting off for All Souls.

Fildyke greeted him at the door of his shop, dressed now in his shopman's apron. He took Felix straight into the stuffy little parlour with the birdcages, where Mrs Fildyke was on her couch as before. She was wearing a dirty yellow silk wrapper which made her look even more grey-faced and miserable. She was obviously in great pain and had recently vomited, for the chamber pot stood full nearby. It was no time to be squeamish, and Felix got on with his examination.

He noticed a slight burn to the corner of her mouth, as if it had come into contact with something extremely caustic.

"Have you taken any medicines or powders, Mrs Fildyke?" There was no knowing what she might have taken. People were quick to dose themselves with things that did more harm than good, encouraged by the quacks who passed for medical men amongst the common people. She may have taken a purge too violent for her to withstand.

Felix had some personal experience of this. As a boy, in the wake of some childish indisposition, he had been given one by a Pitfeldry apothecary. It had almost killed him. He could remember lying in his bed, his mother washing him down between those debilitating bursts of vomiting, while outside in the hall the Rev. James Carswell, who did not lose his temper easily, could be heard berating the apothecary. Later, Lord Rothborough had been there, coming into his bedchamber, a circumstance which until then he had entirely forgotten, and now which struck him forcibly and disturbed him. He had woken from sleeping to find his Lordship on his knees by the bed, apparently praying.

"No, no, just a little gruel." Mrs Fildyke's pained and raspy voice pulled him back to the present. "The gruel my son makes for me."

"You are sure of that, Mrs Fildyke?" Felix said. The sweetmeat dishes and the port bottle were still to hand. The sugar plums looked particularly unpleasant: was that discoloured powdered sugar or dust?

"Yes... oh my God..." was all she managed to say, for she was starting to retch again. There was no suitable vessel to hand other than the already full chamber pot which Felix was obliged to hold up to her to assist her in her distress.

Finally it was over and she fell back panting, tears running down her face. She gripped at Felix's hand and said, in a pathetic hoarse whisper, "I shall not die, shall I, sir?"

"No, I do not think it will come to that."

"Sometimes..." she began, and glanced around her, with the same abstracted mania as the feathery creatures in the cages above her.

"Do not trouble yourself with words now," Felix said. "You must rest."

She nodded and closed her eyes.

There was not even a bowl or cloth to clean her face to hand, so carrying the wretched pot he went back into the shop where he found Fildyke anxiously waiting.

"Where is the kitchen?"

"Down there, sir, if you don't mind." Fildyke indicated the entrance to a dark, sloping passageway which led to an unsurprisingly depressingly apartment. A maid-of-all-work, a rough-looking creature, was on her knees in front of a smouldering fire, trying to coax it into life. There would be no hot water to wash in, then, he thought with resignation.

"Is the closet out there?" he asked, indicating the door.

"Aye," said the girl, staggering to her feet.

"Deal with this, will you," he said, holding out the pot.

She did not look best pleased with him and took her time in taking it from him.

"Water?" he asked.

"There's a pump out in the yard," she said as she stomped towards the back door.

"I'll do it myself," he said.

"What has your mistress been eating?" he asked, noticing the pile of dirty crocks on the draining board as he followed her out into the yard. "Anything unusual? Some spoilt meat?"

"What would I know?" said the maid, banging the privy door.

"Don't you do the cooking?" he said, beginning to crank the pump.

"No, mister Fildyke does it," she said, coming and thrusting the pot under the pump.

"Scrub it out well," he said, "with vinegar if you have some." She gave him an evil look at that. "And I want you to bring out clean basins, clean cloths and a jug of water."

The actual cleanliness of these items could not of course be guaranteed, but it would be better than nothing.

He returned to Mrs Fildyke and found her dozing, so he gently cleaned her face as best he could.

"So what do you think, sir?" said Fildyke, who was waiting in the shop.

"What have you been feeding her?" said Felix. "What is this gruel of yours?"

"Nothing that would harm a soul," said Fildyke. "Just a little barley in broth."

"Well, it doesn't seem to be doing your mother much good. You haven't given her any powders or anything to induce a purge?"

"No, no, of course not."

"That doctor she spoke of the other day – Joyce, was it? – he has not give her anything?"

"No, no, I haven't called anyone except you."

"I think something has poisoned her – she's eaten something spoilt, most probably. She will need looking after a good deal better than this. Surely you can get someone else in to help, other than that girl?"

"Well, I suppose I might – but my mother doesn't like strangers."

"She will not mind in her condition," said Felix. "And you would do well to get rid of these wretched birds. In fact, you ought to clean out that entire room. And what sort of life is it for them, in those cages? It is a barbaric custom."

"Oh, I couldn't do that, sir. Those birds are part of our livelihood."

"You sell them?"

"Of course," said Fildyke.

"Did you sell one recently – a linnet?" he asked. "To a foreign woman, perhaps?" He was thinking of Mrs Morgan's coldly beautiful maid, whom he did not trust, although against whom he had not the slightest evidence. But if Major Vernon was correct in his guess that the threats came from within the household, then she was surely a prime suspect for putting the bird on the bed.

"Not to a foreign woman. I did sell one to a lady, though," Fildyke said. "From London, I'd say she was. And definitely a lady. I was a trifle surprised when she came in."

"When was this?"

"Day before last."

"Could you describe her to me? Her clothes, perhaps? Was there anything distinctive about them?"

Fildyke shook his head. "Not that I remember – other than she was nicely spoken and of the quality."

Felix frowned. It was less than helpful.

"If you remember anything else about her, you must tell me."

"Of course, sir," said Fildyke. He scratched his temple. "My mother – you will call again and see her?"

"Yes, of course."

"And how much do you charge, sir?" Fildyke said.

Felix had not really considered this.

"You will not be much out of pocket," he said, knowing only that he should charge such people moderately. "I will send a bill when your mother is well again."

"I only ask because, well..." Fildyke came a little closer. "I am a little short of the ready money at present, and I wondered if I might pay you in kind."

"In kind?" said Felix, looking around at the shop at the cheap prints and artificial flowers. "I don't know about that."

"I have items that might be of interest to a young gentleman such as yourself. Specialised items that I have found extremely popular." He gave a sly little smile. "You might wish to accept one instead of the usual fee."

"What are you talking about?" Felix said.

"Books," said Fildyke. "Rare books. Books of a particular sort. Special books. Do you get my drift, sir? I think you do," he added, taking a key from his waistcoat pocket. "Books that are not for everyone's eyes. I have a very choice volume indeed which it would be my great pleasure to give to you in return for your kindness."

He brought a pine box up onto the counter and unlocked it.

"Quite a treat, this one," he went on, handing Felix a slim, green Morocco volume. "You may have heard of it."

Felix flicked it open to the title page. *The true and uncensored memoirs of the Comtesse de Mortvilliers. Translated from the French by a gentleman.'*

"I have," Felix said, colouring slightly. He had been nineteen years old, in his cups in a howff in Edinburgh, with a gaggle of fellow students, all talking of lewd books and which were the most engagingly obscene. One of them had actually read a copy of the 'Comtesse' and it had made him, he claimed, priapic for a week.

Felix hesitated a moment and then attempted to hand it back, but Fildyke would not allow him to.

"Keep it, sir. I believe gentlemen value it greatly for its philosophical content."

Seeing that Fildyke was determined to make him have it, he tucked it quickly inside his coat. It would, at the least, save him the trouble of drawing up a bill.

Chapter Twenty

"Mr Sledmere is away today?"

"Yes, he's gone over to Righouses. He's preaching there tonight. He won't be back until tomorrow." Was that relief in her voice, Giles wondered?

"May I speak with you, Mrs Sledmere?"

"Yes, sir, if you like," she said.

Giles followed her into the kitchen, which at first glance seemed more cheerful than the rest of the house. There was a bright fire burning, a well-scrubbed floor of pale stone flags, and rows of bright crocks on the blue painted dresser – in short, all the signs of well-ordered domesticity were there and it would usually have been a calming sight. But Giles could take no pleasure in it, since for him the room was dominated by the sight of Rose Sledmere, sitting hunched in the corner on an old high-backed settle.

She was now dressed in black and she was turning a piece of white ribbon in her fingers. Her face was as pale as the ribbon, and she met his glance with that same blank, insolent stare that he recognised too well. Laura had once sat in the same sort of sullen silence, fiddling with a length of wool for hours on end. He had tried to take it from her, and had been attacked in return. That same sense of latent anger and violence he had suffered from Laura, he felt now; or did he merely imagine it? He was not sure how much his experience was colouring his impressions of Rose.

Mrs Sledmere picked up a stocking and sat down to start darning.

"If you don't mind, sir, I must get on with this. The light in this room, it's shocking after noon, and my eyes are not what they were."

"I wanted to ask you about your nephew and Mr Harrison," he said. "Did you know him?"

"I knew about him, that they were friends."

"He never brought him here?"

"No, Mr Sledmere would not have stood for it."

"Did you meet him, Miss Sledmere?" Giles ventured to the girl in the corner.

"She won't answer you, sir," said Mrs Sledmere. "She hasn't said a word since... well, the news."

"She is very affected, then?" he said.

"She is more strange than ever," said Mrs Sledmere. "She's been sitting there for hours. I don't know what to do with her, sir, and that's the truth of it."

"Was Rose aware of your nephew's friendship with Mr Harrison, do you think?" Giles asked.

"I suppose so, since I was. But who is to know what she knows? She is so... so away, if you take my meaning."

Giles nodded.

"Does she ever leave the house alone?"

"Not if I can help it, because there is no knowing where she might end up. But sometimes she slips out, and then..." She broke off and sighed. "Charlie always knew where to find her. I don't know how I shall manage now."

"I gather from Mr Harrison that there was some talk of going to London together and that your nephew was considering it," Giles said, sitting down opposite her.

"He may have thought of it, but I don't believe he would have gone. He knew his duty, no matter what my husband says – Charlie was a good boy. Charlie was going to look after her. I always took comfort in that, no matter what talk there was, what horrible things we heard. That he would stay and do as he should, that in his heart he was there for us – for Rose. Charlie was everything to her, everything. And that wretch Harrison – well, he corrupted our Charlie, turned him to sin, and I shouldn't be surprised if he wasn't – well, you know what I mean, sir. Hell will be too good for the likes of Jos Harrison!"

He glanced back at Rose who was shredding the frayed end of the ribbon with her fingernails.

"And as far as you recall, on the Wednesday morning, Rose was at home with you all that morning? She did not slip out?"

"No, I don't think so."

"What were you doing that morning? Can you remember? It was market day, I think." Mrs Sledmere nodded. "Perhaps you went to the market?" She nodded. "And Rose went with you?"

"No, I left her here. Mr Sledmere was in his workshop, of course, so she was not alone. I was not long gone. An hour or so."

"Do you think Rose might have slipped out?"

"Yes, I suppose, but... what are you suggesting, sir?"

"Let us go back a little earlier in the day, Mrs Sledmere. Charlie was in the workshop that morning. Did he have breakfast with you?"

"Yes, but he went out. Mr Sledmere and he had words about something and he went storming out. That was the last I saw of him. I told your sergeant all this, sir, I am sure of it, when he came and first told us what had happened."

"And you don't know what the quarrel was about?"

"It might have been anything. It was like a tinderbox between them – it has been the past few weeks. The slightest spark..." she sighed again and laid down the sock. "I wish I had gone in and put a stop to it. I could have seen him then, for one last minute. All I heard was the banging of the door and then my husband was in here, raging away, as he does, and it took all I could do to calm him. I worry he will rage himself to death sometimes!"

"And Rose, where was she?"

"Here, I suppose. I can't say for sure."

"And can you remember seeing Rose between your husband coming in here and your going out to the market, Mrs Sledmere?"

"I don't know. I suppose I must have done. I don't know."

"So she might have slipped out? Gone after Charlie?" Mrs Sledmere stared over at him and then gave a fearful sort of glance to the girl in the corner. "She is not always so tranquil, I imagine," Giles went on quietly. "It is my experience that there is often –"

"What do you know of it?" said Mrs Sledmere rather sharply.

"A great deal, ma'am, unfortunately." There was silence between them for a long moment, and then Giles went on. "I recognised something in your daughter that I have seen before. A passion and an anger."

Mrs Sledmere bit her lip and said, "I am sure she did not leave. I am sure of it. We are always so careful."

He did not pursue the discussion after that. He had no stomach for it. Instead he asked Mrs Sledmere if he might look over Charlie's room again. He had no idea what he was looking for, precisely, only that he hoped he would find some unregarded trifle that might hint at the truth of the matter.

People were diligent in the art of concealing things they valued. In a city where so many people flocked anew each year, and were forced to lived in lodgings, to share with strangers and to be spied on by over-circumspect landlords, a safe place for their scanty possessions was a necessity. If people did not even have the luxury of a box with a lock on it, they would stash their valuables in all manner of places – some more obvious than others. There were thieves in Northminster, knowing rogues, who could find the weak spots in any room in a matter of minutes and yield up the treasure. One such, a woman called Mary Nuttall, had just been transported after a spate of burglaries in lodging houses. He felt it would have been useful to have her there, for she had had a great talent for uncovering well-hidden silver spoons and purses heavy with shillings.

He imagined how Mother Nuttall might have set about her nefarious work, looking about him with the eye of a hunter. He paced the room carefully, feeling for loose boards, and found one at the end of the bed. He pulled it up without much difficulty and found under it a small but heavy box, wrapped in a piece of old sheeting. Uncovering it, he saw it was a handsome piece, with a keyhole of ivory and brass scrolls inlaid in the figured wood. An expensive box that was, of course, locked, and he wondered if the key was concealed elsewhere in the room. Keys – was his life to be bedevilled by them? He continued his search and but found nothing else.

When he went downstairs again, Rose Sledmere was sitting at the foot of stairs, still holding her mess of white ribbon. She did not move as he came past but simply stared up at him with a cool, hard eye. It was not the look of a grief-stricken victim or a person with something weighing on her mind. It was the look of an animal, cautiously appraising a stranger. Was he her enemy or her ally? It was not a question he could answer.

Chapter Twenty-one

Thomas O'Brien, master printer and the owner of The Bugle newspaper, welcomed Giles into his tiny office. There was a brisk fire with a kettle sitting by it, and O'Brien set it on the hob. "I will make some tea," he said. "I don't see why the womenfolk should be the only ones to put the world to rights with tea. Although by the look of you, perhaps you'd like something stronger?"

"No, tea, if you please," said Giles sitting down.

"This may be the last time we sit here," said O'Brien, taking a canister of tea and a teapot printed with a chartist slogan from the mantelshelf. "I'm taking Royd's old warehouse in Wharf Street and setting up there. The Bugle is getting too big for this place. Bridey is complaining about it taking over her kitchen."

"If you move The Bugle out of the yard, Mrs O'Brien will never see you at all."

"I'm not sure she'd mind that. I am a trial when I'm working. And I need a proper office. Especially if I am to set up another venture."

"Oh?" said Giles. "That's interesting."

"Another paper. The Bugle is doing well enough, but I feel there is a limit to what I can do with it. I feel a need to stretch my wings – and probably empty my pocket at the same time."

"But you have the capital?"

"Not enough, but some. I've a few investors interested. Some of the Dissenters, in fact."

"It would still be radical?"

"Of course, but not so as to alarm anyone. It's a delicate

balance of course, but I think it can and ought to be done," said O'Brien. "Radical and reformist, but designed to appeal to the middling sorts and above. A city this size ought to have a serious paper – and The County Gazette is hardly that."

"It's an interesting idea," said Giles, and added with a smile, "you should talk to Lord Rothborough. It's exactly the sort of thing he likes, from what I can judge."

O'Brien laughed and said, "If I talk to him, my Dissenters won't put up a penny. They may like his politics but they can't stand his morals." He was measuring out the tea into the pot.

"That is to do with our visiting diva, I suppose?" said Giles with a sigh.

"Well, she is staying in his house."

"She seems beyond reproach to me," said Giles.

"You've met her?"

"Yes, I am undertaking a little investigation for her. Someone has been sending her unpleasant letters."

"That would be like looking for a needle in a haystack," said O'Brien.

"Is she spoken of so badly?"

"It isn't pleasant."

"Poor creature," said Giles. "But she is not one to accept pity. She's as brave as her voice. I heard her sing last night, and one might forgive anyone anything with such a voice. Not that there is anything to forgive, I think."

O'Brien glanced at him across the table.

"You don't sound as sure as you'd like to be on that point."

"It's a difficult matter. Rothborough is certainly besieging her – at least from what I can observe; but whether she has succumbed is another thing entirely. A matter of conjecture – and town gossip, it seems. And I should not add to it. It is not honourable, let alone kind." He rubbed his face. "I wish she were not here, to be honest. I have enough to do with this murder. Any insights on that, by the way?" O'Brien had been at the inquest, taking careful notes.

"I wouldn't presume," said O'Brien.

"If you hear anything interesting –"

"I'll let you know, of course. And I'll put out another appeal for information."

"Thank you. Oh, and there was another thing," said Giles. "Your wife's sister – the one you mentioned – the widow. She was looking for a place as a housekeeper, I think? Mrs – I'm sorry, I don't remember her name."

"That would be Susanna," said O'Brien. "Susanna Connolly. Did I mention her to you?"

"I think it was Mrs O'Brien," said Giles, after a moment's reflection.

"She's with my brother-in-law in Manchester at present."

"But she's still looking for a place?"

"Yes, I think so. Bridey would know more about that than I do. You have heard of something for her?"

"Yes, well, it's a rather delicate thing," said Giles. "It might not suit her. There would be a great deal of responsibility. But if she's anything like her sister that wouldn't be a difficulty. I'm looking for someone capable, calm and intelligent."

"She's all that," said O'Brien.

"And she has no dependants?"

"No, which is just as well, given the state her husband left his finances in. And that wasn't Susanna's fault. He looked solid – it turned out he wasn't. You know how it is, sometimes?" Giles nodded. "She could do with a bit of luck," O'Brien went on. "What is it you have in mind for her?"

"I have taken a small house – one of those new ones on the far side of Martinsmount, with the large gardens. I need a housekeeper for it."

"What!" said O'Brien, with a smile. "And desert your HQ? I'm shocked, Major – how can you think of it? How will they manage without you?"

"No, I don't intend to live there," said Giles. "It's... it's for my wife."

There was a little silence while O'Brien digested this.

"And I apologise for never having mentioned her to you before, O'Brien," Giles went on, "but it is only that our circumstances have been difficult. She is not well. At present she is in a place where she is not being looked after as she should and I wish to have her near me and cared for properly, decently. I do not know if she will ever recover from her condition, but things cannot go on as they are. I must do something."

"Her condition," O'Brien said, after a moment. "It is not that she is... distressed, in some way, is it?"

Giles looked across at O'Brien, who sat with his elbows on the table, wringing his fingers together. His concern was palpable and comforting, and deserved honesty.

"She is in a madhouse," Giles said, and then rubbed his face. "There is almost a sort of relief in saying that aloud."

"I should think so," said O'Brien. "My God, man, how have you stood it?"

"Because I have no choice," Giles said.

O'Brien said, after a moment, "We've wondered often enough, Bridey and I, why there was no Mrs Vernon. Oh dear God in Heaven, but that's cruel, beyond cruel. And that you, of all people, should be tried like that –"

"Oh, it is not so hard for me," said Giles. "But for her – that is the worst of it. If I could lift the suffering from her in some way, bring her some relief from it, bring her back to what she was..." He could not prevent himself from sighing.

"How did it happen?"

"There was no sign of it when we married – she was high spirited – but that was nothing to alarm a man. Rather it charmed me. But it was when our boy was born, that was when it all began. Apparently it is not so uncommon."

"You have a boy?" said O'Brien.

"He died at three months. Like your little Eliza."

There was silence for a long moment.

"Yes, you must bring her here," said O'Brien, breaking it. "That is the right thing to do. And Sukey may be just the woman for the job."

"Will you have Mrs O'Brien write to her and explain? Tell her that it will not be easy – she will have control over the household and supervision of the nurses. I will, of course, be on hand, and Mr Carswell will be in charge of the medical arrangements. He is up to date in his information, so I am hopeful – well, I must be hopeful, always, must I not?"

O'Brien nodded.

"She'll write today," he said. "You will want this settled as soon as you can. You've enough to worry about just now, as it is."

"Thank you," said Giles, getting up and picking up his box.

"By the way, what's in the box?" O'Brien asked.

"I don't know yet. It belonged to the dead man."

"The solution you hope for?"

"Unlikely. But it may tell me something of use."

~

Dean Pritchard had talked of skeleton keys. Giles had such a key in his possession. They had got it from a notorious local housebreaker he had caught in his first year in the post. At the trial it emerged it had proved an effective tool for this rogue, and for many years.

It was clearly a cast from another tool – how many of the wretched things were in circulation nobody could know – and Giles kept this example safely locked up in his writing desk.

The skeleton key was not the easiest tool to use, and

naturally the man from whom they confiscated it had declined to give them a demonstration of his skills. Ever anxious to know his enemy better, Giles had however attempted to master the technique. As he now tried to open the box he had found under the boards, he was not entirely unprepared as to how to use it, but it still took some time, determination and patience. Lock-picking, even with the right tools, was regarded as a skilled trade amongst the criminal fraternity for good reason. At last he felt the lock turn and yield to him. Housebreakers had their uses, after all.

The box was as fancy within as it was without: lined in green satin trimmed with gold braid. It contained a bundle of letters; a badly executed miniature of a woman and a leather purse filled with coins. This explained the weight of the box. The miniature, judging by the look of the woman's hair and dress, looked as if it had been painted twenty years ago, and the subject looked a great deal like Barnes – his mother, Giles supposed. The purse was of greater immediate interest. He tipped out the contents onto his writing table, and was surprised to see a great many sovereigns among the silver. He reckoned it up and found it came to just short of a hundred pounds. Where had such a quantity of money come from?

Then he turned to the letters, all in the same hand. He plucked one out at random.

> You are my heart's darling. If I were only to see you and speak to you again, as we did last night, if you would only permit me to hold you in my arms again, and kiss your sweet lips, then I would be the happiest man on this earth. My darling boy, you are everything to me.

They were the sort of letters a man would write to a woman, except they were written from a man to a man, for they were all signed *"Jos Harrison"*.

Giles frowned. Harrison might not be a murderer but he might well be a sodomite. That was an indictable offence and

Giles had strong evidence for it, enough to bring it before the Justices.

Yet he hesitated.

Such acts went against the accepted morality of the day, and yet he knew that such inclinations were sometimes unavoidable. Human passion was a strange thing. A man might find himself bewitched by another man, as another man might be enslaved by the face of a pretty woman.

The acts might not be vicious in themselves if there was an element of consent. But a court might well argue that Harrison had seduced and corrupted Barnes. His youth and inexperience in the hands of an older man made him a victim.

He locked up the letters in the box. He needed to talk to Harrison again.

Chapter Twenty-two

The lady then smiled, and took his hand saying, 'Dear sir, your pleasure would be mine entirely. Do as you will with me.' I was still standing behind the screen, but I had a perfect view as my good aunt then stretched herself out upon the sofa, throwing back her silken skirts and displaying all her charms to the young officer, who could not restrain himself from gasping at the beauty revealed to him. Her snowy belly, rising in a gentle curve above that exquisite region, the summit of all pleasures...

Felix could scarcely believe what he was reading. He turned the page, half afraid to go on. He rapidly scanned the passage of description, which if anything became more deliciously lewd, and found himself fingering his cravat as the couple set to on the sofa. Such was the power of the words, he felt he too was concealed behind the screen, watching the action for himself, and as the breathless narrator gave into her own excitement and felt the urgency of her own arousal, he felt a fury of lust which brought him as much pain as pleasure.

A brisk knock at the door startled him back to reality. He felt he had been caught *in flagrante delicto*, and he realised he could scarcely decently rise from his chair.

"Yes?" he called out cautiously.

"Mr Carswell?"

It was, of course, Major Vernon.

"Come in, sir."

He found he was forced into a rather disrespectful sort of salutation, twisting in his seat and giving a mere lazy wave of the hand.

"We need to go and talk to Harrison," said Major Vernon.

"Why do you need me?"

"I want to know what you make of him."

"I am rather busy..." Felix managed to say.

"With what?"

"I am working up some notes. For The Lancet."

He reached for a pencil, attempting to look a little more studious. As he did so the book went flying to the floor, where it lay open, all its charms exposed, just like the heroine's wanton aunt. The Major stooped and picked it up before Felix had a chance to. He glanced at it and then his glance became a moment's study.

"The Lancet, you say," he said, snapping it shut. "You really do not have enough to do here."

"I was merely –"

"There is no need to go into details," said Major Vernon. "Such books exist for a reason, but there are times and places for such things. And this is neither the time nor the place. I think you know that." He strolled into the bedroom and tossed the book onto Felix's bed. "Come now, I need you with your considerable wits about you, Mr Carswell. We need to get some sensible answers from Harrison. There is a good chance he is our murderer."

~

"He's upstairs," said Harrison's landlady.

"And how's your boy, today?" asked Major Vernon.

"Much better, sir. On the mend, I'm pleased to say."

"I'm glad to hear it."

They went up the narrow stairs.

"Mr Harrison," she said, knocking on the door in front of her with a loud rat-tat. "You've got visitors." She knocked the door again, with more force.

There was a lengthy pause and then Harrison's voice, slurred and hoarse, answered: "Yes, yes, Mrs M, for the Lord's sake..."

The latch was lifted, the door partially opened and Harrison was revealed to them, wearing a dressing gown, with a long red scarf wound about his neck.

"What is it?" he said.

"Visitors for you."

"I thought I said no visitors," he said sourly.

"There are visitors and there are visitors," said Mrs Marling. "Major Vernon and Mr Carswell."

Harrison exhaled loudly and wandered back into the room. Mrs Marling bustled in after him and looked about her.

"Well, this is in a fine state, I must say," she said, clearly offended by what she saw.

It was not surprising. The place was squalid and disorderly, although it was probably the best room in the house and furnished handsomely. The air stank of stale brandy, tobacco, urine and vomit and the curtains across the two large windows had been tightly drawn to keep out the sun, making the room both gloomy and stuffy. There were books and papers scattered about, among Harrison's abandoned linen and the dirty crockery. In one corner was an old bedstead, hung with embroidered curtains, but the bed looked as though the clothes had been dragged off by force, and were cascading down onto the floor, revealing the striped mattress beneath.

"I've been ill," Harrison said with shrug.

"And we all know what with," said Mrs Marling, ripping open the curtains and throwing up the sash. "I'm sorry for this, gentlemen," she said, turning round to Felix and Major Vernon. "This is not how I usually keep my house."

Seemingly finding the light of day too much for him, Harrison staggered back to the cave-like sanctuary of his bed and climbed in, dragging the bedclothes with him. He pointedly would not look Major Vernon in the face.

"I think we need to start again from the beginning, Mr Harrison," said Major Vernon, when Mrs Marling had left. He removed a dirty shirt from a chair and set it down near the bed so that he could lean on it. "There are a few discrepancies in what you have already told me that I would like to clarify."

"This had better not take long. I have a rehearsal at three," Harrison said.

"It will take as long as it needs to," the Major said. "You said you did not leave this house on the day of the murder, yet Mrs Marling clearly remembers hearing you leave in the morning. Well before ten, she says."

"She says she remembers," said Harrison. "She may be wrong."

"Maybe," said Major Vernon. "So you stick by your story?"

"It is not a story. It is the plain truth. I did not leave the house that day until I went to sing Evensong."

"Are you sure?"

"Yes, as I said to you before."

"So how are we to account for this banging of the front door that Mrs Marling so distinctly heard?"

"The wind," said Harrison. "She left it open a little and it banged shut."

"Or rather you left it open a little when you came in the night before? That would be a most extraordinary door, that managed to stay a little ajar all night." Harrison said nothing. Major Vernon went on. "And I suppose the wind caused your footsteps on the stair as well? She heard those too. For it is a noisy staircase. I noticed that as we came in. A man could not come down it without making a fair bit of noise, and the door has a heavy latch on it, even when it is not bolted."

"I did not go out!" Harrison said. "The silly creature has it all wrong. I was here all that day. I swear it! I was here in my bed."

"You may have to swear it yet," said Giles. "And perjury

is a serious matter."

"I would be telling the truth! I did not leave this room!"

Major Vernon nodded and consulted his notebook but Felix suspected that he had no real need to do so. He merely wanted to make Harrison uncomfortable with a long silence.

"You decided to leave it a long time to settle your quarrel, then," said the Major at length.

Harrison glanced at him suspiciously. The Major went on, "I have had experiences of this kind myself. I have quarrelled with someone the night before, slept badly and then gone to them straight away the next morning in order to make amends. Given the strength of your regard for Mr Barnes, I am surprised that you left it so long. These things can be such a torture otherwise."

"I don't know what you mean," said Harrison.

"When one's affections are engaged, then these things cannot be left to chance. Why did you leave it so long before seeing him again?"

"What are you implying?" said Harrison.

"I have come to understand that relationship, Mr Harrison, and I see that it went a little beyond friendship." Harrison stared across at him. "Certain letters have come into my possession."

"Letters," said Harrison rather dully.

"Letters," Major Vernon said. "From you to Mr Barnes." There was long silence.

"You have no right to read such things," Harrison said.

"I have every right in this case," he said. "You know the law about such matters, I take it?"

"Letters are simply letters," said Harrison.

"Letters indicate a great deal. A court would not look kindly on these. And we are talking about more than just letters. There is the matter of what happened at Mr Geoffrey's house. Singing for your supper, I think you called it. A nice euphemism."

"You have no evidence of anything."

"I have plenty. I have the evidence of my own eyes, Mr Harrison," the Major said, picking up an empty brandy bottle. "You have been living high with no debts. This is expensive stuff. You could not afford this on your salary from Carr or from your singing. You have been lining your pockets another way. Yes?"

"No, no, absolutely not. No." He staggered out of the bed as he spoke.

"Think before you speak, Mr Harrison. And remember that the truth is always the safest course."

Harrison stood there, his dressing gown wrapped round him, biting at his knuckle, shaking his head.

"I am not saying a thing more. You will not worm anything out of me. I know what you are trying to do. I see your game but I will not play it, sir, I will not! Now I have to dress. I have a rehearsal."

"Very well, Mr Harrison. But be aware I will be watching you. We have not finished talking yet."

~

"What do you think?" Major Vernon asked when they had left the house.

"I don't know, sir, to be frank. He seems cantankerous and proud of himself, but whether that means he could throttle the person whom he — well, loved, if that is the word for such relations."

"That is the word he uses in the letters. Which are as frank in their way as that little volume I found you with."

"That was..." Felix wondered how he could begin to explain it.

"There is no need for you to explain," said Major Vernon.

"At least not that. I am far more interested in who you were talking to last night. The young woman who ran away."

"I really cannot say," Felix said, pushing his hand through his hair. "A promise is a promise especially when a lady is involved."

"Yes, yes, of course, but do you wonder why she has sworn you to secrecy? Is that honourable of her?"

"Should one question a lady's actions?"

"In an ideal world, no," said Major Vernon. "But this is not the realm of the saints. We are all imperfect creatures. We all have our secrets, our flaws, our shortcomings. Ask yourself, does she deserve this protection and what harm would it do her if you were to tell me? A great deal may depend on it. The fact she has asked you to lie and –"

"I cannot say, truly, I cannot."

"She has bitten into you, then."

"No, not at all. No, that is not the case."

"Are you sure about that?" Major Vernon said. Felix did not answer. "Well, think on it, if you please. It would be helpful if you could bring yourself to tell me." He looked at his watch. "Now, the rehearsal at the Minster is at three. I propose we attend and observe Harrison. Yes? And you will have the chance to hear Mrs Morgan. I will see you there, Mr Carswell, if no medical emergencies intervene."

"I doubt that," Felix said. "And you, sir, what will you do until then? It is only one."

"I have a few errands to run," he said, and set off down the street at his usual formidable pace. He stopped, though, and turned back to Felix. "Perhaps you might call on that young woman and clarify the situation," he said, and then started off again.

Chapter Twenty-three

Felix began with good intentions, the Major's counsel ringing in his ears, and he walked up the hill into the Minster Precincts, intending to go and speak to Miss Pritchard. But as he approached the Deanery, he found himself thinking again of Mrs Morgan and he could no longer resist the impulse. He turned towards Avonside Row.

He found Mrs Morgan alone, which surprised him. She was stretched out on a long couch in front of the fire. There was a pencil in her hand and a score open on her lap, but she was not paying it much attention. She had put her head back on a cushion, and was at first sight in such perfect profile and so still, her gaze focused somewhere other, that he felt she might be sitting for her portrait, or in character for some operatic role. He wondered if she were about to rise and sing some aria of longing and loss.

For a moment he wished that was the case. If she had been on stage and he sitting in the audience, then he might have been able to enjoy the moment. It was far easier to manage such desire when one did not have to make conversation with the woman in question.

"You're not unwell, I hope, ma'am?" he managed to say, his throat as dry as ashes.

"No, I am just resting before my rehearsal." She looked up at him rather searchingly. "I don't usually allow interruptions. I was in two minds whether to let you in or not, but my curiosity overcame me."

He could not think how to answer that. The idea of her being curious about him created a heart-pounding sense of anxiety, mixed with excitement.

"May I sit?" he asked, indicating the chair which sat near the couch, almost as if it had been placed especially for visitors, the visitors which she said she did not usually permit.

She nodded but he hesitated, imagining Lord Rothborough sitting there, in his usual languid way: ankles crossed, one arm hooked over the back rail of the chair, and his head thrown back in amusement. He imagined her laughing too, both of them on easy terms, so companionable and comfortable with one another.

He perched there, his hat in his hands, wishing for a moment that he had the grace and polish that Lord Rothborough complained that he lacked. It would have been pleasant to be able to simulate some façade of ease, however thin, but he could not. He felt his every gesture betrayed him as the provincial booby in the grip of romantic passion, a feeling not helped by her continuing to look at him in the same penetrating manner. He had lain awake half the night thinking how glorious it might be to have her to himself for a moment, but now he had been granted this private audience with her, he wished he could be anywhere but there, such was his confusion.

"I am inclined to be a little offended by you," she said.

Felix swallowed.

"If I have given offence, then I am sure —" he began.

"You did not stay to hear me sing last night," she said.

"Last night?" he said.

"Last night," she said, with a gracious nod.

"I..." He looked down at his fingers and his hat. He had not thought she would have noticed him go, let alone take it as a slight. He had imagined that she was only looking at Lord Rothborough. "The wine was very strong. I needed some fresh air." He managed to look at her directly again.

"Are you sure it was just the wine, Mr Carswell?" she said, with a slight smile.

The smile relieved him, but only a little. He felt it was

tinged with mockery.

"It was Lord Rothborough's singing that drove me from the room," he said, with as much lightness as he could muster.

"Can you do better?"

"No. I have no ability. I sing like a bear."

"You ought to have been taught. A man ought to cultivate his voice."

"Is that what he says?"

"He?" she said. "Who do you mean?" Her manner of asking implied she knew the answer, but she waited for him to speak.

"I mean Lord Rothborough."

"No," she said with a frown. "I am not his parrot, Mr Carswell. If we are to have good music in our houses, the men must play an equal part. An accomplished man can play and sing as well as a woman."

"Such accomplishment is incompatible with learning a profession," said Felix. "I wouldn't have had the time."

"You must have been a dull student, then. Now, the French surgeon Monsieur Lebreuve – you have perhaps read him, he is something of an authority on the larynx – well, he is a most brilliant pianist, good enough to play duets with Maestro Liszt himself. And he told me that he attributes all his surgical dexterity to his mother making him learn his scales."

"Is this my punishment for leaving last night?" Felix said.

"Yes, and you deserve it. It was not civil."

"I am not made for society."

"Nobody is. It is something one must learn."

"And you say you are not his parrot," he said. The words tumbled out without his meaning them to, and he regretted them almost the moment he had finished. He flushed.

She picked up her pencil, twisted it in her fingers for a moment and then pointed it at him.

"You seem to be labouring under a misapprehension about Lord Rothborough and myself," she said.

"I do not like to think what he has said to you."

"But you do think it. Rather you imagine it, and wrongly."

"I don't know. He gives the impression to me that –"

"Yes?" she cut in. "What impression might that be?"

"That, that..." He broke off again and she sighed.

"You ought to take me at my word," she said.

"I would dearly love to believe you, Mrs Morgan, and I know I ought, but –" He stumbled out of his chair and strode across the room to the window, where he stood with his back to her. He was so desperate for air he felt he would like to have thrown the window up, or perhaps break it with his fist. "He has said – he has implied that..."

There was a long silence, and then she said, "Of course, you must think what you must think. In your condition there is really nothing else you can do."

"My condition?" he spun round. "What do you mean by that?"

"You know perfectly well. You are not an idiot, after all. Although some physicians are notoriously bad at self-diagnosis, I am sure you are not."

"I do not know what you mean, ma'am," he said. "Truly I do not."

She got up from the sofa and walked over to him.

"Don't lie to me," she said. "Do you think I have never seen this before? I know the symptoms. It is a hazard of my profession. Men of all ages, throwing themselves at my feet." She was close to him now and he could smell the lavender on her skin. Suddenly he ached with longing. "It happens all the time."

"That is not the case with me, ma'am," he said, as coldly as he could. He could not bear the thought of all those others, fawning and drooling over her, feeling those same indecent thoughts about her that he felt. He could not be in such company. His pride would not permit him, and yet...

"Liar," she said and slapped him across the cheek.

It was not a very violent blow, but it was a shock. For a moment he could do nothing and then he caught her hand in his, anxious not to let her strike him again, but having possession of it, he found he could do nothing but bend and attempt to kiss her palm. His lips had scarcely touched it, before she had pulled her hand away.

"There, can you deny it now, Mr Carswell?" she said.

He rubbed his cheek, feeling the smart now.

"A most elegant demonstration," he managed to say.

"Good," she said, and walked away to the piano. She opened the lid and sat down, and began to play some complicated piece, full of notes and fire.

"And did you do such an experiment on Lord Rothborough?" he said, going over to the piano, feeling his anger rising up in him now. "Is he just one of my wretched cohorts, that you clearly take such a delight in humiliating? Or is that another matter entirely? After all, you seem pretty comfortable here, ma'am, in this house!"

She broke off playing and stood up again. They were face to face.

"Do you wish me to slap you again?" she said. "Do not think I will gratify you with an answer."

"Why not?" he said, and grabbed her by the shoulders. "I will go away, if you will just tell me that. I will be the obedient whipped dog and slink away if you will just tell me what there is between you."

"No!" she exclaimed and tried to push him away, but he still had her in his grip. "I have said enough on that subject, and you must take my word. Let me go, sir!"

But Felix could no longer help himself and pulled her closer so that he might kiss her. He felt in doing this that she would understand and relent, that she would feel all that he felt. Like some creature in a fairy tale, he for a moment believed that his kiss might transform her, that she would melt in his arms, and permit all the liberties described in 'The

Memoirs of the Comtesse'.

Yet of course she did not. A second or two of horrible struggling followed, and he was properly repulsed by her, with a strength that surprised him. She finished by cracking him across the face again, this time with enough force he felt he might have a bloody nose as a result.

Then, just as he was getting back his balance, the door opened and Mrs Ridolfi came in. She looked at him, he felt, with utter contempt.

"Ah, Paulina, is it time for me to warm up already?" said Mrs Morgan.

"Yes, dear," said Mrs Ridolfi.

"Mr Carswell was just leaving," Mrs Morgan said, and turned away from him.

Chapter Twenty-four

Why had he attempted to kiss her? In what part of his disordered brain had he imagined that might improve matters? Had that wretched book somehow contributed to his reckless, wanton behaviour?

He had gone into the Minster in order to meet Major Vernon, but he could not yet face him, and had turned into one of the gloomy side chapels, relics of another age, that were such a feature of the building. This one still contained an altar with a smudgy old painting of the Virgin Mary above it, and he considered throwing himself onto his knees in front of it, out of habit as much as anything. He felt ashamed enough to repent – to have kissed her was an act of incalculable folly, the actions of an idiotic boor. But he did not prostrate himself. He had spent enough time on his knees and it never seemed to profit him. He ran his hands through his hair and turned away.

He saw then that he was not alone. In the dustiest, darkest corner, partially obscured behind a vast white marble tomb covered in swooping putti, he noticed a woman was sitting on the bench built into the wall. There was something familiar about her, and as he approached her he saw it was Kate Pritchard.

"We seemed destined to discover each other," he said, and wondered if fate was trying to tell him something, for after Mrs Morgan, he was again presented with the very different charms of Miss Pritchard.

"Because we are both looking for places to hide, perhaps," she said. "I saw Lord Rothborough out there."

"And I saw your father," said Felix. "Though he can't have any objections to your being here, I am sure."

"You have no idea of the extent of his objections," she said.

"May I?" he said, indicating the bench where she sat.

"Of course."

"Have you come to hear her sing again?" he asked.

"Have you?"

It was a little disconcerting to be asked a question in response to his own, but he supposed she was trying to avoid answering him directly. He wondered why she was so cautious and why she was hiding.

"No, most definitely not," he said. "The less I have to do with Mrs Morgan the better."

"Then why are you here?" she said.

"I am here to meet Major Vernon. Have you seen him?"

She shook her head.

"What has Mrs Morgan done to offend you?" she asked. "You sounded so vehement – you don't mind me saying so, I hope."

More questions, he thought, and wondered if he ought to adopt the same defensiveness. But there was something about her that made him unable to be anything but candid.

"It is rather what I have done to offend her," he said, and pressed his hands to his face. "I have been excruciatingly foolish. Beyond foolish."

"I'm sure that is not the case." He felt her hand press his shoulder. He glanced at her pale face in the shadows, and her enquiring yet sympathetic expression moved him. He put his own hand over hers which remained on his shoulder, and squeezed her hand in return.

"You're too kind," he said, and removed her hand and laid it on her lap. "I don't deserve sympathy, that I do know."

"Everyone deserves sympathy, no matter what," she said. "And love is a great tribulation. Is that what this is about?"

"Love – well, I'm not sure it's as noble a sentiment as that. I rather think it's – well, you know..." He pulled away his hand, feeling ashamed to touch her with such thoughts in his head.

"You should not be so harsh on yourself. She is impossibly attractive – so beautiful and talented. I should be surprised if a man did not find her like a siren. Her voice is so faultless – it cuts into one."

"Yes, a siren," he said, "that is what she is. Then I must stop my ears with wax and tie myself to the mast."

"Perhaps, Mr Odysseus," she said.

"He had his Penelope and his Ithaca. To keep him on course."

"Yes, indeed he did."

The choir began to sing and silence fell between them as the music surrounded them.

He watched her listening again, just as he had the other night. She displayed the same concentration, but not the rapture. That had clearly been Mrs Morgan's doing.

Now Miss Pritchard was beating time with her finger, her head moving with the music, and she frowned once or twice, as if displeased at what she heard. Then after a particularly pronounced wince, the choir stopped, almost as if she had been directing them herself and had thrown up her own hands to stop them.

"I knew they wouldn't manage that," she said. "The tenors are so ragged at the moment without poor Mr Barnes." She added with a sigh, "Poor, poor man." He saw her shiver, and he reached for the shawl that lay pooled on the bench and arranged it about her. "Thank you," she said and gave him such a warm smile of gratitude that for a moment he felt his misery lift. "You did say you had seen Lord Rothborough?" he said.

"Yes."

"Then I will stay here a while longer, if you don't mind. I doubt he will find me here."

"And Major Vernon?"

"He may find me. He is far better at searching things out."

"That I had heard. Do you think –" She broke off. "Do you think he will find who murdered Mr Barnes?"

"I am sure of it," said Felix. "He has a great talent for getting the truth out of people. He was curious about last night, by the way. A ribbon fell from your dress and he picked it up."

"Oh, that is where it went!" she said. "Oh dear."

"I did not tell him who you were, but he has a way of guessing at things. You must forgive me if he does realise it was you. He is so acute."

"I could not blame you for that, Mr Carswell. It was my conduct that was at fault. I should not have asked you to do such a thing, I know, but..." She broke off, biting her lip.

"We are back to the siren again, I think," said Felix, pushing his fingers through his hair, and looking up at the vaults. "I wish she had never come here."

"It will pass, I'm sure of it," she said. "Sooner or later."

"I suppose so. And I have friends to help me – you will let me call you a friend, Miss Pritchard?" he said, glancing at her.

"It would be an honour," she said.

And in that moment he believed he might have found a cure for his folly: marriage and a sweet, companionable wife. He found himself thinking of the house that Lord Rothborough had spoken of, and although he disliked the implications of Lord Rothborough's actions, it was possible to see the utility of them. If a house was to be forced on him, he might as well use it for his own ends.

"You must come and see my house," he said, with decision. In his mind, embarking on this conversation was akin to talking of marriage. For what man could marry without a house?

"Your house?" she said.

"I told you that I am probably going to be a man of property. Some place belonging to Sir Robert Arden."

"Not Ardenthwaite?" she said.

"You know the place?"

"I've seen over it," she said. "It is a fine old house – and very large. And the gardens are so pretty. It is all old-fashioned, though. Perhaps you don't like that sort of thing."

"I don't know what I like, to tell you the truth. Well, I did not care for Holbroke. You have seen over that?"

"Yes."

"A great showy soulless monster of a house," said Felix decidedly. "Ardenthwaite is not like that?"

"No, not at all. It is as I said, old-fashioned, and romantic. There are mullion windows and stained glass, and some of the floors slope alarmingly. But there is a great gallery at the top of the house which has the most wonderful view over the moors. You can see the sea from there on a fine day."

"You liked it, then?"

"Yes, I did. Very much."

"It sounds pleasant," he said.

"It is. You are a lucky man, Mr Carswell."

"It sounds like the sort of house that needs a mistress," he said.

"I'm sure there will be no difficulty about that," she said with a smile.

"We did discuss the question of our eloping," he said as lightly as he could.

"That was just a piece of nonsense."

"Nonsense can turn into sense. Sometimes?" he said. She looked at him. "It would not be so ridiculous, would it, to consider?"

"You are pragmatic, Mr Carswell."

"Yes, well, perhaps, but you don't find me objectionable, and I certainly don't find you objectionable. You would have everything you wanted. I could do that for you – you'd have an establishment, and you'd be someone in the county, should you wish it – Lord Rothborough would see to that – I am sure he would love you as a daughter –"

"Enough!" she said. "This *is* nonsense. You cannot make a silly joke into a marriage proposal. You don't feel a jot for me. You are only tired of being in thrall to Mrs Morgan. Do you think that making love to me will cure you of that?" He could not answer. "And what am I to do if it doesn't cure you? If we find ourselves in Switzerland on our wedding journey and you pining for Mrs Morgan still? That is not how good marriages are made. There must be mutual passion. There must be mutual love. It is not a business arrangement."

There was a silence while he took in what she had said.

"Forgive me, it was ridiculous," he managed to say.

"Of course I forgive you. You are half-mad over Mrs Morgan, that excuses it," she said. "We cannot expect reason from you."

She laid her hand over his, and he was moved to take it up and kiss it, feeling thankful for her good sense and mercy. Another woman could have used such a moment entirely for her own ends, but she had not. When she did marry, her husband would be a lucky man, he thought, and in the spirit of friendship he leant forward and kissed her cheek, just as one might kiss a bride.

And as he did, he heard footsteps behind them. He turned, and to his horror saw Dean Pritchard accompanied by Lord Rothborough.

"Katherine, what are you doing here?" Dean Pritchard said. "Did I say you could leave your mother? Did you have my permission to leave the house? And what are you doing here, with this man?"

"There is nothing going on, sir, I assure you," Felix said, jumping to his feet and putting some distance between himself and Miss Pritchard. "We were just talking –"

"Mr Carswell, please, the truth," said Miss Pritchard. "My

dear, it is better that we tell the truth at once." And she reached out and grabbed his hand. He was so astonished by that "my dear" that he did nothing to prevent it. "Mr Carswell has just proposed to me, Papa, that is what has been going on." She was now squeezing his hand so violently that he thought she might crack his fingers. Her hand was so strong, he supposed, from all that piano practice. He was obliged to put his other hand over hers in a covert attempt to get her to release him, but she held fast, and the impression given must have been one of a couple hand-fasting in front of witnesses. *Which is what she wants,* he began to realise.

"Is this true, sir?" said the Dean, turning towards him.

"Yes," he managed to say. "I did, and –"

"And I have accepted," Miss Pritchard said, clear as a bell.

In Pitfeldry, they would be as good as married after that, Felix thought. His father spent a great deal of time trying to persuade people to come and marry in church, but the old system still prevailed.

But this was Northminster, and Scotch marriages were not legal. Neither would the Dean's daughter and the Marquis' bastard be allowed to enter into any such contract independently. He felt the depressing truth of that as much as the disapproving eyes of Lord Rothborough on him. They were not free agents. Their position made slaves of them. A farm servant and a maid had more liberty.

Even before Miss Pritchard had finished saying "accepted" the Dean marched forward and pushed Felix roughly to one side, breaking their handclasp. Felix could not help being a little relieved, but he did not at all like the way Pritchard shook his daughter roughly by the shoulder. He was moving to pull him away for himself, when he felt Lord Rothborough's restraining hand on his arm.

"Take your daughter home, sir," said Lord Rothborough, quietly and mildly. "This is neither the time nor the place." At this Dean Pritchard released her and she turned so that Felix met her glance, which was imploring him. She was begging for his collusion. But why? What on earth was she doing, when only a moment ago she had spoken so plainly?

"You are right, you are right..." muttered the Dean, gathering his thoughts. Then he drew himself up and turned to Felix. "You, sir, will be so good as to call on me first thing tomorrow morning and explain yourself! Katherine, we are going home!"

Felix was left alone with Lord Rothborough. There was a long, rather uncomfortable silence, and then Lord Rothborough spoke.

"What a pretty business," he said. "And I thought you had learnt your lesson in this department. You understand what I expect of you, I trust? When you speak to him tomorrow you will retract your proposal. You can find some excuse for it. It isn't pleasant, but you are not marrying that girl!"

And then to crown it all, in another part of the Minster, Mrs Morgan began to sing.

"Ah, *cara*," murmured Rothborough. He turned and walked away towards the sound of the siren.

Chapter Twenty-five

Giles sat with his brother-in-law in the Minster, listening to Harrison and Mrs Morgan sing the duet "Who calls my parting soul from death?" from Handel's Esther.

Harrison was a transformed man. He had shaved and was now dressed with considerable elegance in a well-cut frock coat and immaculate linen. He wore a figured silk waistcoat that would have cost at least three guineas – a discreet and handsome design with which Giles could not find fault. He perfectly matched Mrs Morgan in both looks and bearing, and he did not look the least out of place. He was every inch the professional singer. Of the disgraced, truculent and resentful clerk there was little sign. Giles found it hard not to be impressed by this, and as for his voice – even though he knew he was no great judge, it struck him as excellent. It was sweet-toned, perfectly controlled and still suitably manly. His performance was full of emotion but did not veer into an excessive show of passion. In short, it was appropriate for his part as the virtuous hero and lover of a queen.

When the duet was done, Lambert said with a sigh, "I think we have lost him. He will never stay now Mrs Morgan has heard him sing like that. Northminster's loss will be London's gain. I have never heard him in such good voice before. It is as if he has come into bloom."

"He does not seem much affected by his loss," Giles said, thinking of those letters.

"He has an excellent technique," said Lambert. "Look how pleased Mrs Morgan is with him. So she should be. Their voices matched beautifully. We can only hope he will come back to us occasionally," he added.

Mrs Morgan and Harrison were looking over their scores together and then she left the platform, and the orchestra began to play again. Lambert was in a sort of ecstatic rapture, following his score as Harrison again began to sing.

Giles slipped from his place in order to study him better as he sang. Harrison was not acting the least bit like a guilty man, but perhaps that excellent technique allowed him to conceal a great deal.

Leaning against one of the great Romanesque pillars, Giles turned over in his mind what he knew of the man. Harrison was undoubtedly a risk-taker, already plunged deep into a way of life that was both dangerous and illegal. He was a man who wrote passionate love letters to another man, letters that were also graphic enough in their content to get him hanged for buggery. He was also, it seemed, willing to sell his sexual favours.

Did this calmness, this remarkable control he was witnessing, indicate that Harrison was amoral? If that were the case, then the murder of Charles Barnes might be just another act that did not much trouble his conscience.

He was so absorbed in his train of thought that he did not realise until the end of the aria that Mrs Morgan was standing beside him.

"I am glad to see you," she said, when Harrison had finished. "I need to speak to you."

"Oh, why?"

"I've had another letter," she said.

"When did it arrive?"

"I don't know. We simply found it in the house."

"We?"

"My sister-in-law found it."

"And where was it?"

"It was lying in a basket in the hall, apparently – the card basket."

"And none of the servants took in a letter?"

"No, they say not."

"And it was addressed to you in the normal way?"

"Unfortunately not," she said. "It was addressed – well, may I show it to you? I have it here."

"Let us go into the library," he said. "I don't think anyone will disturb us there."

He showed her to the south door and they made their way along the ancient cloister until they reached the small nail-studded door that led to the medieval library.

"How beautiful this is!" she said, looking about her as they went in.

"I like it better than the Minster," said Giles, "although it is heretical to say so."

"Books are always comforting," she said, touching the gilded spine of a great old volume with her lavender-gloved finger. "I always think so. So much wisdom... the wisdom of all the ages. I would like nothing better than to sit here and read them all. Then I might make fewer mistakes, perhaps?"

"Great scholars are sometimes the greatest fools, in my experience," said Giles.

"Yes, I have met some of those," she said with a smile. "No, wisdom comes from knowledge and common sense, I think, and experience."

"That is the harshest tutor of all," Giles said.

"Yes," she said, with a slight shiver. "Oh yes indeed."

He had been carefully objective about her – he knew that much, but in that moment, her soft voice seemed to tempt a part of him he never could entirely control. She was wearing a silver-grey bonnet that framed her face, and in the fading light of the room, her pale beauty was eloquent and her companionship seemed infinitely desirable.

He reached into his coat, fetched out a box of lucifers, and turned his attention to lighting the candles that were arranged in a great branched holder. They sat down on either side of an ancient blackened oak table, and Mrs Morgan opened her reticule. She pushed the letter across the table to him.

"This is not pleasant," she said.

She was correct.

The envelope was addressed in gummed paper letters and read:

> To Nancy Morgan, a dirty whore.
> You are all found out. Your wickedness is known. You are a whore and a destroyer of all that is good. You are a stain on the earth. You will fuck any man for a penny. But beware – the time is coming that you must pay, and you will pay with your life. A knife will come and give you what you deserve. You will choke on your own dirty blood. A constant friend.

"I have to admire your coolness under fire, Mrs Morgan," he said, laying the letter down on the table.

"What other way is there to be?" she said. "You heard me singing just then. Handel's heroines are full of virtuous resistance in adversity. I have learnt from their example."

"Did Mrs Ridolfi open the letter?"

"No, seeing the address was enough for her and she brought it straight to me."

"You have discussed these letters with her?"

"I have – but in no great detail. I did not want to alarm her. Especially after that business with the bird, which shook her badly."

"Of course not," said Giles. "Given that she knew of the other letters and how they distressed you, she might have dropped it in the fire, wishing to spare you the pain of it."

"Oh, Paulina would not do that. She knows I would want to see it."

He studied the letter, turning it in his hands, and then said, "I must say, I do find it curious that Mrs Ridolfi discovered both the bird and this letter."

"What are you implying?"

"That she may have been the origin of the letters."

"That is a harsh accusation, Major Vernon."

"It would not be the first time such mischief has been made by a person close to the victim. It is a possibility that must be explored."

"No, no, I cannot agree with that. Not in this case. Paulina is as dear as a sister to me. We grew up together – we were pupils with Mrs Watkins. I would trust her with my life – as I trust her with my child. You are mistaken, Major Vernon. Paulina could not, would not do anything like this." She frowned at him reproachfully, but he was not to be deterred.

"Was she living in your house in London when the first of these letters arrived?"

"Yes," she said, "but that is a coincidence. It is nonsense to even think it."

"And how long have your brother and his wife been living with you, I must ask?"

"A couple of years now."

"They have no house of their own?"

"A house in London at a good address is a great expense and Dick is not as prosperous as he might be. He needs to be in the heart of town, as do I. It is convenient for all of us."

"So your husband does not object to his wife's family living in his house?"

"I don't see what my husband's opinions about anything have to do with this."

"Is that because he no longer lives under your roof?" he ventured.

There was a little pause.

"That is not supposed to be common knowledge," she said, quietly, "for obvious reasons."

"I understand," he said. "And it is not common knowledge."

"I am glad to hear it," she said.

"However, it would have been useful had you told me of

it," he said. "After all, an absent husband, a difficult man by all accounts – an aggrieved husband – could he not be responsible for this trouble?" He tapped the letter with his finger. "That must have crossed your mind, surely?"

"Perhaps," she said after a long silence. "Perhaps."

"And where is your husband at the moment?" said Giles. "Do you know?"

"I think he is engaged in Paris at the opera there. That is what I heard."

"But you do not know any more than that?"

"No. I don't really want to know. I don't like to think about him at all."

"Naturally. He has obviously hurt you a great deal," he said, "but in this case – if you wish to put an end to this, you must force yourself to consider it. I know it is painful, ma'am, but –"

"Yes, yes, it is a possibility I suppose!" she said. "It would not be out of character."

"How well does he know your sister-in-law?" Giles said. "Does he know that she is afraid of dead birds, for example?"

"He may do." She was silent for a moment and then said, "Do you think he might be here?" she said. "In Northminster?"

"Do you?" he countered, hearing the fear in her voice.

"I hope not, but..." She took the letter from Giles' hand and looked over it again. "This does suggest, does it not –" She broke off, and after a moment said quietly, "I have been a great fool. I should have told you. I am sorry, I did not think properly, I suppose. I did not think that he – even he – would stoop so low. I thought we had settled it. Goodness, I gave him enough!"

"You gave him money?"

"Yes, I paid him to go – it was a great deal of money. It was all the money that I had managed to save from my fees over the last few years – money that I managed to keep him from spending. I hid some away, even from the start, because – well, I knew soon enough what a mistake I had made in marrying him. In the end it was all I could do to get rid of him. He discovered I had it – and of course claimed it was his, which I suppose it was by rights, and that I had no right to hide it from him. So I gave it to him, on condition that he left Harry and me alone for good. I thought it would be enough, but perhaps I have been deluding myself. He is an extravagant man. He could have run through it already. Is that what all this means? Is he trying to scare me into giving him more money? It is a strange way to go about it."

"Was he glad to go?" Giles said.

"I don't know. I think so. He said he was, but I know it was a humiliation for him. And he had an easy life when we were together. I did everything I could to make it pleasant for him. I tried not to be a bad wife. I looked after his linen and ordered what he liked for dinner. I was too afraid of him not to do my duty, but I wanted to be a good wife to him. I wanted it to be right and straight between us, especially when Harry was born. I thought that would make him happy, but it never did. I could never do enough. There was always this terrible resentment. Professional jealousy, of course. He would have liked me never to sing again, but then we would have been paupers. He wanted what I could earn, but at the same time he hated that I could earn so much more than him."

Giles scoured the letter for any new meaning that had yet escaped him. He wanted to ask about her position with Lord Rothborough. For Rothborough had enemies enough, and one of those might think of getting at him by tormenting his mistress. But it was not at all clear if she was his mistress, and in the moment he could not find a way to ask her that would not be extremely offensive. In the quiet intimacy of that library he disliked the thought of offending her.

The door opened and George Watkins came in. Giles folded the letter and put it in his pocket.

"There you are, Nan," Watkins said, looking pleased to have found her.

"Oh, am I late, George?" she said, rising at once. "I am sorry – Major Vernon and I had a little business."

"No, no, we begin again in five minutes," he said. "I just wanted to discuss the tempo of the finale with you."

"Of course. Though I thought you had it all straight the other morning?"

"Well I did, but I was looking at the score again and I thought –"

"Have the courage of your convictions, George," she said, laying her hands on his shoulders. "It is your performance. The more conviction you show, the more convinced we will all be. Players and audience alike."

"You're right," he said, "yes, yes, of course. And the others are all here from town now."

"Dick?"

"Yes."

"Good, good," she said, with a smile. "I must go, then. Excuse me, Major Vernon, I must go and see my brother."

"He has come to play the flute in the band," George Watkins added helpfully.

"I'm glad he could get away," Mrs Morgan said. "His employers can be so awkward."

"Who are his employers?" Giles asked.

"He is a visiting music master," she said. "Only to the best families, of course, but such people can be difficult, and inclined to treat him as if he is nothing more than a servant. It is aggravating as he is a fine teacher, and his pupils all love him dearly, but their parents – well, some of them really do not know how lucky they are!"

Giles went back with them into the Minster and was able to witness the reunion of Mrs Morgan and her brother. Like her, he was tall, golden-haired, and good-looking, but he had a washed-out air about him, as if the business of hearing the scales of all those noble misses had drained the life out of him. He had neither the vigour nor the fire of his sister. He struck Giles as a disappointed man, a point rather underlined by the appearance of his wife and Mrs Morgan's little boy. Harry greeted his uncle like the dearest of fathers and would not let go of him, despite being told by his aunt several times that "Uncle Dick must go to work now." Finally she was obliged to drag him away, and young Harry was only pacified by Ridolfi running over to him and whispering something in his ear that made the child grin with sudden happiness. The action of a man who loved children, perhaps, a man who wanted children of his own but had failed in that respect? It would have been another mortification to add to living in his more prosperous sister's house, like a poor relation.

Mrs Morgan's success, he reflected, seemed to be both a curse and a blessing for the men in her life.

"Mr Harrison?" George Watkins was saying, as he stood in front of his freshly assembled orchestra. "Where is Mr Harrison?"

A few moments passed and Harrison still did not appear.

Giles glanced at his watch. He had been out of his sight for only twenty minutes. Had Harrison seen him leave with Mrs Morgan and decided to make a bolt for it? Had he lost sight of his prime suspect? He sincerely hoped not.

~

Giles emerged from the Minster and noticed his niece Celia Fforde crouching on the grass. She was attempting to persuade Samson Agonistes, the big white cat who was habitually seen about the Minster Precincts, to come to her, but he was remaining aloof.

"He does not like me at all, Uncle Giles," she said. "I

must smell wrong or something."

"You do not smell of rats, that is it. Have you been here long, Celia?"

"About a quarter of an hour," she said. "I am waiting for Papa."

"Have you seen Mr Harrison come by? You know him, I'm sure?" She nodded. "Did he come out of the Minster?"

"I haven't seen him, no. Not today at least," she said, and then added a little hesitantly, "why do you want to see him, Uncle Giles?"

"I want to talk to him."

"Is it about poor Mr Barnes?" said Celia.

"Yes, as a matter of fact," he said. "What do you know about that, Celia?"

"Well, I did see Mr Harrison. I saw him the other day. You see, yesterday I heard Cole and Betsy talking in the kitchen – talking about what had happened to Mr Barnes, and that he'd been left dead in that chapel above the gatehouse, that you can see from my tree, and I remembered that the other morning when I was up in my tree I saw Mr Harrison coming out of there. Along that little lane."

"Which morning?"

"Tuesday. The day it happened. It was Tuesday, wasn't it?"

"You are sure it was Tuesday?"

"Yes. I know it was Tuesday because it was before geometry."

"And you are sure it was Mr Harrison?"

"Oh yes. He had that big long red scarf on and he has a particularly shiny high hat. Mama is always fascinated by it. She pretends not to be, but she is always saying it: how is Mr Harrison's hat so shiny? Then Papa says he must use champagne and bootblack."

"When is your geometry lesson?"

"Half past ten. Mr Smithson comes at half past ten on

Tuesday and Friday."

"And your lesson before that – when does that finish?"

"Miss Frey lets me out at ten."

He nodded.

"That is extremely useful, Celia. Thank you for telling me."

"I hope it doesn't mean..." she said. "Well, you know... that Mr Harrison isn't – is he? You don't think that, do you?" Giles did not get a chance to answer, because Celia then said, "Oh look, there's Mr Carswell."

Giles turned. Carswell was striding along at great speed and would not have noticed them had not Giles called out to him, "Just in time, Mr Carswell! We need to find Harrison."

"Harrison – oh?" said Carswell, pushing his hand through his hair.

"You do think it is him!" said Celia. "Oh no. I wish I hadn't said anything now."

"You did exactly the right thing," said Giles. "And it may mean nothing at all that you saw him then. I only need to talk to him again."

"But it may mean everything," she said. "You're going to arrest him, aren't you? – just because of what I said. And then he'll be hanged." She covered her face with her hands.

Giles crouched down and put his hands on her shoulders.

"No, no, that isn't the case at all. We simply don't know. I have to make sure that he was not involved in any way, that is all. There may be a simple explanation to his being there, one that has nothing at all to do with Mr Barnes."

She did not look convinced. She glanced up at Carswell for confirmation.

"Major Vernon is right," he said. "It doesn't mean that at all."

She pursed her lips and nodded.

"Come, let me take you home, Miss Fforde," said Carswell offering his hand. "I need to speak to your mother. I seem to remember I promised I would dissect a bull's eye for you, and we must arrange a time."

The prospect of this treat, which would have made most eleven-year-old girls squeak with horror, seemed to mollify her, and the pair of them went off towards the Treasurer's House while Giles was left to think where best to start looking for Josiah Harrison.

Chapter Twenty-six

Several hours later, Harrison had still not been located. He had not returned to his lodgings, neither had he been seen in the taverns he was known to favour. All the obvious and the less obvious places had been checked, and despite exercising a fair bit of ingenuity on the subject, Giles and his men drew a blank. He seemed to have vanished into thin air.

Very much the actions of a guilty man, Giles could not help thinking, as he poured himself a glass of claret and sat down to dinner. With the addition of Celia's evidence it was damning enough. He could only hope that Harrison could be located before too long. He decided he would go out again later and continue the hunt.

Carswell was equally elusive in his own way. He came in late to dinner, and did not seemed much inclined to conversation. He picked at his food and avoided Giles' glance. When they had finished, he took his wine and stood by the fire, staring gloomily down into it, apparently preoccupied by some private trouble. Giles wondered whether he ought to enquire about it or whether such an intrusion would be resented. He decided that if Carswell wished to talk to him, he would choose his own moment. A rational distraction would be a better strategy.

Giles got up from the table and spread the latest letter Mrs Morgan had given him on his writing table next to the earlier letter. He had been thinking about them as they ate, and now wanted to confirm his suspicions.

"Interesting," he said looking down at them. "I'd value your opinion on this. This is the latest piece of polite correspondence to reach Mrs Morgan. Pretty shocking, wouldn't you say?"

Carswell eventually came and stood beside him, and looked the letter over. He said nothing, apparently determined to be indifferent to it.

"How different they look side by side," Giles went on. "Cut from different paper, and pasted on different paper. Even the way the letters are cut out seems different. This person is a great deal more accomplished with the scissors. Look how the large letters have been so precisely cut round. It is like that fancy work women sometimes do with prints and so forth. Looking at them I wonder if we are not looking at the work of two different people."

"But the sentiment is equally vitriolic," said Carswell, his interest apparently now piqued, "and the language is similar."

"That's the puzzle of it. Is person B," Giles said, tapping the most recent letter, "imitating letter A, and by implication person A?"

"Or have they just taken more care on the second letter?" Carswell said.

"That is a possibility. But this one is done so finely, so carefully. It is like an arrangement in a commonplace book. My sisters used to do these things — Mary would cut entire castles out of paper. Now if you have a skill, and you are a meticulous person — as the maker of letter B clearly is — it is difficult surely to leave off being meticulous?"

"You think it is a woman who has done this?"

"It's possible. I have had a look at some old cases — there was an example fifty years ago in Lincoln when a widow tormented her daughter-in-law with poisonous letters, alleging she was having an affair with another man. In the end the son believed the letters and attempted to kill the man in question, which was how it came to court. It was the prospect of her son being hanged which made her admit to it."

"I am sure there are plenty of women that Mrs Morgan has offended," Carswell said. "Sirens must run the risk of being disliked by their sisters."

"Or more specifically their sisters-in-law?" said Giles, holding up the second letter to the lamp, and peering at it. "I'm willing to swear that this is all cut from The Bugle. Oh, how I wish she had kept those other letters. It was understandable of her to destroy them, but —" He laid the letter down, unable to make any more conclusions. He felt in need of a brisk cold walk in order to think clearly.

Carswell had returned to the fire and was staring moodily into it. It struck Giles that he was also in need of a distraction.

"Get your hat and bag, Mr Carswell," said Giles. "We are going to call on Mr Geoffrey again. Let us see if we can't get something useful out of him. Perhaps he will know where Harrison has got to."

"Do you think that's possible, sir?" said Carswell.

"I don't know, but it's better than sitting here in idleness, don't you think?"

~

The door was opened to them by the grim-faced butler.

"Mr Holt, good evening!" said Major Vernon.

"I don't think my master will want to see you, sir," said Holt.

"We will deal with your master later," said Major Vernon, going boldly into the house. "But first, I would like a word with you."

"As you like, sir."

"Have you seen anything more of Mr Harrison — since Monday night, I mean?" asked Major Vernon.

"Yes, sir, he was here this afternoon, as a matter of fact — at about half past four."

"He was? That is excellent information, Mr Holt. You

opened the door to him yourself, not one of the other servants?"

"Yes, sir, I did."

"How did he seem?" Major Vernon said, taking out his notebook. "Was he calm, for example, or agitated?"

"Agitated," said Holt. "He was up on his high horse, as he always is with me, but more than usual. Trying to show me how much a gentleman he is, which of course he is not. Demanded to see the master at once. I told him to wait. I went to ask Mr Geoffrey if he'd see him, but he followed me in, which of course set the master at loggerheads with him at once."

"What did your master say, precisely?"

"He told me to put him out at once. So I had a go, but Harrison was in fighting mood, and started yelling at Mr Geoffrey, saying that the game was all up, and that Major Vernon would be onto him unless he gave him some tin to clear out of Northminster."

"And how did your master take this?"

"He sent me from the room."

"I don't suppose you went far away?"

Holt hesitated for a moment before saying, "No, sir." He hesitated again. "I stayed outside the door to hear what I could of the rest of it. I thought, since a man was dead, I had better."

"I understand," said the Major. "There are indeed times when eavesdropping is necessary."

"I thought you would see it, sir," said Holt. "Trouble was, it's a solid door, and I didn't hear anything else. But then about five minutes later, Harrison marches out and straight through the front door."

"And you think your master gave him some money?"

"It seems possible, because the master was locking his desk drawer when I went back in to see if he was all right. I know he keeps a bit of ready money in there, so I suppose he did."

"And how did he seem?"

"Rattled, I'd say. He asked me to fetch Nickson – that's his man – to him at once, and asked for a large brandy and water. Oh, and he wouldn't take his dinner, which surprised me, for the man's a glutton and never misses a meal."

"Mr Holt, that is extremely useful. Now, go to your employer and announce Mr Carswell, will you?"

"Yes, sir." Holt went off obediently.

He came back a few moments later and said, "The master will see you, sir. This way, please."

They followed Holt into an impressive apartment, lined with glazed bookcases. There was also a considerable amount of statuary about the place, giving the atmosphere of a museum. It was brilliantly lit up as if a great company were expected, with a huge fire burning in the grate. Felix wondered if this was the room where the *poses plastiques* took place and felt some disgust at the thought. If what they had surmised about these events was correct, then it was inexplicable to him. Man's lustful urges were surely linked inextricably with the desire to propagate the race. How could a man be driven to desire something that could only be futile in terms of the forces of nature? But then from his own bitter experience of the last few days, he knew that desire for a woman was not always rational. Perhaps, then, he in his own inconvenient concupiscence had more in common with these affairs than he liked to admit. He tried for a moment to imagine himself in lustful pursuit of a man, but could not twist his head about the notion.

Clad in his dressing gown and night cap, Geoffrey was sitting at a round table in the dazzling pool of light given off by a particularly large and elaborate Argand lamp. On the table were trays taken from a medal cabinet, and Geoffrey was squinting at some treasure through a magnifying glass. He looked up and stared at them as they entered.

"Who the devil are you, sir?" said Geoffrey.

"Forgive the intrusion at this hour, Mr Geoffrey," said Major Vernon. "I am Major Vernon of the Constabulary. I have taken the liberty of accompanying Mr Carswell on his call."

"Major Vernon, well – I have heard something of you, sir," said Geoffrey putting down his glass and the medal on the baize-covered table. "A military gentleman is an ornament to any society," he said after a moment. "We shall take some wine – Holt, fetch up some Madeira."

"Not for me, thank you," said the Major.

"How are you feeling, sir?" said Felix. "I am glad to see you up and about."

"I have only been up this last hour or so," Geoffrey said. "I have been in a miserable condition. I thought I would take a little consolation in my medals. But I am glad to see you again, Mr Carswell. I have been on the verge of calling you back."

"Let me feel your pulse, sir," said Felix, taking him by the wrist. "Splendidly regular."

"You think so?" said Geoffrey, doubtfully.

"An improvement, certainly. Being out of your bed will always help you, sir, as will moderate exercise and mental distractions – such as your fine collection here."

"Do you like medals, Mr Carswell?" said Geoffrey. "I would imagine that you have an eye for such things. Perhaps you are a man of taste." He picked up a medal and held it out to Felix. "What do you think of that? A rare specimen. Fifteen century Italian – the finest quality. Florentine, of course, from the days of Lorenzo the Magnificent. A nice piece of work."

"I am afraid I am no judge," said Felix.

"Perhaps Major Vernon has an opinion?"

He held out the medal to Major Vernon, who took it and scrutinized it in the light of the lamp.

"A fine image and a handsome profile," he said after a moment or two. "It reminds me a little of Mr Barnes," he added, laying the medal down on the green baize.

"Ah, yes," said Geoffrey with a sigh. "Yes, indeed. How observant of you, sir."

Major Vernon pulled out a chair and sat down next to Mr Geoffrey.

"I understand you had a visitor this afternoon," he said.

"No, I have received no one today. I have not been well."

"Are you sure about that, sir?"

"I do not know what you mean."

"Your man mentioned you had a visitor this afternoon, Mr Geoffrey," Major Vernon said.

"He is mistaken."

There was a little pause as Major Vernon picked up another medal and examined it.

"This is a serious matter, Mr Geoffrey. I am investigating a murder. I would appreciate your cooperation."

"Yet you take a servant's word over mine?"

"Your servant has nothing to hide from me."

"What are you implying, sir?"

Major Vernon put down the medal and knotted his fingers together, fixing his gaze upon Geoffrey.

"In the course of my enquiries into young Barnes' death, certain letters have come into my possession. Letters written by Josiah Harrison to Barnes. They make for illuminating reading."

"I cannot see how such letters concern me."

"You are frequently referred to in them. You and your entertainments. It is all laid plain." Geoffrey said nothing but began to put the medals back into their trays. "Now, sir, will you please tell me who called this afternoon," Major Vernon went on.

"I would have thought you would know better than to trust anything said by a scoundrel like Harrison."

"He is a scoundrel, is he? I understand he was a frequent guest in this house."

"He is a scoundrel! An ungrateful scoundrel and whatever

he says about me in these letters, it is a lie! How dare you take his word against mine, sir? How dare you?"

"Be plain with me then, Mr Geoffrey. Tell me the nature of his business with you this afternoon. I cannot judge you fairly when you will not tell the truth. Mr Harrison was here this afternoon, I think?"

"He may have called briefly," said Geoffrey after a long pause.

"There, that was not so hard," said Vernon. "And what was the substance of the visit?" There was another long silence. "Come, sir, why did he call?"

"He... he asked me for money. The insolent wretch – I sent him packing soon enough!"

"Yes, very insolent. What was the money for? Did he say?"

"I haven't the slightest idea. I did not give him any, of course."

"Are you sure about that, Mr Geoffrey? After all, you have given him money in the past."

"I beg your pardon, sir!" said Geoffrey with something like a splutter.

"Please, a little less innocence, Mr Geoffrey! I am not a fool. I have found purses full of sovereigns in both Barnes' and Harrison's possession. Where did they come by those? How is it that the pair of them could afford such fine tailoring and not be in debt for it? You are the only person of means with whom they have any sort of intimate relationship." Major Vernon put considerable emphasis on the word intimate, and Felix noticed Geoffrey finger the cuff of his nightshirt in agitation.

"I may have made them gifts of money, from time to time," he said, after long consideration.

"Gifts? Not wages for services rendered?"

"No, most definitely not. I resent that suggestion, sir."

"Then perhaps it was money for staying quiet?"

"No, no! What do you mean by that?"

Major Vernon reached into his coat and brought out a folded letter.

"I mean you were paying them for their discretion. Harrison writes here to Mr Barnes: *We may screw that old tart Geoffrey for an extra fifty. He is scared as a man can be. That will get us nicely settled. But you must do it, for he dotes on you.'* What I am to make of that, now, Mr Geoffrey?"

"You can make of it whatever your vulgar mind pleases, Major Vernon, but I will sue you for slander if you continue to make such allegations about my character."

"The burden of truth will be yours to prove and it will not be pretty. You would do better telling me exactly what passed here this afternoon. Harrison is a wanted man and if you have aided him in escaping justice, then..."

Geoffrey gave a great sigh.

"He asked me for money," he said. "And I gave him twenty guineas. He said he intended to leave Northminster tonight – if I gave him the money I would hear no more of him. He begged me for it. He told me he had nothing to do with Barnes' death but that you would not believe him – that the circumstances were all against him and that you were determined to hang him for murder – and if not for that, for... for..."

"For buggery, sir?" said Major Vernon.

"He threatened me!" exclaimed Geoffrey. "The scoundrel! He said if I did not give him the money he would spread dreadful slanders about me."

"Twenty guineas?" said Vernon mildly. "Is that all?"

"It is not true! Whatever that devil says it is not true! Nothing of that nature happened here. Nothing! It is wicked nonsense. I am a good Christian and I would never sully myself with such unspeakable behaviour."

"Then why did you give him twenty guineas, Mr Geoffrey?" asked Major Vernon. "If it was all lies, and you had nothing to hide?"

"I have a reputation as a charitable man, Major Vernon,"
said Geoffrey, drawing himself up a little. "It is something that
you would do well to cultivate yourself."

~

"So," said the Major as they walked away from the house, "has
Harrison taken flight because he is guilty of murder, or
because he is worried about being wrongly accused of murder?
He is scared, that's clear enough. If I could just lay my hands
on him again... The worst of this is that if I hadn't gone to
speak with Mrs Morgan, then I should have never have lost
sight of him."

Felix glanced at him.

"I told you she was a siren," he said. "Bound to put us all
on the rocks."

"Perhaps there is something in that," he said. "But it is
hardly gallant. I do not think she intends to lure us into
destruction. It is just an unfortunate consequence of her
charisma – and of her distress."

There was a sound of footsteps behind them; turning,
they saw Holt running towards them.

"If you have a minute, sir!" he called out.

"Yes, of course, Mr Holt," said Major Vernon. "What is
it?"

"Thought you might like to know, sir, that the master has
ordered for his bags to be packed. He intends to leave town
tomorrow."

"Did he say where he intends to go?"

"The continent. I have given my notice."

"Then you are in want of a place."

"It seems so, sir," said Holt.

"Come down to see me tomorrow morning," said Major Vernon. "I have been looking for a man – my own is getting old and wants to leave me. I cannot offer you French cooking or many perks, but you might find I suit you better in many respects."

"You may be right there, sir," said Holt. "I will be there."

"You seriously mean to employ him?" said Felix when Holt had gone. "A dour fellow like that?"

"Dour but loyal. Men like that are useful about the place, in any capacity. I shall try and persuade him to be more than my servant. I want him on the Force. I'm thinking of setting a few of the more quick-witted men about the town in plain clothes. They have a detective department at the Bow Street office now. I think we would do well to arm ourselves similarly. And Holt is our man, I am sure of it."

Chapter Twenty-seven

As he walked to the Deanery the next morning, Felix wished
he had been able to confide in the Major. He would have had
some good advice for him on how to approach this delicate
situation. As it was, he felt he was going unarmed into the
enemy's camp with not even a good night's sleep to give him
strength and succour.

He rang the bell, and was surprised that the door was
answered not by a servant, but by Kate Pritchard herself. She
at once hurried him through the nearest door into an austere,
formal room with old-fashioned high-back chairs arranged
about the walls and a black-and-white tiled floor. There was a
Bible sitting open on the round table in the centre of the
room, and he wondered if this was where the Dean read
prayers to his family and household each day.

The March light fell grey and cold through the windows
and did nothing to flatter Miss Pritchard. She looked wrecked:
her complexion was ashen, and her eyes red and puffy. Had
she been crying all night? Had she been made to cry? He
wanted to be angry with her but he could not. The sight of her
moved him, despite everything.

"Do not, I beg you, contradict him," she said, in a low
hoarse whisper. "Accept everything."

"But, but —"

"I beg you," she said, grabbing both his hands and
squeezing them in hers. "Please, for the sake of friendship.
You said you considered me a friend!" Then she bent and
swiftly kissed his fingertips. "Please?"

He sensed her passion and her desperation — this was no
manipulative game, surely, but his mind still demanded

answers. He pulled away his hands.

"But why? Why did you say that, when only a moment before –"

"I cannot explain now. Please, just for me – would you – could you?"

"But –"

The door opened and Dean Pritchard entered. Kate jumped away from Felix, but a fraction too late. He marched up and pushed them apart.

"Good morning, sir," Felix managed to say although he was considerably startled by the force of the gesture.

"There is nothing good about it!" the Dean said. "Nothing at all. Go to your room, Katherine!"

"Yes, Papa."

She ran off without another word. Felix was tempted to run after her. The Dean was looking at him as if he were the Devil incarnate.

"Well, well, sir, here you are – at last," the Dean said. "At last. And where do we begin? Where?" He shook his head. "I am still incredulous. That is my difficulty. I cannot credit that a man of your position in society – a gentleman – could even consider behaving in such an outrageous fashion as you have. No gentleman would pursue an honourable courtship in such a way, with secret meetings –"

"There have been no secret meetings," Felix cut in.

"So what was that yesterday?"

"We met by chance."

"Do you expect me to believe that?"

"I give you my word on it."

"You word is worth nothing to me!" said the Dean. "You have been lying all along. Do you think I am a fool? Do you think I see nothing? I saw you talking the other night, when you came to dine here. Your heads together, full of secrets – the pair of you. I saw you and so did the whole company."

"We were only talking," Felix said.

"That was not talk. That was seduction. You were pursuing her, you cannot deny it. You have made love to a pure and innocent girl and seduced her from the path of virtue and duty. You have tempted and flattered her and led her into wickedness and sin. You have made her write to you and meet you in secret. You have stolen my sweet innocent girl from me and made a harlot of her!"

"I have not laid a finger on her!" said Felix. "Do you truly think, sir, that I —"

"You have had her. That is plain enough. She is ruined — and it is your doing."

"That I absolutely refute!" Felix said, astonished by this. "I have not seduced Miss Pritchard! I have not so much as touched her!"

"That is not what she says," said the Dean. "Why would she lie to me? Her own father? She admitted it all to me last night. That you had overwhelmed her. That you took her virtue from her."

"Dear God in Heaven!" Felix could not help exclaiming. Had she really said that or was the Dean suffering some sort of delusion? Or perhaps she was?

And if she had said that, what could have possessed her to do it, unless she wanted after all to be marched to the altar and married to him, post haste? Was Ardenthwaite worth such a dangerous piece of brinkmanship? He knew that young women were sometimes eager to get themselves an establishment of their own, especially when there was an overbearing parent in the case, but to try and trap a man in this way! To accuse him of *that*, to her own father. It seemed to go entirely against what he knew of her character, but then, what did he really know of that?

"Yes, you may as well get on your knees and beg your Saviour for forgiveness, young man!" said the Dean, and with that pushed him to the floor with such force that Felix found himself on his hands and knees. "There may yet be hope for you, if you humbly repent of your licentious and disgusting conduct!"

"I cannot repent of a sin I have not committed," Felix said, struggling to get back up onto his feet, but the Dean had him by the shoulders and held him there, on his knees. "You are completely mistaken. I have not – I would not – do such a thing to your daughter. You have mistaken what she says, I am sure of it. This is a mistake!"

"Fornicator!" The Dean spat the word into Felix's face, increasing the pressure of his grip on his shoulders at the same time. "Seducer!" he shrieked, again right in Felix's face, leaning over him, shaking him. Felix let himself fall backwards in order to extricate himself, crashing painfully onto his backside in the process, but it at least allowed him to scrabble back onto this feet.

"This is a misunderstanding, sir!" he managed to say.

"It is worse than I thought," the Dean said, advancing on him again. "You are prepared to accuse a lady of deceit in order to extricate yourself. Are you not prepared to face your responsibilities?"

"We are at cross-purposes, sir," Felix managed to say, with all the calm he could manage. But he had his hands up to stop the Dean coming any closer.

"You still deny it?" said the Dean, his hand raised menacingly. "Do you?" And then he struck him, plain across the face.

Felix felt his shock turn to rage in being so treated. It took all his self-control not to return the blow, such was his mounting fury.

"I will not stay here and be treated like this!" he said. "And if I find you have treated your daughter in such a fashion, then you will have to answer for it! You shall not slander or intimidate either of us, sir! I will not have it! A man in your position should know better than to take on so, like a common hoodlum!"

That seemed to stop the Dean in his stride. Felix wondered for a moment if he had overplayed his indignation, but the man was being outrageous and needed to be brought to heel.

"You forget," he went on, "I am not without connections, I am not without friends! I am not a nobody to be treated in such a fashion. Take care, sir, take care what you are doing!"

Dean Pritchard gazed back at him for a long moment, his eyes glassy, and in Felix's opinion, somewhat crazed. What was he dealing with here?

"Get out of my house!" he said.

"With great pleasure," returned Felix.

It was not until he slammed the front door behind him that he realised he was apparently still engaged to marry the wretched man's daughter.

Chapter Twenty-eight

Of Harrison there was still no sign. The night watch, even with the extra men, had turned up nothing.

Draining a cup of coffee, Giles realised he was going to look splendidly incompetent for letting his most obvious suspect slip from his grasp. The Watch Committee, to whom he must report later in the day, would no doubt have expected him to take Harrison into custody at once. His pride could take the blow well enough, but it irritated him beyond belief that his quarry was proving so elusive.

There was, however, another message from Mrs Morgan.

> Dear Major Vernon, you will forgive a letter so early, but there has been another letter and I would value your advice once more. Your faithful servant, A. Morgan.

On entering the house, Giles was met by the startling sight of Lord Rothborough lounging on one of the hall chairs, looking for all the world like a bored footman waiting for a reply to a letter.

"What are you doing here?" Rothborough said.

"I have been asked to call," said Giles.

"She asked to see you?"

"Yes."

"And yet she will not see me. I am made to wait!" he said. "What does she want to see you about?"

"I am afraid it is confidential, my lord." Rothborough gave him a rather dark look. "Police business," Giles added carefully.

"And I do not have her confidence! Of course not!" He rubbed his face and exhaled. "Heavens, what a morning," he went on, pulling himself up from the chair as if with great effort. "Still, while I have your ear and we are waiting for madame to honour us with her presence, there is another matter I must discuss with you – young Felix and this ridiculous business with the Dean's daughter. Did he tell you of his intentions?"

"No," said Giles. "This is the first I have heard of it."

"That is as I feared. I had hoped he might have confided in you – but then if he had done, you would most certainly have dissuaded him from it."

"From what?"

"Making the girl an offer – which she, of course, accepted."

"That is a little surprising," said Giles.

"That she accepted? Why wouldn't she? She is no fool."

"No, that he offered. I had no idea she was anything more than an acquaintance."

"I don't believe she is. But she has manoeuvred him into it somehow – the minx. I told him to retract it, of course. I hope he has done so. I shall have to go and make sure he has, then deal with Pritchard, who is a ninny of the first order and no doubt will be as difficult as he can be. What he was thinking of I do not know!"

Giles would have responded, but Mrs Morgan had appeared on the half landing. She was wearing a dressing gown, a golden damask affair that was more theatrical than utilitarian, and her pale hair was still flowing over her shoulders. It was an intoxicating sight and he found himself admiring her rather more than he would have liked.

"Ma'am," he said, nodding to her.

Rothborough turned at once and said, "Anna, my dear, there you are! What have I done to offend you? Why wouldn't you let me come up?"

He bounded up the stairs towards her.

"Nothing, I'm simply not well," she said, putting up her

hands to deter him.

"What? We must get you a doctor, my dear."

"No, no, it's not at all serious," she said, gently repelling him with a light touch of her hand. "I just need to rest. First I must talk to Major Vernon, and then I will rest."

"You are sure?"

"I am sure. And if I do feel worse, I will get a doctor, I promise."

"I am so glad to hear it." He took her hand and kissed it with some fervour. "I will not have you neglecting yourself." He let go of her hand, and came downstairs. "Don't keep her long, Vernon."

"I shall not, my lord."

Rothborough took up his hat and stick and went to the door.

"I shall call later, my dear, be assured of it!" and with a wave he was gone.

"Shall we...?" Giles indicated the door to the ground floor sitting room.

"I would prefer to go back upstairs," she said, "if you don't mind?"

He was a little surprised, but he tried not to show it, especially as he followed her into the bedroom. Fortunately her maid was in attendance, though Giles was not entirely sure whether that made it less or more indecorous. The sight of one beautiful woman helping another out of her dressing gown and back into bed had nothing of ordinary domesticity about it. It seemed to him suggestive of another world and customs different from those of Northminster. He was obliged to look away, for it gave him an unsettling amount of guilty pleasure, a little like reading a French novel on a Sunday.

"Forgive me," she said. "I was going to send Berthe down to dismiss him, but he never listens to servants. He would only go if I dismissed him in person, so I was obliged to get out of my bed."

"Are you sure you are well enough to talk to me?" said Giles, allowing himself to turn and face her again. She was now installed in her bed, the damask dressing gown replaced with a shawl draped about her shoulders. Modesty was perfectly observed, but the sight of her was still disturbing enough for a man who had no woman in his bed with whom he might take regular comfort.

She did not answer until the maid had left.

"I would rather not talk about this at all," she said, "but needs must. Do please sit down, Major."

He had retreated to the window and was obliged to take a chair and move it to the bedside.

"So, another letter?" he said.

"Yes," she said, and reached under her pillow for an envelope. "And this one is worse."

He examined it. It was fashioned in the rough-lettered style – the style of the first letter she had shown him.

> Death to you whore. You are a dirty whore who deserves to be treated like a whore so COUNT the days. There will be no mercy. You are discovered. Your deeds are known. You and your child must suffer the consequences of your vile actions.

"It is that threat to Harry – that is what so disturbs me."

He nodded. "Where did you find it?"

"It was with my wool work, in the bag I keep it in – it is on the chair there. You saw it the other night, I think – I took it to Canon and Mrs Fforde's."

"And where was the bag when you found it?"

"By the piano downstairs. I went to fetch it after dinner last night, as Paulina needed my scissors. It was fortunate I was alone when I found it, I think. I have told no one about this. I did not want to alarm anyone."

"Why did Paulina need your scissors?"

"She said she had lost hers. But I keep mine on a ribbon in the bag so they are always to hand."

"And when did you last do any of your work – before this, I mean?"

"At Mrs Fforde's – that was the last time. That is why it was by the piano. I came straight back in after dinner and did a little practice before I went to bed – that is my habit. And the whole of yesterday I did not touch it, I am sure of it."

"And the bag was where you had left it?"

"Yes."

"So anyone might have put it in there, at any time yesterday?"

"Yes, I suppose so."

Giles took the letter to the window to get a better light upon it. He glanced out and saw Dick Ridolfi playing energetically with his nephew in the garden, while Paulina looked on.

"Your son looks pleased to have his uncle here," said Giles.

"They are a pair of rogues together," said Mrs Morgan with a smile.

"Perhaps it made you sleep better to know you had your brother here last night – after you discovered this?"

"Yes and no. I am not sure what Dick would say if he saw that. He would be..."

"But your sister-in-law will have told him about the others?"

"Yes, I imagine so."

"But you did not want to tell him?"

"Why should I disturb him unnecessarily? Last night we were such a happy family party, I could not bear to break it up. So I decided I would let it lie a night and seek your opinion this morning."

"You have not questioned your servants?"

"No."

"And none of them has mentioned anything strange to you?"

She hesitated a moment.

"Hannah did say something – but I don't know what to make of it."

"Hannah, that's your son's nurse?"

"Yes. She said she saw a man in town who was the double of my husband. She did not think it was him, but that she and Harry passed him in the street, and she was surprised at the likeness, as was Harry. But that doesn't mean anything, does it?"

"It might mean something," Giles said.

"I am sure it does not," she said. "I hope it does not."

She looked away, twisting her fingers in the fringe of her shawl.

"You clearly have a theory, Mrs Morgan," he said.

"You have put it in my head, then, and it is just a theory," she said.

"But the thought that your husband might be here in Northminster disturbs you?"

"Of course."

"From what you know of his character, do you think him capable of something like this?" asked Giles, tapping the letter.

"I don't know. Perhaps," she said. "I don't know what your experience has been, Major Vernon, but it was my thought that when one marries and becomes intimate with someone, one will then know that person, truly know them; but I found I did not. He was unpredictable, at the best of times. I found I could not master his character – he was not like a part all written out for me to be interpreted. He was a mystery, I suppose."

"Was he jealous?"

"Yes – I can say that. Very jealous."

"It must be said that the letter-writer seems preoccupied with the idea of your infidelity."

"Yes," she said, "that is true."

"You must not mistake what I am about to say to you,

Mrs Morgan – I mean no slight by it – but these impressions on the part of jealous men often spring from some seed, unintentionally sown. Do you think you at any time gave your husband cause to think that you had not been constant? Does your husband know of your...” – he hesitated, choosing his word with care – “friendship with Lord Rothborough, for example?”

“He may do, yes.” She sighed heavily. “Oh dear Lord, I suppose that might provoke him, if he had heard of it. For he must think as I suppose everyone does, that it means – well, I suppose you have wondered about that yourself.”

“Yes,” he said, “I admit I have.”

“You were doing as you should, given what I have asked you do,” she said. “And I owe you some honesty in return.” There was a little pause before she began to speak again. “I am not Lord Rothborough’s mistress.” She went on, “And if we were in some way more deeply involved, it would not be as the world would imagine it, I am not one of those –”

“No, of course you are not,” he said.

“But perhaps I *am* deluding myself,” she said with another great sigh. “Trying to make nice distinctions when there are none. Perhaps I am everything those letters accuse me of being, and more. Perhaps I deserve to be tormented.”

“An anonymous letter is the act of a coward,” said Giles. “And no one who writes one in such a fashion as these are written has the right to judge another. We will get to the bottom of this, ma’am, I am sure of it. Do you have a likeness of Mr Morgan, by any chance?”

“I do – if you look in that lacquered box on the chest.”

“This one?” he said, rising and pointing to the box. She nodded and he brought it over to her.

“Why I keep it here I don’t know,” she said, opening the box and looking through it. “Out of habit, I suppose, or sentiment. I... felt so differently about him when this was taken. Here.”

She handed him a miniature. The man in the portrait was strikingly handsome, enough to make him memorable, even allowing for the flattery of the miniaturist.

"May I borrow this?"

"Yes, of course," she said. "It is nothing to me now," she added with a slight shrug.

"Thank you. I will go and speak to your nursemaid," he said.

Chapter Twenty-nine

Giles found Hannah, the nurse, sitting by the fire darning a small sock. She started up when Giles came into the room.

Giles motioned to her to sit down again.

"Mrs Morgan has told me that you think you saw Mr Morgan in Northminster the other day. Can you give me some more information?"

She hesitated for a moment before she answered him. "I'm not so sure now that I did, sir," she said rather quietly.

Giles frowned and took a chair and sat down opposite her.

"You don't think you saw him, then?"

"No, sir."

"Yet you told your mistress you did?"

"I didn't say that exactly, sir," she said, "I only said it might have been him, and now I think about it, I'm not so sure."

"Well, perhaps you could tell me what happened."

"If you think it matters, sir."

"It might, a great deal."

"I was mistaken."

"Tell me anyway, if you will. What day was this and when?"

"Yesterday morning. I generally take Master Harry for a walk about ten. We usually go about the Precincts here – but we went through the big gate at the end down the shops – I can't remember the name – the one with the big confectioners on the other side."

"Minster Gate?"

"That's the one. We went through that one. You see, his

Lordship had given Master Harry sixpence the day before and he wanted to spend it."

"Lord Rothborough, you mean?"

"Yes, sir. He had it when they came back from their drive the other day. And of course Mrs Ridolfi was scandalised by that, but Master Harry, he does like his own way, and he hid it from her, for she told him he must put it in the poor-box. So when we were out of the house that morning – the morning after, he digs into his pocket and shows me it and says, with a great big grin on his face, and says, 'Hannah, I want to spend it all now.' And bless him, he didn't want to buy anything for himself, but for his mama. So that's why we went down to the shops, and Master Harry was excited as anything, and going so fast, it was all I could do to keep up with him, and there were so many people about that I'm not sure what I saw now. I just saw this gentleman in the crowd and I thought for a moment it was him, but that was all it was, sir, I swear it!" she finished, with a touch of desperation.

"Yet you thought enough of it to mention it your mistress? Why was that?" She did not answer and looked down at her work. "Hannah, why was that?" She glanced up at him for a moment and he saw the confusion in her face. He pressed on: "Are you sure that was all that happened? A face in the crowd?"

She bit her lip and looked away. Now Giles asked, "Did Master Harry see him, this gentleman who looked a little like his father? Children can be very observant. Did he point him out to you, perhaps?"

It was a guess on Giles' part, but it made her stare back at him.

"How did you know that, sir? Has Master Harry said something to you?"

"No, but I may have to speak to him. What are you afraid he will say?" said Giles. "You are afraid of something, Hannah, I am certain of that, but surely you know it will be better to tell me everything?"

"But..." she began and twisted up her mouth.

"But?" he said. "I think there was a little more to this sighting of Mr Morgan than you are telling me, is there not?" She nodded. "Did he in fact speak to you and Master Harry?" She nodded again. "So, the whole story, if you please."

She hesitated for a long moment and then said, "I'd hoped I'd never see him again, to tell you the truth. I was as glad as anyone when the mistress sent him packing. It was a relief, and when I saw him there yesterday, in the street, and there was Master Harry tugging at my hand and saying 'Look, it's Papa, it's Papa!' I didn't know what to do, and then next minute there he was talking to Master Harry. I knew I should take him away at once, that it wasn't right, but when I tried to say that, Mr Morgan looks at me and says, 'You mustn't rush away, Hannah, you must respect a father's rights', and then he said that it was God's law that he should be allowed to see his boy, and if I stopped him I was doing wrong. And he's not an easy man to stand up to, sir, he's a big man and he... well..."

"Did he threaten you?"

"He said he wanted five minutes with his boy and if I didn't let him – well, he had my wrist, and he squeezed it so hard, and –" She held out her hand and rolled back the cuff, showing a bruise. "So I let him, I stood there and let him talk to Master Harry."

"And why didn't you tell your mistress all this?"

"Because... because..." It was clearly becoming hard for her to speak. "I only told her what I did because, well, I wanted to say something, give her a hint, but he told me if I breathed a word of it I could expect the consequences, that he was watching us all and he could come and get me any time he wanted. Just like he did before." She looked away.

"Before?" Giles said. "What do you mean by that?"

"He used... sometimes he used to come up to my room and once, well, you know, he..." She broke off, looking down at her hands which were now furiously twisting up the piece of darning.

"Can you bear to tell me a little more plainly what he did?" he asked gently, hearing the rapidity of her breathing.

"He got into my bed," she managed to say. "I couldn't push him off – he's a big man, like I told you. He – well, you know, sir, don't you, what I'm talking about?"

"Do you mean he forced himself on you?" She nodded.

Then she burst out, as if she had been dying to speak of it, "He said he'd tell Mrs Morgan that I'd lured him in, if ever I breathed a word of it. That it was all my fault. That I mustn't make a sound. It was..." She was clearly struggling to continue. "I tried to push him off, but I couldn't. I just couldn't. It was... it was..." She could no longer speak, her arms wrapped tight about her, her body hunched up, her faced screwed up in pain.

He would have liked to have comforted her, but he had the good sense to know that she would have flinched at any man's touch.

"I am glad you have told me this, Hannah," he said. "You have done the right thing in telling me. What he did was unpardonable. If I can lay my hands on him, I will make sure he goes to the gallows for it."

"But what if he finds out, what if he comes back here tonight?"

"You won't be here for him to find you," said Giles. "I want you to take Master Harry out when he comes up from the garden. Just leave the house as if you are going for a walk, but instead you are to take him to my sister Mrs Fforde's house. I will write a note for you to give to her. She will make you both welcome, and you will stay there as long as needs be. You will be perfectly safe there."

"But what about the mistress?" said Hannah. "He said... when he was... he said that he gave her the same treatment – he said that she was a dirty whore who deserved to be treated like a whore..." She stumbled over her words.

Just as the letter had said, Giles thought.

"She will be safe too," said Giles. "I will make sure of it."

"May I go now, sir?" she asked.

"Of course."

She made a bolt for the door.

These revelations made him both depressed and angry. He was used to catalogues of misdeeds – the darker side of human nature was familiar to him – but it was still shocking that a man could prey on the women of his household, treating both his wife and a trusted servant as soulless objects.

He forced himself to wonder what and how much Mrs Morgan might have suffered at her husband's hands, though it disturbed him to think of it. She had only hinted at unpleasantness, masking it all in that bright gilding of her personal courage, but Hannah's bitter testimony suggested a routine callousness that would have made her life beyond miserable. In the eyes of the law, if Morgan forced himself on a servant without her consent and the facts could be proved, he would be found guilty of rape. However, his wife was afforded no such protection by the law. Rape within marriage did not exist – it could not when a woman's body was effectively the property of her husband. Giles suspected it was a more common state of affairs than anyone with a shred of decency or feeling would like to admit. That Mrs Morgan had managed to evict him from her life seemed a remarkable achievement – if unfortunately a short-lived one. There was now no doubt that Morgan was in Northminster and if the tone of his letters was anything to go by, it was a dangerous development.

He went downstairs and found Mrs Morgan dressed and sitting in the large drawing room, a score open on her lap, pencil in her hand. He was glad to find her alone.

"I am going to conduct a little experiment," said Giles, "if you do not mind. I am going to make you vanish."

"Vanish? What do you mean?"

"I am going to hide you and see what sort of reaction that provokes. Your husband is in town and he knows where you are – therefore I think we had best remove you to a safer place, at least for the time being."

"And Harry?"

"Hannah will take him to my sister's house. That is the best place for him. I do not think your husband is interested in harming him."

"And where I am to go?"

"I have another idea about that. Can you contrive to go out for a walk alone, in about half an hour?"

"Yes, of course."

"Go through the Minster Gate and into the Blue Boar. It is a perfectly respectable establishment, and I will leave instructions for you there."

She put down the score and stood up, scrutinising him.

"I do not like this grave tone in you at all. What have you found out?"

"We will talk later. You must trust me."

"Yes, of course, of course. How could I not?" and she reached out with both hands, and briefly and warmly squeezed one of his hands.

Chapter Thirty

"So, Mr Carswell, what is all this about you and Miss Pritchard?" Giles asked, coming into his consulting room.

"How did you hear of that?" said Carswell, jumping up from his desk.

"From Lord Rothborough."

"Oh, dear Lord," muttered Carswell.

"What has been going on, if you don't mind me asking?" Giles asked.

"I wish I knew!" exclaimed Carswell. "I have been embroiled into something I cannot begin to understand. She is... I do not know what she is or what she is about!"

"The young woman – the other night, outside the Treasurer's House – was that Miss Pritchard?"

"Yes. I wanted to tell you. You must believe me."

His distress was apparent. "Of course."

"I do not know what she is up to. I asked her – well, it was not in earnest, and –"

"What did you ask her?"

"To marry me. Yes. Ridiculous though that sounds – and I was being ridiculous. I was not in my right mind, and she saw that and said no, just as any decent girl would, thank goodness, and then her father and my lord arrived. It looked a trifle compromising but it need not have been had she –" Breathless in his agitation, he paused for a moment. "Had she not decided to announce to them the fact that she had accepted to me. In flat contradiction of what she had just said to me in private. A public declaration of intent. It could not have been worse, or at least so I thought!"

Giles reached into his coat pocket and felt for the key

decorated with the plaid ribbon and the matching rosette.

"I went to the Deanery this morning in an attempt to sort it out, only to find she has now made an accusation against me," Carswell continued. "An extraordinary accusation. I cannot think why, unless she is a fool or something, which I do not think for a minute she is."

"What did she say?"

"She has told him – her father, that is – that I have ruined her. And now Lord Rothborough will hear that and he will – well, God knows what he will do."

"He will doubtless disbelieve it, as I do."

"You believe me?"

"Of course."

"Oh, thank God! But why on earth would she say a thing like that? Why would she take it into her head to slander me? Lord Rothborough will not believe me. He will take her part."

"I doubt it. He knows you would not do such an dishonourable thing."

"You do not know him as I do, sir. He will be ready to believe the slightest thing against me."

"I do not think so," said Giles. "And although it is distasteful to have to conclude a respectable young woman is lying, I think anyone who knows you will give you the benefit of the doubt."

"So what on earth is she doing? Is she trying to trap me? But that makes no sense because she could easily have got me when I was a fool enough to ask her. But she was clear as anything on that point. And then –"

"I think there's a great deal Miss Pritchard is not telling us," said Giles, taking the ribbon rosette from his pocket and studying it. "And with luck she will be prevailed upon to come clean sooner rather than later."

"Or I shall be forced to the altar by Dean Pritchard," said Carswell. "He has a vile temper – you would never know it to look at him. One of those people who is too mild for their own good and then: *soudain!*"

"Did he strike you?"

"Yes. That's the worst of it – I worry for her. There was such a look of desperation about her this morning, as if he'd threatened her with the Lord only knows what. She can't be doing this lightly – I must say that for her."

"I will talk to them both," said Giles.

"You will? If anyone can make sense of this it will be you, sir!"

Giles went back to his office and found Holt sitting patiently on the bench in the passageway.

"I am glad you took me at my word, Mr Holt," said Giles, showing him into his office. "I have a particular job for you to undertake, if you are interested. I have to ensure the safety of a lady."

Having briefed Holt and made his arrangements for Mrs Morgan at the Blue Boar, Giles made his way back to the Minster Precincts, thinking he might go directly to the Deanery in search of Miss Pritchard. But as he passed the front of the Song School, he suddenly remembered George Watkins shuffling the music on his grand piano, and casually, yet carefully, putting aside a named portfolio. *K. Pritchard.*

He had heard Kate Pritchard play at his sister's house. She did not play like a young lady. She had played like a professional musician. Who in Northminster would a young woman of such talent find attractive? Perhaps a man of equal talent and the same passion for music. Someone young, energetic, handsome and talented who was at the same time completely unsuitable.

He decided he ought to talk to George Watkins again.

There was no answer when he rang the bell to the Master of Music's house, so Giles tried the door. It opened, and he called out, "Mr Watkins? Are you at home?"

There was still no answer. Giles decided to seize on the opportunity presented by an empty house. He went into the music room where they had previously spoken. There were still great piles of music on the piano. He soon found what he wanted: an unbound volume of nocturnes by Field, marked "K. Pritchard" in a woman's hand.

Just as he had laid his hands on the folio, he heard the bang of a door somewhere in the house.

He went back into the hall, and down a passageway which led to the kitchen, where the fire was burning and a kettle sat on the hob. There was also a dressy bonnet lying on the table and a coloured shawl draped over the back of a chair – neither item looked like the property of a servant.

He could hear that someone was moving about in what he assumed was the scullery beyond.

"Hello!" he called again.

There was a long silence, then Miss Kate Pritchard walked out, wearing an apron, with a cloth and a teacup in her hands.

"Major Vernon," she said.

"Miss Pritchard," he said. "I am glad to find you."

"Are you?" she said, with a shake in her voice.

"I think it will do you good to talk to me," he said, pulling out a chair for her.

"I was making tea. Would you like some?"

"If you like," he said.

She made tea and did it slowly. She had something of the air of a bride entertaining a guest for the first time, laying out the cups on the kitchen table with some ceremony, however incongruous that might be. She was certainly not in the position to be acting as the mistress of this house, and yet it was entirely as if she was.

"So," he said, when she had poured a cup for them both. "Where shall we begin?"

She took her time to answer, avoiding his gaze. He had long enough to observe her red-rimmed eyes.

"You have spoken to Mr Carswell?" she said quietly.

"Yes."

She nodded. "Of course you have. Is he... very distressed?"

"He is certainly confused. He does not like to malign you, Miss Pritchard, but he feels you have maligned him."

"I have," she said. "It's true." She pressed her fingertips to her mouth and closed her eyes. "Oh, it is all so... so..." She sighed.

"Perhaps we should start at the beginning," said Giles, taking out the key and the rosette from his pocket and laying them on the table. She flinched at the sight of them. "Do you recognise these things?" She nodded. "Perhaps you could explain to me what they are."

"That is the key to the gatehouse chapel," she said. "And that is a rosette from one of my dresses."

"And the ribbon?"

"It is the same ribbon, yes, Major Vernon."

"So the key, which was given to me by Mr Watkins, has a piece of ribbon on it that matches the ribbon on your dress – that is even finished in exactly the same manner?"

"Yes, it is the same."

"And is that because you put it there?" he asked. She nodded. "You put a piece of ribbon on a key belonging to Mr Watkins?"

"Yes, of course."

"Why?"

"To mark it."

"So he would remember which it was?" Giles asked.

"No," she said, and then went on after a pause, "it was so that I should."

"Because you had the key in your possession?"

"Yes."

"And why was that?"

"So that... so that I could go and wait there for Mr Watkins. Because – well, you have guessed, surely, sir, that he and I..."

"Are lovers?"

"We are engaged to marry, yes." She looked away.

"And the chapel tower was your trysting place?"

"Yes."

"And you met there often?"

"Yes, often. As often as we could." She looked away. "You must understand, sir, we were desperate. I would not have done this had not my father... he is impossible! Quite impossible!"

"I am not here to judge you, Miss Pritchard. I only want the facts."

"But you will judge me. You already have." She covered her face with her hands again. "I know what you must be thinking. How can you not think it?"

"Let us concentrate on the facts," Giles said. "Tell me when you last went to St Anne's Chapel to wait for Mr Watkins."

"A day or two ago."

"Can you be more precise?"

"Yes."

He gave her an enquiring, prompting glance. She twisted up her mouth.

"Yes," she said again. "It was on Wednesday morning."

"And did you find anything unusual there?"

She looked across at him.

"Yes, yes, I did."

Giles picked up the key and turned it in his fingers.

"What was that?"

"I... I... found Mr Barnes. Or rather I found his body," she spoke quietly, avoiding looking at him directly.

"What time was this? Can you remember when you got there?"

"It was some time after eleven. We had arranged to meet at half past eleven, but I left earlier, because my father had gone out and my mother was busy. I had the opportunity to get away."

"Did you see anyone at all on your way to the tower?"

"I don't remember seeing anyone. The Precincts are quiet that time of day."

"So you found the door locked?"

"Yes. Just as it always is."

"And you went straight upstairs?" She nodded. "Describe what you saw."

"He was stretched on the floor. For a moment I didn't know what to think. I thought he was asleep."

"Did you touch Mr Barnes?"

"Yes, yes, I suppose I did. I wanted to see if he was dead. I shook him a little."

"And was he warm when you touched him?"

"Yes, he was. But it was obvious he was dead."

"And you did not think of raising the alarm?"

"No," she said, after a long moment. "I knew that if I did that, then... No, I went and waited at the bottom of the stairs for Geor– for Mr Watkins to come in. And then we decided..."

"You decided you would tell a slightly different story?"

She got up from the table and walked away, her arms wrapped about her.

"What was I to do?" she said. "It seemed the only thing to do at the time."

He watched her as she stood over the fire. A lover's tryst interrupted by a dead body. Was it really as simple as that?

"How well did you know Mr Barnes, Miss Pritchard?"

"I knew him a little. We both studied with Mr Watkins – at least we did before my father stopped me going for lessons with him."

"Did Mr Barnes know about you and Mr Watkins?"

"No," she said. "No one knew."

"Are you sure?"

"As far as I know: no one."

"These things have a habit of becoming known. You

would be surprised. Perhaps Mr Barnes saw something."

"What are you implying?"

"That he was trying to make trouble for you and Mr Watkins. That he was not dead when you found him. That he made accusations to you and when Mr Watkins arrived, there was an argument."

"No, no, no. He was dead – please Major Vernon, believe me, he was dead. That is not what happened. He was dead!"

"Your word is a little unreliable, Miss Pritchard," he said. "I must test it."

"What has Mr Carswell said to you?" she said.

"That your father thinks you are a ruined woman because of him. Did you imply that to him?"

There was a long silence and then she said, "Sometimes when a person is angry it is better to give them the answer they want to hear. And I wanted to put him off the scent. I wanted him to think that it was someone else. If he was to be angry with someone else, then... Mr Carswell has friends and position, and I thought that..."

"Kate!" Watkins' voice echoed out through the empty house. "Kate, are you there?"

"I am here," she called back.

A moment later Watkins came in. He stopped in his tracks at the sight of Major Vernon.

"He knows everything," Kate Pritchard said simply.

Chapter Thirty-one

"But I've told you all this before," said Watkins.

Giles had taken him into his music room. He wanted to speak to him alone before Miss Pritchard did.

"Hardly," Giles said.

"Does it honestly matter which of us found the body?" said Watkins.

"It matters a great deal," Giles said. "Now tell me, what state was Miss Pritchard in when you arrived?"

"She was upset! Of course she was. She'd just found a dead body."

"Where was she?"

"Upstairs. I went upstairs and there she was – with Barnes on the floor. Kneeling over him."

"You are certain of this?" Giles said.

"Pretty certain. Why?" said Watkins with some hostility.

"That needn't concern you."

"Why – what are you implying, sir? Has Miss Pritchard said something different? If she has, it means nothing, I'm sure of it. She may have forgotten what she did. She was distressed."

"Describe it to me, won't you? Was she hysterical?"

"No, not exactly. But she was in a state of shock. She was shaking and agitated, naturally enough."

Giles nodded. "About Mr Barnes – do you think he might have been aware of your meetings with Miss Pritchard? He hadn't come upon you together at some point? I understand at one time you were giving lessons to Miss Pritchard – that they were not so much lessons as courtship."

"I do not like your implication, sir."

"It is true, surely, Mr Watkins? You are engaged to her."

"Yes, well, I suppose..." There was a long pause, then Watkins spoke again. "He may, perhaps, have seen us once."

"Perhaps? Did he or did he not know about you and Miss Pritchard?"

"He did see us once – together, as it were."

"And the upshot of that was?"

"I told him to hold his tongue about it, of course! And he said he would."

"How did you ask him?"

"What do you mean?"

"Did you ask him humbly as a favour, as a fellow musician asking for his discretion, or did you speak to him as you might speak to a servant?"

"He was practically spying on us!" exclaimed Watkins. "How was I supposed to speak to him?"

"Spying on you? Then you were angry with him."

"Of course I was! Any man would have been angry at such impertinence!" Watkins exclaimed.

"Especially a man conducting an illicit courtship with a young woman of superior rank," Giles said. "A man who felt he was on dangerous ground in the first place."

"What do you mean by that, sir?"

"If you had openly declared your intentions to Miss Pritchard's father, as I am sure you know you ought to have done, then you would have nothing much to fear from Barnes seeing you. It would have been a minor annoyance, not a threat to your secret. And he *was* a threat to your secret if he saw you."

"I told him to hold his tongue. I have said that already!"

"And as far as you know, did he hold his tongue? He didn't speak to Miss Pritchard about it?"

"Why would he do that?"

"Because she has more to lose than you? Because she was the weak point? A man who sees something of that nature might well be tempted to take advantage of it, and who is the easier prey in this case?"

"You think he spoke to Miss Pritchard about this?"

"It is possible."

"What are you implying? That... no, I won't have that, sir!"

"I have to consider all angles, Mr Watkins. And I have evidence that Miss Pritchard has been behaving strangely – in some respects like a desperate woman."

"What do you mean by that? Desperate? Do you mean to imply that Miss Pritchard killed Barnes? She could not hurt a flea!"

"Are you sure, Mr Watkins?"

"If you are so determined to find your murderer, sir, well, you may have me! I will confess to killing him and go to the gallows for it. But you shall not accuse Miss Pritchard of this. I will not have that!"

"That is noble, Mr Watkins, but I am after the truth, not the stuff of old romances. If there is anything about her behaviour that disturbed you that day, that seemed not quite right, I ask you to tell me it. Put aside sentiment – for your own protection. You are not yet her husband."

"In the eyes of God I am!" he exclaimed. "And I will not have her insulted like this!"

"You are actually married?" Giles said.

There another pause.

"We have made our promises to each other before God. That is a wedding contract in all respects."

"But these promises were not made in front of a clergyman, with witnesses present? Nor with a licence or the banns having been read?"

"It was a marriage in the eyes of God," said Watkins. "She is now my wife in all respects."

"All respects?" Giles said. Watkins looked away. The implication was clear enough. "That is interesting, Mr

Watkins."

Watkins sat down and covered his face with his hands. His shame was palpable.

"It was not what we intended," he said rather quietly. "Not for the world would I have chosen it to be this way. It is simply that her father would never hear of it. He is impossible, Major Vernon. He would have separated us for ever and that I could not bear. I was half a man before I met her. I was nothing."

~

Giles went back to the kitchen where he had left Miss Pritchard to wait. He half expected her to have slipped his grasp, but she was still there, holding her bonnet as if about to put it on and leave. She looked as if she had been crying again. Had her conscience been preying on her? Was it possible that she had murdered Charles Barnes in a fit of angry passion, to conceal her love affair?

"May I speak to Mr Watkins?" she asked.

"Not at present, Miss Pritchard, I'm afraid. I am going to take you home now." She nodded and put on her bonnet. "Tell me, Miss Pritchard — and do not take it as a liberty — do you think you are with child?"

"It is possible," she said after a long silence.

"And that is why you took Mr Carswell's name in vain? You wanted to conceal the identity of the real father?"

"Yes. Mr Watkins has told you that we...?"

"And a great deal more besides," Giles said. She screwed up her face for a moment. He went on, "It does not matter to me whether you tell me the truth now or later, Miss Pritchard — but for the sake of your own peace of mind I urge you to consider a speedy confession."

"I have nothing to confess," she said after a moment's hesitation. "You have got all our secrets, Major Vernon."

"Have I?" said Giles, who knew well enough from experience that a pause before a statement often indicated a lie. She avoided his gaze. "Well, Miss Pritchard, I will take you home now, and I want you to think very hard about all that has passed between us."

She nodded, and then said, "What will you say to my father? Will you tell him about this?"

"It is not my place to do that."

"Thank you," she said. "I would rather he did not know – not yet, at least."

"You would do well to tell your father everything as soon as possible. He will, I'm sure, be far more understanding than you imagine."

"You do not know him, sir," she said a little sharply. "You really do not."

They walked back to the Deanery in silence. He took her to the front door and rang the bell. The moment the maid appeared, Miss Pritchard ran in, and went straight upstairs, without another word or a backward glance.

Chapter Thirty-two

Felix left his consulting room to attend to a prisoner in the cells, and returned to find two women waiting to see him.

For a moment he was annoyed, for the usual custom was that prospective patients waited on the benches outside in the passageway. However, a quick glance revealed that these were not wives or relatives of any of the constabulary seeking his advice. They were both handsomely dressed. The woman who was seated was wearing an ornate black lace veil which entirely obscured her face, while the other, standing in attendance, had the look of a superior lady's maid.

The veiled woman rose as he came in, and addressed him. "Mr Carswell?"

For a moment he did not know what to say. Who she was, he had not the least idea.

"Ma'am," he said. "How may I help you?"

She came forward and put out a gloved hand.

"If you might spare me a few moments I would be so grateful," she said. Yet she did not put up her veil.

"Of course," said Felix, shaking her hand, so he might feel her pulse. It felt steady enough. "Please sit down." He pulled out the Windsor chair on which his patients usually sat. "What seems to be the trouble?" He now wanted her to fold back her veil – it was starting to irritate him.

"Jenkins, you may leave us," she said to the other woman in attendance. He had been right to think she was a servant. Jenkins nodded and went to the door.

"You wouldn't prefer that she stay while I examine you?" Felix said.

She said nothing until the maid had closed the door

behind her.

"Ma'am?" he prompted her.

"Oh, this is so difficult," she said in a quiet voice.

He took a chair and sat down beside her.

"Whatever you tell me will be in confidence, ma'am," he said. "Please be assured of that. Now, if you might tell me what is troubling you. Perhaps it would help if you took up your veil?" he ventured.

"I would rather not, if you don't mind."

"A physician may gauge a great deal from the state of the complexion," he said.

"I have not come to see you as a physician, Mr Carswell," she said.

"Then why are you here, ma'am?"

"I am here because of your connection to Lord Rothborough."

"Oh," said Felix, beginning to feel distinctly uncomfortable. Who on earth was she? Some rather unpleasant suspicions were overtaking him. Her clothes were extremely elegant – any fool could see that she was a person of great wealth. She was not young, and he had felt a wedding ring under her glove. Could it possibly be Lady Rothborough herself? It would explain the thickness of the veil and her reluctance to raise it. After all, he had seen her portrait at Holbroke.

He found himself peering through the scrolling black silk, attempting to match the features of the painting with what he could see.

"Mr Carswell!" she said, and leaned away. "Please!"

"Since you know who I am, ma'am," said Felix, "it would only be common courtesy for you to tell me who you are."

There was a silence for a moment and then she said, "You have his manner. It is true what they say."

"Ma'am, if you are who I suspect you are..."

She laid her hand on his arm.

"No, no, I am only her envoy. I am her friend," she said.

"She has sent you to see me?" he said. "Lady Ro–"

"Yes," she cut in. "Yes. That lady."

Felix leant back in his chair, almost too astonished to speak. He did not know whether to take this at face value. It was such a common ruse that he was still inclined to believe that this really was Lady Rothborough.

"If you would put up your veil," he said after a moment, "I think this business between us would go better."

"Very well," she said, and folded back her curtain of lace, revealing her features to him.

He saw at once it was not Lady Rothborough, and felt extremely relieved. This woman was a great deal more handsome. Even after the flattery of an expensive portrait painter, Lady Rothborough was still notably plain, in a sweet, round-faced fashion. She was also dark-haired. This woman was fair, with pale gold hair, not unlike that of Mrs Morgan, although in the stranger's case the gold was touched with grey and the dullness of age. She also had the most striking blue eyes, and she looked up at him through thick lashes in a manner which suggested she knew exactly what effect it would have on him. He tried not to be moved, but he could not help it. It was astonishing that a woman of that age – and he judged she was well over forty – could still exude such powerful beauty. He wished she would put down the veil again. It was disconcerting.

"And your name?" he asked.

"That is not important," she said. "I am merely a humble envoy."

He supposed he would have to accept that, although there was nothing humble about her.

"So what does Lady Rothborough wish to say to me?" he said.

"She begs you, sir, to use your influence, for the sake of a wife and mother."

"My influence? With whom? I have no influence."

"Your influence with her husband, of course," she said.

"I do not have any influence over Lord Rothborough," said Felix.

"There you are wrong," she said. "The regard in which he holds you – it is well known. Lady Rothborough is aware of it."

"There might be regard, but I cannot influence him. She ought to know that. Indeed, she should take comfort from it."

"You have no influence with him because you have not tried to exert it," she said. "But such is his feeling, he will be vulnerable to your opinion, Mr Carswell. That is the plain truth – an unhappy one of course, for Lady Rothborough, but she is desperate and hopes you will help her. This woman, this dreadful creature..."

She looked away.

"Do you mean...?" Felix began, but could not bring himself to continue.

"The Morgan woman, yes," she said. "That is why she has sent me to you. To put it plainly, sir, she is desperately unhappy about this situation."

"Then why does she not speak to him about it?" Felix could not help saying.

"He will not listen to her. We thought, we hoped, indeed we prayed he might listen to you. You must help her, sir, I beg you. You must tell him to end it with her." She grabbed his hand and although he tried to free himself, he could not. "She begs you to intercede. She does so out of great love for her husband. She does not want him ruined by her, and she is certain he will be."

It was on the tip of Felix's tongue to say that Mrs Morgan was far more likely to be ruined by Lord Rothborough, but instead, having managed to disentangle his hand, he said, "Are you sure about this?"

"Mrs Morgan is a wicked woman," said the lady. "She will

ruin him. She is capable of it. She has enslaved him and she will lead him to destruction."

"What evidence do you have for that?" Felix said.

"Will you not take my word for it?"

"Well, no, I cannot. I do not know you from Eve, ma'am, do I? I cannot condemn a person without evidence. I cannot believe mere tale-bearing."

"Do you think I would have come here, taken all this trouble, just to bear tales, sir?" she said. "For pity's sake, you must believe me, Mr Carswell. I would not have come here had I not feared for my friend – and she is a dear friend. I have seen how wretched this is making her – she is suffering grievously knowing what this hideous creature is determined to do."

"Which is?" Felix said. She said nothing. "Give me some evidence and I will do as you ask."

There was a silence, and she got up and crossed the room to the window, where she stood – Felix could not help thinking – arranged to look as elegant and as desirable as possible.

"Of course," she said simply. "Of course, it was a great deal to expect that you would take a part against him. Blood will always speak, and you must be a loyal son. That is to your credit, Mr Carswell, although I think you are pitiless not to consider the feelings of the unfortunate woman who loves him so dearly. She only asks you to help her in helping him. She asks you to think of the affection you bear him, and which she bears him, and she prays that it may make alliance in such a good cause."

"Then you must explain to me – why do you think Mrs Morgan will ruin him? What can she be capable of that Lord Rothborough is in such danger now? After all, it is common enough knowledge that he has had mistresses before. Lady Rothborough must know that. She may be unhappy and he may be the cause of that, and a cruel husband, which I do not condone –"

"I am glad to hear it."

"But how is Mrs Morgan any different from these other women? He has accommodated them without any great scandal."

"Yes, but she is different – very different, and she is dangerous."

"In what way?"

"She is dangerous to him. She has awoken his passions in the most terrible way. That is the danger of it."

"Oh, I do not think that –"

"There is a precedent for this, Mr Carswell, as well you know. The circumstances of your own birth – need I say more? Your own mother, well –"

"What of her?" Felix said, feeling his throat dry.

"I don't know what he has told you. It is a painful subject with him, of course. When she broke with him, he was on the verge of self-destruction, such was his despair. He nearly killed himself. His valet found him with a pistol in his mouth – if he had come in a moment later he would surely have been dead!"

Felix stared at her. This story was entirely new to him – but it made an uncomfortable sort of sense. Why else would have he warned him so much against falling in love if he had not suffered such misery himself? *You must remain captain of your own heart.* Felix had imagined it was cynicism speaking, not bitter experience.

"Dear Lord..." he muttered.

She sat down beside him and took his hand again.

"That is what Lady Rothborough is afraid of. And that is why you must warn him against her – you must tell him that he cannot trust his heart to her. She will not keep him as tenderly as she ought. She is not a good woman – she is no better than a common whore, Mr Carswell, and she will use him for her own mercenary ends, of that you may be sure. And then when she is done with him, he will be wrecked, just

as he was before. She will drive him to self-murder, we are
sure of it. Will you help us?"

Chapter Thirty-three

It was Felix's ardent wish to go straight to Mrs Morgan and demand that she refute these charges. He ached to know her side of the story, for he felt there was too much painful possibility in what his strange visitor had said. How would she defend herself? Could she defend herself? He hoped she could, for it hurt him to hear her slandered.

But first he had a call to pay on the unfortunate Mrs Fildyke – an unpleasant but necessary duty. As he walked there, he decided he would go to Mrs Morgan afterwards, and take another tilt.

Of course, she was likely to be cryptic on the subject, and angry with him for speaking of it. He would probably get his cheek slapped again; not that he cared – he had taken a perverse pleasure in that. To provoke her had meant something. Though his head told him she would never yield, especially when faced with those dreadful accusations, his heart – that diseased organ – still held out the belief that she would, with time, relent. His heart treasured the sting of her hand on his cheek, and hoped that the force of his passion and the memory of his kiss would by now have had some effect upon her, that she too would be in some way infected. He even hoped that she was suffering as he was with the torment of confused feelings.

Yet why did he wish her to suffer? That he could not comprehend. This love of his had no nobility to it. It made him peevish and cruel as well as supremely foolish. It made him suspicious and possessive. He did not know if this was some basic defect in his character. He wondered if he were even capable of generous, disinterested and pure-hearted love.

That was what he would have liked to have felt for Mrs Morgan, something that had a touch of the sacred in it; but he did not, and he hated himself all the more for it.

If only he could rid himself of that bodily desire and those constant, flickering images that his mind conjured up from the darkness in him. How easily he slithered into picturing himself bedding her with no ceremony and very little kindness so that he felt more like a beast than a man. It distressed him greatly. He seemed to constantly stumble over them, even when he was making a great effort to think of other things. He wanted a violent conquest. He wanted to overwhelm her and show her that he had mastery over her. He wanted her to be enslaved by him, just as she had enslaved him.

And was she truly wicked? Beneath all that brilliant surface was there really a vile and corrupted whore? Were those dreadful letters telling the truth? It seemed to him, as he struggled with his unruly mind, that she did indeed possess some dreadful, wicked power over men and that it was not his weakness but her malicious intentions that were driving all this. That was what his anonymous visitor had said, after all.

Women were mysterious continents at the best of the times, but she was like a distant planet for which there was no hope of a guiding chart. It was all speculation, and as a man of science, that gave him no comfort. Then there was the matter of Kate Pritchard, another impenetrable, impossible mystery of a creature. Perhaps that was why men loved other men – at least there was a hope of comprehension there!

The slatternly maid admitted him to Mrs Fildyke's bedside. Of Mr Fildyke there was no sign, and the shop was closed up. Felix supposed that he made plenty of money from those books – enough not to have to keep regular shop hours.

Mrs Fildyke was a great deal improved – she had not vomited for some time and the maid had seemed to take heed of his instructions and had taken reasonable care of her.

However he was depressed to discover she was still confined to the same wretched dirty room, with the birds twittering and twitching in their miserable cages above.

"Where is your son?" he asked, when he had finished examining her.

"Oh, I don't know," she said.

"Where is your master?" Felix asked the maid who stood on the threshold, her arms folded across.

She pointed upstairs. "He's got company," she said.

"Go and get him," said Mrs Fildyke to him. "I want my boy."

The stair was concealed behind a door, and Felix climbed up into darkness. As he did so he became aware of a peculiar muffled bellowing and groaning. It sounded for all the world like someone in distress.

"Mr Fildyke, are you all right?" he said, for the voice sounded like Fildyke's.

There was a door directly ahead of him from which the sounds seemed to be coming and he went and knocked on it.

"Mr Fildyke? Are you there?"

The noise stopped abruptly.

He seemed to wait there for an eternity and as he did so he began to realise what it was he might have heard. Company, the girl had said, and it was apparently a particular sort of company for a particular purpose.

Cursing his naivety, he was about to turn down the stairs again and slip away when the door opened and Fildyke appeared, fastening the belt of a snuff-coloured dressing gown, his hair disordered, his cheeks red. From the way the folds of his dressing gown were hanging Felix could see that Fildyke's prick was still up and Felix, to avoid looking, found himself looking through the open door instead, into a room that was darkened despite it being the middle of the afternoon. However there were a few candles lit, by which he could see that the other occupant of the room was none other than Jos

Harrison, also in a state of undress.

Fildyke quickly shut the door behind him.

"Was that man –?" Felix said.

"Is my mother all right?" Fildyke said, ignoring him.

"She is much improved," Felix managed to say. "If that is Harrison –"

"Thank you so much for calling on her," said Fildyke.

"If you were doing what I think you were doing in there, then it is a serious –"

"That little book, Dr Carswell, did you enjoy it?" Fildyke cut in.

"I don't see what this has to do with anything."

"If it were to come out that you were interested in that kind of literature, well, this is a God-fearing town, Doctor. A word or two in the right ear and your fine reputation – well, well – it would be such a pity, wouldn't?"

"Are you threatening me?" Felix said, after a moment.

"I am just suggesting you think a little before you speak. About how things might appear. That book is a disgusting thing for a fine young man to have in his possession. Shocking. If I were a father I would never ask you to treat my daughter, if I knew that you had a taste for such things."

"You are a fine one to talk about tastes," said Felix, pushing past him and opening the door.

His eyes met those of Harrison who was pulling on his trousers.

"What the hell is he doing here?" Harrison said to Fildyke.

Felix did not wait to hear Fildyke's answer. He spun round and grabbed Fildyke by the shoulder, propelled him into the room with Harrison, and slammed the door. He was fortunate that the key had been left in the lock, so he pocketed it and dashed downstairs in search of a constable.

Chapter Thirty-four

"Mrs Sledmere, I would like to speak to Rose again, if I may."

"You are welcome to try, sir, but what good it will do..."

Giles had been in two minds himself about disturbing the girl again, but he felt there was still something he might find out about Charlie's death from her.

If Charlie had been blackmailing Miss Pritchard or Watkins, he might have confided this to her. Neither was it entirely clear that Rose herself was actively involved – she may have been out of the house at the time of his death and she may actually have murdered him in a fit of lunatic passion. Her tendency to violence had not been denied and it was a line of enquiry he must pursue, however unpleasant it might be.

"The morning your nephew died, when you went to the market, you are still not sure whether or not she left the house?"

"No, sir, I am not."

"Then I must try to talk to her."

She nodded. She perfectly understood the implication of his visit.

"But I do not know how you will get her to speak," she said, with a shrug.

"I have a little experience of such a case." He hesitated and then said, "In my own family."

They were standing in the darkened hall and were alone. He felt her hand suddenly press his forearm.

"I try to tell myself it is God's will," she said, "that it is His plan... but..." He nodded. "Who in your family, sir?"

"My wife."

"Is it God's will?" she said, her hand still on his arm. "I

pray each night for the Lord to send the Devil out of her, to bring back my child, but He never seems to answer. I must be very wicked – sometimes that is the only way I can bear it – to think I am being punished. But then, if God is good, how can He make my child suffer so? That is tormenting me, sir – is this my faith being tested? I do not know." She was in tears now, her words choking her. "As if I do not have enough to bear, I cannot even have His comfort. I am lost, so lost..." She turned away, overcome by her misery. "Forgive me, sir... I ought not... what will you think?"

He had to struggle a little to reply.

"I see a loving mother who will never desert her child, no matter what."

She turned away and let out a low, miserable moan, as if she had read a great tragedy in his words. Then she turned back, steadying herself with a deep breath.

"No matter what," she said. "Aye, if it must come to that, it must, but I will never believe it was my child. It is the Devil in her, not my Rose, it is the thing that has her imprisoned in there that will be at the heart of it. She is an innocent prisoner. That is what I must believe – always."

"Has Rose said something to you since my last visit?" he asked. "Or done something to make you think that –"

"It's that ribbon," said Mrs Sledmere. "She will not stop with it. She had it wound about her neck as if... You see, Charlie had a piece of it. He used to keep a key on it about his neck – at least for the last twelve months or so. I used to worry that he would throttle himself with it, a great heavy key."

"Did he always wear it?"

"Always – even when he took his shirt off to wash himself in the yard. He was cross with me if I made to mention it, so I stopped. You can never get all a man's secrets from him." She gave a great sigh. "You see, sir, that ribbon, it's from the same spool. He bought it for her and must have kept a length for himself for that key. She was so happy that day when he gave it to her, almost like her old self, and I thought, well, perhaps Charlie will bring her back to us, for he did love her, in his funny way. He was always bringing her back trifles and singing her songs. I so hoped, but…"

"And you think that this ribbon is significant, Mrs Sledmere?"

"I don't know what I think, sir! I don't want to think it, but you did say my poor lad was strangled and she will not leave off with that ribbon. Perhaps it is just her grief speaking, but…"

"Yes?"

"Once, in one of her rages, she did fly at him and the key and the ribbon were about his neck and she was pulling at them as if she meant to…" She stopped and there was a silence before she spoke again. "They do not hang the mad, do they, sir? Tell me they do not."

In the most reassuring tone he could manage, Giles said, "I shall try and talk to her. Most likely we shall lay all these fears to rest."

She nodded quickly.

"Aye, most likely." She laid her hand on his arm again. "Thank you, sir, for listening to my troubles. Sometimes it seems there is not a soul in the world who understands."

"I know."

"You will be in my prayers, you and your lady," she said. "I will take you to her. I have locked her door, for she was dancing about the whole house last night. She is a little calmer now, I think."

Rose was sitting on her bed, her knees tucked up under her chin, her fingers busy again with that shock of white ribbon, which was now grey and grubby.

Seeing her, in the light of that conversation with her mother, it was hard not to give in to despair. He had observed through his own bitter experience the tendency of the patient to turn on those closest to them, as if intending to cause the greatest pain and misery. But that turning, that violence, was it not a means of communication for someone for whom all other methods of communication had failed? This girl, like Laura, had become a prisoner of her own body, for whatever reason. The normal means of expression were denied her. Instead she was forced into a primitive, animal-like communication, to use a language of signs, unintelligible to outsiders but eloquent and meaningful to the poor soul forced to such ends. It was then a question of interpreting this imperfect language, of finding meaning in the apparently meaningless. And had not Mrs Sledmere already begun to see a pattern of significance in that ribbon? She had begun to learn her daughter's language. And I must learn Laura's, he thought; I will do my best. I will find some way of understanding her.

He came in quietly and sat down on a bench against the wall, and did as little as he could to disturb her. She gave him a glance and returned to her tangle of ribbon, turning it over in her fingers as he turned her mother's words over in his mind. A key on a length of ribbon about the lad's neck, a key he would not remove because it surely meant a great deal to him. The fact that Rose had attempted to strangle him with it suggested she might also know what it meant, that she felt its importance and it roused her jealousy.

There had been no key on a ribbon on the body of Charles Barnes, but he had been strangled, there was not a shred of doubt about that. Giles thought back to Carswell's detailed drawing of Charles in death and how he had carefully recorded the ligature marks. Would this ribbon, an inch or so in breadth, match those marks on the dead man's neck? If there was some correlation between them it would be reasonable to conclude that the ribbon about Charles' neck had been the thing that killed him. Whoever had strangled him had therefore removed the ribbon and with it the key. How else would the door have been locked when Kate Pritchard got there?

In which case, Harrison's flight became even more significant. Celia had seen him leaving the tower. She might even have seen him lock the door.

He took Miss Pritchard's key to the tower room from his pocket and began to turn it in his hands. He became aware the girl was watching him. He held it out to her, as if offering her a plaything. Wary and slow, she climbed off the bed and came towards him, pressing her mess of ribbon to her heart.

Giles put the key down on the floor, in the space between them.

After a moment of hesitation she sank down on the floor and picked it up, but with caution as if it might burn her.

"Do you know this key?" he said.

Suddenly she had lifted it to her lips and kissed it before she laid it down on the floor again.

"Mary's mother," she said. He was startled, as he had hardly expected her to speak. But she went on, "Mary's mother's house." She began to rock back and forth. "Mary's mother."

"Did you ever go to this place?"

She shook her head and then said, "Secret."

"A secret?"

"Charlie's," she said and picked up the key again. This time she threw it across the room. He did not get up to retrieve it. Instead he thought: Mary's mother – does she mean St Anne?

"Is this house by the Minster?" he asked.

"His sweetheart's house," she said, and began to play with the ribbon again. "Mary's mother."

"You don't have a key like that one?" he said. "On a piece of white ribbon?"

"When is he coming back?" she said. "Have you seen him? He's coming back for me, he promised."

"He told you he was leaving?"

"With his sweetheart," she said. "But he is coming back for me. He wouldn't go without me. Oh no."

"When did you last see Charlie?"

"Market day morning. It's a long time."

"What did you do on market day, Rose? You didn't follow him, did you? You didn't go to his sweetheart's house?"

She shook her head emphatically. "He told me to wait here. So I am waiting. When will he be back?"

Chapter Thirty-five

"Where is Major Vernon?" Felix asked Superintendent Rollins, when they had got Fildyke and Harrison into custody.

"Major Vernon is out, sir, and we are not sure where," said Superintendent Rollins. "However, Lord Rothborough's carriage is in the courtyard. He wants to speak to you, I believe."

"Can no one send him away?"

"The only man who could do that would be the Major, Mr Carswell," said Superintendent Rollins.

That was true enough, Felix thought, as he crossed the yard and opened the carriage door. Lord Rothborough was sitting with his travelling desk on his knees, writing. He glanced up and smiled.

"Good, good, I hoped I would find you eventually."

"Will this take long?" said Felix. "I have duties –"

"Let's go and dine, shall we?" said Lord Rothborough.

"I am not dressed to dine with you," Felix said.

"For once, I will overlook that," said Rothborough. "Get in, will you?"

They drove to the Minster Precincts and the carriage drew up in front of the east door of the Minster.

"That will be all today, Mr Hopkins," Lord Rothborough said to the coachman.

"Eight o'clock tomorrow, then, my lord?"

"Make it half seven, Hopkins," said Rothborough, and the carriage rumbled off.

"Where are we going?" asked Felix, as Rothborough started walking down a lane he had never noticed before. He stopped in front of a tall, narrow red-brick house that seemed wedged in like the keystone in an arch, between two much older buildings.

"What is this place?" Felix said.

"This is where I lay my bones when I am in Northminster. I am deliberately obscure."

"Why?"

"Because sometimes I do not wish to be found."

"Oh," Felix said, with a slightly bitter laugh. "I see."

"No," said Lord Rothborough, opening the door, "I do not think you do. And less of that tone, if you please. You are in no position to lay judgements on my head, sir."

"What?"

"I spoke to the Dean."

"Oh."

"Indeed."

"What she says —"

"This is not a conversation for the street," said Lord Rothborough and gently propelled him into the hall.

Their entrance was marked by the enthusiastic scuffle of Lord Rothborough's little troop of spaniels, followed moments later by James Bodley, his valet and factotum.

"Good evening, my lord, Master Felix," he said.

Bodley had known Felix since he was a child, and Felix felt he still regarded him as one.

"We will dine at once, Bodley," said Rothborough, as he was helped out of his overcoat.

"Of course, my lord," said James Bodley and opened the door to the dining room.

The dining room was the first room off the hall, a respectably-sized square room. If this had been an ordinary house it would have been plainly furnished, but because this was a Rothborough house it was fitted up in dazzling style, better suited to a country mansion or a great house in town. The walls were covered in red damask, and hung with choice pictures, most notably a vast and colourful depiction of a group of nymphs bathing that was both indecent and utterly fascinating.

There was a generous fire burning and a couple of powerful Argand lamps blazing away. Felix found himself blinking at the light. It made the white linen cloth shine, and the silver gilt cutlery and glasses flashed their worth at him. It was also too hot, and he wanted to throw off his coat and sit in his shirt sleeves. But even when he was being obscure, Lord Rothborough would have taken great offence at that. This dinner was going to be an uncomfortable sweat of an affair.

"Sit you down, sir," said Lord Rothborough, indicating his place. It was a round table, with no head, but such was Lord Rothborough's inherent consequence that when he sat down it was at the head of the table, as if this were a great long table at a banquet. Behind him the voluptuous nymphs, dawdling by their pool, gazed enticingly out at Felix. One of them looked alarmingly like Mrs Morgan, or rather how Mrs Morgan might have looked with her hair down and her shift fallen to her waist.

Felix ran a finger down his collar and downed in one gulp the glass of sherry that Bodley had just poured for him. Lord Rothborough frowned.

When Bodley had gone, Lord Rothborough said, "I should really send you to the servant's hall to drink small beer, but then you will never learn."

Felix picked up his soup spoon without replying. It was a fine, full-flavoured clear soup – it seemed the French chef from Holbroke came even to this obscure little house along with Bodley.

They drank the soup and then Rothborough put down his spoon.

"Commendable restraint," he remarked.

"I am rather hungry," said Felix.

"A man cannot be civilised until he has dined," said Rothborough. "We will eat, and then we will get to our business. In the meantime, we should be thankful for the blessing of a well-kept table. There are plenty in this city tonight who will not be so fortunate." Felix stared at him. "You look surprised. Do you think I am without compassion, Felix? Or perhaps you think I have no conscience."

"No, sir, of course not. I know well enough how good you are to your people. My father often says that as a landlord he does not know any like you."

Rothborough inclined his head a little.

"One does what one can. It is the obligation of wealth to take responsibility for those less fortunate. In this place, for example, there is much that could be done here to improve the lot of the ordinary man and woman. All those poor souls working in the manufactories, for example – they are not well served by their employers, and although I do not at all like the principle of the government interfering in a man's business, I can see no other way, in the present conditions. Factory legislation is a pressing need. Small steps have been taken already, but it is not, I feel, enough. Progress must be balanced with the needs of civilisation, yes?"

"Yes, always," said Felix, finding that this speech went strangely with the removal of the soup plates and the arrival of a quenelle of pike. Pike that had, he supposed, been pulled from the great fish ponds at Holbroke, which were strictly reserved for the use of the family, and fiercely guarded from poachers. Anyone rash enough to poach at Holbroke found himself bound for Van Diemen's Land.

Felix took a forkful of fish. It had been whipped up into an ethereally light paste and set on little rounds of toasted bread. He let it dissolve in his mouth, enjoying it far more than he felt he should. Lord Rothborough was playing an artful game – as he always did – but Felix could not yet discern what it was. If he had seen the Dean and Miss Pritchard then there was no end to the calumnies that would be heaped on him. In the normal course of things Lord Rothborough would be preparing to excoriate him for his conduct. Yet he had deferred his anger. It felt ominous.

Perhaps Mrs Morgan was at the root of it, he thought, catching sight of the half-naked nymph who so resembled her. Perhaps, as his mysterious visitor had said, Mrs Morgan had so taken possession of him that he was distracted from his usual hobby-horses. For this Felix would ordinarily have been grateful, but instead recalled the terrible story his visitor had told him.

"Oh, I forgot to mention it when you came in, my lord," said Bodley, bringing in the joint, "Juno has gone into pup. Three of them so far, all little beauties."

Watching the servant move across the room, Felix wondered whether Bodley had served Lord Rothborough back then. Was he the one who had pulled the pistol from his master's mouth and saved his life? Could Bodley be persuaded to tell him the full story?

"Excellent news," said Lord Rothborough. "Mr Carswell will carve, Bodley." Bodley put the joint down in front of Felix. "I thought I might give one of them to young Master Harry Morgan," Rothborough went on. "That boy needs a dog. Perhaps you might like one too, Felix? Major Vernon is right to keep that beautiful hound of his – a gentleman needs a good dog. By the way, you don't know if he has plans to breed from her?"

"No," Felix said.

"If he does, you must tell me. The girls have been demanding a greyhound ever since they met Prince Albert's charming Eos – but I think, with the greatest respect to his Highness, that the points of Major Vernon's bitch are better. Now carve me a slice of that, will you, my boy? The end piece will suit me perfectly. Indeed I much prefer it, and I remember that you don't care for it."

It annoyed Felix that Lord Rothborough should remember this detail about him. If it had been his mother, he would have felt some pleasure in it, although she would have scolded him for having a preference, and told him even now, as a grown man, that he ought to eat what was put in front of him and not question it.

He carved the slice as he was bid and Bodley conveyed the plate to Lord Rothborough with his usual stateliness. Rothborough dismissed him after he had offered the vegetables and Felix, with a full plate in front of him, wondered how the conversation would now proceed.

"Do you think Mrs Morgan will allow her son to accept a puppy?" he said as mildly as he could.

"I cannot imagine why not. Children ought to grow up with animals – it's good for them. Harry is a trifle timid. A dog will do him good. You would be a poorer soul had your father not had that raggedy white mutt of his! He is with us still, I trust – what was his name, now?"

"Keeper. No, he died last winter."

"I had no idea," said Lord Rothborough, with sudden gravity. "I am sorry to hear that. Your father must have been greatly grieved. I must write to him. I wish I had known earlier." Then after a moment, during which he took a reflective sip of wine, he said, "I shall definitely give the boy one of the pups. It is what he needs." He looked across at Felix and smiled. "He is a charming little fellow. Very much like his mama, which is just as well given all I have heard of his father." Lord Rothborough went on: "It is odd how children much resemble one parent or another and never seem to be mixtures. I find it fascinating. There is nothing of your mother in you, thank God, Felix. You have all our family's qualities, and our weaknesses. But your sisters – three of them are their mother's daughters, but Charlotte, well – she and you are very alike." He took another sip of his wine. "I know it offends you for me to speak like this, but –"

"I would not worry about offending me," Felix said. "But Lady Charlotte, on the other hand..."

He did not like to be reminded of Lord Rothborough's daughters, and he was sure they did not like to be reminded of him. Yet at the same time, he had often felt a fierce longing to know them.

"If you could meet them, I am sure you would love them," Lord Rothborough said. "That would be my greatest pleasure – to see my children together."

Felix looked across at Lord Rothborough, unsettled that he should have guessed at his private inclination.

"That is a fancy that not even you, with all your powers, can accomplish," he said.

"Regrettably," said Rothborough with a great sigh. "I am thinking of having a painting done – a group portrait of you all, before any of you are married, while you are all young and at the height of your beauty. I have even discussed it with Axelmann; he thinks it possible to combine two separate sittings."

"Axelmann?"

"He's a clever young German. You would be interested to meet him, I'm sure. I would like to get him to Holbroke, this summer at any rate. That is one of his," he added, indicating the nymphs above him. "He is painting the Queen and Prince Albert – a wedding portrait. I think he will be one of the great masters of the century. I shall get him to do the girls in a group, for the London drawing room, and then you will sit for him, for a cabinet portrait. We will have a copy done to send to your parents, of course," he added.

"You've obviously given this some thought."

"Yes, I have."

"Then perhaps you should get Mrs Morgan to sit for him," Felix said, unable to restrain himself. "For another private portrait."

"He would certainly do her justice, but I sense you are not making a serious suggestion, Felix."

"No, I am not!" said Felix, laying down his knife and

fork.

"I thought we would save business until after dinner. Come now, eat your beef – you are far too thin for my comfort these days. A physician must be strong and you are always in the way of danger working here – you must be fortified."

"I am never ill, you know that," said Felix.

"There comes a point when our constitutions fail us all," said Rothborough. "At your age I believed I was indestructible – and I would like to spare you the misery that I endured when I realised I was not."

"Do you mean..." Felix said, searching for the best way to begin on the subject. "Was this after you had been in Paris?"

"Yes," said Rothborough.

"What form did this illness take?"

"I was half-paralysed with exhaustion and racked with pains that no one could explain. I could not bear light, nor noise for at least two months. It was wretched – to be shut up in my room with no power to make myself any better – and being bled by all the quacks my dear mother could summon to the house. I was like a pin-cushion after all those leeches."

"It sounds like a form of melancholia," Felix said. "Feelings can work powerful effects upon the body's systems."

He was aware of Lord Rothborough's eyes upon him. There was a long moment of silence and then Lord Rothborough said, "That is true – and that is why I am anxious that you are sensible in this regard. I know the dangers, more than most."

"I think you can trust me to avoid them."

"I am not sure I can. This business with the Dean's daughter –"

"I thought we were waiting until we had eaten," Felix said.

Rothborough crumpled his napkin and laid it by his place. "Point taken," he said. "Finish your meat."

"I have had my fill," Felix said.

"Then we will go through to my book room," said Lord Rothborough, getting up from the table.

The room adjoined the dining room, and was equally lavishly furnished.

"Sit," said Lord Rothborough, pointing to one of the chairs. He was pouring wine. "Let us get down to business. Why did you offer for her?"

"Because – does it matter?"

"I must press you on this – why did you offer for her? Why?"

"Because, I suppose I thought it would do me good to be married. That a wife would make me comfortable – if you get my meaning."

"I do entirely," said Lord Rothborough and to Felix's great surprise and concern, he smiled broadly. "And I think I have solved our problem."

"Our problem? It is my affair. This is what you will not understand."

"Yes, yes, of course, you think I am a heartless meddler, do you not, Felix?"

"No, sir, but –"

"Yes, you do. And I will have to do my best to persuade you otherwise. Now, we were speaking of young Axelmann just now. You must admit he has a great talent in capturing the female form."

"Yes, I suppose so."

"He and I have been in correspondence. At the moment he is Germany, and he was good enough to send me this." He took from a drawer a piece of pasteboard and held it out to Felix. "As good a draughtsman as he is with paint. A great talent."

Felix looked at the card. It was a pencil sketch of a young woman, not much more than a girl. She did not smile or simper, but looked out intensely, her dark hair neatly parted in the centre.

"Very pretty," he said, as blandly as he could, and handed it back to Lord Rothborough.

"You are not intrigued to know who she is?"

"You will tell me, whether I ask or not."

"This charming girl is Lady Nina Dundas, only child of the late Earl of Thornhill. She is at school in Lausanne at present, but she will be coming home after Easter. She is apparently an accomplished botanical painter – Axelmann thought her work exceptional. She also speaks French and German fluently, which will endear her to the Queen and Prince Albert, since they speak German at home. How is your German, by the way, Felix?"

"Not as good as I would wish," Felix said, thinking how he had recently struggled over an article in German.

"Ah, then she could tutor you."

"Sir, I do not think –"

"I would like you two to become acquainted before the season, so I have invited her to Holbroke after Easter, by which time you will be in possession at Ardenthwaite."

"No, no," said Felix. "I have no intention of meeting this young woman, let alone making myself agreeable to her."

"You will meet her and you will make yourself agreeable. And I think you will be delighted with her. From everything I have heard, and particularly from young Axelmann's account, she would be an ideal wife for you."

"Then your damned Herr Axelmann should offer for her! He has as much right to try his luck as I do. And even if I did like her, there is little chance that she would like me," said Felix. "She will not want to make a match with me. If she has any family pride, and if she has any regard for her inheritance, I will be nothing but a speck of dirt. How on earth will I appear to her otherwise?"

"That is not how it will appear. The way has been smoothed. Lady Thornhill and I have been in correspondence.

She is prepared to consider the match – if, of course, you make a good impression on her."

"Are you in earnest?" said Felix.

"You have admitted yourself that you need a wife, and you know that a suitable match for you has been in my mind for some time. The question is an important one and this is an opportunity that we cannot let slip. She is expecting to make your acquaintance."

"Then she is a fool – a poor fool! I dread to think what her people may be saying to her, and what a puffed-up, false picture of me you have been peddling them out of your own sense of vanity. I will have nothing to do with such schemes. Tell your young lady that I will not play this idiotic game and that she had better take her chances in the season and find a husband whose rank matches her own! Marriage to me would be a debasement and she would be laughed at. You will be laughed at if you persist in this nonsense, and I have too much regard for you to allow you to make such a fool of yourself. Leave me be, for God's sake. Leave me be!"

"You must accept who you are, Felix," said Lord Rothborough.

"I do accept who I am!" he exclaimed. "I am the son of a whore!"

"Your birth was an accident."

"An accident? That is putting it mildly."

"An accident, and regrettable, but you are my child, my only son, and that means more to me than I can describe to you. You have no sense of it now, my boy, but you will feel it, and all the pain and pleasure of it, when you have a son of your own – though I hope he spares your feelings more than you spare mine! I pray to God each day, that He will grant you a son in wedlock, and that you may rejoice in him, as you ought, without having to shift and swivel and suffer as I have done!" He broke off and went to the fireside, and looked down into the grate. "It is not my vanity but feeling that drives me. Now you may think I am meddling when I put this young woman before you, but I think she and you would make a good match."

Felix shook his head but that, of course, did nothing to silence him. He went on: "I have looked through the ranks of all the young noblemen of marriageable age, Felix, in respect of my daughters, and they are a pack of boobies compared to you. She is an intelligent young woman. She will see the same."

"I do not think so," Felix said.

"In her eyes you are a prize worth getting – a man of talent, of character, a man of this century. Look at the young Prince – he is a German, threadbare nobody, but the Queen utterly dotes on him because he is a man of talent, of intelligence. He is new blood – as you have new blood. You and this young woman could form a dynasty – imagine that, Felix, a dynasty. Think of the great men you might people the nation with from your own nursery!"

It was now as if he were addressing a public meeting and Felix, realising that it was futile to argue with him, let him continue, while thinking how he might actively resist this ridiculous plan.

"The country is changing," Lord Rothborough went on, "and we must change with it. This young woman is intelligent enough to see the possibilities of marriage with you – now allow your intelligence to work upon the problem for yourself, Felix. It will prevent you getting into disagreeable scrapes for one thing, and you will have all the pleasures of the marital bed to keep you comfortable."

Felix turned the picture which was lying on the writing table face-down, for her eyes were a little too well drawn and expressive for his comfort. There was a great deal of life in such simple sketch. Axelmann was indeed talented.

He decided it was time to go on the attack.

"I understand that you submitted to a marriage of this nature and I do not think you have been happy. I certainly do not think Lady Rothborough has been happy. I had a visitor this morning, a friend of Lady Rothborough's, and she said things that —"

"She?" said Lord Rothborough.

"Yes."

"Who?"

"She would not tell me. She would not put up her veil until I begged her to do it."

"But it *was* a lady?"

"Yes, she had her maid with her. She was clearly a person of rank."

"What was the maid called?"

"Oh, I don't know," said Felix, a little astonished. "Well, perhaps it was Jenkinson or something like that."

"Good grief," said Rothborough. "Not Jenkins? A tall, stout woman?"

"The maid, you mean – yes, I think so. The lady was not."

"Describe the lady to me."

"Flaxen haired – with a touch of grey. About forty, I would say. Very handsome – once a great beauty, probably."

Lord Rothborough had pressed his folded fingers to his lips. He looked more alarmed than Felix had ever seen him. He reached into the drawer of the desk again, the drawer from which Lady Nina's picture had been taken, and this time took out a little golden miniature case, which he flicked open and held out to Felix.

"Like this?" The miniature was of a lustrous young beauty, her hair dressed in the style of twenty years ago, but it was unmistakably the same woman.

"That is she," Felix said.

"Lady Limpersleigh," said Lord Rothborough, snapping shut the miniature and putting it away. "She is not a friend of my wife's. Not by any stretch. She is my cousin, though – and yours. So what did she want?"

"She wanted me to use my influence with you. I told her I

had none."

"About what?"

"Mrs Morgan, of course!" Felix exclaimed. "She told me that you are in danger of being driven mad by her wiles and that your poor, neglected wife cannot bear the thought of it."

"And you believed her?"

"I don't know! What was I supposed to think? When she told me what happened in Paris, about my mother – I had never heard before that you tried to kill yourself over that."

"Oh, I see," said Lord Rothborough. "I see." He grimaced and rubbed his hand across his face. "She's jealous, of course. Hell hath no fury like a woman scorned."

"Then that woman was your mistress?" Felix said. "Or one of them, I should say?" Rothborough shrugged. "And you think that marrying me off to this girl will turn me into some virtuous husband who is never tempted to stray, when you yourself have never had any qualms about pleasing yourself when and where you choose? Or am I to marry this poor girl and dabble where I like, is that it?" And he snatched up the picture of Lady Nina and waved at Lord Rothborough. "I should throw this in the fire! She would be far happier if she never has anything to do with us! You told me not to fall in love – to guard my heart. I thought that was out of sentiment when I heard you tried to kill yourself, that you were looking to protect me from that, but I see now it is out of convenience! No, poor girl, she does not deserve us, she does not!"

He would have thrown it in the fire, but Rothborough caught his hand and took the picture from him. It went back in the drawer with the discarded mistress.

"Us?" said Rothborough, rather quietly. "So, you did tup Miss Pritchard?"

"No, of course I did not! I am not your pattern in all things, my lord! I have not laid a finger on her. How could you believe that of me?"

"The young lady was most convincing," said Rothborough. "And given your conduct towards Mrs Morgan..."

"What has she said?"

"That she was the recipient of a most undignified mauling. Very intemperate behaviour, Felix – and you wonder why I recommend the safe harbour of marriage to you? Mrs Morgan agrees with me."

Felix turned away. The thought of the pair of them discussing him was unbearable, and the fact she had told Lord Rothborough about his desperate kiss was a crowning humiliation.

"Though not to Miss Pritchard, of course," Rothborough went on, "however inevitable a course the Dean seems to think that is. He is not a reasonable man at best of times and you have done an excellent job of riling him up."

"He struck me!" exclaimed Felix. "He was insupportable."

"At least we may agree about that," said Rothborough. "And we will both go and call on him tomorrow and put an end to this ridiculous business."

"If my patients permit," he muttered. "I had better go."

"Take this with you," said Lord Rothborough, reaching into the drawer and taking out the sketch again. "It was intended for you."

He held it out most insistently. Felix took it at last, just to silence him, and tucked it into his coat without looking at it. "I am not marrying to order, sir, and that is my final word!"

"We shall see about that," said Rothborough, waving his hand to dismiss him.

Chapter Thirty-six

"Fildyke?" Giles said, looking at the custody register. "And Josiah Harrison?"

"Mr Carswell and Constable Jones brought them in, sir," said Sargent Boyd.

"So I see," he said, consulting the charge sheet. "Harbouring a fugitive and gross indecency. Is this correct, Boyd?"

"According to Mr Carswell."

"Harrison is not technically a fugitive, only wanted for questioning," said Giles. "Where is he?"

"In the infirmary cell. Alcohol poisoning, Mr Carswell said."

"So not in a fit state to be interviewed tonight?"

"I would say not, sir; you would have to ask Mr Carswell about that, but he's gone out."

"With Lord Rothborough," said Superintendent Rollins, joining them at the desk. "About an hour since."

Giles went down to the cells and found Fildyke looking sullen and petulant.

"You've no right to keep me here, sir," he said, jumping at the sight of Giles. "I demand to be released. I have friends, you know, who will not take kindly to my being treated like this."

"These friends, who might they be?"

"The Dean."

"Oh yes, the Dean. That's interesting, Mr Fildyke. What *is* the Dean to you, precisely? He has mentioned you to me, as well."

"A friend. Cannot two gentlemen be friends, sir?"

"You make quite a claim for yourself there, Mr Fildyke," said Giles. "I would not imagine that Dean Pritchard would see it in that light. He might consider it degrading to be associated with you in any way, given the activity in which Mr Carswell found you engaged."

"The Dean is my friend and will soon put this to rights. I must write to him. I demand that I may write to him. You cannot deny me that!"

"Very well, you may have the materials to write," Giles said. "In the meantime, I suggest you spend the next few hours thinking straight about the situation you are in, and how you may best save your sorry skin by cooperating with us as fully as possible. We will talk again tomorrow, Mr Fildyke, and at length."

He then looked in on Harrison who was fast asleep, like an innocent child. He decided that was another interview that could wait until morning; he was not yet clear enough in his mind what line to take with him. This business with Fildyke had confused everything. A night of waiting might make both men more tractable and the threads more easy to untangle.

Giles went and ate his own dinner, with only Snow for company. When he was done, he stood staring at the papers he had pinned to his wall, trying to make sense of them. Snow pressed against him, demanding exercise and attention. It was developing into a foul night, but he decided that a cold walk in the rain was a good remedy for the fog of his mind. Besides, there was a call he needed to pay. He put on his mackintosh cloak and ventured out, with Snow trotting happily alongside him.

~

The little house looked different in the dark. He had only seen it by day before, and now with a lamp sitting in the bow window of the sitting room to signal that it was occupied, it looked as charming as he had hoped. He stopped at the gate, looking up the brick path, for he could hear the sound of the piano, and the melody caught his attention. He felt a shiver of pleasant surprise when a woman's voice began to sing with it. He stood there for some moments listening, despite the rain, wondering if what he heard was real or whether it was some strange dream of domestic bliss.

Snow did not care for the rain and barked with annoyance at being made to wait; so Giles opened the handgate and went up to the door. The music continued and he had no wish for it to stop. Since he had the key in his pocket he unlocked it, opening the door quietly and only a little. But it was enough to fill his nostrils with the sweet scent of a wood fire.

"Mrs Morgan?" he called out, knowing he must break the spell and not wishing to alarm her unduly. "Good evening!"

She came out of the sitting room a moment later.

"Major Vernon! Well, what a pleasant surprise! And you have walked all this way, in this weather. And you are drenched!"

"Not really," he said. "And I needed to walk. I had a few things to think of – I needed to settle my mind on some points."

"Have you dined?"

"Yes, thank you. Do you mind my dog? She is very tame, but I can shut her in the kitchen if you prefer."

"No, no, not at all. How could I mind such a beautiful creature? What is her name?"

"Snow."

Mrs Morgan came forward and gave Snow a generous embrace of welcome, to which the dog submitted for a moment before giving herself a violent shake to free herself of the rain, showering Mrs Morgan in the process. She laughed, not the least offended.

He took off his mackintosh cloak and cap and left them hanging on the large hooks in the vestibule.

"Are you sure you will not have some supper? I am well provisioned. Your man has thought of everything. There is an excellent cheese and some game pie. Oh, and curd tarts. I have made sure Mr Holt has eaten his fill, by the way."

"Good. I am glad he looked after you."

"He is reassuring, I have to say," she said. "Where did you find him?"

"By happy accident," he said.

"I am great believer in serendipity," she said. "Now, there is a good fire in here. Come and get dry. Oh, after you, Madame Snow..." She laughed again, as the dog slipped past her skirts and into the sitting room. As was her custom, Snow at once prostrated herself on the hearth rug and proceeded to roast herself.

It *was* a good fire and Mrs Morgan had lit many candles as well as the lamp at the window. The sparsely furnished room looked inhabited and alive. The low chair had been brought up to the hearth and an Indian shawl lay thrown across the dull brown velvet of the sofa. On the round table sat the tea-tray with the silver pot, glittering a welcome.

"I have been so curious – whose house is this?" she asked, picking up the shawl and wrapping it about her.

"Mine," said Giles. "I hope you don't mind."

"But you do not live here – not yet at least?"

"I have only just taken it. It was an improvisation on my part to bring you here. I only signed the lease a week ago."

"It is very pretty."

"My sister has been seeing to the domestic details. One of her servants has been here, as well as the excellent Mr Holt, of course."

"You are preparing it for someone, I think," she said, tracing her finger along the empty music stand of the piano.

"Yes," he said. "What did you think of the piano? I heard

you playing as I came up the path."

"It is a surprisingly good instrument," she said.

"You know, I think I took the place for the piano," he said.

"A man after my own heart!" she said, and then said, "forgive me."

"I am glad to know it is a good one. I thought it was. I hoped..." he broke off. It was impossible not to stare at her with her patterned shawl about her, her deep red dress beneath glowing in the light of the candles.

"She will be very happy with it," she said.

"I hope so." He rubbed his face and looked away into the fire.

"Hope," he heard her say, "that is a strange thing. We wear it like armour and yet it does so little to protect us."

He turned to look at her again, feeling the acuteness of her remark. She had sat down on the sofa and was twisting the fronds of her shawl fringe about her fingers.

"That's true," he said. "But we cannot do without it."

"No, we cannot," she said, and looked over at him. "Life would be dry without it."

He crouched down on the hearth to scratch Snow's head. He watched her again as she fiddled with the shawl fringe.

"Will you tell me about her?" she said at length. "When are you to be married?"

"Why do you ask that?"

"You are not the sort of man to keep a mistress," she said. "And when you said your sister, well..."

On other occasions he had resented such questions and deflected them. He never wanted to speak of it, but there was something in her straightforward tone that unlocked his tongue.

"We are already married. We have been married eight years," he said. "It is just that she is ill in her mind and of necessity away from me. But I want her here. I am hoping she will be improved by living here, a mistress of her own house instead of a wretched inmate in the place she is now. That she might come back to me a little. That we might find again –" He broke off.

There was a long silence.

"Buckle on your hope, Major Vernon," she said. "And I will pray it protects you."

"Yes, pray for us, Mrs Morgan," he said getting to his feet. "He does not much listen to me, but He may listen to you."

"He does not listen to anyone much," she said. "I think He is fading away. He is dying, that old man in the sky. There, now you know how bad I am for saying that – but there is such wickedness and cruelty in the world that I cannot believe in it any more. How can a loving God permit such suffering? That is what I always struggle with."

"It is a struggle, yes," he said.

"We are better off believing in ourselves and the powers we have," she said. "I think you would agree with that, Major Vernon, being such a practical, sensible man." She got up and walked about the room. "And perhaps to hope is not such a foolish thing. Perhaps you will be happy here. If I had a glass of wine I should toast your future happiness, Major Vernon. I would drink to you and your wife." She made the gesture of a toast. "And I will send flowers and kind letters and music for the excellent pianoforte, if you will permit it? I even have a Berlin work parrot cushion nearly done that would look handsome on that chair in the corner, if you would not object to such a gift?"

"How could I?" he said, with a smile. "I am fond of parrots."

She laughed and then said, "Yes, we must live always in the expectation of a good outcome. And see off all our enemies with defiant good humour."

"Quite," he said. "I wish we had a bottle of champagne to

hand now."

"A bottle from your brother in law's cellar, perhaps? I have never tasted any nicer than the wine we had the other night."

"He will be pleased to hear you say that. He takes great pride in his cellar."

"He is such a kind man," she said. "It was very pleasant for me to be treated as he and your sister have – indeed as you have done – as someone ordinary, if I might put it like that. I find I am always damned or praised, but never accepted for myself."

"But you are not ordinary," he found he must say.

"My voice is not ordinary. But I am, I think," she said.

Snow got up, stretched, and ambled over to her hostess. She was looking up approvingly at Mrs Morgan, Giles felt, although he knew he was allowing his own pleasure to colour his interpretation of Snow's behaviour.

Behind them, the sashes rattled with a sudden gust of wind and there was the sound of hail against the glass.

"I do apologise for the lack of curtains," he said.

"It promises to be an alarming night," she said.

"Yes, perhaps."

"I am rather worried about you walking back in that."

"It will be no trouble," he said.

"You will never find your way. Why do you not stay here? Then you and Mr Holt may take turns in guarding me." She smiled. "Not perhaps that I deserve such attentions."

It was on the tip of his tongue to say something foolish and gallant. The invitation was a tempting one – it made a certain sense, although there was very little danger that Morgan would find his way out to such a remote spot. There was no real justification for him remaining there except to gratify himself, and it would be gratifying, there was no doubt about that. He could not much longer deny the peculiar pleasure he took in her company.

"A good night's sleep by a good fire," she went, sensing his hesitation. "It is what you deserve, when you do so much for us all. But I suppose you never have a fire in your room, Major?"

"No, never," he said.

"This couch is not so comfortable," she said, testing the spring with her hand. "So that will more than compensate for the temperature being over-luxurious, do you not think?" she said. "Will that satisfy your puritanism?"

"I hope you have a fire in your room."

"No, I did not order one," she said.

"Then I will get Holt to make one up at once," he said. "You will excuse me a moment."

She nodded her assent, and he left rather briskly.

It was pleasantly cool out in the passageway and he allowed his mind to clear before going to speak to Holt in the kitchen. Was it a proposition she was making, or merely an innocent invitation to take shelter? Was he guilty, like so many men seemed to be, of misinterpreting her, imagining her to be what he wanted her to be, instead of what she was? She was, he reminded himself, a respectable, modest creature, who would be horrified by the thoughts which now filled his mind.

Holt had made himself comfortable in a Windsor chair by the kitchen hearth, but he jumped to attention when Giles came in.

"I heard you come in, sir," he said. "But I thought I'd best not disturb you. Is the lady comfortable?" he added. "I did what I could but that chimney didn't want to draw at all, when I first got there. You should speak to the landlord, sir, and have it looked at."

"You've done well, then," Giles said. "Could you make up the fire in her bedroom?"

"Of course, sir, right away. Let's hope that chimney has a better draw." There was a spatter of hail against the kitchen window. "It's not a night for a Christian to be out," Holt said, as he went towards the scullery to get logs. "Will you be going back in that, sir?"

"I don't think I'll risk it," Giles said. "I'll stay here."

"Quite right, sir. Why leave a pleasant billet with such handsome company?"

Chapter Thirty-seven

"Is Mrs Morgan at home?" Felix asked.

The maid looked extremely flustered.

"Monsieur, I think you should leave," she said in a whisper. "This is not a good time."

"Is your mistress at home?"

"Monsieur, please leave."

"Not until you tell Mrs Morgan I am here. Let her decide if she will see me."

A man's voice came roaring through the hall, deep and Welsh accented: "Who the devil is it, Berthe?"

The maid tried to shut the door in Felix's face, but he caught it and held it open.

"No one, monsieur," the maid called over her shoulder and again addressed Felix imploringly: "Please, Monsieur, please leave! I beg you."

They had a little tussle with the door, until Felix got the better of her and stepped into the hall, just as a man in his shirt sleeves came out of the sitting room.

"Who the hell are you?" he demanded of Felix. "Eh, sir?"

He was tall, broad-shouldered and robustly built, and in the dim light of the hall he looked faintly satanic. It was also clear that he was somewhat drunk. "Another young buck who thinks he can paw my wife, yes?"

"I wish to speak to Mrs Morgan," Felix said.

"Speak? I doubt very much that's what you want from her," the Welshman said, seizing Felix by both lapels. "At this time of night? Do you think I'm stupid, boy? Do you think I'm a fool?" Felix found himself with his back to the wall. "I know what you want, you dirty little bastard!"

Morgan had the physique of a prize fighter and his spirit was well-stoked by brandy and righteous indignation. Felix found his mouth was dry with terror and that his muscles seemed set rigid. Her husband; this monster is her husband – it was all he could think. "Think you can have her, boy? Is that it? Think she's yours for a tumble, for a nice fuck? Is that it?"

"No!" Felix exclaimed, and summoning up what strength he could, attempted to push him away.

This attempt seemed to amuse Morgan rather than anger him. He let Felix go and said, "Ha! Spoiling for a fight, then, are we? That would be a pleasure – to give you a good thrashing. That's what you're going to get, you know. A good thrashing, you presumptuous little shit-bag."

"Edward, Edward, leave him be, for goodness sake," said a woman's voice. It was Mrs Ridolfi. "That's Lord Rothborough's son."

Morgan spun round. "Rothborough's son? What are you saying? Have both of them been sniffing at her? Is that it?"

Mrs Ridolfi said nothing but Morgan took her silence in the worst light, and Felix wondered if she had seen something that day he attempted to kiss her. Or perhaps Mrs Morgan had confided in her. If that was the case, he was in deep trouble here.

"Father and son – well, well, well," said Morgan turning back to Felix. He looked him up and down. "He doesn't look much like a swell."

"He's a bastard," Mrs Ridolfi said. "But his Lordship is sentimental about him."

Morgan lumbered a little closer to Felix again and Felix thought he was going to strike him, but instead he let his hand drop and wandered away.

"Filthy whore! Father and son. Father and fucking son."

"I'm so sorry, Edward," Mrs Ridolfi murmured, patting him on the arm as he wandered past her to go and sit mournfully on the bottom of the stairs.

"Well, Master Bastard," he said. "I'm afraid you are too late. You and your father. The bitch has already gone. Already taken for the evening, ain't that so, Lina?"

Paulina Ridolfi nodded.

"Where?" Felix managed to ask.

"She didn't say."

"Of course she didn't," Morgan rejoined.

"She went somewhere with Major Vernon," Mrs Ridolfi said.

"What?"

Felix got no answer. At that moment another man came staggering out of the sitting room, holding a bottle.

"What's going on?" he said, his voice slurred and confused. "What's all the fuss?"

"Oh, get to your bed, you silly man!" Mrs Ridolfi said to him with exasperation in her voice.

"That's no way to s...s.... speak to your husband!" he said with some difficulty. "I sh..sh.. shall go to bed when I am good and ready. But first there is a bottle of port that needs my attention." And he went back into the dining room.

"With Major Vernon?" Felix said again to Mrs Ridolfi. "Are you sure, ma'am?"

"I heard her say something to her maid. I am sure of it."

"But why?"

She went and opened the front door.

"Why do you think, Mr Carswell?" she said. "Good night."

Chapter Thirty-eight

Finding the room had grown warm, Giles stripped down to his shirt. He stretched out on the couch, not attempting to sleep, but allowing his mind to turn over the events of the day, trying to take his ease. But he too keenly felt the unfamiliarity of his surroundings and the stimulation of having been so much in the company of a woman whom he found it impossible not admire. She was intelligent, courageous, and full of wit and spirit. He liked her playful mind and how she had endeavoured to smile throughout her trying circumstances.

The rain had turned again to hail, and he could hear it spattering like gravel thrown against the window panes.

There was a sudden loud bang and he heard her cry out. He leapt up from the sofa and headed for the passageway. The door to her room was open, and he could see that the window had also been forced open by a violent gust of wind. He could just see her crouching in the darkness on the bed.

He leant out into the storm and hauled the casements shut, his face lashed with hail as he did so. He fastened the catch tight, and turned back to her.

The room was dark except for the white-hot glow of the fire, and in this eerie light he watched as she pushed her hands through her loosened hair, her shawl falling from her shoulders leaving only her shift to cover her, which also slipped inopportunely down to reveal the generous curve of her breast.

He turned away quickly and searched for a candlestick. There was one on the washstand which he relit from the fire. Then, having set it on the mantel, he set to making up the fire again, putting on fresh logs and raking up the embers into new life.

"There," he said.

"What a fool I am," she said. "I thought – I don't know what I thought – I think my fancies have got the better of me at last. To be scared half to death by a window blowing open in a storm! You must think I am a fool."

"It's understandable in the circumstances. It made quite a noise. What a night!"

"I am frightened by shadows now," she said. "What must you think of me?"

He took the candle from her bedside and lit it. The room became tolerably light.

"I think that you are frightened of someone who has treated you badly and who may be dangerous. You are allowed to be frightened. Besides, fear makes us vigilant. It is a useful emotion at times."

"Yes, I suppose I know that well enough. I have experienced it sometimes before a performance and it is indescribably terrifying. It feels as if utter failure is imminent and disaster is inevitable." She wrapped her shawl about her. "So I should know better." She pressed her hands to her face and breathed deeply, attempting to steady herself. "Really I should." But he could see she was shaking, and he heard her teeth chattering – whether from fear or the cold, he could not say.

"You are hard on yourself," he said. "And you should get back under the bedclothes. You must not catch cold. Lord Rothborough would never forgive me."

"He will never forgive you if he hears you were here," she said, managing a slight laugh. "Poor dear man! I really wish he did not feel so... so! My life would be a great deal simpler if I did not seem to make Cupid fire off his arrows indiscriminately!"

"It must be a terrible affliction," he said, glad to hear the levity in her voice. He went to adjust the logs on the fire and stir up the flames while she got back beneath the blankets.

He was making for the door when she said, "Oh, must you go?" Then she sighed. "Oh dear, you will think everything that is said about me is true from that tone of voice. What I meant is – I do not feel safe alone. I ought to try, of course, but... I know the moment you are gone and the door is closed that I shall..."

"Would it help if I were to sleep on the floor?" he said.

"I would feel ashamed to make you sleep on the floor on my account," she said. "No, I am being foolish. I will manage."

"I will sleep on the floor. It will be no hardship for me, and I will rest easy knowing that you feel comfortable."

"I will not be comfortable if you are on the floor," she said. "I can't bear the thought of such unnecessary gallantry. This is a large bed – if it is not indelicate to point out that fact. Would it be so wrong if you were to lie here beside me? You will die of cold on that floor. If I am under the covers and you wrapped in your blanket, we will be like a bundling couple tucked up by a vigilant parent, and the Bishop of Northminster himself could not find fault with it!"

He could not help laughing.

"I am serious," she said.

"I know you are," he said, still laughing.

"A grown man and a woman – we ought to be able to contain ourselves," she said, and she reached out and patted the space beside her.

"Very well," he said, and went and fetched his blanket from the other room.

When he returned, she had tucked herself up under the covers, facing away from him, but he could see she was still shaking from the cold.

"I am not very hardy, am I?" she said. "I can't seem to get warm."

"This is ridiculous," he said. "Excuse my pragmatism,

Mrs Morgan, but there is one way we can solve this, if you will permit me?"

And he climbed beneath the covers and pulled her into his arms.

"You are a bold man," she said, with a gasp, but she relaxed at once in his embrace, pressing herself against him as she did so. He relaxed too. She had issued an invitation and he had accepted it, it was clear enough now.

"I cannot have you losing your voice," he said. He could smell her hair now, for she had moved so that she lay in a crescent against him and there was not a chink between him and her. Somehow their fingers had knitted together, too.

She began to shake with laughter. It was indescribably pleasant to feel it, and he could not help laughing too at the absurdity and outrageousness of what they were about. Yet he felt a deep sadness at the same time, knowing it was nothing but a mockery of something he profoundly desired. This was how a husband would treat his wife on a cold night when she was in distress. He would pull her close for comfort and whisper into her ear, filling his nostrils with the sweet fragrance of her warm hair.

"If I did not laugh I would cry," she said, speaking aloud his own thought. "This is too..."

"Yes," was all he could manage to say, and buried his face in her hair. Her fingers tightened in his grasp and then she rolled about to face him, and pressed her lips to his for a long moment. Her cheeks were wet with tears.

"Now, don't cry," he said, "please."

"I am crying because you understand me," she said.

He reached out and dried her tears with his fingertips, near to tears himself.

"I have recently been a great fool with a woman," he said, tracing his finger again down her cheek. "I don't deserve to trifle with you."

"Nothing you do is trifling," she said. "I have watched

you this last week – I have seemed to see nothing else but you. Last night I dreamt of you. I dreamt you took me away to America and chopped down a grove of trees to make a me a garden with a view of a river. It was as clear as something I read in a book."

"But I can never do that," he said. "I wish that I could, with all my heart..."

"I did not say it to reproach you," she said, "or to taunt you. Just to tell you, that is my heart's desire. I am not such a fool as to think we will ever have more than this."

"No," he said. "But we can have this," and returned her kiss. "We can and we shall."

Chapter Thirty-nine

Over breakfast, they agreed that there would be one last embrace and then she would go away directly to his sister's, driven in the trap by Holt. Nothing more would be said of the night before. They had agreed to lock up the remembrance of it in their hearts. It had happened, and nothing more could come of it, no matter what they might wish.

But that last kiss was hard to break from, and she clung to him as much as he did to her, and he knew she was stifling a sob as she let down her veil and made for the front door. He did not see her into the carriage. They had agreed on that, too. He remained in the house, and only went to the window to see the carriage drive away. When he saw her later it would be only as an acquaintance. The night was over, and that was that.

He left the house soon after, taking a householder's care to damp down the fires and leave all in order. One of Sally's servants would be there to clean and tidy, but he rather furtively smoothed one set of pillows, wondering whether the bed looked as though it had been occupied by two bodies and not one. He was used to looking for such incriminating details. He realised he was thinking like a rogue, seeking to cover his actions.

But what had passed between them brought him no shame. It had not been furtive. It had been like a night in a marriage that could never exist between them, but which they had both wanted ardently. The sleep that had come after had been sweet, and Snow had climbed up onto the bed and joined them in the small hours, as if she too understood it all.

Now Snow leant against him and whimpered. She had liked her new mistress and did not care to see her leave. He caressed her head and was thankful at least to have a companion. Nancy's road was far harder.

He walked back to Northminster with Snow across the field road by which he had come, a path he knew would soon become familiar. The facts of his life could not be avoided, nor could the facts of Nancy's existence. She had confided that she planned to go to America; she had been asked to go some time ago. Now her mind was made up. She would leave Northminster, in two days' time.

He quickened his step. He had work to do.

~

Felix had not slept well. Two large drams had done nothing to help. He lay twisted up in the blankets on his narrow bedstead. The ancient structure of the building had been set shuddering and groaning by the fierce wind, but it seemed to him like a diabolical chorus, brought on to deny him any rest when he most wanted it. Oblivion he could not find. Even his pillow was determined to attack him – a feather escaped the casing and ripped across his face, threatening another scar.

He threw the pillow across the room, feeling at the scratch with his fingertips, and then the scar on his cheek. It was a woman who had caused that, and now it was a woman who again seemed to be intent on sending him to Hell. Mrs Morgan... oh dear God above, Anna Morgan!

Mrs Ridolfi's words were etched into his being, like acid on glass. Had Major Vernon really succeeded with Mrs Morgan? If he had, what did that say about her? If she was apparently so liberal with her favours, then why had she rejected him? What had he done, or failed to do? Was there some vital step in this game that he had failed to learn? He felt peevish with envy and unable to find any satisfactory answers.

For several long hours, he found himself unable to do anything but imagine in some detail what might be passing between them, and his entire body ached with an agonised mixture of disgust and fascination.

He felt he might have stood it better to know that she was with Lord Rothborough. That would have been explicable – there was a lot for a woman like that to gain from being the mistress of Lord Rothborough. If she was that sort of woman, which was the thing he could not establish for certain. But Mrs Morgan and Major Vernon – he was the last person in the world he imagined permitting himself to get involved in such an imbroglio. He had shown no signs of susceptibility, neither had he seemed much moved by her beauty or her charm, beyond conventional compliments. However, he was a man good at keeping his opinions to himself, and apparently his actions as well.

At length Felix did sleep, waking later than he ought, and was obliged to scrabble to get dressed and decent. The water in the washstand had frozen in the night, meaning he would have to defer his shave, and his clean shirt felt as if it was fashioned out of ice. He wondered if he should employ a man to bring him a little domestic comfort.

As he pulled on his coat, the little drawing of Lady Nina fell out of his pocket and went flying across the room as if with a will of its own. It lodged itself under his bed and he was obliged to lie flat on his belly to retrieve it. Getting back onto his stockinged feet, her eyes looked at him reproachfully at his ungallant treatment. It was indeed a beautiful and intriguing face. She did not simper, and there seemed to be little affectation about her. He turned it over and noticed that there was a competent sketch on the reverse showing, curiously, some form of fungus, with the Latin name written beneath it and initialled 'N.D.' Had Axelmann taken an abandoned piece of sketch board from his subject to draw upon? That suggested a comfortable intimacy, Felix thought. He hoped she were madly in love with him and at that moment planning an elopement.

That would serve Lord Rothborough right, Felix thought, and turned the card back so the portrait faced him, finding he did wish to look at her again. Lord Rothborough had got his taste so right and that annoyed him extremely. Although the scheme seemed ridiculous, it was impossible for him not to wonder what it might be like to marry such a girl, and indeed what marriage might mean in general. A warm bed and a calm night, perhaps. In that moment the idea was infinitely desirable. He put the portrait on the mantelpiece, hoping it might act as a lesson to him.

He had just put on his boots when he heard knocking on the door to his consulting room. He went to open the door, expecting his usual morning queue of patients. Instead he found the Major himself, dressed in his mackintosh cloak and looking as if he had come straight through the storm, which was still hard at work outside.

"May I come in?"

Felix gestured that he might, not entirely trusting himself to speak. He went to the fire and stared down at the dirty grate, full of last night's ashes.

"I need a fire," he said.

"Let's go to my quarters – I've got one," said Major Vernon. "I have some good news for you as well. About Miss Pritchard." He started off down the corridor.

Felix went along after him, wondering how he might begin his attack. He felt it would have to be an attack of some sort. His spirit was demanding it, but it was no easy matter to cross swords with Major Vernon.

There was a pot of coffee as well as a fire in the Major's office. A mud-spattered Snow lay sprawled asleep on the hearth rug. "She is going to need a bath," remarked Major Vernon as he poured the coffee.

The coffee was strong and sweet, just as Major Vernon

always took it, and Felix was grateful for it. He turned to the papers relating to Barnes' death which the Major had pinned on the wall, and the Major came and stood next to him, looking over them also.

"I have forgotten to congratulate you," he said.

"For what?"

"For bringing in Harrison, not to mention Fildyke."

"Oh," said Felix. "Well, yes, it is hardly a matter for congratulation. A lucky chance."

"Did he say anything of interest to you?"

"About Barnes' murder?" Major Vernon nodded. "He denies it."

"Of course," Major Vernon said, scratching his temple.

"You think it is Harrison?"

"He is a candidate. But then again, we have an interesting business with Miss Pritchard and Mr Watkins – I am not convinced they have told me the whole truth about the discovery of the body."

"Miss Pritchard and Mr Watkins?"

"They are secretly engaged. That was the good news I had for you."

"Watkins?" Felix said, struggling to understand this. "She is engaged to Watkins?"

"Yes, and has been for some time. You have been employed to throw the Dean off the scent. A decoy fiancé."

"But that makes even less sense," Felix said.

"Miss Pritchard went to the tower for a tryst with Watkins – and it was she who discovered poor Barnes' body. When Watkins arrived, they decided he would report the discovery of the body in order to preserve their secret engagement. At least that is what they have told me, but there are a few inconsistencies there. I think there may have been more to it."

Felix said, "But why would she slander me – and herself for that matter?"

"Yes, it is a desperate strategy – which makes me wonder if she has not something heavier on her conscience than deceiving her parents. Barnes may have been blackmailing her. She may have lost her temper with him."

Felix scanned the notes pinned to the wall.

"White ribbon?" he said, pointing to the piece of paper on which the Major had written the words in large letters.

"Ah yes, I wanted your opinion about that. It may be a possible ligature. Barnes habitually wore a ribbon with the key to the tower about his neck. About one inch broad. Would that have been enough to do the trick? Judging from the marks you recorded on your drawing, it looks about right to me."

Felix studied his own sketch of the dead man again for a moment. "It's plausible."

"And either a woman or a man could have had the strength to do it?"

"Yes, but Miss Pritchard? Surely not."

"You are very forgiving considering all the difficulty she has caused you."

"If she is in love with Watkins, I suppose it makes sense that she should use me to hide the truth. It is not flattering, but then..." After a moment he went on, "I could not imagine she would actually murder anyone. She is spirited, but not aggressive."

"People do the strangest things under extreme circumstances," Major Vernon said and stood looking at his papery aide-memoires, his arms folded, his brow furrowed. "There is still something missing here. Still something..."

Felix decided after a moment or two he must speak.

"I was surprised not to find you here last night, sir, when I got back. So was Rollins, for that matter."

"You managed very well without me," Vernon said.

"Yes, but..."

"Do you want to know where I was?" said Major Vernon.

"I believe I know that," Felix said. "You see, I went to

call on Mrs Morgan. And I was told —" He broke off. "You should be careful, sir."

"I'm sorry?"

"Morgan was there. He's a brute and a jealous one. He knows you were with her last night."

"Morgan was there?" said Major Vernon. "Why on earth didn't you say so before? It is just as well I took her away. Tell me exactly what happened."

"You don't deny it, then?" said Felix. "Taking her away?"

"Of course not. What are you implying, Mr Carswell? Do you think something has passed between us?"

"Does it need to be implied? It seemed self-evident."

"I am glad you think so highly of me," said Major Vernon, after a moment. "Not to mention of the lady."

"It is difficult when all I hear of her is so —"

"Yes?" Vernon said. "What do you hear?"

"That she is —" he broke off. He could not bring himself to actually say it. "And you, sir, well, you yourself would be the first to admit that you have not been blameless in your conduct. If what happened in January is anything to go by, then —"

"That does not answer my question. And do you really think that I would be such a fool? My record may not be impressive but I assure you, in respect of Mrs Morgan, there is nothing remotely questionable going on between us. You should not believe anything you hear about her. She has been cruelly misrepresented."

Was he lying? Felix really could not decide and neither could he give him the benefit of the doubt. The fact remained they had very possibly been together all night — that was bad enough. It implied nothing and everything.

"Tell me what happened when you went to the house," said Major Vernon, pouring more coffee. "This is of utmost importance."

"Morgan was extremely rude and unpleasant. There isn't

much more to be said than that. And roaring drunk, as was that brother of hers, Ridolfi. He threatened me."

"Morgan, you mean?" Felix nodded. "What does he look like?"

"Big, burly, dark hair thinning on top, but with long sideburns. Manner swaggering and very Welsh. You could not mistake him in a crowd – he was at least six foot tall. He looks like a stage villain – not that he isn't one in real life, which he is. There is no mistake about that. A brute."

Major Vernon rubbed his face.

"We shall just have to make sure his crimes catch up with him now, Mr Carswell. I am determined on that. Your description will be extremely useful. You might do one of your sketches, if you have a moment."

"You think he is behind the letters?"

"Yes, but not just him. I have an idea that –"

There was a knock on the door and one of the constables came in with a message.

"It's Inspector Jackson's wife, Mr Carswell. Can you come at once? The midwife can't deal with it."

"You'd better go," said Major Vernon, with some concern.

Felix did not need to be reminded of the urgency of the case. Mrs Jackson had a history of miscarriages, and had never yet carried a child to full term. He arrived to discover that she had passed a most miserable night in the early stages of labour. Her situation was now very painful, and although he had observed his share of human distress, Felix felt shocked by the intensity of her suffering. It seemed that all those ancient beliefs about the pains of childbirth being a perpetual punishment upon women for the sin of Eve might indeed be true. If not, it was appalling that the natural process of labour could in itself be responsible for such misery. It went against reason that birth, a process which ought to be as natural as breathing, and which in the animal kingdom was attended by so little distress to the mother, should in humankind cause such torture.

Her husband never left her side and he seemed to suffer in his way as greatly as she did, and his tender diligence was so at odds with the man he had seen swaggering about The Unicorn in his silver-laced coat and high hat. It was a revelation, and Felix wondered again at the business and meaning of marriage; of husband and wives and how they were linked by something profounder than the mere vagaries of sentimental love and hot-blooded lust. This connection, so strange and deep between them, was something he did not understand. He wondered if he would ever manage to make such a contract. He did not think he could bear to stand by and see someone he loved suffer as this woman was suffering.

The morning did not go well with them. By eleven he had brought out, by means of forceps, a dead boy – perfect in every way but strangled by the cord. It was all he could do to remember his duty and help her through the last stages of the birth. Her wretchedness was beyond words, and he was glad to see her drift at last into an opiate stupor, her own life preserved as best it could be for the moment.

He went down to the parlour where the curate was praying over the body of the child with Mrs Jackson the elder, the Inspector's mother. She was fighting her tears back as she tried to say the Lord's Prayer. He stood in the doorway, unable to go in. The dead child had been shrouded in one of the little sheets carefully sewn for his birth and placed in the basket that would have been his bed. These things were commonplace, and he knew he ought to be hardened to such things now. But he was not, and he left at the first opportunity, knowing he would have to return soon enough.

Chapter Forty

Harrison was lying on his bed in his cell, wrapped up in a grey blanket that matched his complexion.

"You have no right to interview me," he said in a hoarse voice.

"What on earth gives you that idea?" said Giles.

"I will not speak to you."

"Then your actions will speak for you. If you had stayed put, Mr Harrison, and had not attempted to leave Northminster, I would be inclined to take all your denials a little more seriously. A man who takes it into his head to run is bound to look more suspicious."

"That is precisely why I decided to leave. You are all suspicions and supposition, Major Vernon. You will not take me at my word. I may as well put the noose about my neck."

"Then give me something else, Mr Harrison," Giles said, "give me something I can work with. I need more than flat denials to accept your story. At this moment I have nothing."

"I don't know what I can say to convince you."

"Perhaps you could tell me something about Charlie's relationship with Mr Watkins."

"Why?" said Harrison.

"Just tell me what you know. I believe he was teaching him the organ."

"Yes."

"Did Charlie tell you any gossip about him?"

"Gossip?"

"That he was courting someone in secret, for example."

"Oh, that, yes – the Dean's daughter. Yes. He mentioned it."

"And Charlie caught them together, I understand?"

"Yes, apparently. Swore me to secrecy about it. How do you know that?"

"That's beside the point," Giles said. "Now why did he swear you to secrecy?"

"He wanted that cat kept well in the bag."

"Are you sure there wasn't any ill-feeling between them because of that?"

Harrison stirred a little under his blanket and then answered, "For my own sake, I'd like to say there was — because since Watkins found poor Charlie, that's as suspicious as my apparently being the last person to see him alive, is it not?" Giles nodded. "But if there was, I wasn't aware of it. Watkins is a good fellow — he taught Charlie for free, and his wanting to murder Charlie over that — well, it seems as ridiculous as my wanting to do it. You've only got straws to clutch at there, Major Vernon, if you don't mind me saying."

There was no timbre of apology as he said it and Giles wondered again if he was dealing with a clever liar.

"What about Miss Pritchard?" Giles asked. "Did Charlie have any dealings with her? Did he ever mention her to you?"

"He said she was terrified of the Dean finding out — that he was apparently the heavy father *par excellence,* which isn't really surprising if you listening to him thumping out a text from the pulpit."

"You have the advantage over me there, Mr Harrison. I haven't heard the Dean preach."

"There are three sorts of sermons, if you ask me," said Harrison, addressing his remarks to the ceiling of the cell. "There is the sort that is easy not to listen to. Then there is the sermon good enough to be worth listening to, and then there is the bad sermon which you cannot avoid listening to, because generally the fellow is a noisy ranter who shouts his way through it."

"And the Dean is a noisy ranter?"

"Heavens, yes! Like a dissenting demagogue. It's pretty shocking."

Giles was amused that Harrison, of all people, could be shocked by a clergyman's way of preaching.

"And it brings the wrong people in," Harrison went on. "People who don't care for the music and talk through it, and then sit in dumb silence while he harangues them about hell-fire."

"Charlie was not profiting in any way from that information, though?" Giles asked. "After all, you and he were not averse to a little blackmail, were you?"

"I refuse to comment on that," said Harrison.

"There is no need. I have enough evidence to charge you with blackmail should I choose. But finding Charlie's murderer takes precedence, don't you think? If you are innocent you must want to solve this as much as I do – if not more so, given your relationship with him."

Harrison gave a grimace.

"If there is anything," Giles went on, "any little fact that you think might be of consequence, I do advise you to tell me, Mr Harrison. Let's go back to that last argument you had with him – that refusal of his to come with you to London. What reason did he give you?"

"I told you – he didn't want to leave Rose."

"Is that all?"

There was a long silence. Harrison still stared at the ceiling. There was clearly something more that needed to be said.

"Harrison, come now!" Giles said, and reached out and yanked the blanket off the bed.

"All right, all right," said Harrison, scrabbling up from the bed, anxious to get the blanket back. "There was something; someone settled a tailor's bill for him and he would not say who. We had an argument about it – but he would not tell me who it was."

"Mr Geoffrey?"

"I suppose it must have been, but then why didn't he say? After all – well, you know."

"Do you think there was a possibility Charlie was involved with someone else?" There was another long silence.

"That is possible," Harrison said. He spoke rather quietly as if it pained him.

"Why do you think that?"

"There was a box, this fancy box. He got this box from somewhere. He turned up with it, having been given it, but he would not say who it was from. It drove me mad."

"Can you describe it to me?"

"I only saw it the once and I was glad not to see it again – but it was a fancy sort of box – about a foot long, with inlay on it. You know the sort of thing."

"I believe I have it. It was where he kept your letters."

Harrison turned back to Giles. He looked as if he had just been dealt a body blow. He sat down.

"Well, well, that is just fine," he said.

"And you have no idea who this mysterious person was?"

"No. I wish I did. Or do I? I don't know. But there was someone, yes. Yes." He gave a great sigh.

"You are sure this topic did not feature in your last conversation with him? I'm wondering – since you have failed to mention this before – if that was not deliberate, Mr Harrison, rather than simple forgetfulness. This secret rival for your affections – well, it is rather provoking for you – and you have already admitted you were extremely angry with Charlie for refusing to go with you to London. Perhaps this person's existence was the spark that lit the tinder. It would be more than understandable. He'd betrayed you. That is enough to provoke the most steadfast lover."

"I did not kill him!" exclaimed Harrison. "How many times must I tell you that?"

"Tell me this man's name," Giles said. "I assume it was a

man?"

"I don't know! If I knew I would tell you – like a shot. Charlie would not say. All I know is that whoever it was gave him that damned box."

"And who was the tailor?" Giles said. "The tailor whose bill was settled?"

"Loake," said Harrison. "Who else is worth patronising in this place?"

"Thank you. That is most useful. Now, tell me about Fildyke. Why did you go there last night? Money?"

"That and a bed for the night."

"And you offered him your services in exchange?" Harrison did not answer. "I am surprised Fildyke was interested. You are not known to be friends. Apparently you pressed to get him removed from the choir."

"Watkins asked my opinion, yes. But it was obvious enough. He can't sing. He'd only lasted so long because the Dean – well, I don't know what it was with the Dean and Fildyke. Or perhaps I do, if you get my meaning. I think you do," he added.

"Are you implying that Fildyke might have had some improper relations with Dean Pritchard?" said Giles. "You are certain that Fildyke was of your inclination, Mr Harrison?"

"Oh yes," said Harrison. "He likes a pretty face. He used to leer over Charlie."

"But Dean Pritchard – you know what you are saying, Mr Harrison. Are you certain?"

"There are plenty of men who pretend to be other than they are," Harrison said. "You know that as well as I do, Major Vernon. Men in all ranks and walks of life. The law – your law, sir – may oppress us but it cannot stop what will be."

"You have no evidence for this, though," Giles said.

"Evidence is your business, sir," said Harrison. "Not mine." And he folded his hands behind his head and lay back down on the bed.

~

"So will you speak to Fildyke now, sir?" said Rollins. "I have his letter for you, by the by."

"To the Dean, just as he said," said Giles taking the folded paper from Rollins. He glanced it over. He had a florid, cramped hand that was not pleasant to look at. But the contents were better than Giles could have hoped for.

> The powers that be have me falsely held. I am helpless. If promises mean anything, sir, I ask you to help me now. I have kept my promises to you. You must keep your side of the bargain, and help a poor Christian in distress. I do not know if they will give you this letter, but if they do, come at once, I beg you, or I shall be forced to take matters into my own hands. As I have kept my promises, I ask you to help me now.

"He can wait a while longer. I have a few calls to pay first," Giles said, tucking the letter into his coat pocket.

~

Mr Loake was disappointed that Giles had not come to order a new coat but merely to ask for information. He had launched into a paean of praise for a bolt of fine Melton cloth almost as soon as Giles had come into the shop. Giles stated his business and the tailor frowned, puzzled by the question.

"Barnes, sir? Would that be old Mr Barnes at Shilton Hall?"

"No, Charles Barnes. A young man."

"Oh, yes – that Mr Barnes," said Mr Loake. "Yes, I have made one or two coats for him."

"Do you have his account to hand?"

"I think I have it somewhere, sir."

"I understand that the bill on one occasion had been settled by another person?"

"Yes, perhaps..."

"Might I see the ledger?"

The tailor went and fetched it. He found the page, and then turned it reluctantly towards Giles.

"That is a hefty sum," Giles said. "And settled on last quarter day, I see. By whom?"

"I'm afraid I cannot say. I promised I would not. It was an act of private charity."

"Strange sort of charity to pay for such fine clothes," said Giles.

"I suppose," said Loake with a slight shrug.

"Who was it, Mr Loake? Mr Barnes has been murdered, as I am sure you know."

There was a little pause and then Loake turned a page in the ledger and revealed the name to Giles.

"What did he say to you?"

"He said that the young man had got himself into debt – that he was helping him as any Christian would and that I was not to say a word to a soul."

"And that is all you know about this, Mr Loake?" said Giles tapping the open ledger.

"Yes, Major Vernon, all, I swear it."

Giles glanced about him for a moment, his mind suddenly alert to various possibilities, a picture forming in his mind of what might have happened to Charlie Barnes.

"Thank you, Mr Loake. That will be all for now."

Chapter Forty-one

Berthe opened the door to Giles. A look of relief crossed her beautiful face.

"I am glad you sent Madame away," she murmured as they went into the hall. She shut the door behind them quietly, glancing about her fearfully. "He has been here, sir – your young doctor, he came last night and he saw him. Did he tell you?"

"Mr Morgan, you mean?" Berthe nodded. "Is he here now?"

"Non!" said Berthe. "I saw him leave last night at about one. May I go to Madame now? I have her things all ready."

"Yes, she is at the Treasurer's House, across the Precincts. Do you know which house that is?"

"Yes, Monsieur, it has a little courtyard, in front."

"That's the one. My sister is expecting you. Now where is Mrs Ridolfi?"

Berthe indicated that she was upstairs, and Giles was about to go up when suddenly she appeared, alerted no doubt by the sound of his arrival.

"Major Vernon," she said. "I am glad to see you indeed!" She had her hand laid on her breast, in a slightly theatrical gesture. "I have been so worried. My nephew and my sister-in-law, where are they? What *is* going on?"

"Sometimes actions have to be taken decisively, without consultation. I apologise if you were disturbed, but these letters are a serious threat, and cannot be taken lightly."

"Oh, surely they are not? A few most unpleasant phrases, yes, I will admit, but in essence they are just paper threats, with no real force behind them. Of course, you are most gallant,

Major, but —"

"You were upset by that dead bird."

"Yes, well, that was unfortunate, but I do think you are making a great deal about nothing at all. I hate to say it, but I think she has talked it up rather. She admires you — I suppose you have guessed that? A woman will shape her words and her actions to plead her cause, and you must not forget my sister-in-law is celebrated for her histrionic skills."

Feeling the smart of that, Giles wondered how on earth Nancy could have stood to have this woman live with her. He marvelled at her reserves of tolerance. She had been most unwilling to lay any blame on Paulina. But perhaps Paulina was such a fine actress that she could not suspect her.

She was certainly good at smoothing the surface of her extensive resentment, and presenting only smiles. This was not uncommon, especially among women. He remembered the wife of a fellow officer lauding another woman to her face, only to turn on her with alarming savagery in her absence. Paulina Ridolfi had taken a nasty habit and turned it into a way of life. Those letters were a way of realising the considerable force of her anger — and Giles sensed her anger now, as cold and sharp as the steel of her scissors snipping away at the words and letters.

"Perhaps," he said. "But I do not like to take chances. Even a paper threat against a child is something I must take seriously. I am sure you appreciate that."

"Where is my nephew?"

"Safe and in good hands, Mrs Ridolfi. I will not let him come to any harm. And if there is no danger, and I, like you, fervently hope there is none, then we will be able to comfort ourselves with the old maxim 'better safe than sorry.' And given that Mr Morgan does indeed seem to be in Northminster..."

He watched carefully to see how she reacted.

"He is?" she said, placing her hand on her breast again.

"Are you sure? Oh dear."

There it was: the blatant contradiction. How many other lies might she have told him, he wondered, and how long would it take him to wear her down into an admission that she had sent at least some of those letters?

"That is a pretty performance, because you are lying. Come now, ma'am," he said, "if you please!"

"I do not know what you mean. I told you yesterday that I thought it more than unlikely that Mr Morgan would come to Northminster."

"Mr Carswell tells me he was here last night."

"Mr Carswell must be mistaken."

"Come now. Mrs Morgan's maid has told me he was here last night and your husband will no doubt confirm it, though from Mr Carswell's account he is probably our least reliable witness, being somewhat in his cups. I know he was here. Why deny it?"

"He may have been here," she said after a moment.

"Thank you, Mrs Ridolfi, for your candour," Giles said. "Perhaps he told you not to tell," he went on. "I understand that he can be intimidating. Did he intimidate you?"

She frowned slightly.

"Let us go and sit down," he said, indicating the drawing room door. "Shall we?"

They went into the room, and she sat down and began knotting her fingers nervously in her lap.

"You see," he said, placing a chair in front of her, and speaking gently, "you have spoken kindly of him when others have not. But you must not be afraid to tell me the truth. I can and will protect you from him."

There was a long silence and then she said in a small voice, "It was not always so. When I first knew him. Before... before she..."

"You mean Mrs Morgan?"

"Sometimes people are very bad for each other," she said.

"You have perhaps seen that."

"Yes, I have."

"And people always fall in love with the wrong people," she went on.

"You mean, I suppose, and I hope you don't mind my being so frank, that he did not fall in love with you?"

"She turned his head," she said. "There was nothing anyone could have done about it – well, not without behaving like a hoyden. That I would not, could not do. Perhaps I should have done. What do you think? Should I have thrown my cap at him, to use that dreadful phrase? I might have saved him then – from her and from himself!"

"When a man has set himself on a particular course, it is hard to divert him," Giles said.

"Yes!" she exclaimed. "It was a lost cause, and I have had to sit by all this time and watch him suffer at her hands. She has ruined him in every possible aspect, driven him to wickedness with her caprices. If she had only attempted a little to be a good wife then I might be able to forgive her for it, but she has not even tried. Poor Edward – he is such a sorry creature now – he is angry, miserable and depraved. He is wicked because of what she has done to him and she has no sense of it!"

She must have loved him very much, Giles thought, to absolve him of everything. Perhaps she loved him still. It was an interesting possibility.

"And what form does this wickedness take, Mrs Ridolfi?" he asked. "Is there anything specific you would like to tell me about? You must not be afraid now."

"I am not sure what you can be talking about," she said.

"You know what I mean," he said, standing up. "I have two sets of letters in my possession, both couched in the same deeply offensive and terrifying language, but clearly constructed by two different people. There is one set that is made of torn scraps of paper – a clumsy job – whereas the other is as neatly made as the lace of your collar and cuffs. Did you make those, by the way?"

"What if I did?" she said.

"Lay it open to me, Mrs Ridolfi," he said. "You will feel better for it. Tell me all about those letters you so carefully made and placed about the house to scare your poor sister-in-law!"

She leapt up from her chair.

"I had nothing to do with them! How dare you, sir, even suggest that I could..."

"Then Morgan made them all? That does surprise me." Significantly, she turned away from him so he could not read her face. "Do you know what I think happened, Mrs Ridolfi?" he went on. "I think he asked you to do it. He asked you to make some of the letters and leave them here to scare Mrs Morgan, and you all too willingly agreed because of what you feel for him — and more importantly what you do not feel for her, which you have not concealed in the least from me. You wanted to make her suffer, to punish her, I think, for taking the man you loved!"

"What utter nonsense!" she exclaimed, turning back to him. "How dare you even suggest such a thing?"

He was not convinced by this denial. It seemed shrill. He contemplated what to do. He was tempted to take her back to The Unicorn with him at once and scare a full confession out of her. He was sure she was close enough to it — a little judicious pressure would see to it — and yet he decided that he would delay a little while. He wanted to know where Morgan was and what his intentions were — and she was the person most likely to know the answers. Besides, her confession would not necessarily be the whole truth of the matter. It would still be the version of events that she imagined would best suit her purposes at that moment. She was manipulative — that was clear enough.

"I suggest it because I think it is the truth," he said. "And you may be sure that we will be returning to this conversation, soon enough, Mrs Ridolfi. Just one last time – perhaps you might consider telling me where I might find Mr Morgan?"

"No," she said, "because I do not know where he is! And why you think I would – well, I don't know!"

He decided he would leave her be for the present. If she had a conscience it might now trouble her into further honesty – that was often the case – or equally, if she had none, it might be that she would be provoked into a different sort of alarm. She would no doubt want to speak to Morgan and tell him they were rumbled. He would have a constable keep a close eye on her movements.

Besides, he wanted get to the Deanery.

Chapter Forty-two

"Miss Pritchard," Felix said, getting up as she came into the room. He had been made to wait in the same room as before, without even a fire in the grate to give any semblance of cheerfulness. He felt chilled to the bone. It was a cold morning, for all the first glimmering of spring sunshine, and his mood matched his temperature. He was still tired and shocked by what had transpired with Mrs Jackson and he was in no mood for games. He certainly could not manage to smile at her as she came up to him.

"Mr Carswell," she said, and she did not smile either.

"I am glad for a moment alone with you."

"It will only be a moment," she said. "I think my father —"

"Yes, of course. And Lord Rothborough will be here as well. So I will get to the point. Major Vernon has told me about you and Mr Watkins."

"I see. I suppose he would."

"Of course! At least he has been straight with me."

"You must be angry."

"I am trying not to be," he said. "I am trying to be rational and comprehend your behaviour, but it is not easy."

"I will try and explain," she said. "Please?"

"Yes, of course."

"I needed to hide," she said. "It was perhaps not the best hiding place, but you were there and I was desperate. My father had half-discovered that I had a lover, but I could not bear him to know it was Mr Watkins. He was not ready to hear that, and I knew that my mother thought you were suitable, and that generally you would be a far less objectionable

285

candidate. So I used you. It was wicked of me, but I had to do it. My father is so, so —" She covered her face for a moment. "He never used to be like this. He has been so difficult these last months. Ever since that awful business with Sophie's fiancé, no, perhaps even before — something has come over him, some strangeness. I don't know what it is. But the moment I met George, I knew that I loved him, and I knew at the same time my father would never be able to accept it. And so I decided that secrecy was the best course until such time..." She sighed and then glanced round at the sound of the door bell. "That will be Lord Rothborough."

"Yes, and you must not go on pretending, Miss Pritchard, I beg you. If you are afraid of what he will do to you, come with me. I will make sure that no harm comes to you, though I am surprised that Mr Watkins has not taken you away already. How he can stand this, I don't know!"

She did not answer, for at that moment Lord Rothborough was shown in by the servant. His glance took them both in somewhat caustically as she stood close to Felix, her head bowed. Felix quickly took a step away from her, and she suddenly sank in a pool of her skirts, sobbing violently, hiding her face from both of them.

"My dear young woman," Lord Rothborough began, going over to her. "Please." He helped her to her feet and led her gently to the chairs ranged against the wall. Solicitously he sat down beside her and offered her his handkerchief. After a moment's hesitation she took it, and then buried her face in it, twisting away from him, as if she could not bear his kindness any longer.

"She is engaged to Mr Watkins," Felix said. "I was a decoy."

"Aha," said Lord Rothborough. "Mr Watkins, well..."

Felix wondered if he ought to contrive to hint to his Lordship that Major Vernon had further suspicions regarding Miss Pritchard and Barnes' death.

Miss Pritchard seemed to wrench back her dignity then, and got to her feet, scraping her tear-stained face dry.

"It is not as it sounds!" she exclaimed. "You will think it shabby, my lord, no doubt, but, but —"

She broke off, for the Dean himself and Mrs Pritchard were now coming in.

To Felix's surprise, Lord Rothborough went and took Miss Pritchard's hand and patted it.

"Calm yourself," he said. "We shall all proceed calmly," he added, glancing at the Dean and Mrs Pritchard. "That will be the best way to go on, I think."

The Dean looked as if he were about to begin on a torrential speech of rebuttal, when the maidservant came scurrying in and said, "Major Vernon presents his compliments, sir. Says he must speak with you urgently."

Miss Pritchard made a sharp intake of breath at the mention of his name, and aware she had betrayed herself, walked away a little, turning from them all. Perhaps Major Vernon was right in his suspicions, Felix thought, watching her. Could it be possible that she had strangled Barnes?

"He had better come in, had he not?" Mrs Pritchard said, glancing from her daughter to her husband.

"Oh, very well," said the Dean, as if he were granting a great favour.

"Good morning," said Major Vernon. Having acknowledged the company, he turned to the Dean. "I had hoped, sir, that we might speak alone for a moment."

"About what?"

"I have been hearing your name mentioned in interesting quarters."

"What do you mean by that?"

"In the course of my inquiries into the death of Mr Barnes, various individuals have been making allegations."

"It sounds as if you have been listening to malicious tittle-tattle, Major Vernon, in which there can be no truth."

"Indeed, it is more than possible. I have come to get a refutation, which I am sure you will happily give me."

"That sounds less like an opportunity than a threat, Major Vernon," the Dean said.

"Forgive me, it was not intended so," said the Major.

"Allegations?" said Mrs Pritchard. "What sort of allegations?"

"Nothing that you need concern yourself with, my dear," said the Dean.

"But if people are insulting you – I cannot bear the thought of it. Who are these people, Major Vernon? Can they not be stopped? Should you not be stopping them? Why are you giving them credit?"

"A man has been murdered, ma'am. I must turn over every stone. It is not pleasant, of course, and that is why I am here, in order that your husband may put his side."

"But what is it? What are they saying?" she went on.

"Do not disturb yourself, my dear," said the Dean. "Tittle-tattle. You must not worry."

"I will try," she said.

"Mrs Pritchard, may I trouble you a moment?" Major Vernon asked. "Are those your household keys there on your belt?"

"Yes, Major."

"Might I see them?"

"Really, Major Vernon, I must protest –" the Dean began, but she was already holding out the bunch of keys to him.

As she lifted the bunch of keys that hung from a chain on her belt, Felix saw why Major Vernon had asked to see them. Dangling down was a trail of inch-wide white ribbon that stood out strongly against her dark brown skirts. Felix went a step closer to see better for himself.

"What is this key for?" Major Vernon said, pointing to the one suspended on white ribbon.

"To tell you the truth, I do not know," she said. "I found

it the other day. I think it may be to a cupboard upstairs, but I am not sure. I meant to try it but I forgot."

"Where did you find it?"

"In the – er –" she pointed at the window. "In the garden – well, in the necessity."

"The privy, ma'am?" Major Vernon said gently. She nodded. "And that ribbon was on it when you found it?"

"Yes." She turned to her husband. "I forgot about it. I was going to ask you about it, my dear – I thought it might be one of yours. I just put it on here for safekeeping."

"Might I have it?" Major Vernon said. "With the ribbon, if you please."

"I don't see why not," she said. "Perhaps you will solve the mystery of it." She unfastened the key from the metal hoop and handed it to him. He looked at it for a moment.

"Mr Carswell?" he said, glancing round. Felix stepped to his side and examined it, then nodded, answering his unspoken question. The ribbon looked perfectly consistent with the ligature marks on Charles Barnes' neck. Felix wondered if under his microscope he might detect some traces of skin on it. That would settle the matter.

"Thank you, ma'am, you've been most helpful. I am afraid I shall have to keep it."

"What is all this about?" said Dean Pritchard. "First you come here making most unpleasant suggestions, and then you are rifling through my wife's keys –"

"This key is not one of your wife's," said Vernon. "I think we will find this is the missing key to St Anne's Chapel. How it came to be in your privy is another matter. Do you have any thoughts on that, sir?"

"I do not like your tone!" said the Dean.

"You do not have to," said Major Vernon. "You only have to answer my question." The Dean said nothing, so Major Vernon went on, moving one of the chairs and putting it by the fire. "Perhaps the ladies might prefer to sit down; I think we will be a while. Ma'am, would you prefer to sit?"

"Thank you," said Mrs Pritchard, taking a chair. "Miss Pritchard?" asked Vernon, moving her chair for her.

She shook her head.

"But I do have something to say," she said. For a second or two she seemed to be trying to speak but failing. Major Vernon offered her the chair again with an emphatic gesture and she did as she was bidden.

"Miss Pritchard?" he said, crouching down beside her so that their faces were level. "What is it you wish to say?"

There was a long silence and then her words emerged, in a tiny, dry whisper: "I wish to confess to the murder of Charlie Barnes."

"You are sure?"

"Yes," she said, looking Major Vernon directly in the face. "Yes. I killed him."

Major Vernon stood up and shook his head.

"I'm afraid that won't do. Commendable, but it won't do."

"What do you mean?" she said, jumping up. "I killed him! Isn't that enough for you? I killed him. Arrest me. Do what you have to do! I don't care. Just do it!" She thrust her hands out at him as if she meant him to clap the irons on her wrists.

"I cannot arrest someone who has done nothing," said Major Vernon. "Please, Miss Pritchard, do sit down again. You can help me a great deal more by telling the truth. The whole truth. What exactly happened in the tower that day?"

She sat down and Major Vernon again crouched beside her.

"You see," he said, rather quietly. "I think Charles Barnes was not dead when you found him. Perhaps he died in your arms." She looked up at him, as if at an oracle.

"How did you know? How did you guess?" she said.

"I think he told you something that you could not forget — something that prompted your own strange behaviour. If you discovered your own father could murder Mr Barnes, in a fit of outrage, then what might he do to your own dear George? Therefore it became imperative to put him off the scent. Let your unpredictable, violent father take out his fury on a man that you did not care about. Let him think Mr Carswell was your lover. Is that not it, Miss Pritchard?"

She nodded and looked away.

"Major Vernon, are you sure about this?" Lord Rothborough said.

"Oh yes, very sure," said Major Vernon, springing up again. He turned to face the Dean. "John Pritchard, I am arresting you on suspicion of the murder of Charles Barnes."

Chapter Forty-three

Arresting the Dean of Northminster for murder was, of course, no small thing. He noted the surprise on Lord Rothborough's face – Giles wondered if he was shocked by the actual facts of the case or the inevitable political ramifications. The scandal would be considerable. Questions would probably be asked in the House.

Even as the last pieces had begun to fall into place in his mind, Giles had wondered how it ought to be done. He had felt certain of the truth of it the moment he had seen the length of white ribbon dangling from Mrs Pritchard's chatelaine. Fildyke's letter, so pregnant with mystification, was mysterious no more. He was calling in a favour. *"As I have kept my promises, I ask you to help me now."* Fildyke had guessed at the true meaning of the relationship between Barnes and the Dean.

However, to arrest him there and then – he knew that was taking a risk. He only had circumstantial evidence and his instincts to go on, but he wanted to shock Pritchard into a full confession. When Kate Pritchard stepped up to take the blame, unnecessarily, he knew it was a risk he had to take and the moment had to be seized.

Dean Pritchard at once began a great filibuster of protest.

"This is in an outrage, sir. I cannot conceive what you think you are doing –"

Giles reached into his pocket and brought out a pair of cuffs. He did not think he would have to use them. He wanted to scare Pritchard thoroughly.

"You can either leave this house like a gentleman in your own carriage, or I can have you taken away in the police van," he said.

"On what grounds do you make this outrageous –"

"We will discuss that by and by," said Giles. "Now, will you send for your carriage, sir? Ring for the servant, would you, Mr Carswell?"

Carswell obediently went to pull the bell rope, and suddenly the Dean went after him and pushed him away with so much force that Carswell stumbled. Pritchard stood there, looking as if he meant to take on all comers, all his clerical dignity fallen away from him, looking more like the common bully he undoubtedly was.

"My constables are outside," Giles said to Carswell. "Will you fetch them in?" Carswell left the room.

"Do you imagine you will get away with this?" said Pritchard. "Do you know what you are doing?"

"Yes," said Giles. "Your wrists, please."

Needless to say Pritchard did not offer them, so Giles was forced to grab hold of him and do it by force. Pritchard put up lively resistance and it was only when Rollins came in and assisted him that the deed was accomplished.

Rollins took him from the room. When the door had closed, Kate Pritchard choked back her tears and said, "You were right. I came in and found him lying on the floor, he was writhing about – it was terrible. It was clear he was in agony, that he was... I knew George would be with me shortly – I was going to send him to get help, if it was not too late for that. So I sat on the floor with him in my arms, and tried to give him what comfort I could – and he would insist on talking, although his voice was so faint. And he told me... he told me that Papa had attacked him. Of course, I could scarcely believe it, but at the same time, what reason could he have for lying?"

Mrs Pritchard, who was still sitting opposite her daughter, gave a pained gasp and covered her mouth with her hands. Miss Pritchard went across to her mother and knelt in front of her, taking her hands in hers.

"We knew, we all knew, he could be violent, unpredictable, that over time he has grown more difficult," Miss Pritchard said. Mrs Pritchard looked away from them all as her daughter spoke on earnestly, quietly, "And then he died – the poor, poor boy – in my arms, exhausted by the telling of it, leaving me... well, you can imagine how I was by the time George did arrive. I was... oh, it was too dreadful. Too dreadful... I have had nothing but nightmares since then. The thought that my own father could take an innocent life..." She laid her head in her mother's lap and began to cry. Mrs Pritchard made a few ineffectual gestures to smooth her daughter's hair and then gave herself up to her own emotion, which was not pleasant to witness.

"I think we should move your mother to a warmer room," said Carswell, intervening gently. "This is a terrible shock for her." Miss Pritchard seemed to be rallied by being made to be useful, and together they helped her from the room.

"This is going to cause some difficulties," Lord Rothborough said when they were alone. "A more politic man would have given him warning, Vernon. His family might be spared a great deal if you had allowed that. It is dreadful how these things punish the womenfolk. He could perhaps have slipped away to the continent."

"My lord, I trust you are not being serious?" Giles said. "If he is guilty, he will have to swing for it. There can be no bending the law because of his position or profession."

"The Dean of Northminster hanged for murder – the ballad sellers will have a field day. The populace already has scant respect for the clergy and this will not help. And of course, the Dissenters will use this to have an excellent pop at the established Church."

"I think the Church can survive a little mud-slinging."

"At least he did not get his mitre," said Rothborough with a shudder. "That is a mercy for which we should be grateful."

Felix made up a mild sedative for Mrs Pritchard, and, with Miss Pritchard, helped her into bed. She was still shaking with shock, but gradually the opiate and the warm room calmed her.

"You'll need someone to watch her."

"I will not leave her," said Miss Pritchard, who stood by the bed, her mother's hand in hers.

"And you...?" he searched for what to say.

"I will be all right," she said. "Thank you – you have been so kind, when you have every right to be furious with me."

"Would you like me to fetch Mr Watkins?" he said, after a moment.

"He will be busy with the Festival," she said. "I don't wish to disturb him."

"Will that go on now?"

"I think it should. More than ever. Music is a great defence in time of trouble, and we have plenty of that, don't you think?" She sighed and turned back to her mother, who was now sleeping peacefully, and passed her hand over her forehead. "Oh, how is she going to bear all this? How do people bear it?" She adjusted the cover and went over to the window. "I think it made me mad when I knew what he had done. For which I apologise, Mr Carswell, for what it made me do to you. I did not mean –"

"That really doesn't matter."

"You made me an offer, and it was so kind, and I was most ungracious. I do hope you do not think I am really so false. I am not like that. It was just that things were so complicated. In other circumstances, then..."

She looked across at him, her eyes red and wet with tears, her face blotchy, her hair half falling down, and he saw the beauty in it. He thought of all those odd moments of intimacy he had shared with her, and how she seemed to understand him. If she were married to Watkins, it would no longer be possible to continue with any sort of friendship with her, and the thought pained him.

She put out her hand to him.

"I am so sorry," she said again.

He took her hand briefly and squeezed it.

"Will you be all right? I have to go and check on one of my patients. She lost a baby this morning and I am not sure she will pull through. But I can come back later."

"Then you must go at once. We will manage here."

So he left and walked briskly down from the Precincts to the Jacksons' house. The heavy rain of the previous night had cleared but the wind remained, ferocious, pursuing people down the steep, damp cobbled streets of the city like a wild animal. On entering the Jacksons' house, the door slammed violently behind him, and the crone-like old neighbour, who had come in to help, muttered to him about the darkness of the day and God's wrath. He wondered, as he made his way upstairs, what she would think of the Dean being arrested for murder. It would probably sound like the end of days to her.

He was glad to discover that Mrs Jackson was much improved, and although weak and miserable from her loss, Felix felt that she would recover her full strength with some careful nursing, though it might be inadvisable for her to attempt another pregnancy. This was a delicate matter to discuss with a man and his wife at the best of times. Now, as Jackson pumped his hand and thanked him heartily for all he had done, it was not the moment to tell him that he ought to embark upon a course of chastity for the sake of his wife's health. One of the chief prizes of marriage could not be easily relinquished, Felix thought, imagining himself in Jackson's boots. How would he feel being asked to forswear that?

As he walked back to The Unicorn, he debated the question. Did all men, he wondered, live in this same torment with which he was afflicted – this constant, distracting longing for sexual congress? Perhaps other men felt it less in the first place. Perhaps it was schooled by marriage, and domestic affection, but that brought miseries of its own. Was it better to watch a wife almost die of childbirth or suffer a miserable existence as a bachelor, being reduced to getting dirty comfort from whores?

He stopped to remove a stray piece of paper that had attached itself to his boot and found he was looking at the flyer for the Handel Festival that evening.

"Mrs Morgan: Airs from Handel's Oratorios: Esther, Messiah and Theodora." How extraordinary was the effect that her name had on him, even when it was on a rain-sodden scrap of paper.

He threw it to the ground. He felt he had put his foot into a man-trap.

Chapter Forty-four

Predictably, Dean Pritchard went silent. He refused to speak a word until he had seen his solicitor. He asked for old Mr Eames, but since he was the coroner he could not be asked to act, and young Mr Eames, who might have been acceptable, had gone away for a few days. In the end, Giles had asked Mr Johnson to see him. Mr Johnson was not as lofty a personage as Mr Eames, having his practice among the middling sorts of Northminster. However, he did have a good grasp of the criminal law, being an energetic Methodist with an active conscience which often prompted him to work for no fee. He had often caused problems for Giles in front of the Justices, having a strong sense of vocation to defend the indefensible, and he accepted the challenge of acting for Dean Pritchard with a mixture of proper Christian regret and intellectual excitement.

Giles was waiting impatiently to hear the outcome of their first interview, when he was brought a message from one of the constables he had set watching Mrs Ridolfi. She had indeed left the house in the Minster Precincts, and had gone to The Greyhound Tavern from which she had not yet emerged.

He left at once, taking a sergeant and two constables.

The Greyhound in Bridle Street was a dusty establishment, much in need of a lick of paint. A quick enquiry with the landlord revealed that no one was staying there under the name of Morgan, but there was a tall burly Welshman, calling himself Jones, who had come back very late last night. "Almost didn't let him in, but he was a loud-mouthed bugger, and I didn't want to cross him," he said.

"And he's had a visitor this afternoon?"

"Aye, a woman came in just after noon. A classy piece."

"Take me to his room, would you?"

He led Giles and his men up a dark, twisting stair smelling of boiled cabbage, stale beer and tobacco smoke.

"That's the one," said the landlord, banging on the door. "Open up now, Mr Jones, I've more visitors for you."

There was a delay of a few moments and then the sound of the door bolt being drawn. The door opened, revealing Mrs Ridolfi. She looked Giles squarely in the eyes as she stood back to let them in.

"Where is he?" he said, looking about the shabbily furnished room. There was no sign of another occupant. "Where is Morgan?"

"I don't know," she said. "I told you that this morning."

"Is there another way out?" Giles said to the landlord.

"Down the backstairs," said the landlord. "Takes you into the kitchen and out through the yard."

"You stay there, ma'am," said Giles and went down to the kitchen.

The kitchen boy confirmed that Morgan, alias Jones, had left about half an hour ago. "And in a black fury," the boy said.

He went back upstairs and found Mrs Ridolfi seated on a stool in the window, watched over by Sergeant Baines.

Giles glanced about the room, noting the disordered bedclothes, the flush of her cheeks and the fact that she had taken off her cloak, bonnet and gloves.

"You must have known I would have you followed, ma'am," he said.

She shrugged, and adjusted her collar. The primness of her attitude now seemed assumed and he noted her hair was arranged differently from how it had been a few hours ago. There was something clumsy about it now, as if she had put it back up without any assistance.

"Did Berthe do your hair this morning, Mrs Ridolfi?"

"What has my hair to do with anything?"

"Men notice these things more than you think," Giles said. "It looks different from how it was earlier, as if you have had to take it down and put it up again. Why might that be, I wonder?"

"What an extraordinary thing to say," she said.

"You must expect me to be a little insolent, Mrs Ridolfi, since I find you here, in these compromising circumstances. When you have lied to me about his whereabouts."

"I do not know where he is," she said. "I told you so, this morning."

"That is feeble," he said. "He has been here with you – that is clear enough. You told me that you had not the least idea where he is, and yet here you are, having consorted with him."

"Consorted – what do you mean by that?"

"What do you think I mean?"

"I do not like to say what you are thinking, sir," she said. "And I am very shocked that you could think such a thing."

"This little performance will have to stop, Mrs Ridolfi. It will get tiresome very quickly. You told me yourself you had feelings for Mr Morgan. Everything about this room indicates you have acted upon them. And the fact that you are protecting him still only confirms it."

"Do you mean to imply –?"

"Yes," he said. "You and Morgan are lovers and together you have conspired to send those letters to your sister-in-law. Your hand is all over them and you shall not shift the blame easily from yourself, not now you have proved yourself such a liar. If you had been straight with me, Mrs Ridolfi, and told me he was your lover, and not led me this foolish dance, then things might stand a little better for you, but now..."

She glanced up at him.

"Yes, yes, all right, yes, I did make some of them!" she said after a minute. "But he made me do it. I had no choice about it. I told you he was wicked, did I not? He made me do it. I could not say no. That is what he is like. That is what he has become!"

"And that is why you came here today?" he said. "He forced you?"

"Yes, yes!" she said.

Giles nodded but he still had a nagging doubt in the back of his mind. He wondered who was really at the root of the plot. She was happy to claim to be Morgan's puppet, but was it not equally possible that she might be pulling his strings?

"So why do you think Morgan has come to Northminster?" he said, sitting down again. "Did he tell you what his intentions were?"

"No."

"Did you expect him?"

"No."

"But presumably you told him that you were all coming here? He knew just where to send the letters and where to find you."

"Yes, I told him that."

"It was part of your scheme, yes, of course."

"*His* scheme. He made me, I told you that, Major Vernon!"

"How?"

"I am sorry?"

"How did he make you do it? Did he threaten you? Or hurt you? There must have been some coercion, I think, to make you do something so out of character. It takes something considerable to drive a good woman to a criminal act."

"I told you – he made me do it. That is how he is."

"How, precisely?"

"Is it important?"

"Yes, I wish to establish the degree of his culpability – and how responsible you are. So it is important. Vagueness will not help you at all, Mrs Ridolfi, and you are going to need all the help you can get. What you have done is no small thing; I hope you understand that and are ready to cooperate fully with me. Yes?" She nodded. "So this scheme, let us begin with the scheme – when and how did that come about?"

"I cannot honestly remember," she said with a little shrug. He very much doubted her honesty in that moment.

"Come now," he said. "You must remember something. Perhaps you will remember better if we were to have this conversation at the constabulary headquarters, ma'am."

"Do you mean to arrest me?"

"Yes. But the more you cooperate the better it will be for you. I wish to save you some pain and humiliation by getting the full story. If you please, ma'am?"

He hoped this flourish might nudge her into more revelations, but at the same time he took out his notebook to show her that whatever she said would be on record.

Now she nodded and sat, every inch the submissive woman, her hands folded in her lap, her head slightly bowed.

"So tell me about this scheme of Morgan's, that you were apparently forced into. Did he tell you what he intended by it?"

"To give her a good scare," she said.

"For what reason?"

"I told you – she humiliated him. He wanted her to feel something of the pain she had caused him."

"And so he hit on this idea?"

"Yes."

"It is rather a strange business. Does he intend to act on his threats, do you know?"

"Of course not!"

"But you say he is a monster of wickedness and depravity. Why are you so certain he will not act on them? If he has taken so much trouble and recruited you, by whatever means, to do this thing, how do you know that?"

"Because he... he is not so far gone as that. He means only to scare her. That is all. Is it not bad enough that he has been driven to it?"

He got up and walked up the room a little, and then turned back to her.

"You are so protective of him, even now," he said. "I begin to worry that... well, it is often the case that a woman who is so protective of a man is often his greatest victim. I see a great deal of this. Has he ever been violent towards you?"

"No, never!" she said, and with such firmness that this time he did believe her. She was not a beaten wife desperately hiding the truth of her husband's violence from herself with endless denials – he had seen that enough times to recognise the symptoms. There was something far more complicated and unusual going on.

"Yet you claim he forced you into all this? How?"

"He has a power over people," she said after a moment. "That is it. That is how it happened. I cannot explain. I wish I could."

"And you will not tell me where he is?"

"I swear it, I do not know. I will swear on the Bible I do not know where he has gone!"

Giles wondered if he would be better spending his time now looking for Morgan than listening to Mrs Ridolfi's misdirections.

"Sergeant Baines, escort Mrs Ridolfi back to HQ, and charge her. Tomorrow you can see what the Justices think of your stories, ma'am."

He held out her bonnet to her.

"They will see a woman who has been forced against her will," she said, getting up and taking it from her. "They will have more gallantry and pity than you, sir, as God is my witness!"

After they had gone, Giles went back down to the kitchen, where he found the boy scouring the pots in the scullery.

"When you said he was in a black fury – what made you think that?" he asked.

"He was all riled up, like a mad dog," said the boy. "And he was full of liquor. I could smell the brandy on him. He knocked over that bench on his way out. I only saw his face for a minute, but it was like you'd cross the street to avoid him, if you know what I mean, sir. I've seen my old man like that and know to get out of his way."

Giles left by the kitchen door, making his way along the dank court that lay behind The Greyhound, through a regular nest of rookeries, of the sort that were becoming depressingly common in Northminster. There was only one way out, through a narrow passageway which gave into Fishmonger Street, one of the ancient streets that led up the steep hill to the Minster Precincts. He glanced at his watch as he emerged. Morgan could be anywhere by now.

He caught sight of a clutch of bills, glued to a wall. One read, "Under the patronage of the Handel Festival at the Minster: the celebrated Mrs Morgan."

He ripped one of the bills from the wall, and stuffed it into his pocket. She was in the wretch's plain sight – with a place and time helpfully given.

~

Giles found her alone in his sister's little drawing room, her half-finished needlepoint parrot lying on her lap and her needle in her hand, but her attention seemed fixed on the fire. He stopped at the threshold, partly because he was moved by the charm of what he saw, and partly in order to hold himself in check. It would have been so easy, despite all they had said, to go and kiss the nape of her neck.

"Good afternoon," he said, gently.

She turned her head and smiled at him. It was enough. It implied everything, and nothing else needed to be said.

He went and sat on the other chair by the fire and rested his elbows on his knees, his chin on his knotted hands.

"I have come to ask a favour," he said.

"Ask away," she said, fixing her needle into the canvas.

"You will not like it, I think," he said.

"Ask," she said.

"I want you to cancel your performance."

"Oh."

"I knew you would not like it."

She nodded. "You are right."

"I have failed. I cannot lay my hands on Morgan, and until I have got him where I can see him I do not want to risk it."

"I cannot cancel," she said.

"You must."

"No," she said. "I never cancel."

"Even when your husband sends you death threats?"

"A threat is not a promise. He won't act on it. He is too much of a coward – and too lazy."

"And you are too brave. I sincerely advise you to cancel. We cannot guarantee your safety."

She got up and stood looking down at the fire. Then she turned to him, took his hand, squeezed it and said, quietly, "You are gallant, and loving, my dear, but I cannot cancel. You understand that, I think, or you would not be asking with such trepidation in your voice."

"Is that how it sounds?"

"Yes. You are afraid I will not obey."

"I am not asking you for obedience," he said. "You know that. I am asking you to consider your own safety."

"Yes, I know. I am sorry, that was harsh of me. But I must be plain with you, Giles, I think you are being too careful

– you are letting your heart rule your head, for which I am both happy and sad. I know what it means. But then again, I had thought you might think more of me than to put me in a gilded cage, like all the others." He could not prevent himself wincing. "It is unworthy of you to make me cancel," she said.

He got up and stood next to her, also looking down at the fire.

"I cannot help my fear," he said. "I can't help wanting to protect you. And don't be so cruel, for God's sake, Nan."

"I am teaching you not to care so much. It is necessary. I want you to feel very little for me. Carelessness – that is what we agreed, did we not?"

"Yes," he said. "We did."

"We have no alternative."

He might have pulled her into his arms that moment, such was the fragility of his resolution, but instead he forced himself to walk away from her.

"At least, though, I can put some men to watch over you," he said after a moment. "If you are so determined to do it."

"You should not divert so much of your force to protect such an unworthy object."

"I can never think of you as that."

"Oh dear God, but you must, you must! We agreed – we agreed, did we not?"

"Yes," he said, his throat drying.

"Then will you let me perform?" She stood with her hands stretched out to him, in an attitude of such elegant solicitation that he felt like a piece of melted wax.

"I can't stop you, can I?" he said.

"I am glad you see it."

"The pity of it is, most likely I shall not be able to be there. I would feel easier if I could be, but I suspect that..." He could not prevent a sigh. "I have a man who will not talk and I must make him. When all I want is to..." He gazed at her, ashamed to the degree that he was allowing himself to give in to his feelings. "Forgive me. I am forgetting our bargain. I had better go. The sight of you does me no good. I did not mean to come. I have disturbed you. Forgive me."

He snatched her hand, kissed it briefly and departed the room.

He met Sally in the hall.

"Giles, what is the matter?" she said.

"Nothing," he said carefully, and left.

~

"So, Mr Johnson, what does your client say?"

"He wishes to sue you for wrongful arrest, Major Vernon."

"You have made it clear to him that there is enough evidence to hang him?"

"I am not sure about that, Major Vernon. Miss Pritchard's testimony and her peculiar circumstances will be viewed sceptically by a jury. She has shown herself to be capable of considerable deceit, whereas my client's reputation remains intact."

"What do you think, Mr Johnson, personally?"

"I cannot give you my opinion on that, Major Vernon. I am surprised you asked me. Can it be that you are not too sure about the circumstances that have caused you to arrest him? If you are uncertain at all, you ought to release him. You will save yourself a great deal of embarrassment and a costly lawsuit."

"I have nothing to be embarrassed about," said Giles. "I am perfectly satisfied with Miss Pritchard's testimony, and I am sure an able prosecution advocate will be able to show the jury that her conduct does not discredit her word. And she is not my sole witness." He gestured at the wall where all his papers and notes were pinned. "There is a strong case against him that the Crown can and will make. Tell him that, Mr Johnson, and advise him in the strongest terms to come clean."

"That is for you to do, Major Vernon," said Mr Johnson.

Giles nodded, realising he had no alternative than to wear the man down with questioning. He went along to the room where they were holding him, and looked through the window cut in the door. Pritchard was sitting at the table, looking not the least like a guilty man, but stiff-necked and self-righteous. Giles wondered how he would begin with him.

Find the weak point, he told himself. What was the thing that made the Dean so angry? What had Charles Barnes done or said to make the Dean so incandescent with anger that he had strangled him?

The Dean realised he was being observed and turned his gaze towards the hatch. Giles retreated a little so he should not be seen, and went quietly back to his office. There he took out the marquetry box that had so vexed Harrison. It was a handsome, expensive object, a lover's gift. It was not the gift of some man who wished to steer a young man from a dangerous path, or save his soul. It was a great deal more personal.

He opened it again and studied it with more care than he had previously done. Before he had been distracted by its contents. Now he was looking more carefully at the box itself. There was a piece of baize in the base which slid out of place revealing a slip of folded paper hiding beneath. Giles unfolded it and saw, written out in a careful hand quite different from Harrison's very distinctive scrawl, a single sentence in Latin: "*O crudelis Alexi, nihil mea carmina curas?*"

~

"How is your Latin, Mr Carswell?" Major Vernon asked, coming into his consulting room. "They never managed to knock more than the rudiments of it into me at school, and I have forgotten that much. As a university man you will have the edge on me."

He handed a long thin paper to Felix, who scowled at it.

"It was not my strongest point either," he said. "I think it is something like, cruel Alexi, don't you care for my songs? Virgil, perhaps, but do not quote me on that."

"That's interesting, to say the least," said Major Vernon. "I need a sample of Dean Pritchard's handwriting. He may have written this. Virgil, you think?"

"Are you certain that it was the Dean?"

"Yes, but I want a confession – no, I need one. Otherwise I shall never get it to stick. The moment the news gets abroad that I am trying to get him for this, all the forces of reaction will be against us, and he will be allowed to wriggle out of my grasp. I need this signed and sealed in the next twenty-four hours before his powerful friends come here and make havoc. But this is excellent, Mr Carswell," he said tapping the paper. "A great help. Oh, and I have a special charge for you: Mrs Morgan."

"Mrs Morgan?" Felix said, unable to keep a note of suspicion out of his voice.

"Yes, I would like you to keep an eye on her. I am worried about Morgan and what he might be planning."

"You might well be," said Felix, "given that he seemed certain you had gone off on an assignation with her."

Major Vernon gave him a warning glance which made him wonder more than ever if he was lying. What had really passed between them?

"I have instructed a couple of constables to stay close to her, of course," the Major continued, "but I would like you to assist in this, since you of all of us actually know what Morgan looks like. If you spot him in the crowd, I want you to tell the constables at once."

Felix nodded, not trusting himself to speak.

"You will have the pleasure of hearing her sing when I shall not," Major Vernon said.

"Which you regret, I think," Felix said.

"Yes, of course. She has an extraordinary voice." He frowned. "And whatever fancies you are weaving about the lady and myself, Mr Carswell, I can assure you, as I did earlier, that nothing –"

"I cannot believe you, sir," Felix cut in. "You are the last man in the world to lie, but I cannot take you at your word on this. You are lying to save her reputation, which you seem to care inordinately about, which makes me think that –"

"A respectable woman's reputation is something one must always care about."

"If she is respectable. From what Morgan said – well, and Mrs Ridolfi – the implication was clear enough!"

There was a moment's silence. Then Major Vernon spoke in a careful, quiet voice.

"You are letting your imagination rule your reason, Mr Carswell. Perhaps you have been reading too many lewd books. They are dangerous stuff for an unmarried man. Besides, what may or may not have passed between us is hardly your business, is it?"

He seemed to be waiting for an answer, but Felix declined to give him one. Instead, after a moment had passed he said, "I will of course, do as you wish. Though I doubt she will care much for me as a guard dog."

"If you stay civil, she will not object," said Major Vernon. "And keep your ungenerous opinions to yourself, if you please! You may abuse me all you like – but if I hear that you have broached this with her, you will have to answer to me for it! She is at my sister's house – if you would escort her from there to the Minster, I would be grateful."

Chapter Forty-five

Having assembled Mr Johnson, Superintendent Rollins, and Barker to act as clerk, it was time for Giles to begin his interview.

"I have often observed," said Giles, sitting down in front of Dean Pritchard, "that when I have a man in here, accused of some dreadful crime, he finds it a great relief to talk to me in detail about what has happened."

"I will not talk to you," said Pritchard.

"For such a wretch it is often the first step to redemption. I have seen a great change come over men, when they have confessed it all to me," Giles went on, "and when the burden of the deed is laid down. After that they will often talk to a clergyman and are guided to seek God's grace."

"What do you know of God's grace?" said Pritchard.

"Not enough, probably. I am a sinner who does not examine his conscience as much as he should. But the behaviour of those poor prisoners always reminds me that I ought to address my faults more plainly and also that I can take heart, knowing that I can be forgiven for them by a loving Saviour, if I truly repent of them."

Giles felt a little as if he were parroting his catechism, but he hoped a show of piety might make the Dean uneasy, or at least more cooperative.

"You will have a great deal to repent of when this business is over," said Pritchard. "And I pray you see it sooner rather than later, sir, that I am entirely innocent of this crime, and all your outrageous accusations will turn to dust in your mouth!"

"It would help me, then, if you were to demonstrate

where I am in error. I have put the pieces of the picture together wrongly, perhaps? Is that it?"

"Perhaps?" said Pritchard. "Definitely."

"Then you might help me to rearrange them. That would be better than you staying silent, if you could help me find the culprit. I would be grateful, sir. It would give me great pleasure to be wrong in this case, believe me."

"You *are* wrong," said the Dean, leaning forward, and stubbing his finger on the table to make his point. "Your conclusions are entirely erroneous."

He believes himself cleverer than me, Giles thought with pleasure.

"Then you will help me correct them?" he asked, in his most humble tone, intending to encourage Pritchard to begin a course of lies.

There was a long pause and then Dean said, "Yes, I suppose I must – if only to finish this ridiculous charade."

"Mr Johnson," Giles said, "do you wish to talk to your client alone for a moment?"

The Dean waved his hand. "Mr Johnson may leave if he wishes," he said.

"I do not think, sir, that would be advisable," said Mr Johnson said.

"I am an innocent man!" exclaimed the Dean. "Major Vernon has just admitted as much. I do not need you now, sir!"

A nice show of bravado, Giles thought, and liable to lead him into great trouble. But if he felt he was safe, then let him think that he was. He was far more likely to say something incriminating in such a mood. It was only a question of gently leading him through the maze.

Mr Johnson gathered up his papers and said, "If you are certain, sir?"

"Yes, yes. Send me your account. Thank you for your time," said the Dean.

Mr Johnson left looking uneasy, but the dismissal was clear. If the Dean wanted to hang himself then he could not be stopped from doing so, and Giles felt a quiet triumph at having achieved that much. Yet he would have to proceed slowly and carefully. Once prised open, the oyster might all too easily clam up again.

"I am grateful for whatever help you can give us, sir," said Giles.

"I am glad you are viewing matters in a different light now," said the Dean. "What were you thinking, sir?"

"It is this profession. It makes me suspicious. Forgive me."

"We must not let our work degrade us," said the Dean.

"No," said Giles. "Now perhaps we can begin with poor Mr Barnes. I know that you were taking a charitable interest in him."

"Yes."

"What form did that take, this charitable interest?"

"He was liable to go astray and I wished to prevent that, naturally."

"Naturally," said Giles. "In what manner was he going astray? The more specific you can be, the more it will help me."

"He was keeping bad company, with the people you should be talking to – Harrison, for one."

"Harrison, yes, of course. You considered him a great threat?"

"He is an evil wretch, yes. He corrupted Charles."

"How do you know this?"

"Charles told me."

"So he confided in you?"

"Yes, of course. As I have just said. I was trying to help him back onto a more virtuous path. My interest was strictly pastoral."

"Really?"

"Yes," said the Dean. "Of course."

"Paying a young man's tailor's bill might be misconstrued by some. I seem to have done so myself. The gesture was entirely innocent, then?"

"I did not pay any bills for him."

"Are you sure, sir? Mr Loake seemed sure that you did."

"Mr Loake must be mistaken."

"Then who else might have paid off his bill? Do you have any idea? Mr Loake seemed sure that it was you. Your name is even in the ledger."

"I may have contributed something," said the Dean after a moment.

"If, as you say, you were trying to help him, then it seems admirable to have done so. I ran up terrible bills with my tailor as a young man. I would have been lucky to have such a friend. It would have saved me a great deal of embarrassment."

"I did not wish him to save him embarrassment," said the Dean. "I wished to save his soul. Embarrassment would have done him some good – as no doubt it did you, Major Vernon."

"Do you feel that Charles was sufficiently grateful for your kindness?" Giles said.

The Dean did not answer but twisted up his mouth.

"Then he disappointed you?" Giles asked.

"I would not say that," said the Dean, after a pause, and there was something about the denial that did not convince Giles.

"Might I ask what drew you to him in the first place, as a cause?" Giles went on.

"I try to do good where I can."

"But Charles, specifically? You must forgive me – I did not know him in life. Describe him to me, if you can. What was it about him?"

"I saw a young man being led from the path of virtue into a life of irredeemable vice. I had to act."

"Of course, of course. There is nothing worse than to see something so fresh and beautiful grow tainted. Charles was an extremely handsome young man, was he not?"

"I don't know what you are driving at, sir," said Dean Pritchard.

"Surely that was why Harrison was attracted to him – his great beauty. If Charles had been a pock-marked hunchback he would hardly have been in any great danger from those elements, would he? Even with his exceptional singing voice. It was his beauty that put him in that particular moral danger, I think."

"Yes, I suppose so. It was not something that was uppermost in my mind."

"But it was a consideration, his beauty?"

"I was aware of it, yes, but no more than that. What are you trying to imply?"

"I was only thinking that we are sometimes more aware of the faults in others that mirror our own private inclinations. We are more aware of another man's danger, because we understand the precise meaning of such temptations. You knew Charles was in danger because you felt the danger for yourself. You understood its meaning."

"I hope that is not another accusation, Major Vernon."

"It is an observation I would like you to consider. Charles struck you as in danger, because you understood that danger for yourself. It was something you perhaps once struggled with."

"Major Vernon –"

"Come, come, sir. We have both been away at school. We know what young men may get up to if not properly supervised, the passions that can arise."

"Yes, but God gave me the strength to eschew such degradations. That is what I hoped to achieve with Charles."

"And do you think you did save him?"

"I... I.... pray to God, yes, and that he knew redemption at the last."

"It must have been a horrible death. It will not have left him much time for prayers, to be attacked mercilessly by someone he considered a friend. I cannot imagine what he suffered." Giles studied the Dean to see if this provoked any reaction, but he remained impassive. "Did you see Charles on the day he died?" he asked.

There was a long hesitation and then the Dean shook his head.

"You are certain?" Giles pressed on. "Not even briefly?"

"Perhaps," said the Dean, glancing away. "Briefly."

"Where?" said Giles, quietly, carefully concealing his feeling of pleasure at this small admission.

"I don't remember," said the Dean.

"I appreciate it is painful for you to recall, given the circumstances," Giles went on in his most sympathetic tone. "But please, if you could remember. Did he come to see you?"

"No, it was... a mere chance that I did see him."

"And where was that?"

"In the chapel."

"That would be St Anne's Chapel?"

There was a slight pause and the Dean inclined his head.

"And how did this chance meeting happen?"

The Dean considered for a moment, scratching his temple and glancing about the room.

"I think I saw an open door, and since that door should not be open, I went to see why."

"And you were surprised to find Charles there?"

"Not entirely," the Dean said. "I had sometimes met him there before for our pastoral conversations."

"Did you give him the key to the chapel, perhaps?"

"I may have given him a key at some point."

"So when you saw the door open, you knew he might be there, knowing he had a key?" Again he nodded. "And so you went to see if it was Charles?"

"Yes."

"And you did not see anyone else in the area as you went in?"

"No, no one."

"And can you tell me what time this was?"

"No, I don't recall. Some time that morning. I am sorry I cannot be more precise. I am not in the habit of timing all my comings and goings for the benefit of an officious police enquiry."

"Forgive me," said Giles. "So you went up to the chapel and found Charles there?"

"Yes."

"That must have given you some pleasure. To find him there?"

"I suppose so."

"You went up expressly to see if he was there. In the hope of finding him."

"That was in my mind."

"Was there any particular reason you wanted to speak to him?"

"I do not think so."

"He had not told you he was thinking of leaving Northminster?"

"We may have discussed that."

"I would imagine it would be more than a discussion," said Giles, "given that he was intending to go away with Harrison. Surely you wished to advise him strongly against it."

"Yes, yes, of course," said the Dean rather vaguely, as if he very much wished to avoid anything more specific.

"If I were you, I would have read him the riot act," Giles said. "Did you?"

There was a long pause.

"I let him know my feelings," he said at length. "I advised him not to go."

"And what did he say to that?" Giles said.

"That he was decided. So I left. I was angry, of course, but I left."

"And what time was this when you left?"

"I think it may have been about eleven," said the Dean. "I think I heard the clock chiming the hour as I walked back to the Deanery."

"And that is all that passed between you?"

"Yes. I was there for a few minutes, that is all. It was a fruitless conversation. Very distressing."

"I am sure it was," Giles said, getting up.

He picked up his notebook and began to look through his notes.

"So is that all, Major Vernon?" asked Dean Pritchard. "I trust that –"

"No, not quite," said Giles, "if you please. What I find interesting is that Mr Harrison says that he was angry with Charles because he had said he would *not* go to London. He is specific – they had a heated argument and Harrison left at about ten thirty, and we have a witness who saw him leave. And then you were there at eleven and he was still alive."

"I am not sure it was eleven..."

"But it does not matter, does it, since you left him alive? As did Harrison, which is interesting. Now, whom should I believe?"

"That is a ridiculous question given his notorious character."

"Yes, but facts are facts. I have not a scrap of evidence against Mr Harrison. The key to the chapel did not turn up in his privy. He has never had a key to that chapel. He did not give it to Charles in order that they might meet there for trysts. You gave Charles that key, and he wore it on a ribbon about his neck – a sentimental gesture if ever I saw one. Charles decided to stay because of you, Dean Pritchard. That is what he told you when you went to speak to him. He chose you over Harrison."

"He did not say that, I have told you! Why do you say that? It is foolish of you, Major Vernon. You ruin your own case. Why would I have strangled a man who... who..."

"Who told you he loved you?" Giles cut in. "Is that not what happened? He told you he was not going away, that your affection, your care and your protection meant more to him than Harrison. I am not surprised. Harrison could not afford such expensive tailoring. Harrison did not buy him handsome presents. You treated Barnes like a mistress, Pritchard, that is undeniable."

"I absolutely refute this," said the Dean.

"You may, of course, but you have form," said Giles. "I know you have these inclinations. Fildyke has been most cooperative. He has sold you a fair few lewd books over the years, and he also told me all about a young lodger of his, whom you paid handsomely for the pleasure of buggering – which is, as I think you know, sir, a hanging offence."

Dean Pritchard stared at him.

"I can find that young man easily enough," Giles went on. "And I don't suppose he was the only instance of your giving into temptation. I knew a man once, a senior officer in another regiment, who was addicted to the pleasures of young men. We young fellows all had tales to tell of it, though he had learned to prey only on the enlisted men, who would often submit for a shilling or two. He was a good Christian, that was the interesting thing about him, and he struggled violently against it, but he never seemed able to overcome it. In the end he killed himself rather than sin again. Self-murder – it was a great tragedy. I thought of him when I saw your wife with that key this morning, and again, when Fildyke told me the names of the books he had sold you over the years. You are like that poor fellow, Dean Pritchard, and you do not like yourself for it. You are angry at yourself. No doubt you have thought of destroying yourself. You have probably prayed a great deal for deliverance from your sin, from your dark desires that you know rank high among the abominations in God's sight! And to have Charles say he loved you, to know that this sweet, trusting boy felt something for you, and saw into your heart..."

The Dean seemed to be having a little difficulty breathing. He certainly would not look Giles in the face. Giles went on softly.

"It was more than you could bear. A temptation too great for you to stand. I think you embraced him and then you strangled him so that he could not tempt you any more. You destroyed him because you could not bear your feelings any more, the feelings he produced in you. You put away temptation so that you could live a righteous life once more. You wanted to be at peace."

"I could not, I would not allow him to destroy everything!" Pritchard said.

"So instead, you destroyed him?" Giles said.

There was a long silence, and then the Dean stood up and said, "He was lost. Lost."

Giles stood also and met his gaze. "So you killed him?"

The Dean's hands went up, in a gesture that was both defensive and aggressive.

"It had to be done. I was protecting myself from sin. I looked into his face and saw he had been eaten up by sin. All his protestations of affection, of loyalty, his submission to me – it was false. It was no submission. It was the wiles of the Devil, in the form of Charles Barnes. I had to stamp on the serpent to free myself."

As the Dean spoke he advanced around the table towards him. Giles caught Rollins' eye and saw he was on his guard, and ready if need be. He could press him a little further.

"How did you stamp on the serpent?" Giles said.

"God himself told me to take up the sword of righteousness!" the Dean said. "And He is speaking to me now – of other serpents, who pretend that they are Christian men but who have not a jot of virtue in them!" With which he lunged towards Giles and attempted to fasten his hands about his neck. He was successful only for a moment. Rollins had soon dragged him away from Giles, and in a smart manoeuvre, pushed his head down against the table, and got his hands behind his back so that Giles could put handcuffs on him again.

"Serpents!" the Dean screeched, his cheek squashed against the table. "God will punish you all. He will forgive me! I am sure of it!"

"You had better be," said Giles, "because I don't think a jury will."

Chapter Forty-six

Left alone with his thoughts, Felix could not help but regard the Major's words as a confession. He was again consumed with misery at the thought that she should so lightly bestow her favours elsewhere and yet reject him so summarily. Worse still, he was now obliged to go and be pleasant and civil to her, just to please Major Vernon, whom he had no desire in that moment to please.

She owed him nothing, of course; she had been plain as anything with him – of this he tried to remind himself and put himself in a careless state as he made his way to the Treasurer's House. But his sense of resentment burned within him, like a chemical fire, not easily extinguished. He could only think that if she permitted him some of the liberties that she seemed so readily to allow other men, then her spell might be broken. Only then might he begin to master himself and this foolish obsession. It was the fact that her door was so plainly barred to him that was driving him to distraction. He had not thought he had such a stock of pride and self-love, but apparently he did.

He arrived to find her standing in the hall, drawing on her gloves and thanking Mrs Fforde for her kindness.

"Major Vernon has sent me as your escort," he said.

"Your brother is most unnecessarily solicitous," Mrs Morgan said to Mrs Fforde, and then turned to him: "I do hope you are not being kept from anything more important. You must have many calls to make."

"I am at your disposal, ma'am," he said, offering his arm. She did not take it and he felt foolish, so he went and opened the front door. "To the Minster?"

"I should like to go back to my house first," she said, as they went out into the little forecourt.

"Is that wise?" he said. "I saw your husband there last night. Ought you not send your maid?"

"No, I want some music and she will never find it. And I am sure that you are not my only protector. Major Vernon has seen to that."

There was a touch of annoyance in her voice, he was sure.

They walked in uncomfortable silence to Avonside Row, followed at a respectful distance by Constables Taylor and Lewis. They left them waiting at the gate, and went upstairs to the drawing room with the piano. Mrs Morgan took off her bonnet and shawl and began to search through her music. He laid his own hat down by hers, and watched her, fascinated by her every movement.

"The last time I was here you slapped my face," he said.

"So I did," she said, without turning her attention from her task. "And you deserved it."

"Did I?" he said. "What exactly did I do that was so offensive, Mrs Morgan?"

"You are a stubborn child," she said, "who will not learn his lesson."

"Perhaps. I am confused. It seems you do not slap all men who presume to come within a foot of you. What did I do wrong? That's all I am asking."

"What do you mean by that?"

"You can't guess?"

She shrugged, walked away and began to look through another pile of music.

"Why on earth did Major Vernon send you, of all people?" she said.

"I do not think he is thinking straight. No man can in your thrall, Mrs Morgan. You make us all gibbering fools — that is the plain truth of it. I told him I would make a poor guard dog, but he was so concerned to protect you and your precious reputation. He is your complete slave now, ma'am, another conquest for you to glory in."

She came over to him and looked at him. For a moment he felt sure she would slap him again, but instead she said, "Please, do not speak of something about which you know nothing."

"But I want to know," he said, grabbing her hand. "I want to understand. Why him? Why could you not show any kindness to me, for Heaven's sake?"

She pulled her hand away.

"Must you be so wretched?" she said, angrily.

"I wish I were not!" he exclaimed. "For God's sake, do you think I like this? I wish I did not feel this thing, but I do. I am in torment because of you!"

She threw up her hands.

"Yes, perhaps you are, but it will pass! I know what you are suffering. I have had such feelings myself at your age. The moment I am gone from here it will pass. Believe me, you are not truly in love. You are in a selfish passion. It is not love. You are not fatally wounded." She let a great sigh and turned away. "Anyway, it is good practice for you," she went on, walking up the room. "Renunciation is a skill that life demands of one more and more, as time passes..." Her voice cracked and she began to shake with sobs. He saw her reach out to the piano to steady herself, her other hand covering her face as she gave in to the tears.

He stood, not knowing whether he should go and comfort her or not. He had no wish to add to her misery by some clumsy gesture, and yet he felt he must attempt something to alleviate her pain. To see her crying was too raw, too unpleasant.

"I have a clean handkerchief," he said, reaching into his coat.

She managed to look at him with something like a smile and put her hand out for it. He went to her side and gave it to her.

"Excuse me," she managed to say, taking it from him. "I thought..." And with that she broke down again. "Oh, excuse me!"

This time he could not forbear and put his arms about her. She allowed it, even glad of it, and he felt her bend and rest against him, allowing herself to give into the full torrent of her misery.

"I thought I was stronger than this," she managed to say. "But I feel so utterly broken. What is happening to me?" She pulled herself away from him and stared at him, with her tear-sodden face. "And I have been so unkind to you, when all you have done is allow yourself to feel!" she said, her words clearly a struggle for her. "And there is nothing wrong with that — except it will cause you such pain! Oh why, why on earth is the world so cruel?" she finished, grasping his shoulders, almost shaking him. "Tell me that, Mr Carswell, why?"

"I don't know," he said. Her physical closeness was almost unbearable, and to have the full scorching force of her attention turned upon him made him breathless. He had dreamed of intimacy with her and of being an object worthy of her attention, but now it was too much and he could feel no triumph in it, let alone any pleasure. It was all wrong.

"No, how could you?" she said, and traced her finger down his cheek, her unerring finger finding the tear that had humiliatingly escaped from his eye. "Poor, sweet young man." She bent her head and rested it on his shoulder, as if exhausted. He felt sick with desire, his whole body was stirred into it, and he knew he ought to break away from her. But instead he put his trembling hands on her back, at the top of her bodice, so that his fingertips could feel the warm, soft skin of the nape of her neck. He breathed in deeply to steady himself, but instead found himself dizzy with the scent of her hair. He rocked on his heels, feeling that he might faint, and wished he might and pull her with him into some blissful other-worldly union of oblivion. If he were to die in that moment, he thought, it would be with no regret.

The door to the room opened behind him. She glanced up and suddenly stiffened in his arms. He felt terror inhabit her entire body and instinctively he tightened his grasp, anxious to protect her, but at the same time she wrenched herself free and walked quickly away. He turned to see what had so alarmed her.

Morgan was standing in the doorway in his shirt sleeves, a cigar in his mouth, his arms folded.

"Very pretty," he said, strolling in.

Mrs Morgan stood straight-backed, her hands balled into fists, as if she were a prize fighter about to square up to the opposition, albeit a prize-fighter with a tear-stained face. Her demeanour was simply astonishing, but it seemed not to impress Morgan.

"Please leave at once," she said, in a sort of strangled hiss.

"Why would I do that?" he said, advancing towards her.

"Because we have an agreement," she said.

He took out his cigar and blew a cloud of smoke straight into her face. She turned away as if he had struck her, and began to cough.

Felix, unable to bear it a moment longer, hurled himself forward with the intention of smashing his jaw with his fist. Morgan spun round, grabbed him and threw him across the room, sending him sprawling on to the floor, his head cracking against one of the chairs. Blackness engulfed him.

He awoke to the sound of Mrs Morgan screaming desperately for help.

He struggled to sit up, unable to focus properly. He could see that Mrs Morgan was lying on the floor, Morgan straddling her. He could just see the flash of a blade in Morgan's hand and the sound of ripping cloth, but it was nothing to the awfulness of her cries as she struggled to escape. He realised, as he began to crawl across the room, that she was using the full power of her voice to raise the alarm, that there was a desperate courage in it.

Morgan was slashing her dark skirts to ribbons, and there was blood. Mrs Morgan was suddenly silent and still. Felix felt his own heart stop for a moment.

Then Constables Lewis and Taylor burst into the room and dragged Morgan off her.

The blood-stained knife went spinning to the floor, and Morgan, now restrained by the constables, crumpled to his knees, like a puppet cut from its strings. It was as if a devil had possessed him which had now departed. He looked about him, his expression one of confusion melting into profound agony.

Felix at last got to her side, and grabbed her hand to feel for the pulse. It still remained – it was feeble, but it remained.

Chapter Forty-seven

Giles came out of the room where he had been interviewing Pritchard feeling no sense of triumph. He had his confession, and it was properly done before witnesses, so that it would all stand well in court. But the plain truth of it was that the man had showed no remorse. To Pritchard, Charles Barnes was apparently an obstacle to his own peace of mind, not a human from whom he had savagely stolen life.

He stood in the passageway for a long moment, gathering his thoughts, attempting to master the anger that threatened to overcome him. It was not his place, he reminded himself, to mete out justice, no matter how much he wanted to. He had uncovered the truth of the matter and apprehended the villain. His part was over. But it still rankled greatly with him that a man in Pritchard's privileged position could be so fundamentally base and unscrupulous. It was far easier to forgive his usual quarry, impoverished wretches for whom crime was a desperate step, forced upon them by circumstances. Not so Dean Pritchard. He had every advantage in life and still he had given into evil when confronted by a difficulty. It was incomprehensible and unforgivable.

He was making his way back to his office when he was met by a constable with a handful of messages for him.

"They have got Morgan downstairs, sir," said the lad, who seemed breathless with excitement.

"That is good news," said Giles, allowing himself to feel a surge of the same excitement. With Morgan in the cells, Nancy was safe.

His pleasure lasted only a moment. The first note he

looked at was a few brief lines from Mr Carswell, in an almost illegible scrawl, the script itself seeming to convey intense agitation.

Having read it, he glanced up at the constable.

"When did this news come?" he demanded.

"About ten minutes ago. The order was that you were not to be disturbed."

It was true – he had gone into the interview with strict instructions not to interrupt him until the job was done.

He stared down at Carswell's note again. "Mrs Morgan in v. dangerous condition at Avonside Row. F.J. Carswell."

"I have to go," he said, thrusting the other unread messages back into the constable's hand.

~

Felix had never in his life been so glad to see Lord Rothborough.

He had arrived about five minutes after the constables had taken Morgan away, just as Felix was struggling to deal with Mrs Morgan's injuries. Felix had called for help, but the house was curiously empty of servants, and he was left alone trying to do what he could for her.

She was drifting in and out of consciousness and it was difficult to keep her responsive, and at the same time establish exactly what Morgan had done to her. Her skirts were a bloody, shredded mess and he was endeavouring to see what was a dangerous wound and what was superficial when Lord Rothborough came in.

Lord Rothborough did not ask for explanations – that was the real miracle. He saw a crisis and came immediately to Felix's aid, getting down on the floor and cradling her head and shoulders, calming and comforting her so that Felix could make some progress in his examination. She was in terrible distress, which was hardly surprising as the full extent of the wounds became clear. Morgan had gone at her with such force, slashing rather than stabbing, and that was perhaps more disturbing. Had he meant her to suffer and be scarred rather than kill her outright? Her long stays had protected her chest and abdomen to some degree, and her thighs had taken most of the damage. There was nothing that was immediately liable to kill her, but the overall effect put her in considerable danger.

He set to cleaning and dressing the lacerations as fast as he could. The conditions and equipment were not ideal, but at least he had his medical bag with him, and Lord Rothborough had a flask of French brandy in his top coat pocket. As she grew more and more tired from the pain and the shock, he saw her complexion fade into alarming greyness, and he met Lord Rothborough's eyes.

"She won't be lost," Lord Rothborough said, in a quiet voice. "She is in the best of hands with you." He turned his gaze back to her, stroking her forehead and murmuring to her. "You will not leave here yet, my dear, we will not allow it. Hold fast."

She rolled her head a little and said, "Where is Giles? I want..." and passed out again.

~

As he entered the house, Giles met Lord Rothborough. He was coming downstairs in his shirtsleeves and carrying a pail and a jug.

"She's upstairs and God willing, out of immediate danger," he said to Giles. "She's been asking for you."

He ran upstairs into the drawing room. Nancy was lying

on the floor, supported by a heap of cushions, covered by what looked like Lord Rothborough's great-coat, while Carswell was on his knees, bent over her. Her eyes were closed, her face distorted with pain, and she gave a gasp.

"That's the last one," Carswell said.

She seemed to relax a little and open her eyes. It was then that she saw Giles, and stretched out her hand to him. He went and knelt beside her, took her hand and kissed it.

"I am sorry," he said. "I am so sorry."

"For what?" she said.

"This should not have happened. I was wrong. I should not have allowed this to happen."

"How could you have prevented it?" she said.

"I... I..." he broke off, glancing down at her ravaged legs. "I should have prevented it. I could have anticipated this." He folded both hands around hers and kissed her finger-tips. "But you are safe now. You have Mr Carswell. Thank God you were here!" he said, glancing over to Carswell, who was sitting on the floor, catching his breath for a moment.

"We must get you into bed," Carswell said, staggering to his feet.

"At least I can help with that," said Giles, gathering her into his arms.

Together they got her upstairs.

Gently he removed what remained of her dress and disentangled her from her stays. He found a fresh nightgown and put it on her while Carswell rearranged the bed, improvising with a towel rail to keep the weight of the bedclothes from her body. When she was installed, Carswell gave her a dose of tincture of opium while Giles got the fire going.

Giles turned back to see her imploring hand stretched out to him again, and when he came to her side, she grasped at his hand fervently. What had he awakened in her, he thought, looking down at her, and what had she awakened in him?

"That will work its way soon enough," Carswell said. "And you will be much more comfortable. Sleep is the best thing for you now, Mrs Morgan."

"He's right," Giles said, crouching down and gently pushing back a lock of hair that had fallen across her face.

"Please do not go, Giles, not yet," she said. She knew that he must leave, sooner or later. "Please."

"I will stay until you are asleep," he said.

~

Felix came out onto the landing and closed the door behind him softly. Lord Rothborough was there, pulling his great-coat on.

"I shall be back directly. I am going for reinforcements," he said. "What do you need?"

"A clean shirt," said Felix. He really wanted a bath and a cheroot, but that would have to wait. "Will you get her maid? She's at Mrs Fforde's."

"Yes, and James Bodley and my cook," said Rothborough. "Where the devil did all the servants go?"

"Morgan must have sent them away. He must have..." Felix broke off, suddenly overcome with exhaustion. He sat down on the cane settee on the half landing and tried to steady himself. His head was suddenly throbbing. He reached up, wondered how much damage Morgan had done when he had thrown him across the room.

"I tried to stop him," he said. "I did, but he pushed me over. I was out for... for..."

Lord Rothborough sat down beside him and put his arm gently about his shoulders. Felix, although he scarcely meant to, relaxed against him and accepted the embrace. He felt, for all his confusion, that there was a sense of rightness in it, and it steadied him.

"She nearly died," he managed to say.

"But she did not," Rothborough said, squeezing his shoulder. "Because of you."

"She is not out of danger yet," Felix said. "We ought not fool ourselves. There can always be complications in such cases. She might yet –"

"Courage," said Lord Rothborough. "And remember that she has the will to live. She has a child, and – well, other objects, it seems."

"Major Vernon, yes," said Felix, hauling himself to his feet.

Lord Rothborough stood up also. "It is a hard loss. But there are other prizes, my dear boy. Now, you must rest. Go and sit by the fire in the kitchen. I will be back directly."

Chapter Forty-eight

Morgan sat on the floor of his cell, hunched in the corner, as if he meant somehow to make himself invisible. He looked up at Giles with terror in his eyes, as though he were holding a noose in his hands. Perhaps he might have preferred that – a speedy end to his evident misery.

Giles said, "I am Major Vernon, the Chief Constable. Do you understand why you are here?"

"Yes," said Morgan. "My wife... oh, Christ forgive me. Have you any news of her?"

"She may live, she may not," Giles said.

"Christ forgive me," Morgan said again, covering his face with his hands. "I did not mean... I did not..." He put down his hands and looked up at Giles again. "Vernon – that is the name that she told me – she said that you and Nancy –"

"She?"

"Lina."

"Paulina Ridolfi?"

"Yes," he said, "that evil little bitch. She said... and I believed her. I believed every fucking word. She knows how to play me. She has done these last ten years. She has had me wound about her wicked little finger and now... she... oh, Christ in Heaven..." He began to gasp and shake, racked with sobs.

Giles crouched down opposite him.

"Talk to me, it will be better if you talk," Giles said. "Tell me what Paulina has said to you. I know she came to see you at The Greyhound. What happened then?"

"What happened?" said Morgan, looking at him. "What always happens. She gives me everything but nothing. She is the Devil, and now I will hang for her and Nancy will die, and she will get everything she wants. The thing she really wants."

"Which is?" Giles asked.

"My poor bloody child. My poor little Harry."

~

"How long am I to be kept here?" Mrs Ridolfi asked, rising as he came into the room.

"You may go for the present," he said. "But you will still have to appear before the Justices tomorrow. If you attempt to leave Northminster, the consequences will be serious."

"Thank you," she said. "I will not."

"Would you allow me to escort you home?"

"You are very kind, Major Vernon," she said.

He arranged a carriage, and they drove in silence to the Treasurer's House.

"Why are we stopping here, sir?" she said.

"I have some bad news for you, ma'am," he said, opening the door. "It is better that I break it here. Besides, your nephew is here. I thought you might like to see him."

He handed her out of the carriage.

"Yes, very much. How kind you are, sir, so thoughtful. But what is this news?"

"Let us go in, shall we?"

He told the servant to fetch Sally and sat Mrs Ridolfi down in the large wing chair that stood by the fire in the hall.

"Please tell me what has happened."

"It is your sister-in-law," he said. "I am afraid to say..."

Mrs Ridolfi grasped at her throat.

"What has happened? Tell me, for God's sake!"

"I am afraid she is dead."

"Oh, dear Lord, no. How? What happened?"

"Morgan attacked her with a knife this afternoon. She died of her wounds. There was nothing that could be done to save her, though Mr Carswell tried all he could."

"No... oh, but... Morgan? He did that? Dear God! Oh, but... but..." she jumped up and walked across the hall, in great agitation. Giles watched her, feeling again that he was watching a performance.

At that moment, the schoolroom door opened and Sally came out. Through the open door Celia could be seen entertaining Harry with a game of skittles on the hearthrug. Mrs Ridolfi saw him and ran past them both, and fell down onto her knees beside the child, enfolding him in her arms, hugging him as if she meant to suffocate him. She kissed him with ecstatic pleasure but he struggled in her arms.

"Auntie, no, I'm playing. We're playing!"

"Let him be, ma'am," said Giles. "You and I must talk a little more."

"I must comfort Harry..."

"Not now, ma'am," he said, anxious that she would say too much to the boy. "This can wait."

He put his hand upon her shoulder and she looked up at him.

"No, I will not come," she said, clinging a little tighter. "I cannot. He needs me. My boy needs me. He cannot do without me now!"

"Auntie, let go, you're hurting!" said Harry. "And I'm not your boy. I'm Hannah's boy and Mama's boy, but I'm not your boy!" and he burst free. "Am not! Am not!"

"Harry!" she exclaimed and looked as if she were about to box his ears, but she clutched her hands together.

"Celia," said Sally, "why don't you take Harry upstairs and show him the soldiers?"

"We have a whole regiment of Grenadiers," said Celia, putting out her hand to him. Mrs Ridolfi would have gone with them, but Giles caught her arm.

"No, ma'am," he said quietly. "You and I are going to the Constabulary Headquarters."

"Why?"

He waited until Celia and the child had left the room, before he spoke: "Because, Paulina Ridolfi, I am arresting you for conspiracy to murder."

~

Felix found Major Vernon studying the fire in the drawing room. Since James Bodley and Lord Rothborough had taken command of the house, order had quickly been restored, the fires made up and the lamps lit. It looked as if nothing unpleasant had ever happened in the room.

"How is she?" he asked, turning from the fire.

"Comfortable. And awake again. You can go up to her if you like."

"I don't think I should. I have to get back to The Unicorn. So long as she is out of danger..."

"As much as she can be at this stage," Felix said. "But the problem is always the healing process. You saw how extensive the damage was –" He broke off, seeing a flicker of pain cross the Major's face. "You should go up to her. That would do her good."

"It would and it wouldn't," said Major Vernon after a moment. "I do not wish and neither... So long as she is out of danger. That is all I needed to know."

He went towards the door.

"What is to prevent you, sir?" Felix could not help asking. "Morgan will hang and she will be free."

"I am not free," said Major Vernon. Felix's surprise must have shown. "Forgive me, Mr Carswell, I should have told you earlier. It is a difficult subject with me. She is unwell in her

337

mind and necessarily we live apart."

Felix could not think how to answer this.

"That is why I must leave Mrs Morgan alone," Major Vernon said. "I have done enough damage already. And my apologies for the lectures on moral conduct, Mr Carswell. I am in no position to deliver such things, as you know. It is a bad habit of mine."

Felix would have spoken, but the Major put his hand up to silence him, and left without another word.

Felix went up to his patient. Berthe was sitting with her, holding her hand with a tenderness that made him regret thinking her sour.

"I heard the door close," said Mrs Morgan.

"It was Major Vernon leaving," Felix said. "I tried to make him come up."

"It is better he did not," she said, after a moment. Her words were forced, full of quiet emotion. "Berthe, un moment, s'il te plaît."

"Bien sur, Madame," said Berthe, getting up. She made a little curtsey to Felix and left them alone. He went and sat in her place, but he did not venture to take Mrs Morgan's hand. He was still struggling to understand what had happened between her and Major Vernon, wondering what it could be like to make such a profound connection with a woman and then have to renounce it utterly.

"Lord Rothborough thinks I should go to Scarborough as soon as I am able. He has a house there," she said.

"I think the sea air would be a good idea," said Felix. "As soon as you are able."

She nodded, and there were tears in her eyes.

"My wounds will heal," she said, after a moment.

"All of them?" Felix found he must ask. She twisted up her mouth and reached out for his hand. He allowed her to take it.

"Look after him, Mr Carswell," she said. "And his wife."

Epilogue

April 1840

"I think it might be safer to put this up somewhere higher," said Mrs Fforde, once again tweaking a stem of apple blossom in the vase she had put on the table. As she did so, a little shower of petals fell onto the table. Quickly she gathered them up and looked about the room nervously. Felix did not think he had ever seen her at such a loss.

"Is that the carriage I hear?" said Canon Fforde, who was sitting reading a newspaper.

Mrs Fforde at once went to the window.

"You may be right," she said.

She glanced back into the room and caught Felix's eye. She gave him a brief smile, which he supposed she meant to be encouraging. He did not feel encouraged. Rather, he shared her unease. He had been cramming himself with what he hoped was the most up-to-date and useful information for the management of such cases, but did not feel confident. In truth there was often little that could be done.

The carriage drew up and he joined Mrs Fforde in the window to see Major Vernon handing his wife out. She was a tall, extremely thin young woman, dressed plainly in dull colours. She appeared sallow and undernourished, with hollow eyes, and she looked suspiciously about her as she came up the path with her husband. He had her firmly by the arm as if he were afraid she might bolt.

Mrs Fforde went out to the hall to greet them, and Felix stood on the threshold with Canon Fforde.

"Laura, how good to see you again," she said, with her hands outstretched. Mrs Vernon did not respond. "Let me help you with your bonnet," ventured Mrs Fforde, and undid her bonnet strings. Mrs Vernon stood impassive, as if she was well accustomed to people doing things for her. Mrs Fforde lifted the bonnet from her head, revealing flaxen hair that had been close-cropped. It did little to improve her cadaverous appearance. Mrs Fforde seemed shocked and glanced at her brother.

"It was a matter of hygiene, I understand," he said. "Now, Laura, will you come and see your new room? I hope you like it." He steered her across the hall into the bedchamber. "There is a good fire in there. You will be able to get a little warmer. Nurse, if you would?" he added, to the woman who had come with them.

Felix watched as Laura Vernon went at once to the window, as if drawn by the light. There was a pattern of bars visible through the muslin glass cloth.

"It might be best to let her get used to it alone, sir," the nurse said. "Just to let her rest a little?"

"Yes, I think so."

The nurse closed the door, and Major Vernon came up to his sister, took the bonnet from her hands, and kissed her forehead.

"Oh, Giles..." she began softly.

"I would like something to eat," Major Vernon said. "Where is Holt? You'll join me, won't you, Carswell? Lambert, yes?"

He went down towards the kitchen.

"Yes, that would be excellent," said Canon Fforde, taking his wife's hand and leading her back into the sitting room. She had been staring at the closed door to Mrs Vernon's room.

"What do you think, Mr Carswell?" she said.

"Sally," said Canon Fforde, "how can he have formed an opinion?"

"No, I am afraid I cannot," said Felix, "until I have examined her."

"All in good time," said Canon Fforde. He made his wife sit down by the fire.

"She is so thin," said Mrs Fforde. "And dressed like something from the poorhouse. Poor Giles..."

"Hush," said Canon Fforde. "You will not be thanked for your pity, you know that."

"I know, but –" Mrs Fforde would have gone on but Holt came in with a tray of wine and some bread and cheese. Major Vernon followed him.

"You'll take some to Mrs Vernon, won't you?" he said, as Holt laid the food out for them. "And some broth?"

"Yes, Mrs Connolly is heating some up for her, sir," said Holt.

"Has Mrs Vernon eaten today?" Felix asked.

"They gave her something, but she is liable to refuse food. That is the chief difficulty of the moment." Felix noticed Mrs Fforde wince slightly at this revelation.

"The change of air may stimulate her appetite," Felix said. "Not to mention a change of cook. That bread looks good, by the way," he added.

"Mrs Connolly made it herself, Irish fashion," said Holt. "And it is good, sir."

When he had left them, Lambert, much amused, said, "I think you have found yourself an indispensable fellow with Holt."

"Yes," said the Major. "Not to mention Mrs Connolly," he added, taking a small piece of bread and trying it. "This is excellent."

Canon and Mrs Fforde drank a scant glass of wine each, tasted the bread and then Canon Fforde proposed that they should walk home while the weather held. "Now we have seen the travellers are safe by their hearth," he said, and so they took their leave, though not without an uneasy backward glance by Mrs Fforde.

"My poor sister," murmured Major Vernon as they went back into the house.

"I shall just go and see her for a moment, if I may," Felix said.

"Thank you," the Major said.

"Oh, by the by, there is a parcel for you," Felix said, just before he went in. "It's on the piano."

~

Giles wondered what Mr Carswell would make of Laura, as he took the parcel from the piano and unwrapped it. She had been calm on the journey, if that state of withdrawal might be called calm. But she had not protested. Nurse Beddowes seemed to be able to manage her well, and the journey had passed without incident. Dr Fernham, her physician at the asylum, had told him that she had been quiet for some weeks now, and eating little. It made her tractable but it did not offer much hope for an improvement.

He reached for his pocket knife and cut the string on the parcel, having noticed the Liverpool postmark. Inside the brown paper he discovered a Berlin work cushion depicting a parrot and two folios of piano music by Mendelssohn: "Songs without Words", which seemed painfully appropriate. There were also two letters addressed in a familiar hand, one to himself and one to Mr Carswell. He propped Carswell's letter against the decanter and took his own to the window.

It was a brief note, which both relieved and saddened him.

> I promised you these small tokens. They are no comfort I know, but a promise is a promise. Harry and I sail for New York tomorrow – a great adventure – and he is so excited! I

intend he will be a man before we return. It is for the best, just as we decided. But I will always dream of you clearing a forest for me. That, I am afraid, I cannot do without. N.

He folded the letter and put it away inside his coat. Then he sat down and ate some bread and cheese, and tried to concentrate his mind upon the work of the days ahead.

Dean Pritchard's trial was to take place in a week's time, and he had retained Francis Edwardes QC as his counsel. It was not going to be straightforward. He had already manoeuvred significantly, retracting his confession and entering a non-guilty plea. Edwardes had a reputation for the brutal cross-examination of prosecution witnesses and Giles had been attempting to prepare himself for his appearance on the witness stand by anticipating all possible lines of attack.

Carswell came in after five minutes or so.

"She took half a cup of broth and now she's sleeping," he said. "I gave her a cursory examination. She's weak, but not in a dangerous state. If we can persuade her to eat more, I think physically she will be improved. As to her mental state, I cannot yet say."

"No, of course not," Giles said.

"I am in correspondence with a friend who is studying in Paris. There is interesting work going on there in this field, with some surprising results. I am hoping to pick his brains thoroughly."

"I know you will do all you can," Giles said. "Will you have some wine?"

Carswell nodded and then saw the letter propped against the decanter.

"Was that in the parcel?"

"Yes. It is from Mrs Morgan. She sent a parrot cushion."

Carswell snatched up the envelope and tore it open. Then he hesitated for a moment before pulling out the letter.

"Did she...?"

"A line or two," he said, and forced himself to smile. He got up from the table and went to see to his sleeping wife.

~

Felix was glad to be left alone with his letter.

> My dear Mr Carswell,
> This is perhaps not the sort of gratitude you want from me. But I am conscious that you have saved my life, and you will always have a significant place in my affections because of it. My physician at Scarborough says I have made an excellent recovery and he admired your needlework very much.
> Lord R. writes from town that he has met a certain young woman – I believe he has spoken to you about her. Whatever you may think, I know he will not make you do anything against your will. He simply wants you to be happy. Forgive my advocacy – he did not ask me to do it – it is simply that I also wish you well and happy. It is as much as you deserve.
> Tomorrow Harry and I sail for New York. Perhaps in many years' time we may meet again, DV.
> In the meantime, I am your most humble and always grateful servant,
> Anna Morgan

He stuffed the letter into his pocket and left the room. The door to Mrs Vernon's room was open and Major Vernon could be seen sitting by his wife on the bed. The Major saw him standing there and got up, kissed his wife on the forehead and came out into the hall, closing the door behind him.

"We should get back to our work, Mr Carswell," he said.

They walked back across the fields in a spring dusk that promised much sweetness to come, although the air was still cool.

"Which way is Ardenthwaite?" Felix asked, as they paused to climb over a stile.

Major Vernon gestured, from the top of the stone steps. "North-east of here," he said. "Is that all in hand, then?" Felix nodded.

"I should go and look the place over, I suppose," he said, climbing up the stile and looking over in the direction towards which the Major had flung his hand. "Though what I am to do with it, I don't know. I cannot live there, but I have no wish to be an absent landlord, and I do not want to give up my post here."

"Look it over and then make a decision," said Major Vernon. "The sight of the place may answer your questions. You may find it agreeable – and there may be plenty of work for you there. Of course, that would be somewhat of a loss to me, and the men."

"You think I should turn farmer?"

"I think you should go and see the place," Major Vernon said. "See how your land lies."

"My land," Felix said, shaking his head. "It is not really mine. It is absurd –"

"Land is never absurd," said Major Vernon. "You are a lucky man. You will get a good income from it, whatever you decide, and you will have the consequence of it. Most men would count themselves extremely fortunate."

"Yes, I am grateful – I think," Felix said. "But I feel my hand has been forced. I do not want to desert you, or all this, and become something I am not. I have only just begun to make sense of this profession – and I am beginning to feel that will be a life's work to master it, and not to try, well –"

"Then get a good man to manage the place for you. They can be found. I can help you find one, if you like. I have a little knowledge of these things."

"Thank you. I would be grateful for your advice."

"I'm glad to hear you have no wish to leave us," Major Vernon said. He whistled to bring Snow – who had gone skittering off in search of an interesting scent – back to their side. "You would be hard to replace, Mr Carswell."

"Oh, I don't know," said Felix. "You could get some straightforward, virtuous fellow who reads his Bible and never gets drunk."

"That sounds extremely dull," said Major Vernon, "and I would look shabby in such company, don't you think?" He stopped to put Snow back on her leash, caressing her head extravagantly as he did so. "About Mrs Morgan. I'm sorry I could not be entirely straight with you. The situation was an exceptional one. I do not expect it will happen again. I must keep myself better tethered," he finished, caressing the dog's head again.

"She is exceptional," Felix could not help saying. "I don't think that I –" but then he broke off, realising it was, for both of them, too painful a subject to proceed with.

"Come," Major Vernon said. "Tell me again about your ligature evidence. You will need to be word-perfect in court or we will be routed by that demon counsel, and after all we have gone through I am determined not to let that happen!"

~ THE END ~

Dramatis Personae

The Northminster Constabulary

Major Giles Vernon: Chief Constable of the Northminster Constabulary

Felix Carswell: Police Surgeon, natural son of Lord Rothborough

The Minster Precincts

Canon Lamber Fforde: Minster Treasurer and brother-in-law of Giles Vernon

Mrs Sally Fforde: elder sister of Giles Vernon

Celia Fforde: the Ffordes' daughter

The Rev Mr Pritchard: Dean of Northminster

Mrs Pritchard: Mr Pritchard's wife

Miss Kate Pritchard: the Pritchards' daughter

Mrs Anna Morgan: a brilliant soprano, sometimes called Nancy or Nan

Edward Morgan: Anna Morgan's husband, also a professional singer

Paulina Ridolfi: Anna Morgan's sister in law

Berthe: Anna Morgan's Swiss maid

Harry Morgan: Anna Morgan's three-year-old son

Hannah: nursemaid to Harry Morgan

George Watkins: Master of Music at Northminster Minster

Mr Elias Geoffrey: a gentleman of independent means

Holt: butler to Mr Geoffrey

Nickson: valet to Mr Geoffrey

Lord Rothborough: prominent local grandee and admirer of Mrs Morgan

James Bodley: Lord Rothborough's valet

Northminster

Edwin Fildyke: the proprietor of a fancy good shop and a member of the Minster choir

Mrs Fildyke: Edwin's mother

Charles Barnes: a bookbinder and a member of the Minster choir

Mr Sledmere: uncle and employer of Charles Barnes

Mrs Sledmere: Mr Sledmere's wife

Rose Sledmere: the Sledmere's daughter and cousin of Charles

Josiah Harrison: a clerk and a member of the Minster choir

Thomas O'Brien: printer and proprietor of The Bugle

About the Author

Harriet Smart was born and brought up in Birmingham. She attended the University of St Andrews, where she read History of Art, and married a fellow student. She now lives with her husband in an eighteenth-century house in Northumberland.

Harriet has an M.A. in screenwriting. She has published twenty novels as well as helping to design the creative writing software Writer's Café and the e-book editor software Jutoh.

She has been writing the Northminster Mysteries since 2010.

You can follow Harriet at www.harrietsmart.com and BookBub.

Made in the USA
Columbia, SC
30 November 2023